Praise *for* Rexanne Becnel

"Ms. Becnel creates the most intriguing characters
and infuses them with fiety personalities and
quick minds."
— *Literary Times* on *The Bride of Rosecliff*

"…Becnel skillfully blends romance and adventure
with a deft hand."
— *Publishers Weekly* on *When Lightning Strikes*

"There's magic in Rexanne Becnel's ability to
conjure a story."
— *Baton Rouge Advocate* on *Where Magic Dwells*

"Becnel gives us true insight into the human
spirit."
— *Romantic Times* on *The Matchmaker*

"Rexanne's stories stay with the reader long after
the final page is turned."
— *Literary Times* on *Heart of the Storm*

Rexanne Becnel

Rexanne Becnel, the author of nineteen novels and two novellas, swears she could not be a writer if it weren't for New Orleans's many coffeehouses. She does all her work longhand, with a mug of coffee at her side. She is a charter member of the Southern Louisiana Chapter of Romance Writers of America, and founded the New Orleans Popular Fiction Conference.

Rexanne's novels regularly appear on bestseller lists such as *USA TODAY*, *Amazon.com*, Waldenbooks, Ingrams and Barnes and Noble. She has been nominated for and received awards from *Romantic Times*, Waldenbooks, The Holt Committee, the *Atlanta Journal/Atlanta Constitution* and the National Readers Choice Awards.

THE Next NOVEL™

Old Boyfriends

Rexanne Becnel

OLD BOYFRIENDS

copyright © 2005 Rexanne Becnel

i s b n 0 3 7 3 2 3 0 3 6 2

This edition published by arrangement with Harlequin Books S.A.

® and TM are trademarks of the publisher. Trademarks indicated with
® are registered in the United States Patent and Trademark Office, the
Canadian Trade Marks Office and in other countries.

TheNextNovel.com

 HARLEQUIN®

PRINTED IN U.S.A.

From the Author

Dear Reader,

You'd think an author with eighteen books
under her belt wouldn't be so excited about the
publication of her nineteenth!

Wrong!

Old Boyfriends marks the beginning of a new
direction for me: from historical romance to what
I fondly call "girlfriend" books. Little did I know
when I started writing about Cat and Bitsey and
MJ that a new publishing outlet was being created
for that exact sort of book. I am so happy to be
a part of NEXT and their wonderful lineup of
books and authors. Writing about women *my* age
with my concerns and my fears and hopes has
rejuvenated my creative side. Maybe too much.
You see, I write in a coffeehouse and I know some
of the other patrons wonder about me. I sit at my
corner table, pen in hand, and grin and frown and
mumble to myself. Sometimes I even shed a tear
or two. But I'm too happy with what I'm doing to
care if they think I'm crazy.

Writing *Old Boyfriends* was sometimes hard and
sometimes effortless, but always fulfilling. I hope
you find reading it equally satisfying.

Best wishes,

Rexanne

For my friends on Jackson Avenue
who keep me sane and focused.

CHAPTER 1
Death and Dieting

Cat

My friend M.J.'s husband died on a Friday, lying on the table during a therapeutic massage. A massive heart attack, that's how the newspaper reported it. But that's only because his son and the PR firm for their restaurant chain made sure that's what they reported.

The truth? Viagra and the too-capable ministrations of a pseudowoman, pseudomasseuse wearing a black oriental wig, a red thong and fishnet hose are what did in Frank Hollander. The table was actually a round bed covered with black satin sheets, with an honest-to-God mirror on the ceiling. The House of the Rising Sun serves a very good hot and sour soup downstairs, but the therapy going on upstairs isn't the sort that the chairman of this year's United Way Fund Drive could afford to be associated with.

Needless to say, the funeral was huge. The mayor spoke, the bishop said the mass, and the choir from St. Joseph's Special School, a major beneficiary of the United Way, sang good old Frank into the ground. As pure as those kids' souls were, even they couldn't have sung Frank into heaven.

Afterward, M.J.'s stepchildren entertained the mourners at her home, where everyone came up to the widow and said all the things they were supposed to:

"If I can do anything, Mary Jo, just call. Promise me you'll call."

"Your husband was a great man, Mrs. Hollander. We'll all miss him."

Blah, blah, blah. It was all I could do to keep my mouth shut. But Bitsey had given me my marching orders and I knew my role. I was there to support M.J., not to air my opinion about her sleazy bastard of a husband and his gang of no-good kids.

Thank God for Bitsey—and I'm not using the Lord's name casually when I say that. Thank you, God, for giving me Bitsey. She's like the voice of reason in my life, the perfect mother image for someone sorely deprived of that in her biological parent.

M.J., Bitsey and me. Three girls raïsed in the South, but trapped in California.

Well, I think that maybe I was the only one who felt trapped in the vast, arid beigeness of southern California. But then, I felt trapped wherever I was. I was slowly figuring that out.

That Tuesday, however, at M.J.'s palatial home with the air-conditioning running double time, and Frank Jr.'s Pacific Rim fusion restaurant catering the after-funeral festivities, we were all feeling trapped. Sushi at a funeral is beyond unreal.

Bitsey had explained to M.J. that she had to stay downstairs until the last guests left. She was the hostess, and it was only right. But yes, she could anesthetize herself if she wanted to. Everybody else was.

So M.J., in her perfect size-six black Giselle dress and her Jimmy Choo slingbacks, sat in Frank Sr.'s favorite fake leopard-skin chair and tossed back five vodka martinis in less than two hours.

M.J. drank, Bitsey ate, and I fumed and wanted to get the hell out of there. That awful, morbid couple of hours sums up pretty well how the three of us react to any stress thrown our way. And God knows there's enough of it. When Bitsey hurts, she eats. Even when she was on Phen-Fen, and now Meridia, if she's hurting—especially if her husband, Jack, pulls some stunt—she eats. Considering that Jack Albertson can be a coldhearted bastard, and unlike Frank, doesn't bother to hide it, it's no wonder she's packed close to two hundred pounds onto her five-foot-four frame. The more she eats, the fatter she gets, and the more remote and critical he gets. Which, of course, makes her eat even more.

But I digress, which I do a lot. According to my sometimes therapist, that's a typical coping mechanism: catalog everybody else's flaws and you'll be too busy to examine your own. M.J. drinks, Bitsey eats, and I run. New job. New man. New apartment.

Today, however, I had vowed to hang in there, bite my tongue and generally struggle against every impulse I had.

"So sorry, Mrs. Hollander." A slick-looking man with a classic comb-over bent down a little to give M.J. his condolences. His eyes were on her boobs, which are original issue, contrary to what most people think. He handed her his card. "If I can help you in any way."

After he wandered away, Bitsey took the card from M.J.'s vodka-numbed hand. "A lawyer," Bitsey muttered, glaring at his retreating back. "How positively gauche to hand the bereaved widow a business card at her husband's funeral. Is there even one person in this entire state who was taught a modicum of manners?"

"She's going to need a lawyer," I whispered over M.J.'s head, hoping the vodka had deadened her hearing. "Frank Jr. isn't going to let her get away with one thin dime of his daddy's money. Her clothes, yes. Her jewelry, maybe. In a weak moment he might even let her keep the Jag. But the house? The money?" I shook my head. "No way."

"Shh," Bitsey hissed. "Not now."

M.J. turned her big, fogged-over blue eyes on Bitsey. "I need to use the little girls' room."

"Okay, honey." Bitsey patted M.J.'s knee. "Do you need help?"

Somehow we guided M.J. through the crowd without it being too obvious that her feet weren't moving. Good thing she's only about a hundred pounds. The girl is as strong as an ox, thanks to Pilates three days a week, cross-training two days and ballet the other two. But she doesn't weigh anything.

Instead of the powder room, we took M.J. to the master suite where we surprised Frank Jr.'s wife, Wendy, scoping out the place. The bimbo didn't even have the grace to look embarrassed that we'd caught her in the act of mentally arranging her furniture in M.J.'s bedroom.

But when I spied the delicate ceramic bunny rabbit she held in her greedy, sharp-nailed clutches, I saw red. Bloodletting red. Bitsey had made that rabbit in the ceramics class where she, M.J. and I first met. She'd given it to M.J., and a cat figurine to me. I glared at Wendy until the bitch put the bunny down and flounced away.

Bitsey gave me a scandalized look. "Please tell me she wasn't doing what I think she was doing."

I rolled my eyes, hoping M.J. was too far gone to have noticed her stepdaughter-in-law's avarice. But as M.J. kicked off her shoes and staggered to the "hers" bathroom she muttered, "Wendy wants my house. Frank Jr., too. She's always saying how a big house like this needs kids in it."

M.J. paused in the doorway and, holding on to the frame, looked over her shoulder at us. Tears spilled down her cheeks. She was gorgeous even when she was drunk, miserable and crying. If she wasn't such a lamb, I'd hate her. "Like I didn't try to have children," she went on. "I always wanted children, and we tried everything. But . . ." She sniffled. "I just couldn't get pregnant. She always lords that over me, you know. We're the same age, but she's got three kids and I don't have any." M.J. went into the bathroom and closed the door.

Bitsey looked at me. Her eyes brimmed with sorrow, but her mouth was pursed in outrage. "And now Wendy wants her house?" She fished the lawyer's card out of her pocket.

I snatched the card and tore it in half, then tossed it in a garbage basket. "No. Not that lawyer. If he's here at Frank's funeral it's because he's a friend or business acquaintance. Some kind of way he's connected to Frank Sr., and therefore

Frank Jr. When M.J. gets a lawyer, we have to make sure it's someone who doesn't have any ties to the Hollander clan."

"You're right. You're right," Bitsey conceded. "You have a very suspicious mind, Cat. But sometimes that's good."

"A girl's got to watch out for herself."

Bitsey gave me a warm, soft hug. "And for her friends."

M.J. went alone to the reading of the will. We found that out later. I would have canceled my appointments to be with her if she'd asked. Bitsey would have gone, too, not that she would have spoken up against a room half full of lawyers—all men—and the other half full of relatives—all bloodsuckers. But at least M.J. would have had one person on her side.

M.J. went alone, though, and when I called her that afternoon to see if she wanted to have dinner, all I got was the answering service. Even the housekeeper was gone. That's when I knew something was wrong. Ever since the funeral, M.J. hadn't left the house except for her exercise classes. I called Bitsey.

"Maybe she's taking a nap," she said. Bitsey is big on naps.

"Or drunk."

"Or drunk," Bitsey agreed. "We should go over there."

"What about Jack? Isn't it his dinnertime?" I tried to keep any hint of scorn out of my voice; I'm not sure I succeeded. The thing is, Jack Albertson is an overbearing jerk. Bitsey is the perfect wife, but nothing she does is ever good enough to suit him. She's Julia Child and Heloise rolled into one: perfect meals served in a perfectly kept house. I helped her decorate it, but she keeps it up herself. Even their kids are perfect, good grades, no car wrecks or illegitimate babies—no thanks to Jack. But does he appreciate any of Bitsey's good qualities? Not hardly. In his book she's too fat, too permissive, a spendthrift and a brainless twit. Oh yeah, and did I mention? He thinks she's too fat.

Sometimes I hate the jerk. But then, I'm beginning to think that maybe I hate all men.

"Jack's working late tonight," she said. "His division is entertaining a group of businessmen from South Korea and they're pulling out all the stops to impress them."

What I heard in her determined explanation was, "He's nothing like Frank Hollander, so just turn off that suspicious little mind of yours." For her sake I did.

"Okay, then," I said. "I'll meet you at M.J.'s in, say, twenty minutes. We'll take her out to dinner."

Twenty minutes later nobody answered the door, so we went around to the back. The gate was locked, but through the iron fence and tall border of variegated ginger and papyrus plants we could see M.J. lying on a chaise longue on the far side of the pool. She was asleep. At least, I hoped she was asleep.

When we were hoarse from trying to rouse her, I swore. "That's it. I'm going over the fence."

It would have been easier if I was twenty years younger or ten pounds lighter, or both. I had on high-heeled mules, ivory silk cigarette pants and a sleeveless black turtleneck. Very chic and severe, as befits an interior designer to the quasi rich and famous of Bakersfield, California. But it was lousy rock-climbing garb, and by the time I tumbled into a bed of pothos and aluminum plants, the whole outfit was ruined. "Hells bells. I think I broke something."

"No you didn't. Open the gate," Bitsey demanded. So much for being motherly.

We hurried over to M.J.; for once Bitsey moved faster than me.

"Please, God," Bitsey pleaded. "Don't let her be dead."

"Don't say that. She's not dead," I muttered. "Dead drunk, but not dead."

I was right, but barely. The last bit of margarita in the pitcher next to M.J. would definitely have finished her off. She was breathing but not responsive beyond a few indecipherable mutters.

"We should take her to the hospital," Bitsey said as we wheeled her inside on the chaise longue.

"She's just drunk. Look how big that pitcher is. She drank almost all of it."

"What if she took something else?"

"Like what?"

"I don't know. Sleeping pills. Painkillers. And look how sunburned she is. She must have been out there all afternoon."

M.J. woke up when we turned a cold shower on her. "Stop. Stop!" She covered her face with her hands and curled on her side in the group-size shower stall.

"Mary Jo Hollander, what did you take today?" Bitsey exclaimed in her sternest I-am-the-mother-around-here voice.

"Tequila. Leave me alone."

"What else?" I turned the cold up to full blast.

"Nothing!" She squealed in protest. "Nothing else."

"No pills?" Bitsey demanded, her blond hair beginning to droop in the spray from the five-point water delivery system. "Mary Jo! No pills?"

"Nooo!"

Bitsey and I shared a look. As one we decided to believe her. So I turned off the water, Bitsey found some towels, and together we got M.J. dry and changed and into bed. This was beginning to be a bad habit. After that, completely done in, we threw ourselves onto the twin couches in the living room.

Bitsey kicked off her shoes. "She shouldn't be living alone."

"We both live alone."

"I don't live alone."

I massaged my left ankle, which still hurt from my adventures with the iron fence. "Your kids are gone. Jack's never around. Face it, Bitsey, you're just as alone as me and M.J." I knew I was being mean for no reason, but I was in a pissy mood.

"On the rag are you?" Bitsey was a sweetheart, but she wasn't totally defenseless.

She was no match for me, though. "At least I'm not too old to still have a period."

She glared at me. Bitsey was very sensitive about the impending death of her forties. She'd gone through the same tortures when she was thirty-nine and her first daughter went off to college. Forty was old! Four years later her middle girl went off without too much trauma. But the baby had left last August, she'd turned forty-eight the next month, and according to her gynecologist, she was officially in menopause. She hadn't yet recovered from any of it.

I knew she'd be okay once she actually turned fifty. But we had another year and a half till then. Despite my nasty mood, I probably shouldn't have made that last crack.

"At least I won't die alone," she finally said, but without any real venom in her voice.

I hugged a silk-tasseled pillow to my chest. "Sorry."

She nodded. "Me, too."

We sat in silence, surrounded by the self-conscious splendor of M.J.'s home. Pure California posh. By day it was bright and elegant: white everything—floors, walls, carpets, furniture; art in every shade of red; and the bright green of potted palms and ferns. By night the lighting turned everything amber, dark emerald and the color of blood. Dramatic.

You'd think as M.J.'s best friend I would have been consulted on the decor. But Frank Hollander used a big interior design firm from L.A. for everything: home, restaurants and his latest venture, a boutique hotel in San Diego. Despite my professional jealousy I could appreciate the house's artistic merit. But it didn't suit M.J. She's a big softy at heart, so that slick, polished look didn't come naturally to her. She had to work at it.

"I'll stay with her tonight."

"Good idea," Bitsey said. She sighed. "She needs to get out of here."

"You mean a vacation?"

She shrugged. "Something like that."

"The trouble is, if she leaves—even for a week—Wendy and Frank Jr. would be in here with the locks changed. Possession is nine-tenths of the law and all that."

Prophetic words. Hours later, after we forced two cups of strong coffee into her, M.J. spilled all. "He left me with nothing. Well, practically nothing," she wailed, sitting cross-legged on the bed.

It was a garbled tale, interrupted by a bout of vomiting and lots of tears. By the time we had the gist of it, M.J.'s head was beginning to clear. "All those years," she muttered. "Seventeen years of marriage and he betrays me, not only with that…that freak of nature woman-wannabe, but he lied about taking care of me. The kids inherited the corporation, and everything belongs to it—the restaurants, the hotel, even my house. And my car, too!"

"Wreck it," Bitsey muttered.

I swiveled my head to stare at her. "Wreck it? You mean the car?" M.J.'s Jaguar sedan is the most gorgeous hunk of metal and leather you've ever seen.

Scowling, yet also looking like she wanted to cry, Bitsey nodded. "Wreck the car, wreck the house, wreck his reputation."

M.J. sat up against the leather upholstered headboard of her Ponderosa-size bed. Vindictiveness in Bitsey was enough to sober anyone. "Wreck my car?"

"Wreck the house?" I said. "What do you mean?"

Bitsey got up, turned her back on us and stared out at the pool and the cunningly lit courtyard that surrounded it. "He deserves to be punished."

"He's dead," I pointed out. "That's pretty significant punishment, don't you think?"

She shook her head. "It's not like we have to lie about him. The truth will do just fine." She turned around. "Maybe a little public humiliation will teach those horrible kids of his to mend their ways while they still can."

Personally I didn't think Frank Jr., Celeste and Roger would learn anything from a stunt like she was proposing except to hate their father's second wife even more than they already did. But what the hay. "I'm in. Heck, I'll spread the word to everyone I know about Frank and how he really died.

I'll even write a damned press release and send it to every media outlet in Southern California—if that's what M.J. wants. But Bits, the Jag? I don't think I have it in me to wreck the Jag."

I was trying to lighten the mood, but it wasn't working, at least not with Bitsey. She planted her fists on her hips. "I say burn down the house and drive the car into the pool. What have we got to lose?"

I swallowed hard. I had never seen Bitsey so furious. It wasn't like the stomping around, cursing fury I was prone to. I might fly off the handle, but Bitsey was too much the genteel Southern lady for that. Instead she was cold and bitter, very scary for such a truly nice person. Struck dumb by her outrageous suggestion, M.J. and I could only follow her as she headed for the kitchen.

"We can plant evidence to implicate Frank Jr. as the arsonist," she went on. She was serious.

"And you know how to do this?" I asked. "Don't you watch CSI? You can't hide something like that."

"We wouldn't be hiding it. That's the beauty of it all. We'd just make Frank Jr. look guilty. Or better yet, Wendy. They deserve it. And after all, they'll be the ones to collect the insurance. I'm sure she can think of a hundred ways to spend that much money."

She turned on the steam attachment of M.J.'s elaborate espresso machine. M.J. and I shared a look. Bitsey might be an avenging arsonist, but she made a damned good espresso.

It was after midnight. I had no business drinking coffee, even decaf with lots of milk. But we were avoiding liquor for M.J.'s sake, so coffee it was. We sat in the breakfast nook of M.J.'s kitchen, one of the only cozy rooms in her house. M.J. was wrapped in a pink French terry robe, looking small and childlike with her face washed clean of makeup and her hair pulled back in a ponytail. Even miserable and hung over, the girl managed to still look good.

"Okay," Bitsey said, setting two mugs of perfectly foamed café au lait before us. "Cinnamon or chocolate shavings?"

I've often thought Bitsey should open a coffeehouse. A chain of them. Bitsey's Kitchen Table.

"Okay," she repeated, once we were all settled. "Maybe burning Frank's house down isn't the best idea. But we should at least strip the place and sell off whatever we can. I can't believe Frank left you penniless. Seventeen years of marriage and he does that to you? God, men are horrible."

M.J. stared down at her coffee. "I signed a prenup, you know. But I thought, since we stayed married more than the ten years specified, that I would at least get something. Only it turns out he doesn't own anything in his own name. It's set up so that it all belongs to the company."

"Everything?" I asked. "What about your jewelry? Or the art? " I gestured to a Steve Rucker painting above the sideboard.

"The jewelry's mine," M.J. allowed. "I'll throw it into the ocean before I let Wendy get her greedy mitts on it."

"Amen," said Bitsey. She dumped two spoons of sugar into her cup. I reached for a packet of the blue stuff.

"Who bought the art?" I asked.

M.J.'s face screwed up in a frown. "I bought most of it."

"How?"

"Credit card, of course."

"Whose credit card?" Bitsey asked.

M.J. straightened in her chair. "It's in my name. But Frank always paid the bills."

"Doesn't matter," I said. "The art you bought is legally yours, not some corporation's."

"Or at least half yours," Bitsey said. With eyes narrowed, she looked from M.J. to me and back. "Let's take it. But first let's eat."

She took over the kitchen and made us mushroom omelets and fresh-squeezed orange juice. "I can't believe you don't have any grits," she said as we sat down at the chrome-and-glass breakfast table.

"Even I keep instant grits in my pantry," I threw in.

Though I prefer the real thing, microwave grits are better than no grits.

"Frank likes oatmeal. Liked," M.J. corrected herself. "Liked."

"Another poor choice," I said. "Any man who doesn't like grits should be viewed with suspicion."

"Did Bill like grits?" M.J. asked.

"Kiss off," I threw right back at her. Bill was my second husband, now my second ex-husband.

"Jack loves grits," Bitsey said. "You remember what grits stands for, don't you?" she added. "Girls raised in the South. Grits."

That was us all right. Girls raised in the sweet, green humidity of the deep South, and decades later trying our best to get by in the desert that was Southern California—even if that meant burglarizing our best friend's house.

We worked through the night, stacking paintings, prints, statues and all the silver and china in the garage. By nine in the morning we had a moving van and a storage facility lined up. By noon everything was gone, and by one we were all zonked out at Bitsey's house. Her husband, Jack, woke us when he came home around six.

"What's going on around here?" he said from the door to the master bedroom. His voice carried down the hall to where M.J. and I shared the guest room. "What are you doing asleep, Bits? Why are M.J. and Cat here?" He must have seen the Jag. "And where's my dinner?"

I sat up; M.J. looked at me. We both strained to hear more.

"Honey, I'm home," I muttered. As I said, I don't like Jack. I used to. I mean, on the surface he's a pretty nice guy. Most guys are. But Bitsey was my friend, and more often than not, Jack made her unhappy. That's all I needed to know.

Apparently he closed the door behind him, because although I could tell they were talking, I couldn't make out what they said.

"I think it's time for us to go."

"Maybe so," M.J. agreed.

"What's wrong with the world?" I asked as we slid into yesterday's clothes. "Bitsey's husband is a jerk. Your husband was a jerk. Certainly my two ex-husbands are jerks."

M.J. paused in the process of brushing her hair. "Are you still sleeping with Bill?"

In a weak moment, fueled by margaritas, I'd once revealed that my second ex and I occasionally get together. I didn't say we slept together, but M.J. and Bitsey had drawn their own conclusions. Accurate conclusions, I might add. I searched for my sandals. "Every now and again."

"Recently?"

I looked up at her. "Why do you want to know?"

It was her turn to look away. "Because he called me a few days ago."

"He called you? Bill called you? But why?"

She didn't answer, which was answer enough.

"You're kidding. He hit on you, the bereaved widow? My best friend? And he's trying to get you in the sack?"

"I hung up on him." M.J. stared earnestly at me. "As soon as I realized what he was leading up to, I hung up. And you're right. He is a jerk."

I managed a smile, but my heart was racing. Not from jealousy, though, and certainly not from anger at M.J. Bill was a jerk; I'd always known that. We'd divorced once I realized that he'd never been faithful, not even for one month during the four years we were together. But this was even worse. M.J. was my friend. How could he set his sights on her?

And why did the fact that he was attracted to her leave me so panicked? Any man still breathing is attracted to M.J.

But that sort of logic didn't matter to me.

M.J. put a hand on my arm. "I'm sorry, Cat. Are you okay?"

"I'm fine. Fine. And there's no reason for you to apologize. It's not your fault he's a lowlife asshole."

I raked my fingers through my hair. I thought I was beyond being hurt by the scumsucker, but my hands were shaking. "I wish I was a lesbian. Women are so far superior to men."

"Yes," M.J. agreed. "We are." She gave me a hug, which I really needed. "But despite Frank and Bill, I have to believe there are still some good guys out there."

I let out a rude snort. "Yeah, maybe. But they're all pre-pubescent. The trouble with men is that they all suffer from testosterone poisoning. It shrinks their brains and swells their balls and they're never the same again."

M.J. laughed, but I was serious. "Come on, Cat," she said. "Surely you've known one or two good guys."

"No. I don't think so."

"Well, I have."

"Yeah? Who?"

"My old high school boyfriend, for one."

"If he was so great, why didn't you just marry him?"

M.J. sighed. "I wanted to. But he went away to college on a football scholarship, and Mama had me on the beauty pageant circuit. That was when I really believed I could have a future in the movies. I guess he and I just sort of drifted apart. You know how it is at that age."

I slipped on my shoes and let the subject drop. But her remembered high school passion reminded me of my own. He'd been a skinny Cajun boy and our favorite date had been to go fishing. At least we always took fishing gear when we set off in his flatboat. But we never did catch anything. We were too busy making out.

Despite my cynicism, I couldn't help smiling at the memory. God, how I'd loved that boy.

"Anyway," M.J. went on. "Not to change the subject, but I thought of something, or maybe I dreamed it. Anyway, we have to go back to the house." She smiled like an impish kitten. "Frank kept mad money. I don't know exactly where, but I remember last year when his grandson had a DUI and they wouldn't take credit cards at the jail. He went upstairs and came down with a fistful of cash."

"Is there a safe?"

"Yes, but it's downstairs, and I already checked it."

While Bitsey fed her demanding husband, M.J. and I took

my car to her house. She'd padlocked the gate so we knew Frank Jr. hadn't been in yet. But it was only a matter of time. Two hours and twenty minutes later we found a false bottom in the humidor in Frank's study. It was a large, freestanding piece made of beautiful English oak.

Big humidor equals big hidden panel equals big, big payoff. Frank might have let M.J. collect art, but it was obvious that he collected money. Packets of twenties, fifties, hundreds and five-hundred-dollar bills. In his desk drawer we found three collections of the new state quarters and an odd bag of felt-wrapped coins. Old ones.

M.J.'s eyes lit up as she snatched the bag from the drawer. "These must be valuable or he wouldn't have kept them." Then she grabbed a few more of her clothes, filled a garbage bag with boxes of shoes, and we left.

"Aren't you going to padlock the gate?

"Nope. And I didn't lock the house, either. I'm outta here, and I'm never coming back."

"Maybe someone will break in," I said, "and burn it down. Wouldn't Bitsey be pleased."

"Me, too." M.J. snapped her seat belt on.

I gave her a sidelong look. She meant it. Since Frank's death, M.J. had spent over a week drunk and less than a day sober. But I could sense some sort of change in her, as if she'd turned a corner, from shock to sorrow to really pissed off. I steered my VW onto the boulevard that led to the gate house for the exclusive neighborhood.

"So. Are we heading back to Bitsey's?" she asked.

"No. Not there. Tonight you can stay with me. Tomorrow we'll figure out your next step."

Bitsey came over around eleven the next day. I was working from home, mostly phone stuff, and I had a meeting at a client's home at two. M.J. was in the shower. She'd already exercised for an hour and a half, made us a healthy breakfast of OJ, cracked-wheat toast, organic boysenberry jam and melon balls. Bitsey had a Krispy Kreme napkin in her hand

and a sprinkle of sugar on the stomach of her olive-green jumper.

Bitsey flung her hobo bag onto the kitchen counter, stepped out of her shoes, then plopped down in my window seat. I looked at her over the rim of my red polka-dot Peepers. "Have you been crying? What did he do?"

She shot me a belligerent glare. "Why do you always assume it's Jack? You never give him a chance."

Tread lightly. "Well, since it's only you and him at home now…" I raised my brows and trailed off.

"I talked to Margaret this morning."

Margaret was the middle of Bitsey's three perfect daughters, the one with the most potential for not being perfect. "Is she all right?"

"I don't know." Bitsey heaved a weary sigh. "You know she transferred to Arizona State. Well, it turns out she hates it there."

"The state or the university?" I asked. "Or maybe the state *and* the university?"

She ignored me. "What if she drops out? Jack says if she does she can't come home."

I sat down next to her. "That's not much of a threat anymore. At her age she probably won't want to come home."

Bitsey looked down at her lap and plucked at the Krispy Kreme sugar. She needed a manicure, I thought, then immediately hated myself for noticing. Sometimes I can be so shallow. The last thing Bitsey needed was her friends magnifying her insignificant flaws. Jack was more than up to that task.

She let out another deep sigh. "I wish I didn't have to go home, either."

Uh-oh. This didn't sound good. For all the ups and downs in her marriage, the one thing Bitsey had never done was consider abandoning it. At least not out loud. I might not like Jack Albertson all that much, but I'd been divorced twice and I knew just how hard the process could be. I wasn't so sure Bitsey was up to it.

"What's wrong, Bits?"

She was blinking hard. "What if…" She swallowed hard, then turned to look at me. "What if Jack's having an affair? If Frank could cheat on M.J.—you know how beautiful she is and he was just this wrinkled old man—if he could cheat on her, then what do you suppose Jack is doing to me?"

"Oh, Bitsey, I'm sure he isn't doing anything of the sort," I lied. For friends like Bitsey, you lie even if it tastes like gall.

She stared me straight in the eye. "You're lying. I know you don't like Jack. He's critical and demanding, and he takes me for granted. You've pointed that out a hundred times."

"That doesn't mean he's cheating."

She pressed her lips together and blinked several times. "Maybe. Maybe not."

M.J. came into the kitchen, her hair in a towel. "I don't think Jack's the type to cheat," she said. Obviously she'd overheard our conversation.

Bitsey heaved that same, desolate sigh. "Did you think Frank was the type?"

M.J. shoved her hands deep into the robe's pockets and shrugged. "I tried to pretend he wasn't, but I knew he was. After all, he was married when we met."

M.J. had been a trophy wife. Before that she'd been a twenty-three-year-old beauty pageant winner and aspiring actress, working as a hostess in Frank Hollander's restaurant. He had kids almost her age, and when he'd dumped wife number one for her it must have been as bad as any cliché out there: a middle-aged man and his sex kitten.

Of course, I can understand why he'd fallen for her, and it's not just how she looks. M.J. is one of those good-hearted, loving women who always tries to please the people she loves. And she'd really loved Frank.

There'd been no pleasing Frank's kids, though. Some would say she's getting what she deserves now, and I admit I even thought it. But not for long. To know M.J. is to love her. And I do love her.

"I used to be thin," Bitsey said. "When Jack and I met I wore a size eight. Then I had all those kids."

"I wish I had kids," M.J. said in a quiet voice. "Tight buns and great abs are no substitute for a real family."

"What about me?" I put in. "I don't have kids or tight buns. By rights y'all should be feeling sorry for me."

Neither of them laughed. Bitsey made coffee and we went out into the courtyard.

"That's new," Bitsey said of the plant nestled beside the pond.

"Louisiana Blue Iris," I said.

That made M.J. smile. "There used to be drifts of those back home in the marshy area behind our house. Where'd you get it?"

"That specialty florist on San Pedro Avenue." I stroked the deep purplish-blue flower. "A little taste of home, but without all the aggravating people."

We were silent for a minute, then Bitsey looked at M.J. "Have you considered going home for a while?"

M.J. frowned. "Home? You mean like to Louisiana?"

"Don't talk like that around me," I said. "It gives me hives and I've got a very important meeting this afternoon."

Bitsey didn't spare me a glance. "Now that you're out of that house and have a little money, you could go home to see your mother."

"She moved to Florida," M.J. said. "But maybe…"

"Does that mean you don't have anybody left in New Orleans?"

"Not really. I mean, I have an aunt and two cousins. But I think maybe they've moved, too. The cousins, I mean."

Bitsey stared into her half-empty coffee mug. "My dad's still there, and it's been three years. I guess I ought to go visit him. And I was planning to go," she added. "But now…"

"Now what?" I asked when M.J. didn't. You have to understand that Bitsey isn't the sort to come right out and reveal her feelings. Maybe if she's angry, but not if she's sad. Right now she was seriously down in the dumps.

M.J. reached out and squeezed Bitsey's hand. "Hey, Bits, what's going on?"

Bitsey shook her head and put on her "it's nothing" smile. "I got this invitation. That's all. I was halfway thinking of going..."

"What, to a wedding?" M.J. asked.

"To my high school reunion," Bitsey admitted. "My thirtieth."

"Oh, you should go," M.J. said. "I went to my twentieth and it was so much fun."

Bitsey slowly shook her head. "I don't know. Reunions can be hard and Jack can't get away." She sent me a quick, guilty look.

To my credit I kept my mouth shut and didn't roll my eyes. But there was no way I would be able to restrain myself for long, so I changed the subject. "You never finished telling me what Margaret had to say."

Bitsey gave me a grateful look.

"That's right," she began. "Well, like I said, Margaret's not happy in Tempe. Five years, three majors, and now she's thinking of taking a year off from school."

"Maybe that's not such a bad thing," I said. "Maybe she needs more time to figure out what she really wants to do. "

"Tell that to Jack," Bitsey muttered. Then she shook her head. "The thing is, there's something else going on. I can feel it. I don't know what it is exactly, but she's so unsettled. So unfocused. Something's wrong. I can hear it in her voice. But she won't say what."

Kids and how to deal with them were the one thing M.J. and I had no experience with—unless you count our mutual hatred of Frank's awful kids. Generally we tried to be sympathetic with Bitsey's situation, but we'd learned long ago not to be too forceful with our opinions. I could rag on Jack, but when it came to her kids, Bitsey was very sensitive.

A cloud passed over us, blocking the sun. It was such a rare occurrence that we all paused and looked up at the sky.

"What I wouldn't give for a real thunderstorm," I said. "Remember when you were a kid in the summertime and there was a storm, seems like every afternoon?"

"That's the only time Mama used to let us play in the attic, when it was raining and we couldn't go outside," Bitsey said.

"We used to play under the house." I said. Actually, it was a trailer up on cinder blocks, but they didn't need to know that. Bitsey was a product of a Catholic elementary school and one of the best private high schools in New Orleans. M.J. was a suburban beauty queen. But I'd grown up in one of those spontaneous trailer parks that used to sprout up along the river road above New Orleans. To look at the three of us, we seemed pretty much the same. But we were a blue blood, a nouveau riche, and a redneck. And though we all visited our families now and again, we'd never all been back in New Orleans at the same time—which was just fine with me.

M.J. put her legs up on a wicker footstool. "You know, Bits, you ought to go to your reunion anyway. You could go with one of your old girlfriends."

"Oh, I couldn't do that."

"Yes, you could," I said. "Why should you have to miss your reunion because of Jack?"

"I'm not missing it because of him," she said in this defensive voice. "He told me I could go."

"Big of him," I muttered.

"Be nice," M.J. said.

"Look, Cat. The reason I don't want to go…it's because of my weight. Okay? Are you happy now? I'm fat and I don't want my old boyfriend and all my cheerleader pals to see me like this."

Why am I so stupid? As long as I've known Bitsey, you'd think I could have figured that out myself. Trying to back-pedal I said, "Come on. You don't think anybody else has gained a few pounds?"

She shook her head and looked away. "It's a rule. Only thin people or the really successful, filthy rich ones go to their re-unions."

"Actually," M.J. said, "I'd been thinking you looked a lit-tle thinner lately, especially around your face."

For the first time since she'd arrived, Bitsey smiled. "Really? I've been dieting," she admitted. "I told myself that if I lost twenty pounds I'd go to the reunion."

"Good idea. So, how many have you lost?"

"Nine." Her smile faded. "In two months only nine pounds. Even with the Meridia I didn't make a dent."

"But nine pounds is a good start," M.J. said. "Really, it is. When is this reunion anyway?"

"Three weeks."

The wheels were spinning; I could see it in M.J.'s eyes. "What if you and I took a little trip down south together?" she began. "I could get out of here—I don't mean your apartment, Cat. I mean this town. Southern California. The desert." She leaned forward to grab Bitsey's arm. "I could use a change of scenery, and you could go to your reunion—"

"But I don't want to go—"

"And in between, I'll be your personal trainer."

Bitsey started laughing. "My personal trainer? You mean, like, exercise? I don't think so."

"Come on, Bitsey. I need to practice on someone. Think about it. I have to either get a job or get a husband. And since I'm not ready for marriage—I don't even have a boyfriend—it'll have to be a job. But what kind of job am I eligible for? I suppose I could teach ceramics, but somehow I don't think that would even pay for my manicures. But I could be a personal trainer. I could."

She was right. I leaned forward. "You know, that's a good idea. You're already an expert in all sorts of exercises, and God knows you're a walking advertisement."

"Please, Bits, let's do this," M.J. said. "Let me practice on you and get you gorgeous. We could have a really good time down in New Orleans. By the time I'm through with you, you'll make all your old girlfriends jealous and wow that old boyfriend of yours."

"Hey? What about me?" I asked. Despite my aversion to them ever meeting any of my seedy family, I was beginning to feel left out. Besides, without them here to keep me sane, I might murder Bill. Accidentally, of course. "I could use a little making-over myself, and I could definitely stand to run into one of my old boyfriends, so long as he's single and rich and not allergic to commitment."

"That would be even better!" M.J. exclaimed. "All three of us together." She caught my hand in hers, then took Bitsey's in her other. "Let's do it. We all have reasons to visit, so why not go together? We can make it a road trip, and along the way we'll all get gorgeous. We'll look up our old boyfriends, and we'll have a terrific time. Come on, Bits, what do you say?"

Bitsey wanted to do it; I could see it in her sweet, yearning expression. But she was afraid. Well, damn it, so was I. Bad enough to go back there and deal with my mother and her other lousy kids, but last night after my conversation with M.J., I'd dreamed about making out in a flat aluminum boat with a lanky Cajun boy. Sure as anything, I was setting myself up for disappointment.

But it didn't matter, because suddenly I wanted this trip in the worst way. "I'm in. I'm going with M.J. to Louisiana." I grabbed Bitsey's other hand and stared challengingly at her. "It's on you, Barbara Jean. Are you in or are you out?"

Bitsey

I have been on and off diets for the past twenty-two years.

I diet before every single holiday, before we go on vacation, before every major social event, and afterward, too. My closet is organized with size eights in the back, then tens, and so on and so forth. I wore the eights and tens during the eighties when Jack and I first came to California. During the nineties I graduated to twelves and fourteens. The millennium ushered in the sixteens. Now I'm in eighteens, but I've taken a stand. I refuse to go into size twenty. It's getting mighty tight, though.

When the invitation came from my high school reunion committee, it seemed like an ideal way to motivate myself. I made an appointment with my doctor, started taking Meridia, and vowed that this time I would succeed. And at first I did. I lost nine pounds the first month. That's pretty good. But since then I've lost nothing. I'm stalled. Nine pounds is not enough to return to New Orleans. Nine pounds is not enough to face Eddie.

Eddie, Eddie, Eddie. What is wrong with me? I wouldn't be behaving like an insecure fifteen-year-old if a different name had been listed on the reunion committee. But there it had been: Edward Dusson, Cochair. Eddie Dusson. Harley Ed, I used to call him. Dangerous Dusson, the other cheerleaders had said. My heart hurts just to remember how much I loved him in high school, and how much he'd loved me. But if I walked up to him today, would he even recognize me?

Then again, who's to say that he hasn't gained a hundred pounds himself?

I can't imagine that, though. Not Eddie. Besides, if he's on the reunion committee, he must still be fit and trim, still good-looking, and probably rich by now, too.

If only I could go see him and yet not have him see me. It was almost a relief when Jack said he couldn't get away from work. I didn't have to decide; he'd done it for me. I could be angry with Jack and hide at home, and on the weekend of the reunion, I could sit two thousand miles away and pig out on Oreo and Jamoca Almond Fudge.

But I have more pressing problems than Eddie's weight and his bank account. This morning I telephoned Margaret, and her roommate informed me that Margaret had moved out. I must have sounded like an utter fool, a mother too stupid to know what her own child was up to. "Yes. Two weeks ago," her roommate had said in this "you poor, pathetic thing" voice. The snooty little brat.

It turns out my middle child, the one with the highest IQ but the lowest level of ambition, is living with some guy she's never even mentioned to me.

I knew something was wrong. I knew it. I should never have let her live off campus. I should have made her stay at an in-state university. I should have realized that even at twenty-two she wasn't responsible enough for college. Junior college maybe, but not a big liberal arts school.

I called her on her cell phone, and after three tries reached her. She was in a bad mood already, because I'd awakened her. She is so much like her father, a total grump until he's had his coffee. But it was ten o'clock in the morning. On a weekday most people are up by then.

Except that cocktail waitresses aren't like most people. A cocktail waitress! It turns out that she works a late shift from six until two in the morning, and sometimes even later. But she makes great tips, she told me, so she thinks it's worth it.

Oh, and his name is Gray. "He's a bass player, Mom, in a roots rock band."

A roots rock band. What is that supposed to mean? And what kind of musical roots does Tempe, Arizona, have anyway?

I shouldn't have gone to Cat's house after that call. I should have just crawled back into my bed. After all, Jack wouldn't be home until after eight. All I had to do was order dinner from Gourmet Wheels, put it into my own pans, and he'd never know the difference.

But I couldn't make myself sleep during the day without taking a Xanax, and I didn't want to do that. So I threw on a green linen jumper over a white T-shirt, stuck my feet in my favorite espadrilles, and ran to Cat and M.J.

"It's on you, Barbara Jean," said Cat in that schoolyard bully way she sometimes gets. "Are you in or are you out?"

If they each hadn't been holding one of my hands, I would have said "Out." I would have. Except that when Cat and M.J. gang up on you, there's really no way to defeat them, at least no way for me to defeat them. But it's not because I'm a wimp. It's because they make me brave. They grab hold of my hands, and all of a sudden Cat's loud bravado and M.J.'s determined optimism spread through me like the enticing aroma of fresh-baked cinnamon rolls on a Sunday morning when the girls were little and all lived at home.

"I'm…in," I said, hoping I wouldn't regret it.

"Yes!" M.J. cried. "Here, let's have a toast."

We lifted our coffee mugs and clinked them together. "To road trips," Cat toasted.

"To losing weight," I added. "And fast."

"To friends," M.J. said. "And maybe old boyfriends, too."

The rest of the morning passed in a blur. We had plans to make, a diet and exercise regimen and a travel itinerary to arrange. Cat would have to take time off from work. We decided to drive M.J.'s Jaguar. Cat was ecstatic about that. She hates to fly, and we would need a car when we got there anyway. So we'd make it into a real road trip, and if I wanted, we could stop to see Margaret in Arizona.

I calculated that if I restricted my caloric intake to below a thousand a day I could lose eight pounds in the next three weeks. Maybe even ten.

But only a thousand calories? I'd already eaten that much for breakfast.

That night I told Jack about our plans. I had returned home midafternoon, and in a frenzied burst—of guilt, I guess—I cooked his favorite Fiesta shrimp pasta for dinner. I also prepared a pot of gumbo—his mother's recipe, not mine—and a pork roast stuffed with garlic. Tomorrow I planned to make a pan of spinach lasagna as well as a pot of Chicken à la Bushnell. That way I could freeze more than a dozen meals for him to eat while I was gone. All he would have to do was supplement them with salads and a hot roll or two.

"Why are you driving there?" he asked. "That's a four- or five-day trip, assuming nothing goes wrong."

"What can go wrong? As long as we stay on I-10 heading east we can't get lost."

He made a sarcastic sound. "The way you three jabber, you'll miss a turn and end up in Idaho before you notice."

"We will not!"

He got up from the table and without responding, headed for the television in the den.

I hate when he ignores me like that. It's like getting in the final word, without saying anything. I wanted to scream, but of course, I didn't.

After I loaded the dishwasher, I followed him into the den. He was reading the latest issue of *U.S. News & World Report* with the television on.

"I'll leave the freezer stocked so you won't have to worry about meals."

"That's all right," he said, without looking up. "I can always order out. Just leave the phone number of that place you use."

"The place I use?" I stared stupidly at him. "What place?"

"I don't know the name. Meals on Wheels. Something like that."

My heart did this great big, guilty flip-flop in my chest. He knew I sometimes used Gourmet Wheels? I was ready to abandon the trip right there. The one value I still had to Jack was my cooking ability. But if he knew about Gourmet Wheels and they were good enough for him, what did he really need me for?

He tossed the magazine on a side table and glanced at me. "So, when do you leave?"

"Um...next Friday," I mumbled. "I'll call you every night."

"Okay." He reached for the remote control and flipped through the channels. "You'd better tell the girls. Oh, look. They're rerunning that Jackie Gleason biography, the one with the guy from *Raymond.*"

I went into the bedroom, closed the door and burst into tears. Then I called Cat and M.J.

We stayed on the telephone for two hours. You'd think we were teenagers the way we talk. Cat can make anyone laugh, she just has that way about her. She's sarcastic and totally irreverent. She could be a stand-up comic if she wanted to, which always makes me wonder about her upbringing. I read Roseanne Barr's biography, and Louie Anderson's, and I know that the best comedians usually come from awful childhoods. The fact that Cat hardly ever mentions her family actually reveals a lot about her. But all she's ever told us is that she grew up in one of those small towns strung up and down both sides of the Mississippi. For the most part they're just clusters of little frame houses and the occasional trailer park, the kind that always attract tornadoes. My guess is that her father worked in one of the chemical plants.

As for me, I, too, sprang from that part of the state, only my grandfather owned six hundred acres of land there, an old sugar plantation that had been in the family since the early nineteenth century. He sold it right after World War II to one of those same chemical companies, and he made a lot more money from the sale than he ever did raising sugar.

Thanks to Pepere, my family has lived well ever since. He bought a huge Greek Revival house in the richest New Orleans neighborhood he could find, the Garden District, then proceeded to join every private club and exclusive society he could. He lived like a king for ten more years until he walked in front of a streetcar. He lingered three weeks, then died.

A month later my father eloped with my mother, a woman his father hadn't approved of, and moved her into his father's house. He lives there still, but alone now. Memere died when I was six. Mama died eight years ago. But at seventy-seven Daddy is going strong. He'll be overjoyed to have all of us stay with him.

Cat and M.J. were pretty pleased by the idea, too. I just hope they don't become awestruck when they see the way I grew up. The problem is, our house is huge. Magnificent even. It's been written up and photographed for innumerable publications, as much for its architectural value as for the antiques that fill every nook and cranny. Mother bought only the best. Her entire life was dedicated to proving that she was good enough for the La Farges. Even though Grandmother was never as unkind to her as Grandfather had been, I don't think Mother ever felt good enough for either of them, let alone the rest of her in-laws. So she did everything she could to make herself seem good enough to belong in their family.

Mother took classes in all sorts of subjects: art, music, antiques, and she was on so many committees and foundations

I don't know how she kept up. Our house was used for every kind of society fete you could imagine. But she only picked the charities that made her look like a generous benefactress or patron. Forget political fund-raisers. She was terrified of offending someone by taking a position on anything that might be controversial. But crippled children or multiple sclerosis or art education, the museum or symphony or ballet association—those were her charities.

To be fair, she did a lot of good. She was even nominated for the *Times-Picayune*'s Loving Cup. But she didn't do it out of love. She did it to look good.

I always knew I was a disappointment to Mama. I hated all that society posturing, and I didn't want to join a sorority at LSU. But of course I did. She planned my wedding to meet her standards, then helped us pick out an appropriately grand house to live in. But she was always on me about my clothes, my friends and especially my weight. It was a relief when Jack was transferred to California and I no longer had to see her every day.

Fortunately my brother married a woman even better connected in New Orleans society than he was. They were married just before Jack and I moved, and she and Mother became inseparable. I was sick with jealousy for years. Six years, twice a month with Dr. Herzog, to be exact. Then Mama died and so did my jealousy, though I still see Dr. Herzog now and again for other reasons. Anyway, my brother and his wife live in a monstrous Palladian-style mansion on St. Charles Avenue, so Daddy's house is practically empty. We girls would have the entire second floor to ourselves.

Cat yawned into her end of the phone. "Some of us have to work tomorrow. Y'all can talk all night if you want, but I'm turning in."

"'Night, Cat," I said.

"'Night, Cat," echoed M.J.

After the click M.J. started laughing. "You should see her face. She can't stand to miss anything, so you know she must be tired."

"So am I," I said. "Tired and excited and scared."

"Me, too," M.J. said.

"Are you going to stay there? In New Orleans, I mean?"

She was quiet. All I heard was the faint rhythm of her breathing. "I don't know. I don't think so. But maybe. Except that I need you and Cat. What would I do without y'all? So no. I don't think I can stay."

All it would take was the right man to keep her there. I knew it but didn't say so. The odd thing was, M.J. was even more scared than I was to go home. And I think maybe Cat was, too. It was a novel concept. What is it about home and the family and friends we leave behind? Compared to them we were all failures—failed marriages, failed careers. Well, Cat was doing okay in that department. But she's the one with two divorces.

On the other hand, I told myself, marriages unravel in New Orleans, too. Youthful plans fall apart. Children disappoint you. You disappoint you. Maybe the secret to high school reunions was lying, creating another wonderful life that makes everyone else's feel inadequate. I could do that, couldn't I?

"Well, good night," M.J. said. "See you at nine. And wear comfortable clothes and tennis shoes."

"Okay," I said. "Good night." Comfortable clothes? Tennis shoes? I hung up the telephone and went to my closet. Big loose dresses. Too-tight pants. I closed the door and turned away, then reached for the Xanax. Tomorrow was going to be rough. I needed a really good night's sleep to get through it.

I woke up late. Jack had already left for work. I saw his cereal bowl in the sink and his orange juice glass. I hadn't made him breakfast on a weekday since Elizabeth left for college. She's our youngest. Cat was gone, too, when I arrived at her house. The whole world was at work except for me and M.J., and she was doing warm-up stretches. I slunk into Cat's sunroom feeling guilty, but M.J. didn't fuss about the time.

An hour later I was close to tears. "No. I cannot do even

one more." Crunches, lunges, pliés, punches. I couldn't do anything that involved any moving at all. I lay on my back on the floor and wiped the sweat from my brow. "I think I broke something, M.J. I'm not joking."

She ignored me and like a sadistic drill sergeant, fixed me with an unsympathetic gaze. "You didn't break anything, Bitsey. But you did use muscles you haven't used in years."

Somehow I rolled over and pushed up onto my knees. "And I don't want to ever use them again."

"Once we cool down you won't feel so bad. Just remember your goal, to make that old boyfriend of yours sick over what he missed out on."

Of course, that was the precise moment I caught a glimpse of myself in the mirror over the gold-leafed, side table against the far wall. A red-faced, middle-aged woman with ugly hair and wet spots everywhere her too-tight T-shirt snugged up to the rolls in her belly and arms. I squeezed my eyes closed against the sight, and against the tears. "This is not going to work, not in three weeks. Not in three years."

"Oh, yes, it will." She steered me toward the powder room. "Wash your face, comb your hair, then grab your sunglasses and visor. We're going for a walk."

That day I drank ten glasses of water with lemon, and three glasses of juice. Orange juice, cranberry juice and white grape juice. I had a salad for lunch, grilled vegetables and salmon for dinner and an apple for my evening snack.

"No cheating," was the last thing M.J. said as I crawled into my Volvo. "I'll be over in the morning to clean out your pantry and your closet," she said, looking as fresh and perky as a prep school cheerleader.

"I hate you," I muttered, glaring at her in the rearview mirror as I pulled out of the driveway. "I hate you and I hope you gain a hundred pounds. And that your boobs sag down to your waist." She wouldn't be so perky then.

I was in bed when Jack got home, and in bed when Cat called. I didn't answer the phone but she knew I was there.

"I heard what she did to you," Cat said into the answering machine. "And you have my condolences. Call me if you need anything. I have some prescription-strength Advil and three heating pads. Good night, Bitsey. I love you."

The next day M.J. and I walked again, though walking is a relative term. She strode, I staggered. I suppose that averages out to walking. Afterward I watched while she emptied my pantry of every gram of carbohydrates. "Nothing white stays," she said, "except on your hips and thighs."

"But you drink," I protested. "Like a fish," I added, and none too nicely. But since drinking was her only vice, I meant to milk it for all it was worth.

She sent me a cool look. "The difference is that I exercise enough to counteract the calories. You'll be able to drink, too, once you lose the weight."

"So since I never want to drink as much as you do, does that mean I won't have to exercise as much?" My voice was sweet, but I was seriously annoyed.

She gave me a long, even look that made me feel like an evil stepmother. If I didn't want to accept her help, fine. I didn't have to make ugly little digs at her. But before I could attempt to redeem myself, she shrugged one shoulder. "You can do what you like, Bitsey. Meanwhile this stuff can all go to the food bank. Now, let's tackle your closet."

Cat came over after work. She stared at the mountain of clothes on my bed. It's a big bed, a California king, and the clothes M.J. said I could no longer keep smothered it. Cat picked up an ivory silk shell.

"She says I can't wear it," I explained. "Even if I lose weight."

"*When* you lose weight," M.J. corrected me. "The problem is, the blouse isn't your shade of white."

"That's because it's not white. It's ivory."

"And it's too yellow for your complexion. Just like your hair," M.J. said.

I stared at her. First my pantry, then my closet. Now my hair?

Cat took a seat across the room, grinning like a redneck

in a ringside seat at a Dixie wrestling match. Round one might have gone to M.J. But I wasn't down yet. "I've always been a blonde and I'm not changing now," I said, feeling more than a little rebellious.

"I've made an appointment for you with my hairdresser. Tomorrow at eleven," M.J. went on as if nothing I said mattered. "By the way, have you weighed in today?"

I wanted to strangle her. She was as bad as Jack, always honing in on my weakest spot and winning the argument, of course.

To put it mildly, I had a terrible week. My whole body hurt, my pantry and closet were embarrassingly naked, and I decided I hated cottage cheese.

My daughters were no solace. Margaret never returned my calls, Elizabeth couldn't talk because she had a big test and a big paper and a social calendar that left no room for her poor old mother. Jennifer talked, but I made the mistake of telling her I was on a diet, and after that all she could do was lecture me with her theories of what worked for her. Seeing as how she's never been more than one hundred and ten pounds, her theories didn't exactly carry much weight with me. No pun intended.

The only good thing that happened started off as a bad thing. M.J.'s hairdresser, Darius, cut all my hair off. And I do mean all. He had to get rid of the old perm, he said, and as much of the old color as possible. He left me a measly inch and a half. Then he dyed it an ashy blonde. I cried all the way to Nordstrom where, to make me feel better, M.J. bought me a pale aqua sweater and a pair of silver clip-on earrings shaped like shells.

Only after she left my house did I venture into the bathroom and stare at my strange reflection. Jack was going to have a fit.

Or maybe not.

What if he didn't care? Or worse, what if he didn't even notice?

I fiddled with the hair. Smart and sassy was what Darius had said. Hair with attitude.

Actually, I looked like Meg Ryan's mother. Well, maybe her fat older sister. One thing I did notice was that the short hair made my eyes look bigger. And the aqua sweater gave them a sparkle. I decided to reapply my mascara and eyeliner.

When Jack got home I had dinner ready "You cut your hair," he said as we sat down to eat.

I ruffled my hand through the short, thick tufts. "Yes, though the hairdresser went a little overboard. Edward Scissorhands. But I like the color."

He grunted. He probably didn't know who or what *Edward Scissorhands* was. He's not a movie person, even after fifteen years in California. He glanced at me again. "I forgot how much you look like Margaret. Or the other way around."

That was the best part of the day. Of the week. He thought I looked like Margaret, who is probably the prettiest of our girls. That's when I decided I loved my new hairstyle, the cut, the color, and most of all, the attitude.

We planned to leave on Friday. I wasn't going to pack much. Instead I would buy some new outfits during the trip. I'd lost an additional six pounds this week. Six pounds in a week! The first few days I'd been so sore I could hardly move. But there's nothing like success to make pain insignificant. By Friday I meant to lose two more pounds, and along the trip I hoped to lose another three or four. At least I would have met my twenty-pound goal. And I'd still have another week in New Orleans before the actual reunion. Maybe five more pounds?

In between exercise sessions, during all the free time I had left over from my five-minute meals, I'd made arrangements for the housekeeper and gardener. Their checks were already written for Jack to dispense. The refrigerator was stocked with everything he liked, and all he had to do was feed the cat, feed himself and put his dirty clothes in the bathroom hamper.

As I watched him drive off to work that Friday morning, it occurred to me how easy his home life was. No decisions, no responsibilities. He provided the paycheck, and in return he lived here and expected that his every need would be taken care of. I suppose it's the fulfillment of the contract we made when we said "I do."

I have a degree in early childhood education, and I taught two years before Jennifer was born. But for the past twenty-five years I've been a stay-at-home mom with no complaints from him. Or from me. Jack is a wonderful provider and I also have income from my trust fund, which I use mainly to build up the girls' trust funds.

But he's unhappy. I'm sure of it. And I must be, too, if I'm driving two thousand miles and torturing myself to lose weight just so I can see Eddie Dusson smile when he sees me.

I hugged my arms around myself as Jack's Lexus turned the corner and disappeared. He'd given me a quick kiss—a peck, really—and told me to have a good time. Then he'd gone to work.

I gnawed on my left thumbnail. Maybe I should worry more about impressing Jack than impressing Eddie.

Maybe I shouldn't be going on this harebrained trip at all.

Then M.J. and her big champagne-colored cat of a car came purring down the street with Fats Domino blaring "Walking to New Orleans," and my decision was made. I was eighteen again, going on a road trip with my two best girl-friends, and we were going to have a blast.

I fitted my suitcases next to theirs in the trunk, loaded three plastic containers of cut fruit into the ice chest along-side all the bottled water and slid a six-pack of toilet tissue under the seat. I had baby wipes, too, for the nasty truck-stop bathrooms we were sure to encounter, especially if we drank all that water.

"I brought lots of nail polish," M.J. said. "We can do ped-icures and manicures and we'll stop in Dallas to get new out-fits."

"Don't you mean Houston? I don't think Dallas is along I-10," I said.

"The fact is," Cat said, "We can do whatever the hell we want." She gave me a devilish grin, then handed me a pair of sunglasses, cat-eyed glasses with navy-blue lenses and a V of diamonds at each corner. "I'll be Patrick Swayze, you be Wesley Snipes, and M.J. can be John Leguizamo. Like in *Wong Foo*," she added when I gave her a confused look. "We're going glamorous and we're going to leave people staring after us as we go by."

What we got was a speeding ticket before we were barely out of the Bakersfield city limits.

Of course, we didn't actually get the ticket, because M.J. and her fabulous chest were at the wheel. But it wasn't a testosterone-driven C.H.I.P who went gaga at the sight of my gorgeous pal. It was an estrogen-deprived female motorcycle cop, pretty but butch, and not much older than my daughters. She gave us a tolerant lecture, warned us to slow down and left before we did.

"Well," M.J. said. "That was a first. I charmed a lesbian cop."

"I told you. This is *Wong Foo*—the Lesbian Version," Cat said.

"Except that none of us are homosexual. Are we?" I added.

"Oh, no, " Cat said. "I like men. They're usually lousy men, but nevertheless, they're men."

"But if I *did* like women," M.J. said as she pulled back onto the interstate, "I would have liked her. She had the prettiest complexion and a cupid's bow mouth. Did you notice?"

"Especially when she said 'I'll let it go this time,'" Cat added from the front passenger seat. "You know, I wonder why we get turned on by the people we do. I mean, not just straight or gay, but why one guy and not another? Why do I always pick charming jerks? Why does M.J. like sugar daddies, and Bitsey like…" She swiveled around to look at me. "Come to think of it, I don't know what your type is, Bits. I mean, Jack is such a regular hardworking kind of guy."

"Whom you do not like," I reminded her.

"Only when he takes you for granted. So Bits, what *is* your type?"

I put on my cat-eyed glasses. "I don't know. Maybe I don't have a type."

"What about that old boyfriend you mentioned? He was your type in high school. Was he like Jack?"

No. Eddie was nothing like Jack. In many ways he was the exact opposite. He'd been the boy from the wrong side of the tracks, the public school hood who had fascinated the good little Catholic schoolgirl I'd once been.

"Eddie was wild," I said, mainly to placate Cat. "And I was a good girl."

She laughed. "You still are."

There was nothing wrong with being good, with doing the responsible thing. Even so, her words hurt. "I'm sorry I'm so boring." I looked out the window, at the fields of citrus trees in rigid green rows.

"I didn't say you were boring." She turned around to look at me. "Bits, that's not what I said or what I meant."

"It doesn't matter."

"Obviously it does." She reached back and tugged on my skirt. "Is that what this Eddie said when y'all broke up? That you were too boring for a hotshot like him?"

That fast my anger bled away. How could I be angry with Cat? She was my friend, and I knew she loved me. In some ways she even envied me. Stylish, successful, career-woman Cat envied plump mother and housefrau Bitsey. I looked at her and smiled. "He didn't say those exact words, but I knew that's what he meant. I think maybe by then the novelty of dating a rich society girl had worn off."

M.J. glanced back at me. "I knew you went to private schools. But you were a rich society girl?"

Shoot. I hadn't meant to say that. On the other hand, they'd figure it out the minute they saw Daddy's three-story cottage. So I told them my story, all except for the part about

Mother committing suicide because no matter how many accolades she received for her work, it was never enough.

"You were queen of a Mardi Gras ball?"

"Proteus," I admitted. "And a maid for two others. But it was a big pain and I wouldn't wish it on any of my girls."

"Wow," Cat said. "And you're so *not* a snob."

"Debutante does not mean snob," I said. "Check your Funk & Wagnall's."

M.J. hadn't said much, but I could tell she wasn't just concentrating on her driving. We were in a dry stretch of land now, all sand and dried-out everything

"Would you like some water?" I asked her.

"That would be nice."

"You know, although we've been friends for a long time, we never really told each other about our growing-up years. I know why I never said too much about it, because I didn't want y'all to think I was some rich snob. But why don't either of you talk about your childhoods?"

"Because mine was lousy," Cat said. "And I don't want to relive it."

"You already know about mine. I was the beauty queen, from about age two to twenty-one. Then I came to California."

I stared at the back of their heads, M.J.'s dark shiny ponytail and Cat's impeccable blond bob. "This isn't fair. There's a reason y'all decided to go back to New Orleans now, and it has nothing to do with my high school reunion. So tell the truth." I crossed my arms. "We're in this together, aren't we?"

M.J. glanced at Cat, then back at the road. Finally she caught my eye in the rearview mirror. "Okay. I mean, it's no secret. I need to get away from Frank's kids and hide the money and car from their greedy hands. I have a few friends I can visit, and...I need time to think about what I'm going to do next."

Cat laughed at her. "What Bitsey wants to know—what we both want to know, is who's the first guy you plan to look up? An old boyfriend. Who's *your* Eddie? That football guy you told me about?"

A smile brought out M.J.'s dimples. "I suppose he is. My Eddie is a guy named Jeff. Jeff Cole, star running back for the John Curtis Patriots."

I shifted to the side and pulled my feet up under me. "Now we're getting somewhere."

"Don't get all excited," M.J. said. "I doubt he's in New Orleans anymore. He got a football scholarship to Ole Miss and then played pro ball for a few years. I don't know where he is now."

"Is that who you lost your virginity to?" Cat asked.

"Yes," M.J. admitted.

Then Cat looked at me. "And Eddie was your first?"

Slowly I nodded. Then M.J. and I both looked expectantly at Cat.

"Okay, okay," she said. "If you must know, I sacrificed my cherry to Matt Blanchard." She twisted the top off her bottle and took a long drink. "On a picnic blanket on the banks of Bayou Segnette with mosquitoes biting our asses. Classic, don't you think?"

M.J. laughed. "So why did you two break up?"

Cat shrugged. "Because I couldn't wait to blow town, and he was planning to stay forever."

"Who's the first person you're going to call when we get there?" I asked her. "Matt?"

She took a long time answering. The tires hummed along the road.

"No. Not Matt. For all I know, he's married with a house-ful of kids. I'll probably call my sister first."

"Not your mom?" M.J. asked.

"No. Not my mom."

"Why not?" I saw Cat's jaw tense and release. Her mom is a sore point with her, but I wasn't letting her get away with being evasive anymore.

She let out a long whoosh of a breath. "Okay. If you can admit you were once a debutante, I guess I can admit that I was born trailer trash."

For a moment I was struck dumb, not from what she said, but how she said it. There was such contempt in her voice. Loathing, even.

"Trailer trash," M.J. repeated. "You know, I hate that term. It's like people always have to find a shorthand way to categorize people. Dumb blonde. Trailer trash. Beauty queen. Trophy wife. They categorize you because it makes it easier to dismiss you. Debutante, too," she added. "Society deb."

All of a sudden she laid on the horn, I mean mashed it over and over, all the while tearing southeast on the interstate doing at least eighty-five. "Make way for the Trophy Wife, Trailer Trash, Debutante Express! Look out world, 'cause ready or not, here we come!"

We squealed and cheered and laughed until our sides ached. It was a good thing our butch C.H.I.P. wasn't around, because this time she would have hauled us straight to jail.

"We need to find a rest stop," Cat pleaded. "I have to pee."

Which sent M.J. into fresh whoops of laughter. "Well said, trailer trash. You need to pee, but I need the little girls' room."

"Oh, you trophy wives are all the same, " I put in. "You never grow up. What this debutante needs is a powder room. And fast."

We found one, and none too soon. Of course, after we relieved ourselves, M.J. made me walk from one end of the rest stop to the other, the entire time goading me to go faster. Faster. She said it was about a mile round trip, but in the desert heat it felt like five. I did it, though, and when we stopped two hours later for lunch, I gobbled up a huge Cobb salad with fat-free ranch dressing.

Cat drove the next leg. We meant to reach Phoenix by dusk and get a hotel with a nice health club. Three to a room would keep it reasonable. Though I'd consumed probably less than four hundred calories at lunch, I was still halfway into a torpor when Cat said, "So, are we going to visit Margaret?"

I blinked away the beginnings of a nap. "Maybe."

"Maybe?" M.J. turned around to study me. "The perfect

mom doesn't want to see her daughter whom she hasn't seen in months?"

Why did that make me feel so guilty? Because it was true. "I'm planning on calling, but she may be too busy to see us. She works evenings. Besides, if I see her I'll only worry about her."

"You'll worry anyway, so I say we go see her. Okay, Cat?"

"Okay with me. We can go to the club where she works. Maybe I can pick up some young studly college boy. I've been thinking that what I need is a trophy husband."

M.J. laughed. "Sorry, darling, but it doesn't work that way. Trophy husbands are old and wrinkled and very, very rich."

"Like Frank."

"Like good old Frank."

"Is that what you want again, M.J.?" I asked. "A trophy husband?"

"I think she should hook up with Mr. Football," Cat said. "What was his name?"

"Jeff Cole." M.J. smiled and hugged her knees. Damn, but that girl was limber. "Wouldn't that be great if my first real boyfriend was rich and still available?"

"We should try to find out," Cat said. "Bitsey gets to meet up with Eddie at her reunion. You could call Mr. Football."

"And what about you?" she asked. "Are you going to look up Mr. Stick in the Mud?"

"Matt," Cat said. "Sheriff Matt Blanchard, according to one of my mother's infrequent Christmas cards."

"He's a sheriff?"

"Of my old hometown. *Mais*, I tol' you, he's a good ol' boy," she said, slipping into a thick Cajun accent. "He prob'ly has a passel of kids by now, *cher*, an' a kennel of hunting dogs, an' a gun rack in his pickup truck."

"I bet he chews tobacco," M.J. said.

"And has a beer belly," I put in.

"And hates uppity women," Cat said. "Maybe I will look him up, just to be mean."

From the back seat I considered just what we were doing

in M.J.'s semistolen Jaguar on our way cross-country to New Orleans. I was going to my high school reunion because I wanted to see Eddie. I couldn't explain why. I'm happily married, although I'm not so sure my husband is. The fact remained, however, that I wasn't in the market for another man. But M.J. and Cat, my two very best friends, could each use a decent guy in their lives.

I unfastened my seat belt and scooted forward so that my head was even with theirs. "Listen to us," I said. "We've all admitted that we have these unresolved relationships with our old boyfriends. Maybe there's a reason we're making this trip together. Maybe we're supposed to resolve them. You and Jeff." I squeezed M.J.'s shoulder. "And you and Matt."

Cat fixed me with a narrow gaze. "And you and Eddie?"

I sat back. "Maybe."

"You would cheat on your husband?" M.J. asked.

"I didn't say that. God, you have your minds in the gutter. What I'm saying is that things are not…wonderful between me and Jack. I just need some perspective."

"I say go for it," Cat said.

"I will if you will," I said right back.

M.J. frowned. "I don't know if Jeff is even in New Orleans."

I grinned. "I bet Margaret can find out for us."

"Margaret?"

"The Internet. If he was a football player and later a coach, she can probably find out where he is now."

"Maybe there will be something about the good sheriff, too," Cat said. "And Eddie Dusson."

It was decided then. Ahead of us the southern tail of the Rockies formed a jagged line on the horizon. But we would be driving over them and through them, and at the end of our journey we would find the girls we used to be—and maybe the boys we once upon a time loved.

CHAPTER 2
Not Without My Daughter

Mary Jo

Big breasts can be such a curse. They attract attention from everyone, good attention and bad.

Please, don't misunderstand. I'm not naive enough to believe mine weren't directly involved in my husband's interest in me. The odd thing, however, is that Frank was most fascinated by the fact that my breasts were real. Apparently his first wife's enhancement procedure was the beginning of the end for them. Why couldn't life be simple? he used to always ask. So I made it my goal to keep his life simple and pure, first as his employee, then as his wife. Bottled water, organic food, nothing synthetic in his clothing.

Except for his children and our lack of children together, I would have described our marriage as perfect. We were in balance, each with our own area of responsibility. Frank made the big decisions and paid for everything; I made all the small decisions and kept our life calm and organized. But then he died.

Even more drastic than Frank's actual death was the way he died. It made our entire life together a lie—messy, complicated and nasty.

How could he want a man pretending to be a woman, when he had me, real breasts and all?

Thank God for Cat and Bitsey. Those two saved me, and I mean that literally. I don't know what I would do without them, my Grits sisters. And now here we were, cruising through the desert with Cindy Lauper blaring from a Phoenix radio station.

Funny as it seems, my enthusiasm for this trip slipped a bit when we first started off this morning. I was leaving California for good. I knew it and I wasn't really sorry. But I didn't know where I was supposed to go, or what I was supposed to do.

Then we were pulled over for speeding, and for some reason that changed everything. It sounds ridiculous, but when that cute lesbian cop gave me the once-over, it gave me just the boost I needed. Not that I'm interested in women sexually; men are definitely my first choice. But I realized then that no matter the stumbling blocks thrown at me, I can find a way through—at least as long as Cat and Bitsey are on my side. I promised not to speed anymore, the cop let us go, and we were on our way. Best of all, I was back to feeling great.

The sky had begun to turn coral, aqua and rose in the rearview mirror when we exited I-10.

"My butt is numb," Cat muttered, shifting in her seat. "Just find the nearest hotel and let me out of here."

I had visions of a Motel Six. "There must be a Sheraton or Doubletree here. They usually have great spas."

"How about a Marriott?" Bitsey asked, pointing to a billboard. We followed the signs to the Marriott and within a half hour we were checked in, with Cat and Bitsey fighting for first dibs on the shower.

"But what about our workout?" I asked Bitsey.

"Not today, M.J. Please? I'm just too worn-out for any workout more strenuous than searching for a restaurant. But I promise to be a good girl about it tomorrow."

"Yeah, M.J. You're on vacation," Cat said, taking advantage of Bitsey's preoccupation with me to slip past her and into the bathroom. "What do you say we play first—and play later?"

"Fine." I shouldn't have been annoyed, but the idea of helping Bitsey get in shape had become a real challenge to me. A mission. And now she wasn't cooperating. "While you two freshen up here, I'll get in a couple of miles on the bike. You'll be sorry," I added to Bitsey, "When I can have a drink—"

I broke off when she raised her eyebrows sternly at me. "Okay. Okay, Mother," I amended. "You'll be sorry when I can have dessert and you can't." I flounced out, but by the time I reached the elevator I was already reconsidering my behavior. Not the exercising, but the flouncing. How old was I anyway?

An hour and a half later we were dressed and out the door, looking pretty good, if I do say so, and ready to take on Tempe.

"Where does Margaret live?" Cat asked Bitsey.

"I have the address in my wallet. But she's probably not there."

"So where's this bar she works at?"

The waitress at the restaurant gave us directions to it, and we decided to go.

Tavernous was nothing like what we expected. The neighborhood was seedy, the building listed drunkenly to the left as if it were about to collapse, and the windows were papered over with posters for bands and music shows. The bouncer, a hairy-chested behemoth with one gold tooth and a shaved head, carded me.

Bitsey scowled at him. She was already upset by the look of the place, and this didn't help. "Young man, you should be more respectful."

Cat laughed. "Uh-oh, the jig is up, M.J." To the grinning goofball she said, "She's only seventeen, you know, trying to pass for forty-two."

I elbowed her. "Shut up." She didn't have to announce my age to the whole world. Anyway, I was used to guys carding me. It was their awkward way of starting a conversation, of flirting with me. Of staring down my blouse while I was searching for my driver's license.

"Okay, Mary Jo," he said, handing me my license and flashing his gold cap. "You have a nice time, you and your friends." He held open the door for us, letting a wall of noise crash over us. "And just call for Donnie if anybody gives you any shit."

Cat led the way, but I had to practically push Bitsey inside the place. I could feel the poor thing trembling. "What's wrong, hon?" It was so noisy I could hardly hear myself, but she heard.

"What's wrong? What's wrong!" She stared around, appalled. "I didn't raise any of my girls to work in an awful place like this!"

"You have to look at it in a positive light," I yelled over the thunder of drums and the squeal of guitars. The three skinny guys on the stage made more noise than the Rolling Stones, the Beatles and the Who together could do. "Working at a lousy job for lousy pay is the best incentive she'll ever get for going back to school."

"Over here!" Cat called, dragging Bitsey by the arm. She'd found two stools against the wall. Bitsey wiped off her stool with a tissue before sitting down. Cat perched eagerly on hers, craning her neck, probably looking for Margaret. As for me, I wanted a drink and I wanted to dance. That's what my talent had always been in the pageants. Dancing. Sometimes ballet, sometimes tap, later on, modern dance. I loved to dance and I was better at dancing than singing.

I tapped the arm of a waitress going by. "Is Margaret here?" She looked at me askance. I smiled sweetly at her. "Margaret, one of the cocktail waitresses."

"I don't know any Margaret. Wait, d'you mean Meg?"

"Meg. Of course. Could you send her over to us?"

"I could. But this is my zone. You gotta order from me."

I gave her a twenty. "Just send her over, okay?"

She went off smiling, I started dancing in front of the two stools, and in less than a minute Cat's face lit up. "There she is. Look, Bits."

Neither Bitsey nor Margaret was smiling when they spied one another. Bitsey's reaction I understood. Margaret's thick blond hair was now short and black with a Day-Glo red streak over her left brow. She had on a T-shirt made for an eight-year-old, too tight and too short. Sort of like my Pilates outfit, but in a bar it invited all kinds of trouble. Her eyes were ringed with kohl, her lips were maroon red, and her nose was pierced. So much for the sunny California girl she used to be.

But it was the frown she directed at her mother that most bothered me. "Mom? What are *you* doing here?" Her horror obviously included me and Cat, too.

"We're on our way to New Orleans," Cat said when Bitsey didn't answer. "And we decided to stop and see you."

"Yeah? Well, you should've called first. You should've let me know you were coming."

"Why?" Bitsey finally spoke. "Aren't you happy to see me?"

Margaret's—Meg's—eyes slid away, like a feral cat trapped inside the house and searching out an escape route. Finally she looked at her mother. "It's not that, Mom. It's just that…I'm working. I can't like visit or even chat right now. I have to work."

"Okay. But…" Somehow Bitsey managed to smile. "How about we take you to breakfast tomorrow?"

Meg's sullen gaze slid away. "Why? So you can rag on me about working in a place like this?"

"Because I want to visit with you, " Bitsey answered. "Because you're my daughter and I love you."

I'd known Margaret since she was twelve or so, and though she'd always been an independent child, I'd never seen her challenge her mother. Plead and cajole, perhaps, even whine. So the hostility I now saw was something entirely new.

Fortunately this new Meg person hadn't totally taken control of sweet Margaret. For although Meg wanted to say no to the breakfast date, Margaret couldn't quite pull it off. With a sigh she nodded. "Okay. Fine. But not till lunchtime. Or even later."

"She needs her beauty sleep," Cat said as Margaret melted back into the sweaty noise of the crowded club.

Bitsey didn't laugh, and Cat sent me a look that said, "Do something."

I put my arm around Bitsey's shoulder. "She's just stressed out, hon. I mean, look at this place. Working here has got to be tough."

Bitsey was back to trembling again. "I wonder if her boy-friend is here. The one with the 'roots rock' band," she added, a sneer in her voice. Then she sniffed and wiped her eyes, ru-ining the effect of her sarcasm.

"I think you ought to cut off her allowance," Cat said. "The brat didn't even notice your new haircut."

Bitsey smiled, but Cat and I knew it was forced. "Let's get out of here," she said. "If I can't drink or eat, I might as well sleep."

"Or exercise." My jest was no more successful than Cat's. To make matters worse, on the way back to the hotel, Bitsey called Jack, only there was no answer, not at home or at his office. She left messages both places and tried to shine a good light on it. But later I heard her crying in the bathroom.

We went to bed somber and woke up little better. But at least we had the whole morning for exercise.

"You're doing good," I said as Bitsey attacked the stair-climber as if it were Mount Everest. Her eyes were puffy and her short hair stuck out in a punky kind of way.

Across the room Cat pedaled a stationary bike very, very slowly. "You're looking buff, Bits," she said.

"What I need is a punching bag." Bitsey huffed the words out.

Cat hooted. "Damn, the girl's getting tough inside and out. You really are good at this personal training stuff, M.J."

I grinned. It was nice being good at something. "Watch out world, 'cause here comes Bitsey, killer bunny."

"All I want is to not kill them when I sit on them," she muttered. "Except for Margaret. Meg." She made a face as she stretched out the word. "I wouldn't mind squashing that brat."

We went to the brat's house without calling beforehand.

The first sign of trouble was the broken front step. Then the porch had an old couch on it.

"My, my. Looks like home," Cat quipped. "You don't need a trailer to live like trash, I guess."

Bitsey's face took on a pinched expression. "Maybe y'all better wait out here."

I grimaced. "Are you sure, hon?"

When she nodded, Cat and I hung back. We didn't like it, though, especially when, after her third knock we heard a loud, angry male response. "Who the fuck is it?"

I thought Bitsey would fold, but I guess I underestimated the power of maternal love. "Margaret!" she cried. "Open the door. It's your mother!"

Margaret came to the door, but she only opened it a crack before closing it.

Bitsey trudged down the steps. "She's coming," was all she said. Two minutes later Margaret hurried out. She had on jeans, a T-shirt and a pair of chunky sandals, clothes the old Margaret would have worn. But the pale face with the sunglasses, and the blue-black hair with its blood-red streak were jarring in the unrelenting sun of high noon.

"Hi, sweetheart," I said, giving her a hug, wanting to make her smile, but not succeeding.

Cat ruffled her hair. "So. Where's a good place to eat around here?"

Bitsey was the only one who didn't touch her, and Margaret kept her distance, too.

We found a Shoney's. Once we were all settled with our buffet lunches Bitsey asked, "Do you like my hair?" forcing Margaret to look at her.

Margaret stared at her through the dark glasses for a long moment before the difference seemed to register. "You cut it. It looks good. It makes your face look thinner."

"Her face is thinner," Cat said.

"You look thinner, too," Bitsey said to her daughter.

Margaret shoved her mixed greens around with a fork. "I've been working a lot."

"How's school going?" I asked.

Her fork clattered down onto her plate. "Look. I don't want to be grilled, so let's just get it over with. Here's the deal. I dropped out of school and I'm not going back." She glared at her mother. "So if you want to cut off the money, fine. I'm doing just great at Tavernous."

"Yeah," Cat said. "And you're living in the lap of luxury, too."

"Fuck you!" She stood up but Bitsey grabbed her arm before she could storm off.

"Margaret Anne Albertson! What kind of way is that to speak to someone who loves you? We all love you and we're all worried about you."

"I don't *need* you to worry about me. Okay?"

The people at the next table were trying not to notice us, but without much success. I don't like scenes and I know Bitsey hates them, but Cat is a different story. Once you rile her up, it wouldn't matter if the pope himself was watching. Without warning she stood and snatched the sunglasses off Margaret's nose.

The girl froze. So did Bitsey. The bruise around Margaret's left eye was faint and probably old, but there was no mistaking what it was.

"I thought so," Cat said as she sat down, picked up her fork, and began calmly to eat. "She has that same belligerent attitude I used to have in my first marriage. I couldn't stand up to him, but I sure as hell stood up to everybody else."

"Fuck you," Margaret repeated, only it came out a shaky, little-girl whisper. Not very sincere.

Bitsey caught her by the hand. "Margaret, honey. Sit down. Are you all right? Let me see—"

"Mom, no!" Margaret shrugged her off. "I'm sorry. I don't want to talk about it. It was just once and I'm okay. I can handle it. I *did* handle it. He said he was sorry, and I know he is. So just…just eat your breakfast and…and have a good trip."

She scooped her glasses off the table and put them on.

"Wait," Bitsey pleaded.

"No, Mom. I have to go. Tell Grandpy hello when you see him." Then she walked away and left us, three women sitting in a Shoney's booth with a brand-new trouble on the table to worry about.

She walked across the parking lot and headed down the street. She was so thin, but it wasn't that strong willowy thinness. She looked skinny and brittle, ready to break. Though it was only eight or ten blocks to her house, the choice she'd made, to leave the security of our love and reenter the danger zone of that apartment, made the distance seem enormous, a chasm impossible for us to cross.

Only when she turned a corner past a dry cleaner's shop did any of us speak. "We can't let her go back," Cat said. She'd acted so blasé before, but now her jaw was clenched and it jutted forward like a bulldog's. Belligerent and determined. Tenacious.

We both looked at Bitsey. Her face was almost as pale as Margaret's, but she wasn't crying. She looked at each of us. "You're right. We have to get her out of there, even if at first she refuses to come. If she won't protect herself, then we have to protect her. *I* have to protect her," she said.

I leaned forward on the table. "Maybe we should call Jack."

Bitsey shook her head. "Jack doesn't need to know how his little girl is living, or with whom. First of all, it would kill him. And second of all, we can handle this." She grabbed each of our hands. "We can. We have to."

We. My first instinct was to save Margaret. My second was to avoid any kind of ugly scene with her or the creep she was living with. But Bitsey's quiet conviction and Cat's unmistakable fury gave me courage.

"So, how are we supposed to do this?" I asked. "I mean, it sounds like you want to kidnap her or something."

"If I have to, I will," Bitsey responded.

"You can't be serious."

"She was right about stripping your house of all the valuables, wasn't she?" Cat pointed out.

"Well, yes. But her first suggestion was to burn it down. And don't forget, she wanted to drown the Jag."

But Cat didn't back down. "This is different. Those were things. This is Margaret. Little Magpie."

So we made a plan. First we staked out her place. Cat and I took turns strolling by, disguised by big straw hats and white plastic sunglasses. It was about quarter after two when some lanky, shaved-head guy with sideburns and a goatee sauntered out of Margaret's place. He stood on the front steps scratching his belly and lit a cigarette. Then he crossed to a beat-up blue van, climbed in, and with a smoky roar, drove off.

We called Bitsey. "He's skinny, almost six feet tall. No hair, blue jeans and a black T-shirt. With a hole in it."

"You just described every other musician on MTV. So he's gone and she's inside?"

"It seems that way."

"I'll be right there with the car."

The three of us knocked and knocked, but there was no answer. "Maybe she's pulling an M.J.," Cat said.

"Excuse me," I said. "In case you haven't noticed, it's been juice, tea and water for me for over a week."

"Ignore her," Bitsey told me. "Cat is just being her smart-alecky self."

"What? Me, smart-alecky?"

"Y'all! Focus!" Bitsey ordered. "What do we do now?"

Cat and I shared a look. "She's probably loaded. That's why she won't wake up," Cat said. "I say we break in, get her in the car and go."

So we did. I was scared to death, so my job was to back the car into the driveway, move everything off the backseat and keep a lookout for the creep in the blue van.

Displaying a talent she had up to now kept hidden from us, Cat pried open a screen, lifted herself up and shimmied through the bathroom window, then came around and opened the door for Bitsey.

When a woman peered out at us through a window in the house next door, my adrenaline, which was already pumping, started speeding. But she must not have called the cops, because it took nearly fifteen minutes to get Margaret out, and no police cars ever showed up to investigate. I watched fearfully as they walked Margaret out the side door, hefting her between them like a limp doll. "Good grief. What's she on?"

"Probably Vicodin," Cat said. "We found a half-empty bottle."

Bitsey looked as if she'd aged fifteen years in the last fifteen minutes. But she had this superhuman strength, because she maneuvered Margaret as if she were still a little kid, heaving her into the backseat and folding her legs carefully inside.

"Get the bags," she told Cat, who was already on her way back into the apartment.

Just then a van slowed in front of the house. *That* van with *that* man. Seeing his parking spot taken, he passed the house.

"Get in. Get in!" I yelled to Bitsey. "Cat! He's back. Hurry up!"

The woman next door was watching us again, but I didn't care. I was scared and I wanted us out of there. Bitsey pushed me into the driver's seat. Not that I needed much pushing. " Drive!" she ordered, climbing in beside Margaret.

"What about Cat?"

"Just get this car out of here! I'll…I'll go back to get Cat."

So I pulled out, laying rubber like a sixteen-year-old the first time out on his own with his mother's car. A half block down the creep was climbing out of his van, and for a moment I considered running him over. It was only for a very brief moment. But if I hit him the police would definitely come. So we whizzed past him, just a little too close for his comfort. He jumped back, screamed something ugly and shot me the bird. Then he headed for his place.

I stopped two blocks down and around the corner. "Wait here," Bitsey said. Then she got out and ran back down the street.

I made a mental note not to make her exercise anymore today. If her adrenaline was running as high as mine, she was burning calories at triple speed.

Unfortunately, waiting only seemed to increase my anxiety. I leaned over my comatose passenger. "Margaret? Margaret!" I shook her knee but she was a gone pecan. Her soft snores were even and deep, though. Thank goodness.

When another couple of minutes went by and neither Bitsey nor Cat showed up, I got out and ran to the corner. What I saw might have been a scene out of a Woody Allen movie. Bitsey was leaning against a fence as if she was poking a pebble out of her shoe.

Farther down the street the creep was talking to the lady from the window. I couldn't hear what she was saying but she seemed pretty agitated. Her hands were flapping and she was pointing back at his house. Was she telling him what we'd done? Did she know Cat was still inside his house? Did he?

Then I saw Cat. She came out of a driveway two doors down from where Margaret had lived, and turned abruptly toward us. She was loaded down with a suitcase, some sort of gym bag and a couple of big plastic bags. So much stuff she was staggering. But she never stopped moving.

When Bitsey spied Cat, she turned back toward me and started walking, too. Meanwhile the lady from the window, who must have seen them both, just kept on talking and flapping her hands.

Bitsey reached me just as the creep broke away from his neighbor and headed for his place. The woman planted her fists on her hips and watched him go. Then she turned back toward us and waved. As realization dawned on me, I waved back.

"She helped us," Bitsey said, waving, too. "She distracted him so Cat could get away."

We took the bags from Cat, and she gave us each a hurried hug. "She told me to go through her backyard and into the next yard, too. That she'd keep him busy." Cat turned for one last wave to our unexpected savior. "She said he was a fucking dickhead with a bad attitude. And that he couldn't play the guitar for crap."

I grinned. "Come on, let's go." And we ran for the car.

We couldn't get out of Arizona fast enough. This was the day I deserved a ticket. Flying ninety miles per hour down I-10, I was ready to skip New Mexico altogether and go straight to west Texas. But there's that little girls' room thing, so late in the afternoon we pulled over at a speck on the map called Shuttlesworth. Margaret had hardly moved all afternoon, but we made her get up anyway.

"Come on, sweetheart," Bitsey coaxed, wiping Margaret's face with a napkin dipped in the chilly water in the ice chest.

Margaret flinched away. "Stop it," she mumbled.

"Do it again," Cat said. "I'm too old to be hauling people around. If she needs to pee she'll have to get to the bathroom on her own."

"Margaret, please, sweetie. Wake up." Bitsey begged. This time she wiped Margaret's wrists and arms with the cool cloth before moving to her neck and cheeks.

Margaret shifted, trying to get comfortable on the seat. "Leave me alone," she muttered.

"Too bad y'all can't put her in a cold shower like you did to me," I said.

Cat slammed her car door.

Margaret jerked and opened her eyes. "What the fuck?" she mumbled, trying awkwardly to sit up.

"Margaret Anne!" Bitsey exclaimed. "Don't you dare talk like that around your mother!"

"Mom?" The poor girl blinked and stared around her in confusion. "Mom? Where are we?"

"New Mexico," Cat said, leaning in at the window. "But just for a bathroom break. Let's go."

"Go ahead," I told Bitsey. "I'll help Margaret."

The girl was still woozy but she was able to get out of the car, and once pointed in the right direction, she managed to walk. "So," I said. "What're you on? Besides the Vicodin."

"What do you mean?" She tried to look affronted and self-righteous, but she failed. With a shrug she conceded the truth. "What difference does it make?"

"You're right," I said. "It doesn't matter. Alcohol, pills, weed. I've heard heroin's a real trip. Ever tried it?"

"No." She gave me a shocked look, this time sincere. "Geez, M.J., what do you think I am? Have *you* ever tried it?"

"No."

Thank goodness that was the end of the drug talk. I mean, I know there are times when I drink too much. But after all, I'm a recent widow. That has to count for something. Besides, I've never used any illegal drugs. At least not in almost twenty years.

So we took care of business in the little girls' room and headed back to the car. Bitsey was already sitting in the back seat. Cat had finished filling the tank. The question remained, would Margaret get back in?

She stared at the open door, then peered in at her mother. "Where are we?" she asked again.

"New Mexico," Bitsey said.

"New Mexico!" Margaret straightened, then turned to stare back at the lowering sun. "But... But I've got to work tonight."

"Not tonight, hon," I said. "Come on. Let's go."

She shook her head. "No. No, no, no. What's going on? No way did I agree to this. What did you do, Mom? Kidnap me or something?"

When none of us said a thing her face got this stunned kind of scared look on it. She slammed the door shut. "Son of a bitch! You did kidnap me. Jesus!" She raked her hands through her hair and turned in an uneven circle.

Bitsey slid across the back seat and got out. "Now Margaret, listen to me."

"No! What do you think I am, ten? Twelve? You can't run my life anymore, Mom. I won't let you."

"And I won't let some worthless excuse for a man beat you up!" Bitsey might have started off trying to be calm, but she had just lost it big-time.

"I explained about that. And anyway, he didn't beat me up."

"You're lying, Margaret. If not to me, then to yourself. He's not going to stop, so I'm going to stop him."

The two guys who worked at the service station watched Margaret and Bitsey squaring off as if they didn't know whether to enjoy the spectacle or break it up. Cat wasn't nearly so hesitant. She hopped out of the car like a firecracker about to explode and thrust her cell phone at Margaret.

"Here. Call the creep. Tell him to come and get you."

When Margaret just glared at her, she went on. "What's the matter? Don't you think he'll come? Isn't he your white knight, willing to come to your rescue no matter the odds? Surely he'll battle three middle-aged busybodies to get you back."

The girl's face was as pale as ever, but two spots of color burned in her cheeks, nearly as red as the red streak of hair over her left eye. I held my breath waiting for Margaret to snap back with something too ugly for Cat to back down from.

Instead Margaret turned away, bent over and puked into the dirt.

All in all, it was the best thing that could have happened. While Bitsey helped Margaret, I dragged Cat away from them to cool down.

"That ungrateful little bitch," Cat fumed.

"Come on, give her a break. She discovered she's in New Mexico. How did you expect her to act?"

"Better than that."

I tucked my arm in hers. "I wonder how you would've behaved at that age if your mother had done that to you."

She shrugged me off. "Just shut up, M.J." But there was no venom in her words. I had scored my point and, as usual, once she'd spouted off, Cat was cooling down.

Under the watchful eyes of the gas station guys we made our way back through the dusty heat to the waiting car. Bitsey raised her brows at us but said nothing.

"You okay?" I asked Margaret. She nodded and gave Cat a sidelong look. I nudged Cat.

"Sorry I went off on you," she said to Margaret. "But I get a little crazy over the men-slapping-women-around thing."

"But he doesn't—"

"Save it, Margaret. I've been there and I've done that, and I can't stand to see anybody else go through it."

On that sober note we all got back into the car and headed east. Margaret slept again. Bitsey said that she'd agreed to spend the night with us but that tomorrow she was taking a bus back to Tempe.

"We'll just see about that," Cat said, gunning the motor. "We'll just see."

It took twenty-five miles and Tammy Wynette to settle us down. I don't usually listen to country stations, but the choices were limited. Besides, there was something about our situation that called for the messy heartbreak of country music. So when "Stand by Your Man" came on and Cat started singing "Stand *on* your man," the gray cloud hovering over us broke up and vanished.

Bits and I joined in, too, in our best Southern twang. "Stand on your man."

"That's me," Cat said as Tammy kept on singing. "I stand on 'em. You two stand by them, and Margaret, too. But not me. Then I D.I.V.O.R.C.E. them."

"Don't act so smug," Bitsey said. "You may cut and run, but only after they've stomped all over your heart."

"Okay, okay. So we've all been stupid about men, " I said. "But isn't that what this trip is about? Second chances?"

"Or third," Cat said.

"No. It's a second chance with your Boy Scout turned sheriff," I said. "And Bitsey's second chance with her Eddie."

That's when Cat's eyes got big, and she gave me a sharp shake of her head. I didn't understand why until Margaret shifted in the backseat, opened her eyes and stared at her mother. "Who's Eddie?"

Bitsey

I wanted to kill Mary Jo. She should never have mentioned anything about Eddie, even if she thought Margaret was asleep. Even if she thought the girl was comatose.

But once the name was out of her mouth—Eddie—it hung in the air like the loud buzz of a faulty neon light. It sputtered and spat and wouldn't go away.

"Mom?" Margaret said, and for a moment I was reminded of a seven-year-old Margaret who'd just been told by her older sister that there was no Santa Claus. "Who's Eddie?" she repeated.

"Oh, Eddie." I laughed and prayed I didn't sound as nervous and guilty as I felt. "Eddie is the boy I went to the prom with. I told you about my high school reunion, didn't I, sweetie? Well, that's the whole point of this trip. I wasn't going to go without your father," I went on, talking much too loud and way too fast. I tried to slow down. "But he encouraged me to go anyway, and M.J. needed to get away after Frank died, and Cat wanted to visit her family. So we decided we'd all head down south together."

Margaret stared at me; Tammy had subsided and now Randy Travis was singing "Forever and Ever, Amen." Other than that, the car was absolutely silent.

"So...this Eddie was your date for the prom?"

"Yes," I said. "And I'm praying he's gained more weight than I have." Again I laughed, but it was a strain.

"That's why she's been dieting," M.J. jumped in, trying to help. "We've been working out together."

"Yeah," Cat added. "You're too young to know this, but starting around the tenth high school reunion, looking slimmer and better dressed than the rest of your old classmates becomes a major motivator in a woman's life."

"I wasn't going to go, " I repeated. "But M.J. convinced me I could lose twenty pounds by then. And I'm almost there."

Margaret smiled then, and I wanted to breathe a huge sigh

of relief. She said, "You're looking good, Mom. I can see the difference already. This Eddie guy is gonna be sorry he ever let you get away. But I'm still mad at you," she added. "You had no right to kidnap me. I could have you arrested, you know."

I grabbed Cat's shoulder before she could jump into the fray. This was between me and my daughter. "I have twenty-three years of right!" I said to Margaret, trembling with emotion. "I love you, Magpie. I always have and I always will. Even with your hair dyed black and streaked with red. If you ever have a daughter and find out she's being abused, you'll do the exact same thing."

"I'm not being abused!"

God, but I wanted to shake her. Instead I tried to stroke her healing bruise, but she flinched away. I felt as if my heart were breaking. "Would you ignore a black eye on me?" I asked.

"That's stupid. You don't have a black eye—and neither do I."

"You did. What would you think if I told you your father had given me a black eye?"

She shook her head. "Daddy would never do that."

I gave her a grim smile. "My point exactly."

She turned away from me, and the car sped on. Dusk fell before we pulled into a Motel 6 in a dusty town twenty miles or so from Las Cruces. I was exhausted, so when M.J. suggested a quick jog before supper, I didn't even grace her with an answer. By silent assent Cat and Margaret took one room and M.J. and I took the adjoining one. I headed straight for the shower and only then did I fall apart. There was no real reason to cry. Tears never solved anything. How many times had my mother pointed that out in that brusque manner she always used with her supposed-to-be-perfect children? But as I undressed in the unblinking fluorescent glare and the unforgivingly mirrored confines of the bathroom, I couldn't help it. No amount of dieting and exercise would ever erase the soft folds of my belly or the dimpled excess of my thighs.

Arms, chin, jowls. I was fat. And even if I did lose all the weight I wanted, what would be left but saggy skin and shrinking breasts? Just gorgeous.

No wonder Jack found me so boring. No wonder my daughters didn't look up to me as a role model. In the hot, enveloping steam of the pounding shower I cried and raged at the unfairness of it all. No wonder I felt so miserable all the time. I *was* miserable. A miserable, boring excuse of a woman.

I was in the shower so long that M.J. showered in Cat and Margaret's room. I don't know what kind of lecture Cat and M.J. had given Margaret, but by the time I was out, with my stupid short hair dry and spiky and sticking out like a teenager's, they were all dressed and ready to go.

We piled into the car, heading for a Tex-Mex place the desk clerk had recommended, only the car wouldn't start.

"Come on, baby," M.J. crooned as she retried the ignition. "Come on, you can do it." But the motor only sputtered and coughed in a vain effort to turn over and catch.

When M.J. finally gave up, Margaret started to laugh. "Serves you right. Now you're stranded in nowhere New Mexico where they've probably never seen a Jag before, let alone tried to fix one."

Thank goodness she was wrong. We ate at a diner across the street from the motel and discovered there was a mechanic who specialized in imported cars. As it turned out, nowhere New Mexico was a fairly with-it town. Though no Taos, it boasted a thriving artists' and retirees' community. The retirees all drove American with "These Colors Never Run" bumper stickers. The artists drove imports and I even saw three of those electric-gas hybrids.

First thing in the morning, a Eugene's Imports tow truck came for the car. Over breakfast we discussed our options for the day. "Of course we'll exercise," M.J. told me. "Even though we missed out yesterday, you did very well with your caloric intake."

I nodded as I ate my bowl of fruit with fat-free yogurt.

Cat stirred some sweetener—the pink stuff—into her second cup of coffee. "Sorry, M.J. Y'all can exercise, but I think I'll check out the shops, maybe even buy a piece of outsider art. Who knows. I could discover the next great artist to sell to my clients, the ones with too much money and too little taste."

"You ought to be nicer about your clients," M.J. said. "If they had great taste they wouldn't need to hire you."

Cat shrugged and glanced at Margaret. "So. What are you going to do between now and the time the Greyhound leaves?"

My stomach clenched. She'd already checked the bus schedule?

Margaret yawned. "I don't know. I saw a sign for an Internet Café last night. I might head over there. Check my e-mail. See if I still have a job." She shot me a contemptuous look.

"She hates me," I muttered to M.J. an hour later as the two of us stretched and warmed up for our jog. "Worse, she's going back to that creep."

"What can you do, besides cutting off the money?"

I shook my head. "Maybe her sisters can talk some sense into her."

"But not Jack?"

"Oh, no." I stretched my fingers toward the floor. "He'd have a fit."

"Did you just touch your toes?"

I straightened and looked at M.J. "Did I?" I stared down my front. Breasts, belly and toes. I could see my toes without throwing my neck out of whack. Once more I bent down and sure enough, the tips of my fingernails flicked the tips of my Reebok trainers. I would have been ecstatic if I wasn't so worried about my Magpie.

We jogged the length of the town, past a small brick school, an impressive town hall with a clock in the pediment and a combination firehouse, health clinic and sheriff's office. It reminded me of the town in *Back to the Future*.

On the opposite side of a town square framed by gnarled cedar trees and underplanted with an impressive xeriscape garden, a row of wood-framed shops formed the downtown. We saw Cat inside a quaint art gallery haggling with a leather-faced woman and a man with a gray ponytail.

At least my face wasn't all leathery, I told myself, and I wasn't old enough to be an old hippie. But I was forty-eight and soon I'd be fifty. My kids didn't need me anymore, and neither did my husband.

"Look," M.J. said. She was barely perspiring. "There's that Internet café. Why don't we go in and say hi to Margaret? Better yet," she amended, "You go. I'm going to do another fast mile back to the hotel. See you there."

A good-looking cowboy type came out of the café as she trotted off. He was so intent on watching her that he nearly collided with me. I could just see the headlines: Rotund, Red-faced Woman Skewered on a Rodeo Buckle. But he dodged me, then gallantly held the café door open. I had no choice but to enter.

Inside it was cool. An iced coffee seemed like a good idea, but I hadn't brought any money with me. So I scanned the high-tech decor and spotted Margaret at a back table, hunched over a glowing computer screen. I put on a deter-mined smile. "Hi, sweetie."

She glanced up, then back to the screen. "Hi."

Okay. I cleared my throat. "Do you think you could treat me to something cool to drink? I forgot my wallet."

She squinted at the screen, then briefly at me. "Sure." With one foot she nudged her purse toward me while keep-ing her focus on the screen. "When you get back I have some-thing to show you."

I had visions of some diatribe e-mail from her employer, or perhaps the section of the Arizona legal code pertaining to kidnappings. What she showed me when I sat down be-side her, however, was a Web site for my high school class re-union. "This is it, right?" she asked.

time just flew. It turned out that Matt Blanchard was not merely the sheriff of St. Charles Parish, Louisiana, he was also a highly decorated former member and hero of the New Orleans police force. He'd been shot twice, burned while saving a disabled grandmother from a house fire, and credited with busting one of the most vicious drug gangs in eastern New Orleans. He'd moved back to his hometown twelve years ago when the sheriff's position became available, and he showed no indication of wanting to leave.

"No mention of a wife," M.J. said to Cat, who was uncharacteristically silent. "He's probably divorced."

"So who isn't?"

"We aren't," M.J. retorted for the both of us.

"Well, you should have been. A long time ago."

Margaret tilted her head to frown at Cat. "You don't like my dad, do you?"

Cat scrunched up her face. "Sorry, Margaret. When it comes to men I'm in a grouchy mood. But M.J.'s old boyfriend has potential. There was nothing about any wives or children, was there?"

M.J. smiled at a photograph of the coaching staff of the New Orleans Saints and pointed him out to us. Dark brown hair, light eyes and really broad shoulders. Oh, yes, he was quite a fine specimen of a man. "He hasn't changed a bit," she said.

"That's not necessarily a good thing," Cat said. "You want a grown-up, not a teenager. Or do you?"

"I just don't want an old man," M.J. replied. But she was smiling. Maybe Jeff Cole was exactly what she needed.

"So why did y'all break up?" Margaret asked.

"He got a football scholarship and went away to school while I…I became a professional beauty pageant competitor. We lost touch when I moved to California."

"So this trip could actually fire up all the old feelings," Margaret said.

"Did he ever hit you?" Cat asked M.J.

Margaret rolled her eyes, but I smiled. There was nothing subtle about our Cat.

"Of course not," M.J. said. "Even Frank, awful as he turned out to be, he never hit me, either."

With three swift moves Margaret shut down the computer, then sat very still, staring at the blackened screen. "All right." She spun her chair around and faced us. "Here's the deal. I'll go along with you to New Orleans, but no more cracks about me being hit, okay?"

She fixed me with a glare that reminded me of someone. My mother? No, me. "Okay?" she repeated.

I raised my hands in a gesture of conciliation. "Okay, Margaret. No problem."

"And another thing. Chill with the Margaret stuff. I've been going by Meg. It suits me better."

"Meg." I nodded. "Actually, it does suit you. But if I sometimes forget, don't jump down my throat, all right?"

She nodded and for a long awkward moment we just stared at each other. *Your children are grown.* That's the thought that went ricocheting through my head. *They're grown and you're not in charge anymore.* Ridiculous as it was, I think I might have burst into embarrassing sobs if M.J. hadn't grinned with delight, then gathered us both into a big hug.

"This is going to be even better than I thought!" she exclaimed. "Look out, New Orleans, 'cause here we come."

"If the car will make it," Cat said, joining our group hug. "Maybe Bitsey was right. Maybe we *should* have driven it into the pool."

"Mom?" Margaret exclaimed—Meg exclaimed. "*You* wanted to drive M.J.'s car into a swimming pool?"

I could feel my face getting hot. "It was just an impulse. It didn't last long. And I wouldn't have driven it into just any pool," I added, feeling sheepish. "Only Frank's pool."

"But why?"

M.J. arched her brows at me; Cat tried not to laugh. "PMS," I blurted out. Then we all dissolved into laughter, the hard, racking kind that makes your sides ache and your eyes weep. The disapproving glares of the other café-goers only made us laugh harder. We were the Grits girls, and together we would be okay.

CHAPTER 3
Getting the Hell Back to Dodge

Cat

I don't pray much. My parents raised us quasi-Catholic. I hold to the theory that it was the wine part that my father liked, and the confession part my mother craved.

My mother. She sure loved playing the victim. The long-suffering wife; the overwhelmed mother. She thought confessing her misery to everyone cast her in a sympathetic light. She was always sick, and she couldn't manage so many wild kids, but she wouldn't divorce my father, no matter how awful he was.

The irony was that once he died—so drunk that he choked on his own vomit while he was passed out in his car outside a convenience store—she took up the bottle he'd left behind. Naturally, as the oldest daughter, I'd promptly stepped into the role that she'd abandoned. I'd had to leave the state to escape that god-awful, soul-sucking role. Except that now I was heading back.

But I digress. About the praying thing—for the next two days of our Grits caravan I prayed for M.J.'s Jag to keep going. The mechanic had repaired the most immediate problem, but he'd pointed out at least three potentially fatal illnesses plaguing the car. The master cylinder, the transmission and a ring job. Once we got to New Orleans the Jag *had* to go in the shop for all three, he said. And he couldn't guarantee we'd even get that far.

"Spend the night in big cities, just in case," he told us. "You do have triple A and a cell phone?"

So we kept the cell phones charged and the water bottles full, and I prayed off and on through New Mexico and the long flat ride across Texas. I wouldn't be able to relax my vigil until we crossed the Sabine River into lush, mosquito-laden Louisiana. And yet I wasn't really anxious to get to New Orleans.

I always tell people I'm from New Orleans. It sounds better—interesting, exotic and a little decadent. But I'm really from Ama, one more forgettable hamlet among the several strung along the lower Mississippi River. I hated the place. Thank God the art teacher at Hahnville High School encouraged me to go to college. "It's your only sure way out," she'd told me. "That and not getting pregnant."

I clung to those two bits of advice. It turned out she was right. I got a degree in interior design from what used to be Louisiana State University in New Orleans, and then got the hell out of Dodge.

Now I was going back.

It's not as if I'd never been back. In twenty-three years I've been back six or seven times, with each trip confirming the rightness of my decision to live on the opposite end of the continent. But this time felt different. I had an agenda, of sorts. I was going to be a good daughter to my mother and see if there was any way I could make her life easier. After all, she was sixty-six and not in very good health. I didn't want her to die and leave me feeling guilty for having neglected her.

It helped that I had Bitsey and M.J. with me. But they also complicated the situation. And then there was Matt. Although I knew it was idiotic, I'd been spending an awful lot of time remembering him. Wondering about him.

Beside me, Bitsey shifted into a more comfortable position. In the front seat M.J., too, was dozing. She'd decided to let Meg drive, but only if she obeyed the speed limit. Of course in Texas the unofficial speed limit is eighty-five or so. But true to her word, Meg was sticking to seventy. Well, seventy-four and a half.

"What are you going to do once we get to your grandfather's house?" I asked.

She shrugged. "Hang out. You know, hit the French Quarter."

"By yourself?"

"I have cousins. Besides, I'm not afraid to go places alone."

"That's good."

She glanced at me in the rearview mirror. "Meaning?"

I grinned. Smart girl. "Meaning, I was afraid you might be the type who can't go anywhere or do anything without a guy."

A little frown line formed between her eyes. She didn't like that. "You've got your nerve, Cat. I mean, you might be Mom's friend and all, but you don't know anything about me. And just because you're happy without a man doesn't mean I want to be like you. But then, you're *not* happy without a man, are you? Witness this little trip to snag the good sheriff."

"Oh, yeah. Andy of Mayberry, here I come."

"Who?"

I shook my head, suddenly feeling very old. Instead of snapping back at her I said, "Never mind. The point is, I'm glad you're with us."

We drove on and by dusk Houston glowed on the horizon. We limped the car into a Courtyard Marriot, fed her some oil and gas and antifreeze and fed ourselves salads and water with lemon. Meg and I watched a movie in the room while Bitsey and M.J. hit the workout room.

The closer we got to New Orleans, the more excited Bitsey got, and the stricter she became with her health regime. M.J. seemed calmer than she was in California, as did Meg. Was I the only one whose stomach twisted into knots of anxiety?

Bitsey called her father, but he wasn't home. "Where could a seventy-seven-year-old man be at nine-thirty at night?" she asked the cell phone as she clicked it off.

"Call Aunt Ginnie," Meg said. "She'll know where he is."

"I'm not ready to call Virginia. My sister-in-law," Bitsey explained to us as she headed for the bathroom. "If she knows we're coming in, she'll want to engineer some sort of event. And I'm not in the mood."

When the bathroom door closed Meg turned to me. "Does your mother know you're coming?"

"No."

She laughed. "Don't tell me you and she don't get along?"

I shook a bottle of Plum Crazy nail polish. "Imagine that— the mother-daughter conflict isn't unique to you and your mom."

She pushed back on one of her cuticles. "I love my mom. Sometimes she drives me crazy, but I do love her. What about you?"

I opened the polish and flexed my toes. "My mother is not particularly lovable. One thing I know for sure, she'd never kidnap me to save me from a bad situation. She'd yell at me, call me stupid for getting in such a situation. But come to my rescue?" I bent over my left foot trying to paint my big toe-nail, but my hand shook too much. "Shit," I muttered. "Look what you made me do." I shoved the brush back into the bottle and reached for a tissue and the polish remover. "I can't talk and do this at the same time. One of the curses of getting old," I added flippantly.

But she wasn't fooled. "What about your dad?"

"Dead."

"Brothers and sisters?"

I let out a noisy sigh. "One sister, two brothers. All useless."

M.J. came out of the bathroom on a billow of steam. She had on pale pink shorty pajamas and her hair up in a towel. She looked so young, she and Meg might have been sisters.

"You might as well give up, Meg," said M.J. "I can tell you now that Cat doesn't give any straight answers when it comes to her family."

"Really?" Meg looked at me with Bitsey's bright blue eyes, only sharper and a lot less sympathetic.

I grinned at her, but inside it was a grimace. Then I grabbed the remote and raised the volume on the television to an annoying level.

"All right!" she yelled over a commercial for fat-free, sugar-free canned meals that guaranteed skinny thighs and a flat stomach or your money back. "I get the hint!"

But later when we were all in bed and everyone was asleep—at least I thought they were—Meg rolled to face me. "I don't fit into my family, either," she whispered.

I pretended I was asleep, but for a long while I obsessed over her unhappy words. I had never thought of myself as not fitting in with my family. My biggest fear was my potential to be exactly like them.

We sputtered into New Orleans around rush hour the next day, made our way up St. Charles Avenue to the Garden District and stopped in front of an imposing mansion on Fourth Street.

The place was enormous, li   every cliché associated with New Orleans and the deep S   h. Ancient live oaks spread their dark arms wide, shading   h house and garden. Resurrection ferns clung moist and green to the branches, while beards of Spanish moss swayed in the early-summer breeze. I smelled gardenias, or maybe it was jasmine. The sidewalks were brick, a fountain splashed in a circle of azaleas, and a pair of giant palm trees flanked the run of steps that led up to the front porch.

"This is nice," M.J. said as we unfolded from the car. Major understatement

"If this is merely nice," I said, "then I grew up in a cave. D'you think your dad needs a decorator?"

Bitsey didn't smile. In fact, she looked kind of upset. Or maybe uneasy was the right word. Considering her excitement of the past few days, it seemed odd. I leaned closer to her and whispered. "What's wrong? Didn't you tell him you were bringing guests?"

"Yes. He knows. And he was pleased. But I didn't tell him exactly when we'd arrive."

"Because of your sister-in-law?"

She glanced at me. "Partly. And partly because I really didn't know. But don't mind me. Whenever I come home I always get…" She trailed off and shrugged. "I don't know. Moody." Then as if she were shedding a coat, she threw off her mood and smiled. "I see Daddy's car, but I wonder who that old Mercedes belongs to?"

"Not the maid?"

"Veronica doesn't drive. Her husband or her son picks her up. And Miss Ulna lives just across Magazine Street, so she walks."

While we dithered and stretched, Meg opened the trunk and grabbed her bags. "I don't know about you guys, but I'm going inside. I need to use the john."

M.J. and I shared a grin. No euphemisms for Generation X.

A skinny woman with a dark complexion, a severe bun and a snow-white apron opened the front door before we reached the front porch. "Bitsey, girl!" she exclaimed with a warmth that belied her austere appearance. "And…Margaret?"

"It's me, Miss Ulna. Only with short black hair."

"And red. Oh, child, all that pretty blond hair. Your grandfather is gonna have him a conniption. Yes, indeed he will. But I like *your* hair," she said to Bitsey, giving her a closer scrutiny. "Did you lose weight?"

Finally Bitsey gave a sincere smile. "I did."

"Mm, hmm. Well, you better just watch out for your skinny self, 'cause Veronica don't believe in dieting. Now. Who all do we have here?"

Once the introductions were made she led us up a wide mahogany stairwell to our bedrooms. "Your daddy is napping," she said. "He got into the habit of napping every day, and he don't like to be interrupted." She made a faint har-rumphing sound, before adding. "He'll be up in time to have supper with y'all."

"Whose car is that?" Bitsey asked as she heaved one of her bags onto a settee. She was in the pink room, her childhood bedroom. I was across the hall, but I heard Miss Ulna's response.

"Oh, that old thing? That belongs to Doris Sutherland. Mrs. Emil Chauvin Sutherland the third. She's a widow."

In the pause that followed, I imagined Ulna's and Bitsey's eyes meeting in silent communication.

"Was Daddy friends with her husband?"

My question would have been, "If Daddy's napping and the Widow Sutherland's car is in the driveway, where the heck is Miz Doris Sutherland?" But Bitsey closed the door and I didn't hear the rest of the conversation. At the same time some heavy rhythm of quasi music started thumping from down the hall. Meg, of course. Living with rock music would probably be harder on me than on Bitsey's daddy.

The bells rang in the bedrooms at precisely seven o'clock, and like little clock people, the four of us all popped out of our bedrooms and assembled at the top of the stairs.

Miss Ulna had informed each of us that at the La Farge cottage, everyone dressed for dinner, and there was no way I was crossing her. She might only be five feet tall and maybe ninety-five pounds, but she was a formidable woman and clearly in charge of this household. Not that I was opposed to the idea. I'd worked very hard to shed the gracelessness of my childhood, so dressing for dinner sounded wonderful, especially in a house like this.

"You look nice," I said to M.J. She had on a pink silk dress with pink heels and a flower tucked into her upswept hair. Elizabeth Taylor in *Cat on a Hot Tin Roof*, only classier. You'd think she was to the manor born. I had on a black-and-white print linen sheath, very modern but elegant. Even Meg sported toned-down makeup, an ankle-length black skirt and a red sleeveless scoop-neck sweater. Red butterfly barrettes sparkled in her hair, and a black cord was looped twice around her neck with a bow tie in the back.

Bitsey's outfit was harder to understand. M.J. frowned, but said nothing. I, of course, was not so restrained.

"Bitsey. I thought you threw away all your unflattering clothes," I said in a stage whisper.

"Shut up," was her response.

But the shapeless shift in a pukey green shade demanded I press on. "You look fat and sallow in that sack. Put on that light blue outfit that looks so good on you."

"Yeah, Mom, we'll wait."

"It's dirty," she said, then started down the steps.

The three of us shared a look. We didn't get it. After all her hard work, why would Bitsey want to meet her dad looking so dumpy? But we weren't going to argue with her in her own home. So down we went, past a gallery of La Farge relatives in gold leaf frames with a patina of age impossible to fake. We trod on Oriental carpets with threadbare patches, and wide-planked floors, uneven in some places, but waxed to an authentic lemon wax gloss.

A real gas chandelier flickered in the foyer as we crossed to the front parlor where aperitifs were waiting. It was life as lived in an earlier, more privileged time—except that a hundred and fifty years ago the house and all its furnishings would have been brand-new.

"So there you are, " A man's voice greeted us. "Come on over here, Bitsey girl. Let me see you and that pretty granddaughter of mine."

Charles La Farge sat in a large leather chair with his feet propped up on a low footstool needlepointed in a fleur-de-lis pattern. He struggled to his feet, hugged Bitsey and Meg, then turned to us. He was too small for his booming voice; that was my first thought. Though he might once have been of average height, he was thin and stooped now, not much taller than Bitsey. But he had a leonine head of white hair and a gleam in his eye. Probably a hellion of a husband at one time, I decided.

"So," he boomed once we were all settled with Grasshoppers served in beautifully cut Irish crystal liqueur glasses. "You've all come home to New Orleans. Everybody does, you know. No place like it. The city gets in the blood, and you have to come back."

"We're just visiting, Daddy," said Bitsey. "It's just for my high school reunion. I can't stay for long."

"You'll be back," he said with absolute confidence. He winked at Meg. "I've already decided to bribe Margaret to stay, and if she stays you're bound to come back."

"I might stay," M.J. said. "I wasn't certain, but once I started breathing that New Orleans air, well," she giggled, "I can just feel my skin plumping up with all this humidity."

"Don't breathe too deep," I said. "Cancer alley starts just a quick five miles or so up the river."

Mr. La Farge let out a snort. "That's a bunch of pinko California hippie bullshit."

"Daddy!" Bitsey exclaimed.

"All right," Meg chortled.

And that's how the rest of the evening went. Over aperitifs we debated air quality. Hors d'oeuvres were the EPA and the Clean Water Act. We tackled the United Nations over salad, unions over minted lamb chops and the Middle East over bread pudding with hard sauce. Not that I have an opinion on the Middle East any more profound than Rodney King's "Can't we all just get along?"

But Charlie boy didn't need an opponent to fuel his filibuster. He was happy to expound with or without input from us. M.J. had quit trying to talk; Bitsey had never even started. I was beginning to think I was trapped in a new kind of hell when Meg took quick advantage of his need to take a breath. "So Grampy," she chirped. "What do you think of Michael Jackson's nose?"

He paused in midthought, mentally changing gears. "His nose? Who cares about his nose? Michael Jackson is the greatest basketball player that ever lived—though if our boy Pistol Pete hadn't died so young he would've been just as good.

That's the trouble with young people today," he added, waving his dessert spoon at Meg. "They care more about looks than they do about accomplishments."

Meg stifled a grin but didn't correct him. Bitsey, however, was not in so generous a mood. "No, Daddy, not Michael Jordan," she said with a sarcastic edge I wasn't used to hearing in her voice. "Michael *Jackson*. The singer, not the basketball player."

He stared at her in confusion. Before he could reply, Miss Veronica came in with the coffee service, followed by Miss Ulna with the coffeepot. The wiry little woman must have heard the sarcasm, too, because she sent Bitsey a quelling glare. Charles La Farge might be a noisy, overbearing old man, but he had the loyalty of his staff.

But though Miss Ulna disapproved of Bitsey's attitude, I didn't. I'd thought for a long time that she needed to stand up to the men in her life—namely her husband. But her father would do for a start. After all, it was beginning to look like she'd married a man just like dear old dad.

And so had I, I realized with a start. I was the daughter of a drunk, and look at the two AA rejects I'd promised eternal devotion to.

The coffee was served and Miss Ulna started to leave until Mr. La Farge said, "Where's Doris?" He looked at her first, then at each of us in turn. "Why isn't Doris here?"

All eyes turned to Bitsey, whose mouth was looking a little pinched. "Why don't you tell us about Doris, Daddy?"

"I bet she's his girlfriend," Meg said. She stood up, went to her grandfather and bent over to hug him. "Tell the truth, Grampy. Do you have a girlfriend?"

He patted her hand and grinned. "You better believe it, missy," he said, all traces of his confusion gone. "She's quite a girl, my Doris. You're going to love her."

Later on, once Miss Ulna had settled Mr. La Farge in his bedroom, I found Bitsey on the far end of the front porch, sitting alone in a rocking chair. "Hey, pal. You okay?" I sat in the rocker next to her. Somewhere in the yard a frog called out lures to any and all willing females. Somewhere else one of them answered.

She shook her head. "I don't know why I get all snippy with him. But every time I come here I turn back into the insecure little girl I used to be."

"You, insecure? I saw your yearbook. You were Miss Popularity, a cheerleader and everything."

"Maybe so, but I never felt good enough. It used to be Mother—now it's Daddy and Virginia."

"Well, you're good enough for us."

Again she shook her head. "Margaret's mad at me. Meg," she amended. "First because of us kidnapping her, now because of the way I talk to her Grampy."

"We're all tired, Bitsey. Tomorrow will be easier."

A car pulled up alongside the house and after a moment Miss Veronica lumbered down the stairs and out to the curb. A minute later Miss Ulna found us. "I'm leaving now, Miss Bitsey. But my phone number is on your daddy's speed dial. Number one."

"Okay. Thanks, Ulna. You're just as terrific as ever."

"I wonder," I interjected, "Do you know any good mechanics? M.J.'s car needs some work."

Miss Ulna glanced from Bitsey to me, then back. "Miss Doris swears by her mechanic. That Mercedes of hers is twenty-seven years old and it runs like a top. You can call her for his name." She paused. "She's number two on his speed dial."

"Skinny old witch," Bitsey muttered. But not until Miss Ulna was past the gate and a half block down the street. "So she's number one and Doris Whoever is number two. So what?"

"I don't know, " I said, breathing in the warm fragrances of the night. "I think she just did you a favor. You don't have to worry about your father so long as Ulna and Doris are on the job. I wish there was someone reliable like them to dump my mother off on."

* * *

I called my mother the next morning. No one answered, which felt like freedom to me, at least for a few hours. Then I'd be obliged to try again.

Bitsey wouldn't call Doris. I've never seen Bitsey act petulant before. Petulant. It sounds soft and flowery, doesn't it? But it made sense. I'm bitchy, Bitsey's petulant. I don't know what M.J.'s version would be. Pouty? Anyway, Bitsey wouldn't call her daddy's girlfriend so M.J. did. We sat in the brick-paved courtyard sipping coffee. A fountain gurgled, a soft, sprightly sound, and I breathed deep and tried to relax. Bitsey had grown up in this heaven and still she wasn't happy. Like an exclamation point coming after M.J.'s debacle with her husband, it proved what we all should know: it's the people, not the money.

Still with this sort of gracious surroundings it seems like you ought to be able to pick and choose the right kind of people. Assuming you had decent judgment. Then again, none of us get to pick our families.

I looked over at Bitsey who was touching up her toenails. She looked much better today. Her hair was cute and fluffy and she had on a pale blue camp shirt and a pair of blue-and-white-striped Capris. M.J. looked outstanding. No surprise there. She had on a cream-colored outfit with a turquoise belt and turquoise jewelry. A Jimmy Choo slide dangled off her foot as she talked earnestly on the phone.

A wave of emotion washed over me. What wonderful women they were. How lucky for me to be friends with them. My judgment about men might suck, but I was damned good at picking friends. And so were they.

M.J. gave me a smile. "Yes, I'm a friend of his daughter's," she said into the phone. "Mm, hmm. Miss Ulna said you were very pleased with your mechanic." After a moment she gave me a thumbs-up. "No. It's a Jaguar." Another pause. "Oh, aren't you just too kind."

"What a sweetie," she said when she hung up. "She's looking forward to meeting you, Bitsey."

Bitsey squinted at the toes of her left foot. "Did she mention my brother and sister-in-law?"

"No. But she did say she and your father were going to the symphony this evening and that we were all welcome to join them." When Bitsey didn't react, M.J. shrugged. "Okay. Well, I'm going to take care of the car today. How about you two?"

"I think I'll rent a car and take a drive to see my mother," I said. It was only a *little* white lie.

"I'm going to exercise," Bitsey said.

I tried not to laugh, but that phrase still seemed so unnatural coming out of Bitsey's mouth. She shot me the bird. "Then I'm going to go to one of the spas on Magazine Street," she continued in that elegant Southern way she had, "and have a facial and a massage."

"Ooh, I might join you on that," M.J. said.

"Okay."

While they made plans, I got on the phone and arranged for a car. M.J. dropped me off at Avis with instructions for me to pick her up at the auto repair shop afterward. We hadn't seen Meg or Mr. La Farge that morning, but I figured they were both used to fending for themselves. But as M.J. drove off, her Jag coughing and bucking down the street, I couldn't avoid the truth. I was the one at loose ends. I'd come for the fun of the trip, and so far that had been great. But now I was here. So though I didn't want to, once in the rental car I flipped open my phone.

It rang seven times before she answered in that raspy barroom voice I knew so well. "Hello?"

"Hello, Mom? It's Cat. Cathy Ann. How are you doing?"

"How am I doin'? How d'you think I'm doin'? I'm dying, Cathy Ann, not that I expect you to give a damn."

Mary Jo

My Jaguar had gotten me from California to Louisiana, from monthly visits to Rodeo Drive, past dust devils in Arizona, the vast skies of Texas, to the green dripping haven of the deep South. Surely it could make one more mile to Foreign Car Works on Tchoupitoulas Street.

But two blocks away I wasn't so sure. It was as if without the infectious enthusiasm of its four passengers, my poor baby had run out of energy. I suppose I should have called for a tow truck.

"Come on, honey. Just a little farther." She sputtered and jerked and made an unhealthy noise. A cloud of whitish smoke came out of the tailpipes, but there was no going back.

"The car doctor is going to take good care of you," I promised, clutching the leather-wrapped steering wheel and leaning forward encouragingly.

The thing is, I totally understood how the car felt. The trip had totally energized me. Having a goal, a destination, and my best friends to keep me company had been like a Power Pak Smoothie, a megadose of vitamins and a superdose of pure oxygen all rolled into one. But now we were here, and like my car, I wasn't feeling so good. Only there was no turning back. The Jag gave another buck, but she kept going. And so would I. What other choice did I have?

When I finally pulled into the open garage door I felt an enormous wave of relief. We'd made it.

Three men lifted their heads out of the car engines they were bent over to stare at my poor sick baby car. I almost hated to get out, because I knew what would happen next. I mean, I like the attention I get from men. But sometimes I wish I could pull out a key and turn it off.

I suppose I could dress down, wear baggy clothes, no makeup and unflattering colors. But my mom always emphasized the importance of presentation, of making the most of what God gave you. "God gave you a lot," she used to say. "Looking your very best is how you thank Him."

So here I sat in a big warehouse of a garage, with the smell of grease and gasoline and motor oil overpowering my six dabs of Chanel Number Five. Time to get out and pray my cream linen slack set didn't get smudged with car dirt. "No offense," I said to the car as I opened the door.

The three mechanics—the term grease monkey suddenly made sense—all gawked at me. Actually, they gawked at my chest. Though I'm used to it, you never *really* get used to it. Especially when not one of the men says a word.

This was not a good beginning. I wanted to heave a big, frustrated sigh, but that would only give them more to stare at. Fortunately, just to my left I saw a boxed-in room with two windows and a sign announcing Office over the door. I gave the three stooges a nod and headed for the safety of the office. Maybe their boss was more verbal.

Then again, maybe this once I should have worn a loose T-shirt, jeans and tennis shoes.

The guy inside was on the phone. He gave me a quick glance when I walked in, then looked back at the notes on his desk. "Yeah, that's right. I ordered fourteen, not four. And I need them now. So I expect you to overnight them and eat the cost."

I don't know what the person on the other line said, but the man behind the desk didn't fidget as he listened. He didn't jiggle his pen or shuffle his papers or glance up at me again. I could imagine the other person making excuses or protesting the cost or whatever the little buzzing sound of his talking was. But the boss man of Foreign Car Works just listened. Then he said. "Your mistake, Fuller, not mine. I've got customers same as you, and I don't make excuses when I'm wrong. Overnight them," he added in a low growl of a voice.

I suppose Fuller agreed; I know I wouldn't argue with the guy. He had this forceful look about him. Dark hair, square jaw and firm lips. He had on a black T-shirt that showed off his broad shoulders and a pair of arms that could have graced the cover of *Muscle* Magazine. I wondered where he worked out. When he finally hung up, he looked up at me. "Have a seat. I'm Steve Vidrine." He glanced past me, toward the workshop. "That your Jaguar?"

After checking that the seat wasn't greasy I sat. "It's mine."

"What did you do to it?"

"Drove it. From California."

"Put anything in it besides gas?"

Sarcasm was not what I expected. "Excuse me, but I most certainly did. I always use full service, and I always have the attendant check everything."

He didn't blink, didn't look away with those slate-blue eyes, and didn't apologize for assuming I was a brainless twit who thought cars ran on air. Did he want my business or not?

Just to be mean, I took a deep breath and straightened in the blue vinyl upholstered chair. Sure enough, his gaze fell to my chest. But in the next instant his eyes were fixed back on my face.

If he would only smile he would be a handsome man. Under the circumstances it was an inappropriate thought. But then, my mother's second mantra had been "stand straight and always smile." He was doing neither. Rude *and* unpleasant. And he wasn't the least bit impressed by my looks. Even gay men were usually impressed. But not Mr. Boss Grease Monkey.

He pulled out a blank form and wrote the date on it. "So. What's the problem?"

I lifted my chin and tried to remember the exact words the mechanic had said way back in New Mexico. "I believe she may need a ring job, the transmission is failing and something else." I paused. "The master cinder."

"Cylinder. The master cylinder."

I shifted in irritation. "Well, it wasn't gone at the time. But I suppose it is now."

"Yeah. I suppose it is." He hadn't written anything down but just thumped the papers a couple of times with the end of his pen. "All right. We'll run some diagnostic tests, and once we have an idea of what's needed we'll give you a call. What's your name?"

I stared at him. "You don't think I know what I'm talking about, do you?" I had to be seriously annoyed to confront anyone like that. "You don't think it's the rings and the transmission and the—"

"The master cylinder. Yeah, it probably is all that. But this is my shop and I don't take another guy's opinion as gospel. Now. What's the name?"

Did I say rude and unpleasant? But I reminded myself that I was looking for a mechanic, not a new best friend. "M.J. Hollander. Make that M.J. Landry," I amended, then immediately regretted it, for he gave me this "it figures" look, as if no man would stay married to a woman who let her car get that horribly out of shape. I gave him my cell phone number.

"That's a California area code," he pointed out.

"That's right."

"Don't you have a local number?"

Without answering I stood up and reached for the tattered phone book on the shelf beside his left shoulder. I couldn't understand why the man rattled me, but he did. That's why I leaned low over his desk as I stretched my arm for the directory. Let him get a closer look. I'd never been a tease, especially toward men I didn't know. But he was treating me like an idiot and I needed to take him down a peg. The fact is, I wanted to get a rise out of him. Literally.

He leaned back in his chair. I pulled the phone book over to my side of his desk and, still frustrated, thumbed through, looking for Bitsey's father's listing. "I'm staying at this number." He wrote it down. "How long do you think it will take to get the car running?"

"First the diagnosis. I'll call you tomorrow, probably by noon. Shop time will depend on what we find. How long are you staying?"

"In New Orleans?" The question shouldn't have taken me aback, but it did. How long was I going to stay? Until I found a reason to go elsewhere.

"For a while," I said. Then I stood. "Is that all?"

"That's all. Do you need a ride somewhere?"

He didn't stand. So much for good Southern manners. But at least he offered me a ride.

"Thanks, but no." Then knowing an exit line when I heard one, I turned and walked out.

The three guys in the shop stared all over again, but this time I glided by as if I were still Miss Pontchartrain Beach or Queen of the Peach Festival. Chin up, chest out, hips swaying, and very, very confident.

It all wilted once I rounded the corner and stood in the meager shade of a lone crepe myrtle tree and waited for Cat. "Come on," I muttered as a trail of nervous sweat trickled down my side. That man had shaken my confidence almost as badly as Frank's death had. Wasn't I attractive anymore? Those mechanics had been almost drooling, but I hadn't been able to get even a smile out of their boss.

Finally Cat arrived in a white Taurus that smelled of citrus air freshener. "So what's the damage?" she asked as I climbed in.

"He's going to call and let me know."

She pulled up across the garage driveway, waiting for a break in the traffic. That's when I peered back toward the office door, and that's when I saw him come out. Roll out. He was in a wheelchair, propelling it with one hand while he gestured to someone with the other.

"Oh, no," I muttered, just as Cat pulled out.

"Don't worry," she said, as we merged with the traffic. "The cars weren't coming that fast."

I let the misunderstanding go, and on the short drive back to Fourth Street I managed to respond appropriately to whatever she said. Fortunately Cat can pretty much carry a conversation by herself if she needs to. She has a fear of prolonged silence, which Bitsey and I often tease her about.

But today I was glad she was going on and on, for I had something else on my mind. That surly man with the impersonal gray stare would probably coax my car back into perfect shape, just as he'd honed his upper body to perfection. But I was betting that no amount of hard work could make his legs work again. All my animosity toward him dissolved, but it didn't turn to pity. It couldn't. I knew instinctively that he would hate that.

Then I gave myself a mental pinch. Where was I going

with this? He hated me with or without my pity. Well, maybe hate was the wrong word. But he certainly didn't think very well of me.

"So," Cat said as we pulled up at Bitsey's house. "What are we doing today?"

"I need to work out," I said.

"After you got all dolled up to go to the mechanic's, now you're going to get all sweaty?"

"Bitsey needs the work," I said. Then more truthfully I added, "Besides, exercise is a better vice than drinking."

We were at the bottom of the porch steps when she said, "Don't take this the wrong way, M.J., but do you think you might be an alcoholic?"

I shook my head. "No. I mean, sometimes I do drink too much."

"Sometimes?" Though it came out sarcastic, I knew Cat well enough to know she was only worried about me.

"All right, a lot of times. The thing is, I don't feel this need to drink. If I'm busy and I'm happy, I don't even think about drinking. I can go days without it."

"The thing is," she mimicked me. "All alcoholics say that."

"You don't know that."

She looked away for a moment.

I'd always thought Cat was such a striking woman. She can have this hard edge to her, but she's so energetic and funny and smart, and she dresses so beautifully, that it doesn't matter. Then there are other times when she's as soft as anyone. But today, with a patch of harsh sunlight falling on her face, making her squint on top of her frown, she looked not hard, but tired and vulnerable.

She shaded her eyes with one hand. "I come from a family of alcoholics," she said. "A bunch of drunks in denial."

"Oh. Well. That explains why you hardly ever talk about them."

"And never come to see them."

"But you're going to see them now."

"Yeah. But I don't want to. I called my mother, so she knows I'm here."

I reached an arm around her shoulder. "I'm sure everything will turn out all right, Cat. Your family may never change, but that won't be your fault."

"I know." She patted my hand. "I know. I'm more worried about you than them. Promise me you won't turn into a lush."

I shook my head in fond exasperation. "I promise. I'm going to work out with Bitsey, then run with her up to Audubon Park. After that she and I are going for facials." I paused when the image of a beat-up telephone book popped into my head. Then I smiled. "And after that I'm going to sit down with the telephone book and check out all the health clubs and exercise programs in town. I'm going to start looking for a job."

To my surprise, Bitsey put up not one word of complaint even though I drove her like a drill sergeant. Though her face beaded with sweat, and her T-shirt turned dark with perspiration, she never once dropped down to a walk. As we headed down St. Charles Avenue, jogging between the streetcar tracks, she labored beside me, but she never quit. Of course, I was going awfully slow. We could have walked faster than we were jogging. But the point was, she kept going.

"I have a…new…goal." She puffed the words out in short pants as we crossed Louisiana Avenue. Ten blocks to go.

"What's that?"

"After the reunion…I want to lose…sixty…more pounds."

"Sixty? You go, girl."

"I want to be a size eight again…before I die."

"You can do it."

"Of course—" she gasped for air "—I may die today."

We counted down the blocks and once we turned onto Fourth Street, I asked, "So, when are you calling Eddie?"

"After you call Jeff," she threw right back.

The thought of calling Jeff Cole out of the blue made me

ridiculously nervous. Me, nervous about a guy! But the fact was, I needed a push to get the deed done, and Bitsey had just given me one. "All right. Today then."

We reached the elaborate cast iron gate that led into her father's front garden, and she grabbed it for support. "God, you're a heartless witch. But okay. Today I'll call Eddie, too."

"But we don't call until we're showered and primped up with all our makeup on. It's a trick I learned at my momma's knee. Whenever you make an important phone call, be sure to look your very best. And while you're talking, look into a mirror and smile."

Cat was gone, and so was Meg. Mr. Charles had lain down for another of his naps, and Miss Ulna and Veronica were having coffee in the kitchen, watching *Passions* on television. So we had the upstairs to ourselves. With the high ceilings and heavy Victorian furnishings, the ceiling fans whirring, and the shutters on the south side of the house closed to the midday sun, it was easy to imagine we'd stepped back over a hundred years. Except for my Reeboks and the spandex in my jogging clothes.

I poured a cool bath, sprinkled old-fashioned salts into the water in the deep, claw-foot tub, then peeled down my clothes and slid in. Jeff Cole. Another job for the phone book. And yet as I dredged up the memory of the cocky high school kid he'd been, another equally dark-haired image intruded. A scowling image.

Had Steve Vidrine ever played football? Had he always been in that chair, or had he once walked and danced and sprinted through life?

Did his grouchy personality have nothing at all to do with me and everything to do with the limitations he faced?

I straightened up and reached for the fresh bar of soap. It smelled like chamomile, good for improving moods, and I breathed deeply. Why was I even thinking about Steve Vidrine? No matter the cause of his bad temper, it was not my problem. All I needed from him was a car that ran. Meanwhile I had a phone call to make.

I made Bitsey go first.

"It's his machine," she mouthed to me, then abruptly straightened. "Hi, Eddie. This is Bitsey Albertson—Bitsey La Farge Albertson. I'm in town for the reunion. I'm so glad you and the rest of the committee decided to organize one. Anyway, if you have time, I'd love to get together with you. For coffee. Or a drink." She left the number, then heaved a massive sigh once she hung up. "Oh, my God. Why was I so nervous?"

"'Cause we're from the generation that didn't call boys. They called us."

Meg chose that moment to join us. She'd obviously heard the last part of our conversation. "Y'all need to get with it, " she said, plopping down on a pink damask chaise. "Women do the asking now just as much as the men." She slanted her eyes at her mother. "Seeing the old boyfriend makes you nervous?"

I watched Bitsey, praying she wouldn't act guilty. But she must have been prepared for just such an occasion. "Nervous? I'm way beyond merely nervous. You've seen my pictures from high school. Even though I'm losing weight, I'm still awfully fat compared to then."

Meg smiled at her. "Well, I think you look great, Mom. Really."

"Thanks, honey. So. What have you been up to?"

Meg's smile turned to a grin. "Oh, nothing. Just getting a job."

Bitsey gaped at her. "A job?"

"That fast?" I exclaimed. "Maybe there's hope for me, too."

"Does that mean you've decided to stay in New Orleans?" Bitsey asked Meg.

She nodded. "For a while, yeah. You don't think I should?"

"No, that's fine. Fine. So, where is this job? Not a nightclub, I hope."

"Chill, Mom. It's a coffeehouse on Magazine Street. It's close enough to walk, and once I can afford it, there's lots of apartments nearby. By the way, where's the Jag?"

"In the shop," Bitsey said, then looked at me. "It's your turn. Call Jeff."

So I did. Fortunately, I got his machine. Unfortunately, in the middle of my message he picked up. "Mary Jo? Is that really you?"

My heart began to pound. "Jeff. Hi. Yes." I gave a nod to Bitsey and Meg who were all grins and thumbs-ups. "Yes, it really is me. I'm in town and I decided on a whim to try and call you. How are you?"

"I'm great. Really great, especially now that you've called. What brings you back here? I heard you were out West somewhere."

"I came down with a couple of girlfriends."

"A couple of girlfriends, huh? Where are you staying?"

"I'm at one of their houses."

"In the Quarter?"

"No. We're in the Garden District."

"Damn, right in the neighborhood. That's perfect. I have a condo on St. Charles. So how about the two of us have dinner sometime?"

"Okay." Though I hadn't dated in years and had been a lot more nervous about this than I let on, hearing Jeff's familiar voice made everything easier. He was just as I remembered. Casual and outgoing. We could still have been eighteen, the years melted away that easily.

"How about tonight?"

I caught my breath. *Tonight.* "Okay."

"Give me the address and I'll pick you up. Eight o'clock good for you?"

Bitsey's brows were arched when I hung up. "Wow. He doesn't waste any time, does he?"

Meg kicked off her heavy black shoes and shot me a knowing look. "Is he that fast in bed? Not *in* bed, " she amended when her mother gasped. "I mean in maneuvering a girl into bed." My face must have reflected my shock. "You have to think about it, M.J. You're single now. Guys are gonna hit on you."

"He can hit on me all he wants—I'm *not* going to bed with him."

Famous last words. By ten-thirty he had one hand up my skirt and the other on my left breast, and I had to admit that it felt pretty good. At least he wanted me, unlike Frank who'd wanted—I don't know—something else entirely. Still, I wasn't ready to do what Jeff was more than ready to do.

The evening had started pleasantly enough. Jeff arrived right on time. His hair was still dark, cropped short with that bad boy, stand-up-straight-on-the-forehead style. Talk about a man in good shape! His body-mass index had to be below twenty. Well built, but not overbuilt. He was definitely GQ material, and even though I wasn't looking at her, I knew Cat's eyes were bugging out. If there was any man more unlike my late, unlamented husband, it was Jeff Cole.

"Wow," he said when he saw me.

I felt a blush on my cheeks, as if I was still sixteen. "Wow yourself." I'd worn a classy outfit, a white piqué fitted shift with ebony piping at the neckline, armholes and hem. It was one of those dresses that doesn't reveal much but hints at a lot. He was tall, so I had chosen spike-heeled sandals, and my hair was swept up in a loose, about-to-fall-down arrangement.

He had on black slacks, a white, open-collar knit shirt and a black-and-white silk tweed sport coat. Very chi-chi. Again, very GQ.

Bitsey winked at me as we left. Cat whispered "Go for it, or else I will." Meg gave me a hug and slid two condoms into my hand.

I nearly choked when I saw what they were. Somehow I slipped them into my purse without him seeing them. But I had no intention of using them.

Now I wasn't so sure.

"Jeff. Jeff!" I practically shouted in his ear.

"Just relax, babe. Just relax."

"I *can't* relax," I muttered, shoving his palm off my breast, and clamping my thighs in a ninja hold on his other hand.

"Damn, you're strong," he swore. But he finally relented and leaned back in the seat of his Porsche. He tilted his head and grinned at me. "So, you plan to ignore this thing between us, Mary Jo?"

"What thing?" I shifted and twisted in the seat, trying to pull my skirt as far down as it could get.

"C'mon. We're not teenagers, so you don't have to be coy, babe. You and I, we should never have broken up. We belong together. The minute I heard your voice on the phone I knew it. And then when I saw you…"

I shook my head in denial, but I knew exactly what he meant. Jeff was precisely the antidote I needed for Frank's humiliating betrayal. But that was logic speaking. For some reason my heart wasn't in it.

I swallowed hard and stared out the side window. We were parked on Esplanade Avenue, a block from Café Degas, an incredibly tiny restaurant which, despite its odd configuration and crowded dining room, had turned out to be an extremely romantic place to eat. Like a corner restaurant overlooking the Seine.

The sweet scent of night-blooming jasmine drifted on the soft air, and through the open car window I heard the faint strains of Wynton Marsalis, or someone who sounded like him.

It was any thinking woman's dream date, but I guess I wasn't ready to date, because all I wanted was to go home— that is, home to Mr. La Farge's grandiose cottage where I knew Bitsey and Cat and maybe even Meg would be waiting for all the details.

"Look, Jeff." I turned to face him. God, the man was good-looking. "This is all just a little too fast for me, you know? I haven't even been widowed a month yet."

"Yeah. Sorry. I guess I got carried away." He exhaled a breath, and thrust one hand through his short hair. "Considering how delicious you look, I think I was pretty restrained. But okay." He grabbed the steering wheel with both hands and straightened in his seat. "Would you like me to take you home?" He turned the key and the engine roared to life. Then he gave me this sidelong look and a very sexy smile. "Or we could go to my place."

"Home, James," I said. But despite my stern words, I couldn't restrain a grin.

He made a big show of looking disappointed, but he complied. "Well, at least you're still smiling," he said as we pulled into the traffic.

Ten minutes later when he kissed me good-night, it was like every romance novel I've ever read. Standing on the darkened porch, he took me by both arms and slowly pulled me flat against him. My toes barely touched the ground as he kissed me absolutely senseless. But there was no grabbing of any body parts. It was almost as if since plan A hadn't worked, he'd moved on to plan B.

But it only worked while he was kissing me. Once I slipped inside the door and closed it on him, my good sense fortunately returned.

"So?" Cat called down from her perch halfway down the wide mahogany staircase.

"We didn't expect you so early," Bitsey added from her spot right beside her.

Holding on to the massive carved newel post, I bent down and removed my sandals. "Ooh, that feels better." Then snagging them with one hand, I started up the steps. "I must be getting old, but I am *so* glad to be home. I think Jeff may be a little more man than I can handle right now."

"Wanna share?" Cat asked. "Share about what happened, I mean. Not share the man—though that's actually not a bad idea."

I glanced around. "Meg's not here, is she?"

Cat grinned. "No. Why? Wanna talk sex?"

"We did not have sex," I said. They followed me into my room. "But for a while there he did turn into an octopus."

"All hands?" Bitsey asked. My antenna went up at the odd, almost wistful tone of her voice.

"Did Eddie call?" I asked, turning my back to her.

She unzipped my dress. "No."

The big jerk. "So how did your day go?" I asked Cat.

"That's right. Change the subject."

"What do you mean? I told you everything. He tried. I declined. We parted as friends."

"You mean *you* won't go out with *him* again? Or the other way around?"

"Neither." I stepped out of the dress and slipped on a cotton robe. "We're going to get together again, okay?" Then I giggled. "He said we have this 'thing' between us. That we belong together."

"Oh, my!" Bitsey exclaimed, clasping her hands to her chest. "That's so romantic."

"Yeah," Cat said. "Romantic. I only hope that it's a really big 'thing,' Big and hard, and that it lasts a long time."

She was incorrigible, and we laughed until it hurt. Only later, when I was in bed, reliving that good-night kiss, then perversely wondering how my car was doing, did I remember that Cat never had answered my question about how her day went.

We met Doris Sutherland the next morning. She came over for brunch, which Miss Ulna and Veronica served on the back porch. Mr. La Farge presided over the event, and as before, we all dressed. Very old South. I shouldn't have liked it so much, but I did, and I tried to figure out why. It wasn't anything like a Southern California brunch where designer labels were essential on the clothes, the table linens, the flowers and—oh, yes—the food.

By contrast, this brunch was cooked and served by two old servants. The flowers—pentas, impatiens and ham-and-eggs—were still rooted in the ground. The linens were very likely seventy-five years old—probably bleached the old way, with salt, lemon juice and sunshine. And the clothes labels didn't matter at all.

If it weren't for Bitsey's being so obviously ill at ease, it would have been perfect.

At least she looked good. We'd exercised early, since the day was going to be hot. May in the Gulf South is like August in other places, and if you're not used to the humidity, it's unbearable. But I was getting used to it again. You can take the girl out of the South, but you can't take the South out of the girl. That was me. I wasn't crowned Little Miss Satsuma Queen for nothing.

Anyway, it was hot but we were in the shade with cool bricks beneath us and a large outdoor fan keeping us comfortable. Even so, Bitsey was perspiring . Her cheeks were flushed and she kept tugging at the V-neck of her aqua linen blouse, all the while shooting resentful glances at fluttery, oblivious Doris.

Doris had eyes only for Charles La Farge, and under her fond regard, he seemed almost to glow. It was actually very sweet.

"So Doris says to me, she says, 'I always wanted to try ballroom dancing, only Emil never would go.' So I think to myself, my doctor told me to get some exercise, and I tell her 'I'll go with you.' So that's how we started to keep company." He patted her on the hand.

She beamed at him, then turned her fluttery smile on us. "He really is quite a good dancer. You girls ought to try ballroom dancing," Doris suggested. "It's such a lovely, civilized way to meet nice people."

"I prefer a mosh pit," Meg said, dabbing her mouth with her late grandmother's Irish linen. Despite the streaky hair style, she was looking much better, well rested and well fed. Well treated.

"What's a mosque pit?" Doris asked. She was a pretty woman with delicate features and parchment skin. In her prime she must have been gorgeous. Her hands were manicured, her jewelry good but discreet, and her hair professionally styled. All in all, a real Southern belle. Of course she wouldn't know what a mosh pit was, let alone a 'mosque' pit.

Meg giggled. "Well, it's a big circle of dancers. Sort of like ballroom dancing, but not exactly."

Cat raised her brows and shot Meg a warning look, since Bitsey had obviously abdicated her role as parent. But I don't think Meg intended to be rude. "It's a little rougher dancing than some women like," she went on. "But it's a great way to meet guys."

"If that's how you met your last boyfriend," Bitsey said, cutting a sausage in half with a sharp little click of silver blade against china plate, "Perhaps you *ought* to try ballroom dancing."

"Oh, I'm afraid there aren't many young people there," Doris lamented. "This mosque pit sounds better for that." Her eyebrows knitted together. "I assume they let Christians dance there, too."

"What do you want to dance in a mosque for?" Mr. La Farge broke in. "I thought Muslims didn't allow dancing. Hell, I didn't think they allowed women in their mosques at all."

"Mosh pit," Bitsey said, almost angry. "Mosh, not mosque. Margaret, I wish you would stop aggravating everybody."

"How am I aggravating anybody?"

"Well, you're aggravating me."

Miss Ulna took that moment to interrupt us, bless her heart. She put one hand on Meg's shoulder, frowned at Bitsey, then looked at me. "Excuse me, Miss M.J. I wouldn't normally interrupt you at the table, but it's a Mr. Vidrine calling regarding your automobile."

I was glad to escape. Despite the lovely, relaxed ambience of the meal, Bitsey's mood was depressing. I knew it must be hard for her to see another woman in her mother's place, but really, her father was entitled to a life.

I took the call in the front parlor. The moment I heard Steve Vidrine's aggressively masculine voice, however, I was ready to retreat. I crossed to the mantel, stared at myself in the wavy, antique mirror and forced myself to smile. "Hello, Mr. Vidrine. How's my car?"

"Nearly dead," he said. "Call me Steve."

"Okay, Steve. Can you save her?"

"Of course. But it'll take time and it won't be cheap."

He quoted me a price that would almost buy me a new Saturn. Not that I wanted a Saturn. "That's a lot of money."

"That's a lot of car. It's a classic and it deserves the best. But if you just want to patch it up, I'm sure you can find someone who can do it a lot cheaper."

Maybe it was his form of a sales pitch: imply that you might settle for a lousy job, but he never would. Or maybe it was my need to prove that I could make him like me. Whatever the reason, I wasn't backing down. "Can I think about it?" I asked in my sweetest, breathiest voice. "I'm in the middle of something at the moment. Perhaps I can come by your office a little later to discuss it in more detail with you. When would be a good time?"

"You don't have to come here—"

"Oh, but I do. I left something in the car. Besides, I'm sure you have paperwork for me to sign. Don't you?"

There was a short silence. I smiled at my reflection, all the while picturing him in his utilitarian office, frowning at the phone.

"I'm here till six."

"I'll see you before then. By now."

I hung up before he could, then stared at my wavy image. "What are you up to, girl?" I wasn't sure. All I knew was that Steve Vidrine didn't want me around, and for some reason that made me want to make a real pest of myself.

CHAPTER 4
Men and Whine

Cat

Between M.J.'s hot date, Meg's new job and Bitsey's strange funk, I escaped being grilled about my visit to my old stomping grounds. I fobbed off M.J.'s question about the previous day, but the truth was, there was nothing to tell. I'd driven out to Ama, where we lived when my dad was alive. There's nothing left of the aluminum foil box we used to live in except for a few of the concrete blocks that used to hold it up. I continued down River Road to good old Hahnville High.

After that I meant to go by my mother's place, I really did. But I saw a St. Charles Parish sheriff's car parked outside a diner in Luling, and I had to stop. I told myself it was lunchtime, and I could use a bowl of gumbo or a fried soft-shell crab po' boy. The truth, of course, was that I had to know whether is might be Matt Blanchard having lunch there. Sheriff Matt Blanchard.

For some reason, the fact that it wasn't him—or maybe the fact that I would even care that it wasn't him—got me all depressed. I ate my lunch, got back in the car and headed for Boutte.

But I didn't stop at my mother's latest shabby house. I slowed down and squinted at the shotgun double with its tin roof and asbestos siding. There was an old recliner and a plastic lawn chair on her half of the porch, and parked in the driveway a rusty Ford pickup truck with weeds growing out from under it. Obviously things hadn't changed at all.

Then a twenty-year-old Camaro with a bright green home-painted finish and a jackhammer for a muffler pulled into her driveway, and before I could see which one of my pitiful brothers it was—my sister doesn't drive thanks to three DUIs—I peeled out and never looked back.

Cursing my cowardice, I made a beeline down Highway 90, heading back to New Orleans and the safety of Bitsey's Garden District mansion.

I got pulled over for speeding just before I reached the Jefferson Parish line. Seventy in a fifty-five speed limit, the St. Charles police officer said. Where was M.J. when I needed her?

As he wrote out the ticket, I looked at the officer's name tag. "Excuse me, Officer Guillory, but I was wondering, do you work for Matt Blanchard?"

He quit writing and looked at me. "Are you a friend of the sheriff's?"

"No. I mean, I was. But I haven't seen him in, oh, twenty years or so. I'm visiting from out of town."

A scowl line formed between his already thick brows. "If you don't think this ticket is fair, you'll have to take it up with him."

"Oh, no. That's not what I meant. I was just wondering, that's all."

He finished scribbling the ticket, tore it off his pad, then handed it and my license back. "I suggest you obey the speed limit, ma'am. As for Sheriff Blanchard, he's usually in the office till six or so. It's in Hahnville."

Don't ask me why, but I drove to Hahnville. Not to have my ticket fixed. God forbid that I meet Matt again under such circumstances. I sat in my rented car under an oak tree and watched the come and go at the police station. What was I doing here? If Matt came out, was I going to approach him? If he didn't come out, would I go in and look for him?

No to both. I just wanted to see him. I told myself that I wanted him to be bald and fat and sloppy, with nothing left of the dark-eyed boy I still pictured in my mind. That way I could abandon any stupid idea about connecting with him again. Bad enough dealing with the rotten past that included my family. It was impossible to deal with the one good part of that past, the part I'd had to give up along with the bad.

After forty-five frustrating minutes trying to be invisible in a rented Taurus, I finally started the car and found my way back to the Mississippi River Bridge—sticking strictly to the speed limit. Back on Fourth Street I helped send M.J. off on her date, watched *The First Wives' Club* on the VCR with Bitsey and refused to think about Matt Blanchard.

Brunch the next morning was pleasant enough, but the day loomed ahead with no reason not to visit my mother. Meg was to start training at her new job at noon. Bitsey was in a new funk over her dad's obvious infatuation with his sweet old Doris. I told myself that propping up a morose Bitsey was infinitely better than dealing with my mother. Then came the phone calls.

First the mechanic whose brief conversation left an odd little gleam in M.J.'s eyes. Then the phone rang for Bitsey. Eddie Dusson. She was on with him for a long while. Meg left before her mother returned to the table, and it was a good thing. Bitsey was all flushed and flustered, and her eyes were bright with emotion.

"Oh, my goodness," she said as she slid into the chair beside me. "He wants to have dinner. Tonight. What'll I do?"

"Don't worry, pal, you'll be great."

"This calls for a shopping trip," M.J. decided. "You deserve something beautiful to wear as a reward for all your hard work the last couple of weeks."

That's when Miss Ulna came out to say my purse was ringing. My cell phone, actually, but she carried my purse out to me, holding it at arm's length as if there might be a nest of roaches in it.

"Excuse me," I said as I checked the messages. I expected it to be something about work. Instead a bass voice with a faint hint of Cajun lilt spoke right out of my past.

"Hello, Cathy Ann. This is Matt Blanchard. I heard

you've been speeding through my town and didn't even stop to give an old friend the time of day. If you have a minute, give me a call."

I didn't have to write down his number. As he said it, it burned forever into my brain.

Mr. La Farge was holding forth on the local school board and what a bunch of political failures they were, with Doris nodding and smiling and refilling his coffee cup. But Bitsey and M.J. were watching me, and they knew at once that this was no ordinary phone call.

"That was my old friend, Matt," I said when Mr. La Farge paused for a breath.

M.J. grinned. "I didn't know you'd called him."

"I didn't."

"Maybe your mother?" Bitsey suggested.

I laughed, as nervous as a teenager. "I got a speeding ticket yesterday, apparently in his territory. He must have recognized the name."

"Catherine Peterson? He knows your married name?" M.J.'s grin turned into a smirk.

"I bet he's going to ask you out to dinner," Bitsey said, still floating on her own pink cloud of teenage memories and forty-something possibilities.

I was right up there on that cloud with her. "Maybe so," I said, unable to get rid of the sappy grin on my face.

"Go on then," Doris said. "Call your young man. There's nothing to be gained by waiting, dear."

The three of us convened in Bitsey's bedroom as soon as brunch was over. "Call him," M.J. said, sitting cross-legged on Bitsey's bed.

"I can't talk to him in front of y'all. I'll get all nervous and embarrassed."

"Then go call him in your room, but come right back here and tell all," Bitsey said.

So I did. He answered on the third ring.

"Hello, Matt?"

"Well. Cathy Ann."

"Cat," I said. "So. How are you?"

"I'm great. And you?"

"Fine. Just fine." There was an awkward pause.

"Good. So, what brings you back here? Your mother doing okay?"

I laughed, nerves, not mirth. "You're the sheriff. You probably know better than me how she's doing."

"Well, she's not driving. Neither is Sissy."

"The whole parish must be relieved. Of course there's still Hank and Bubba," I said.

"I always wondered if you had the Arceneaux curse."

"You mean, am I a drunk? No. I only marry them."

"I noticed the new name. What happened to the first guy?"

"Don't know and don't care."

He paused. "How's Mr. Peterson doing?"

"Don't know and don't care. How's your wife?" I added. It sounded bitchy but it was a purely defensive reaction.

"She died."

"She died?" I wanted to die myself. Did I always have to be gauche, uncouth and suffer from hoof-and-mouth disease? "God, Matt, I'm sorry."

"It was a long time ago, Cathy Ann. Cat. You couldn't know."

"How did it happen?"

"A drunk driver."

"Oh, my God."

"Yeah. Well." He cleared his throat. "The reason I called you was to see how long you plan to be in town." Another pause. "Maybe we could get together for a cup of coffee."

When I burst into Bitsey's bedroom, they took one look at my goofy grin and jumped up and down along with me. Like a group of high school kids we leaped around in an excited circle.

"We're getting together this afternoon," I said. "I'm going to the West Bank to visit my mother, then I'm meeting him at three."

"Can you believe this?" Bitsey asked. First M.J. and Jeff, then you and Matt, and tonight Eddie and me." She giggled. "Maybe we can go on a triple date before we all go home."

M.J. turned to the vanity mirror and fiddled with the hem of her blouse. "I'm not so sure I want to go out with Jeff again."

I guess I was too excited about my own circumstances to hear the odd note in M.J.'s voice, but Bitsey did. "What's wrong, hon? Is it something about him, or is it just too soon for you to be dating?"

M.J. shrugged. "Maybe a little of both. Anyway," she said, turning to us with a bright smile. "What do y'all plan to wear? It's got to be something that'll really knock their socks off."

I wanted to wear my favorite white linen slacks and a new azalea-red sleeveless blouse, accented with lots of silver jewelry. Very summery. Cool, calm and collected, the exact opposite of how I felt. But M.J. nixed it.

"Men like legs, and yours are good," she told me. "Wear a skirt and pretty sandals, and wear your hair up with dangly earrings. Those silver *fleur-de-lis* would be perfect."

Who was I to argue? I dressed. They tweaked the outfit, then sent me off while they made plans to shop for Bitsey.

"I'm sure I'll be back before you leave, " I told Bitsey.

"So you say. But I bet once the good sheriff sees you—and you see him—you'll forget all about poor little ol' me." She squeezed my arm through the open car window. "You have fun, you hear? And we'll compare notes tonight when I get back."

"Okay. But, Bits, " I said, knowing how much more vulnerable she was than I. "Take it slow tonight, okay? Don't do anything you might regret come the morning."

She shook her head as if that was a ridiculous thought. "I'm not M.J., and I doubt he's any Jeff Cole. We're just old friends. That's all."

I worried about her all the way to my mother 's house, which prevented me from worrying about my mother. This time I didn't hesitate, but turned into the rutted drive and parked behind the old truck. She was sitting in the front room with the television on and the door unlocked. Even the screen door wasn't latched. So I knocked, then walked in. "Hello, Mother."

She didn't move from her position, feet up in an old puke-brown Naugahyde recliner. A pair of pink terry cloth slippers dangled from her toes, and her pink-and-yellow daisy-patterned housedress had bunched up around her knees.

I stared at her, aware of a heavy weight in my chest. She looked more like eighty-six than sixty-six. Worse, with her eyes closed and her head tilted to the side, she looked dead. But her chest was moving, and she even swatted at a fly that landed on her cheek.

The TV was blaring a commercial. I turned it down but not off, then looked around the place. It was four rooms—a living room, a couple of bedrooms and a kitchen at the back. Unlike our home when I was a kid, it wasn't crammed with stuff. Then again, most of that stuff had been my dad's. He'd saved everything and brought home other people's cast-off crap, too. So had we kids. But there was no sign of anybody's stuff here but Mom's. Except for the kitchen sink, the place wasn't too messy. It was shabby, though, and I felt that old familiar guilt. I wasn't rich, but I made a good living. I sure didn't have to shop in thrift stores.

No, you shop in antique shops. The same thing, really—other people's old stuff, only fifty times as expensive. Except for my clothes, my linens and the electronics, hardly anything in my house was new.

For some reason, that realization helped me to relax. I returned to the living room, went outside again, and this time I knocked really loud and called out until my mother woke up.

"Come in," she grunted, heaving herself upright in the recliner, and pushing her glasses higher on her nose. "Oh," she said once I was inside. "It's you."

"Hi, Mom." She let me kiss her cheek but there was no

mistaking her hostility. There wasn't going to be any small talk, so I sat down and said, "Now, what's this about you dying?"

She pursed her lips. "Who told you?"

"You did. Yesterday when I called."

She flicked one hand as if my words were a pesky distraction. "I mean before that. Who told you to come back here to see me before I died?"

She really was dying? I leaned forward, bracing my elbows on my knees. "Nobody called me. I came home for a visit, that's all. Ma, what's going on?"

"What isn't?"

It turned out she has emphysema, high-blood pressure, a heart arrhythmia, and arthritis in her hands. Not a death sentence exactly, but not good, either. There was no liver disease, though. With proper care she could easily live another ten years or more. With proper care.

The problem was, she was living on nothing. Social security and food stamps. That's why Hank Jr.—my youngest worthless brother—had moved out. She didn't have any more money to give him.

"Do Bubba and Sissy ever come around?"

She gave me a sour look. "You don't know anything, do you? Bubba's in jail. Has been for almost a year. As for Sissy, well, she might as well be."

What little optimism I'd had for this visit dissolved. Bubba was in jail? I wasn't surprised, but it was depressing all the same. "Is Sissy still married to that guy? Donnie, wasn't it?"

She shrugged. "So she says. What about you? You got a man?"

I laughed. "No. And I don't need one. They're too much trouble. I would think you of all people would know that."

"Don't you start talking bad about your daddy."

I rolled my eyes and bit my tongue. I wasn't going to fight with her, especially not about him. "Look, I thought maybe we could do something together, Ma. You know, go out for lunch. Or I could pick something up and we could eat in."

She closed her eyes and let her head fall back against the chair. Her skin was so thin I could see the shape of her skull, and once again an unfamiliar panic tightened my throat. I leaned forward and put my hand over hers. At least her skin was warm. "You okay?"

She sighed. "I'm tired, that's all. Tired of feeling sick, tired of waiting to die."

My mother has always been a complainer, a whiner. And for most of my adult life my main reaction had been disgust. But today she was scaring me.

But disgust or fear, my reaction was the same: Get the hell out of Dodge. I stood up. "Okay. I guess today isn't a good day. But I'll come back for another visit. In a couple of days, okay? Maybe we can do something then."

She opened her eyes. "Did you talk to your sister or brother yet?"

"No, not yet. But I'm sure I will." *Unfortunately.* "How about I pick you up Monday at noon?"

She didn't look capable of even making it out to the car, let alone enjoying a meal at a restaurant. But at that moment I didn't care. I just wanted to get away. "D'you need anything before I go?"

Our eyes held, a long moment bursting with forty years of friction and sometimes outright hostility. Then she pointed at the television. "Raise up the sound."

I drove away shaking, hating myself for being such a wuss. So she was old; so she was on her last legs. She'd lived her life without caring how it affected others. Now she was reaping what she sowed. Taking her out to eat, fixing up her place, giving her a few bucks—none of it would help anything. She would probably smoke and drink away any money I gave her anyway.

Except that I realized that there had been no sign of her smoking anymore. And I hadn't seen any bottles in the kitchen.

I glanced at the clock on the dash. I had almost an hour

before my meeting with Matt. Maybe I should try to call Sissy.

I arrived early at Sal's Restaurant and went straight for the bathroom. It took a few tries, but I finally reached Sissy's house. Some guy answered. Donnie, I guess.

"She's probably at work. Want her number?" I took it and thanked him, all the while wondering why he wasn't at work, too.

"Cathy Ann?" Sissy exclaimed in a voice that sounded just like Ma's used to. "Girl, where you at?"

"I'm at Sal's. You know, in Luling. I'm visiting down here for a week or two. I just saw Ma and she doesn't look too good. Is she really dying?"

"Who knows? Look, I can't talk now. We're still pretty busy. How 'bout we get together later?"

We agreed to meet at four when she got off. When I hung up with her, I stared at myself in the mirror above the lavatory. I'd seen Mom and spoken to Sissy. That was two big hurdles already leaped. Since I didn't care if I saw Hank Jr., and I wasn't about to visit Bubba in jail, that left only one last hurdle: Matt.

I took a deep breath and reached for my lipstick, my powder and my hair spray. It took three minutes to touch up my makeup. That left twenty minutes until he came, twenty minutes to sweat off all my efforts to look cool and totally unaffected by the prospect of seeing him. You're a successful businesswoman, I told my reflection. He's an old friend. Just exude that chic, California cool the rest of the world tries to copy and you'll do fine.

I used the toilet, washed my hands, spritzed on a little more Oscar de la Renta, then forced myself back into the restaurant. Only fifteen more minutes to wait, I told myself. I could have a drink to settle my nerves. Except that the minute I left the restroom I practically bumped noses with the man.

"Cathy Ann?"

He stared down at me and I swear I turned into the same stammering idiot I'd been way back when. My face turned red, my palms started to sweat, and I had an immediate and urgent need to pee.

"Matt?" Where did that shaky Southern belle voice come from?

He grinned at me and, oh my God, it was like not one thing had changed in all those years. He was still Matt Blanchard—black hair, crooked smile and impossibly dark eyes—and I was still crazy Cathy Ann Arceneaux.

His gaze ran over me, top to bottom, then he leaned over, put a hand on my right shoulder and gave me a friendly kiss on the cheek. "Now that I've seen you," he said, "it'll be easier to get used to calling you Cat. You sure don't look like little Cathy Ann from up the River Road anymore."

He was smiling when he said it, so I guess it was a compliment. Finally I was able to relax. "And you sure don't look like the skinny Cajun kid I used to know." I used to love, I almost said. "And now you're the sheriff for the whole parish. I should have known."

"The usual table, Matt?" the waitress asked. She was watching us with a curious gleam in her eyes.

"Yes. Thanks, Charlene."

Once we were seated I asked," Does this mean we get the policeman's discount?"

He grinned. Actually, he hadn't stopped smiling and I realized that neither had I. "There are few enough perks being a small-town sheriff."

"So why do you do it?":

"Probably for the same reason you decorate houses in California. Because I like it, and I'm pretty good at it."

Touché.

"So," he went on when I picked up my menu and scanned it. "How long you plan on hanging around these parts?"

"At least a week. Maybe longer. How's the bread pudding here?"

"Great. But the pecan pie is even better."

We ordered two coffees and two pies, then just stared at each other. I wasn't sure what to say, so I asked, "How old is your son?" then inwardly winced. I sounded like I was interviewing a new client before I started designing her decor.

"He's fifteen, going on twenty-five. Do you have any kids?"

"No. I've had two husbands, though, both emotionally stalled at about fifteen. Does that count?"

He chuckled, as I hoped he would. "Same old Cathy Ann. You ever think about moving back home? Considering the amount of construction in these parts, you'd never lack for business."

Fortunately the coffee and pie arrived and I had a minute to bite my tongue into submission. Home? What home did I have here? "I'm pretty settled in California. Do you ever see anybody from the old days?"

"Are you kidding? All the time. You know, I heard that Myra Gaines is planning a twenty-fifth reunion for next spring. You ought to plan on coming."

"Our twenty-fifth, already? How did that happen?" I shouldn't have been surprised. After all, wasn't I here because of Bitsey's thirtieth? She was several years older than me. But still it caught me off guard.

"I'll give her your address and she can send you a notice."

"Okay. How is Myra, anyway?"

We talked about Myra and everyone else we'd known. Who'd made good. Who was dead. He told me my art teacher, Mrs. LeBlanc, had suffered a stroke and lived in a nursing home now, and that our old principal had been killed while cleaning his gun, but everyone thought it was a suicide.

We talked and laughed, and after forty-five minutes and two cups of coffee, I felt like I was eighteen again. In every way that counted, he was the same boy I'd once loved. If he'd made a pass at me I would have leaped into his lap.

It had been a month since I'd been with Bill—two-timing, asshole Bill. That's why I was so horny, I told myself. But the truth was, I could have screwed my brains out last night and I would still be ready to jump Matt Blanchard's bones. He was tall, had all his hair, and though he'd gained some weight, it was in all the right places. Plus, he was still a Boy Scout at heart. One of the good guys.

"I think I need to take you dancing," he said after he paid the waitress.

My heart started to flutter and I tried not to smile too big. "I'd like that. But I have to warn you, I haven't Cajun danced in years."

"It'll come back to you. Some things you never forget."

As he walked me to my car, his hand lightly touched my waist. Not steering me. I hate when men do that, like you can't find your way to the door without them. This was different, a courtly Southern gesture that doesn't imply you're helpless. It says you're valued. Or, it says, I like touching you.

We stopped at the Taurus and I turned to face him.

He grinned. "Is this the race car?"

Embarrassed, I ducked my head and looked at my feet, then at his big, boot-shod ones, which made my size nines look slender and feminine. He made *me* feel delicate and feminine and, oh God, did I like that feeling.

"This is it," I admitted. "But don't worry, I'm sticking strictly to the speed limit now." *Except when it comes to you,* I thought, raising my gaze back to his.

Of course, that's when his radio crackled to life. He grimaced and turned away. I unlocked the car, then waited for him to finish.

"Sorry," he said. "I've got to go. But I'll call you. Keep tomorrow night open, okay?"

Tomorrow! "I will."

He drove one way; I went the other. I was halfway to the bridge before I remembered about Sissy. After glancing in my rearview mirror, I made an illegal U-turn and started back toward Boutte.

Seeing Sissy brought me back to earth. She was sitting on a bench outside LeBlanc's Truck Stop, but I walked right past her.

"Cathy Ann?"

I knew that voice. Even so, when I turned around I still

didn't see Sissy in the neatly uniformed woman who rose to her feet. She laughed, as if she was enjoying my shock, as if she'd expected it. I could see why. She'd gained at least thirty pounds—and that was a good thing. Her eyes were clear. Her hair was clean and dyed a natural-looking light brown. She looked ten years younger than the last time I saw her. And infinitely healthier. "Sissy?"

She was grinning at me like a fool, but there were tears in her eyes. She nodded, then laughed and wiped them away. "Sometimes I forget how low I sank back then, and how far I've come until I see the shock in someone's face. C'mon. Give me a hug."

Maybe I'd just been through too much today. Mom. Matt. Now Sissy. Whatever, when she grabbed me and then clung so hard, I started to cry. She didn't have to tell me what had happened; I could tell by looking. She was sober.

"A year last month," she said when we sat down together on the bench. "I spent six months in Grace House, and now I'm at Lindy's Place. It's a halfway house. I work and turn most of my money over to them. In two months I can move out and they'll give me my money to start fresh in a place of my own."

"I can't get over it. You look so good. Great. But Mom didn't say a word to me about you. Donnie, either."

"Mom doesn't want to know. I mean, I tried to explain, but she ignores me. As for Donnie, he tries but he keeps slipping back. Mostly alcohol, but he likes painkillers, too. The problem is, he's not trying to get sober for himself. He's only doing it because he's afraid that if he doesn't, I won't come home to him."

"Will you?"

She fiddled with her canvas tote bag. It had a screen-printed image of a caterpillar turning into a butterfly. "I don't know. I probably shouldn't. But I just don't know."

An eighteen-wheeler pulled into the lot beyond us, and for a moment we were quiet.

"I wish you'd called me," I said, not looking at her.

"Why?"

"I don't know. Maybe I could've helped you out."

She shook her head. "I had to do this myself. Just me and everyone else in recovery. Besides, you'd pretty much given up on me—on all us Arceneauxes. I'm surprised you came back at all."

"Thank God I did."

I whispered that last part, but Sissy heard me and she put her hand over mine. I swallowed hard. "You know, seeing you…it restores a little of my faith in our family."

She pressed her lips together. "I feel the same way about you."

We never went in for coffee. We just sat on that bench, talking a little but mainly just enjoying being sisters. I drove her home—to the group home she lived at—and we promised to walk the levee together one evening like we used to when we were kids.

"Maybe we can take Mom out to lunch or dinner one day," I suggested.

"If she'll leave the house. She hardly ever does anymore."

I watched her go inside the neat brick house that looked like every other house on the street. But to me it seemed to glow. My little sister wasn't going to die from an overdose or get shot or raped or beaten up by some drug dealer. She was going to live.

But as happy as that made me, when I drove up to the house on Fourth Street, all I felt was depressed. Everything around me was changing. Bitsey. M.J. Even my horrible family. But I was stuck, feet mired in the same mud of my miserably lonely existence. Even my rekindled attraction to Matt wasn't trustworthy. I'd broken up with him over twenty years ago. Was starting up again with him just a panicky reaction to being alone?

My cell phone rang just as I got out of the car. It was Matt.

"Something's come up," he said, "and I won't be able to make it tomorrow night. But I'll call you," he said.

I'll call you.

"Yeah. Sure you will," I said after we hung up. That fast I was sorry I'd come back to New Orleans. My mother didn't need me, except maybe as somebody new to complain to. My sister sure didn't need me. My brothers weren't worth bothering about. And as for Matt...

Well, Matt was just a guy I once dated. I'd probably never see him again.

Bitsey

My mother was crazy.

I didn't realize it until I moved away to the other side of the continent. That's when it became obvious. She suffered from mental illness, manic depression, to be exact, though bipolar is the term du jour. All I knew as a child was that I was terrified of her.

The thing is, she never actually raged at us. She would stand very straight, very stiff, as if the least movement might cause her to explode. But the fact that she held it in made her even scarier. She had this way of pinning you with her eyes, and this laceration in her voice that made you feel like a stupid, ungrateful idiot. I used to wonder why she had kids; it was obvious that for her we were more trouble than we were worth.

But she never behaved that way around my father. In our house he was a god. I suppose she never forgot that he'd lifted her up from nothing to the heights of New Orleans society. He might be loud and demanding, but she catered to his every whim. So did we, for with his children he was generous with his praise and his money, if not always his time. Even now he was the same.

My brother, Chuck, is a junior version of our father—except when Virginia is around. As for me, I've told myself that I'm nothing like my mother. Nothing. Although I do have a few of her traits. The truth is, I bounce back and forth between fearing I'm a clone of my mother and fearing I'm a clone of my father.

Or maybe I'm just my own twisted version of all their worst traits. What other reason could there be for my unreasoning fury at Doris Sutherland? I didn't have to call Dr. Herzog to know how skewed my thinking was. The fact was, Doris Sutherland was a very nice old lady. She doted on my father and he loved every bit of that adoration.

According to Miss Ulna, Doris was too rich to be after Daddy's money, and anyway, Daddy and Chuck's lawyer wife Virginia had arranged his estate a long time ago. Nobody was coming between my sister-in-law and her kids' inheritance, so if she approved of Doris, why shouldn't I?

But all this logic was wasted on my out-of-control emotions. Wasn't there one man in the whole world who remained faithful? Thirty years ago Eddie had dumped me; ten years ago Jack had begun to drift away; and now my daddy was abandoning me, too.

Irrational, I know, and more paranoid than bipolar. But there was one good side effect of all this craziness. I'd substituted exercise for food. The more, the better. I guess I thought that if I lost enough weight I could get Eddie back. Then Jack would come crawling, begging me to come home, and in the middle of all that melodrama my father would realize that this was all his fault. All of it. He would dump Doris, beg my forgiveness and…and… And what?

That's what convinced me I really was slipping off the edge. Banishing Doris would change nothing for me. Furthermore, if Eddie fell in love with the new slimmer me with the attitude hairdo, why would I want Jack back?

I took a half dose of Xanax before my date. It was the only way to slow down my racing pulse and overactive sweat glands.

"You look nice," Meg said, popping her head into my room. "Where you going?"

"Nowhere special," I lied. Frantically I searched for a way to divert the subject from me to her. "How was work?"

"Cool," she said, meandering around my room. "I learned how to make cappuccinos, espressos and mocha lattes." She picked up my bottle of lotion and sniffed. "I was wondering," she went on. "There's this band playing tonight and while I'm in training I don't get a share of the tips, plus payday isn't till next Tuesday. So do you think you could advance me twenty bucks?"

"You're going to some club by yourself?"

"No. I'm going with some kids I met at work." She gave me this patient look. "Mom." She stretched it out to three syllables. "It's perfectly safe. It's not even in the French Quarter, okay? It's this dinky bar called the Dixie Tavern. Anyway, you forget that I worked at Tavernous. I know how to handle myself."

That was probably true. Then again, look how that had turned out. "The Dixie Tavern. It sounds like a country music place."

She grinned. "Yeah, but it isn't. This band, Noodlehead, is having a CD launch party, and Brandon—that's this guy at work—he says they're great. Really out there. So, will you loan me the money?"

I gave her twenty dollars; she gave me a quick thank-you kiss. Once she left I stared at my reflection in the mid-nineteenth-century Victorian mirror. At least Margaret still needed me for something. But not for long. She'd turned into Meg, this independent college dropout of a girl. Once she got her first paycheck she wouldn't need me at all.

I was saved from drowning in self-pity when Cat knocked once, then popped her head in. "What time is he coming?"

"Seven. Oh, God, Cat. What am I doing?"

"Having dinner with an old friend." She dropped onto the settee and kicked her mules off.

"Right, dinner. Where's M.J.?"

"I dropped her at the car repair place. You know, I think she might have the hots for one of the men there. She's counting on him to give her a ride home."

I swiveled around to stare at her. "She would get in a car with a strange man? She's as bad as Meg."

"What's Meg up to?"

"She's going out with some new friends, coworkers. Brandon Somebody."

"Hell's bells. Everybody's got something going on tonight except me."

"You know, you never did say what happened with Matt."

She stared up at the ceiling. "One, he's better looking than ever. Two, he asked me to go out tomorrow night. Three, he called less than an hour later and canceled."

"He canceled?" I studied her profile—set jaw, noncommittal expression. "Did he say why?"

"Nope."

"I swear. Men are such pigs."

Cat slanted a leering look at me. "But not Eddie. Eddie's not a pig, is he?"

"You're forgetting that *he* broke up with *me*. You were the one to dump poor old Matt. Maybe that's why he canceled on you, to show you how it felt."

"I don't know. I don't think that's his style."

"So call him and ask," I said, turning back to the sprawl of earrings on the vanity. "Which ones should I wear?" I wanted to be a good friend, but I was too nervous to think about anything but what Eddie would think when he saw me.

Cat didn't seem to mind. She picked out a pair of pearl earrings, then loaned me a pearl and Austrian crystal pendant of hers to wear with them. I had on a V-neck black cotton sweater with three-quarter length sleeves, a black-and-white ankle-length skirt with wavy stripes—slimming—and my tallest pair of sandals. I looked tall and, for me, relatively slim. Better than I had in ten years. But I was still a long way from how I'd looked at twenty.

The doorbell rang at ten minutes after seven. I got it before Miss Ulna could. Through the intricate cut glass of the front door I saw a tall, lean silhouette. Then the door opened and my young and handsome first true love turned out to be just as old as I.

For a moment we only stared at one another. His hair had gone a striking steel-gray, and though it was a little thinner than it used to be, he still had a lot of it. When he smiled, creases fanned out from the corners of his eyes, and deep furrows bracketed his mouth. He was still good-looking and still trim, but he was forty-eight all the same, just like me.

"Bitsey!" His eyes ran over me and his grin increased. Oh, how well I remembered that wide, masculine grin. "Wow, still gorgeous," he said. "I thought after three kids that you might be an old frump. I should have known better."

Then without waiting for an invitation, he came in and gave me a big hug.

If I'd had any sense I would have gotten even more nervous. But that hug melted away all the years. He might have still been wearing a leather jacket and had his Harley-Davidson waiting around the corner. He hugged me and I turned into a hopelessly enamored teenager all over again.

"Eddie. Oh, my God!" I exclaimed, when he slipped back. "You haven't changed at all."

He rolled his eyes. "What a load of crap. C'mon, Bitsey, did you ever expect to see me in pants with this sharp a crease? Or lace-up shoes?"

"Or a tie? No," I said, unable to stop smiling. "But they look good on you."

He glanced around. "I see your dad's still living well."

"Don't you start on my dad, Eddie. He's an old man and this is his family home. Besides, I think you liked the fact that he didn't approve of you."

His eyes crinkled when he smiled at me. "You're probably right. D'you think he'd approve of me now?"

"I think so. Well, not your politics. But he's impressed with anyone who pulls himself up by his bootstraps."

"That's big of him."

"Now, Eddie," I said in a teasing tone I hadn't used on a man in a million years. "If we're going to have a pleasant evening, we won't be able to talk about my father."

"Don't worry, Bitsey. I'd much rather talk about you. Shall we?" He offered me his arm.

"Yes, but first I want you to meet my friend Cat." She was on the back porch petting one of Miss Ulna's six-toed cats.

"So glad to meet you," Cat said, shaking his hand. "Bitsey's told me so much about you."

Thank goodness M.J. wasn't there, too. As it was, Eddie's obvious appreciation of Cat's classy good looks turned me pea-green with jealousy. Jealousy! I realized as he turned back to me that this could turn out to be a far more momentous evening than I'd thought. Two minutes into it and I was ready to fight my best friend because my old boyfriend had given her the once-over. He'd given me an approving once-over, too, but compared to Cat I was nothing, a hausfrau decked out in new clothes. But at heart still a hausfrau.

But there was a bigger issue here than that. If I didn't get my careening emotions under control, I was liable to venture into territory I was not ready to venture into.

From my house, ten minutes to an odd little restaurant called Nat and Maddies, my heart raced like an overrevved engine. Eddie might be bad for my ethics, but he certainly was good for my metabolism.

In the car we talked about the car. It was one of those hybrid vehicles that ran on electricity and gas, a "green" car like Susan Sarandon's husband and all the other political celebrities were driving. "It gets seventy miles per gallon," he said. "Do you realize that this country could slice its gas usage by two-thirds if the oil and gas industry didn't have ninety-nine percent of the politicians on its payroll? And with the savings we could really work to improve the quality of life for the underclasses here and in the third world."

"Are those the sorts of cases you work on?" I asked as he whipped the little car into a sliver of a parking space.

"Not the oil and gas industry per se, but their partners in crime—the plastics industries, the processing plants. They poison the air and the water, and leave the little people to suffer in silence."

He slammed his car door and looked at me across its roof.

"I work on a lot of first amendment issues, too. Mainly I try to give the little people a voice."

He must have realized he was beginning to sound preachy, because he grinned and said, "But enough about me and my causes. Tell me about you and your life the last thirty years."

We talked nonstop through dinner—I had a wild field greens salad and an eggplant Napoleon, and for dessert, broiled pears and decaf coffee with skim milk and no sugar. M.J. would be so proud. He ordered vegetarian, too, though I think his was more a political statement than a diet decision. But I wanted him to think well of me, so I let him think I was a vegetarian, too. I was cagey about a few other things, as well.

"I do volunteer work in the arts—and for literacy," I added. Actually I threw ceramic pots for fun and had donated a few to a charity auction. As for literacy, I sometimes read to patients in the pediatrics wing of the Bakersfield Hospital.

He nodded his approval; I felt like a fraud.

But I vowed to take a page from his book in the future, and devote myself more to such causes.

"So when are you moving back to New Orleans?" He grinned. "Am I rushing things? You've told me about your kids, your friends and everything else in your life. But you haven't once mentioned your old man."

"My old man? Now there's a term I haven't heard in a long time."

"Aha. You don't want to talk about him. Should I assume that all is not golden in the Golden State?"

Suddenly I felt defensive. "I'm surprised you asked, given the fact that you broke up with me."

He didn't look the least bit repentant. "I hope you didn't marry him on the rebound."

"I might have dated him on the rebound, as I'm sure you remember. But I married him because he was the right man for me. At the time." Now why had I added that?

"At the time," he echoed. "But not anymore?"

I poked my spoon too hard at the uneaten half of my

pears. "I don't know." I looked up at him. "I came home to think about my life and my marriage. I don't know yet what I'm going to do about either of them."

He nodded. "Fair enough. I'm divorced myself, so I know that feeling. Let's just have a good time while you're here, okay? And we'll see how things go."

Just have a good time. That sounded perfect, and perfectly safe—until he kissed me good-night.

Eddie had kissed me in the shadows of my front yard a thousand times in the past, standing just beyond the streak of light from the side parlor windows. When he walked me there I couldn't pretend I didn't know what was to come.

But what I didn't know was how profoundly it would affect me. No husbandly kiss, no dutiful peck. Eddie kissed me the way a hungry lover kisses his woman.

He'd always been a good kisser. It was because he committed himself wholly to the process. He did that with everything, I realized once I came up reeling from a lack of oxygen. Lovers, work, politics. Eddie was an all-or-nothing kind of guy, while my husband was the hedge-your-bets kind.

But I was tired of hedging my bets. So I threw my arms around Eddie's neck and kissed him back.

We were both breathing hard when we came apart. "Are you sure you haven't already decided the fate of your marriage?" he asked. His voice was a warm tickle in my ear, so sexy I could feel myself going all gushy inside.

"Maybe… Maybe I'd better say good-night."

His hands ran down my arms, then up again until he held my face cupped in his hands. He gave me a last kiss that turned my knees to banana pudding. Then he let out a frustrated sound and stepped back from me.

"Yeah." He thrust his hands into his pockets just as he used to and my heart almost beat its way out of my chest. "You'd better say good-night," he said, "And I better go home."

He walked me to the door and with a wry, sideways smile, he left. He didn't say he'd call, but I knew he would. And I knew I'd drop everything when he did. He knew it, too. Just like thirty years ago.

I sat on the stairs a long while before going up to my room. I heard the television on in Daddy's room downstairs, and a different channel coming from Cat's room. Though I knew I ought to go talk to her, I wasn't quite ready. But her door was open and she spied me in the upstairs hall. Since M.J. was there, too, I knew I had to join them.

"Uh-oh," Cat said after a moment. "This looks serious."

I didn't even try to pretend. "It may be."

"Be careful, honey," said M.J. She was curled up on an old love seat that had the same burgundy tapestry upholstery from when I was a little girl. "Just don't let him rush you."

Cat turned the television off. "Okay, Bits, what happened?"

"Nothing," I said, shaking my head.

"Oh no, you don't," she retorted. "M.J. shared about her date. I admitted the humiliating results of mine—"

"Just because he had to cancel doesn't make it humiliating."

"Don't change the subject. We told you our details. Now you have to tell us yours. We didn't come traipsing all the way back to New Orleans with you just so you could shut us out about you and Eddie."

"You wanted to come," I protested. "You're the ones that talked me into coming."

Cat threw a pillow at me. "And aren't you glad we did?"

"Shut up, Cat," M.J. said. At least she was sticking up for me. "Come here, Bitsey. Sit here." She patted the spot next to her. I did as she said, kicking off my shoes as I went.

"Now," she said when I was comfortable. "I'm guessing things got a little physical with Eddie and you're feeling a little guilty. Right?"

A little? Like the emotional idiot I was, I began to cry. Then I started to talk, and in a rush of hot tears and devastating guilt, I told them everything. "I've never cheated on Jack. Never. Even when I saw a guy I could be attracted to,

I never was. Not really. I've been a good wife. Twenty-six years of marriage and then this…" I stared from M.J. to Cat and back. "What am I going to do?" I bowed my head into the pillow Cat had tossed at me and cried a new wave of tears into it.

For once Cat was not so quick with her smart answers to everything, which was one more guilty knife lacerating my heart. "You both know how it feels to be cheated on," I whispered. "How hard it hurts."

Cat had been sitting cross-legged on the bed. Now she lay back and stared up at the ceiling. "It only hurts if you find out." The words came out slowly, as if she wasn't sure they were true.

"So you're saying I can go for it with Eddie as long as Jack never finds out."

"But eventually the truth comes out," M.J. put in.

"So you're saying I should decide what to do about my marriage before I let things go too far with Eddie."

"It sounds like she's gone pretty far already," Cat said to M.J.

"Emotionally, maybe. But she hasn't slept with him."

"But it's the emotional cheating that counts most," Cat replied.

"That's not true," M.J. said. "Was Bill ever emotionally involved with any of his other women?"

Cat snorted. "Are you kidding? He wasn't even emotionally involved with me. And we were married three years."

"Right," M.J. said. "And I doubt Frank was emotionally involved with that…that creature." She shuddered. "Nothing emotional. Purely physical. But you and I were both crushed by what they did."

"So you're saying I need to end it with Jack now," I interrupted them, "before I see Eddie again."

They both looked at me, then at each other. "I don't know," Cat began.

"It's not for us to decide," M.J. said.

I collapsed against the worn back of the settee. "Y'all are

absolutely no help. I mean, come on. This is the worst crisis of my life."

"Okay then." Cat sat up again. "Here's what I think—and I'm trying to be very fair to Jack even though I don't think he deserves you. Even if you were divorced and totally available, I'd still tell you to slow down with Eddie. You're way too confused right now to make a smart decision. And one thing I know, Bits. You need to be smart about this. You're not just talking about your life. There's Jack and your girls to think about."

"Like you care about Jack."

"I care about you and you care about Jack, even if you're not very sure about him these days."

I shook my head and glared at them. "Why can't you just give me a clear-cut answer? Some good, grits girlfriend wisdom. But I'm not going to get it, am I?"

"Cat's right," M.J. said. "You have to slow down with Eddie. Get to know him as a friend first. Find out what he's like now. I mean, he might not be married, but he could have a girlfriend."

"Or a live-in."

"He could be as big a cheat as Bill."

"No. You're wrong about that," I told them. "This is a man whose life is dedicated to righting wrongs, to getting fair play for people who can't get it for themselves. A man like that does not lie and cheat. He doesn't."

"Neither does a woman like you," Cat said.

I wished she hadn't said that. I wished she'd just made one of her flippant, sarcastic remarks that I could shrug off, like swatting an annoying mosquito. But I couldn't shrug this one off. She was right. I wasn't a liar or a cheat. That was the Grits Girlfriend wisdom I needed to hear.

"Okay. Okay. You're right. No more dates with Eddie. We're just old friends trying to see if we can resume our friendship. And if it leads to more, well, we'll just wait and see. But I have to tell you," I added, "I haven't been this horny in a long, long time. Do you think it's because he's an old boyfriend and he's roused up all those eighteen-year-old feelings? Didn't y'all feel that way when you met up with Jeff and Matt again? I mean, M.J., even though you'd been married to Frank for seventeen years, didn't you want to do it with Jeff?"

"I guess I did—at least I wanted to while we were making out. But it's weird. Jeff is so good-looking. Women everywhere just drool over the man. I'd forgotten about that, how hard it is to date a guy like him."

"Look who's talking!" I hooted. "I pity the poor guy who dates you."

"But that's different," she said.

"How?"

"Because I know I'm not going to cheat on any guy I'm committed to. But I can never be sure about the guy I'm with, especially a guy who can have any woman he wants."

"Frank had money as a lure," Cat said. "And Jeff has sex appeal. What about that mechanic?" she went on. "What does he have?"

My head swiveled toward M.J. "The mechanic? You mean the guy who's repairing the Jaguar?"

"He drove her home, " Cat went on. "But not until almost eight. Two hours they spent together," she said, smirking at M.J. who had blushed a very telling shade of pink. "Somehow I don't think they spent two hours talking about her car."

"Shut up, Cat. I told you, he's a very interesting guy."

"How interesting?" I asked.

M.J. took a long time to answer. "For starters, he doesn't like me."

"Come on," Cat said.

"No, I mean it. He didn't want me to come in person to talk about the car and he didn't want to give me a ride home."

Cat made a face. "Maybe he's married and he's that one rare guy who is loyal."

M.J. shook her head. "It's not that. He really doesn't like me. Me, specifically. I thought it might be like what I said about Jeff. I mean, I don't want to sound vain, but I thought maybe he thought I was too good-looking for a guy like him.

Or too rich or too—I don't know—too society. But I think it's more."

"But what?" I asked. "You're sweet and not at all stuck-up. Besides, it's not like he doesn't deal with rich women and their expensive cars all the time."

When M.J. stared down at her lap I realized that even when Frank died she hadn't looked this dejected.

Cat tried to cheer her up. "Ironic, isn't it. The one of us who's not available has something going on, but single me and single M.J. can't manage to get a date with the guys we like. She paused. "Do you think, honey, that the reason you like him is because he's not falling all over you?"

"I don't know. You've got more experience with men than me, Cat. You should be full of good advice."

"Yeah, and look where all my experience has gotten me. Alone at forty-three with two divorces and no prospects."

"What a bunch of sad sacks," I said. "I don't know about y'all, but I'm no better off now than I was back in high school and college. Still whining about men to my girlfriends. Do you think we'll ever outgrow this phase?"

"I don't know," Cat said "The good widow Doris looks to be about seventy-five and she still needs a man in her life."

I lurched up from the settee. "Please. Let's not talk about Doris Sutherland."

"I just use her as an example. Let's face it, we're addicted to men."

CHAPTER 5
Baby You Can Drive My Car

M.J.

I don't know why I didn't tell Cat and Bitsey the truth about Steve. Most likely I was afraid they'd tell me to drop him. But ever since I'd seen him rolling across that shop of his, I couldn't stop thinking about him.

It actually started before that, though, in his office. He's a good-looking man in a rough, capable sort of way. And those arms... But he hadn't come on to me at all when we first met, not even a smile. It had been both irritating and interesting. Irritating because I wasn't used to being ignored by men. Interesting, because given my lack of serious interest in Jeff, I'd started to worry that Frank's betrayal had turned me off to all men. But Steve's wheelchair had turned my annoying interest into fascination, and so I'd insisted on meeting him at his shop at closing time—and with no ride home.

Cat dropped me off without even grilling me about how I'd get back to the house. She was preoccupied with her own plans. But, I was sure we would talk later, all three of us Grits Girls.

I'd dressed very simple for this meeting. No one could tell I'd spent an hour dithering over my choices before I settled on a cotton-candy pink tank top, a black-and-pink cotton skirt and a simple pair of leather slides. Of course as Cat pulled away and I stepped into the cool dimness of the garage, I realized that by emphasizing my legs I might alienate Steve even more.

But it was too late to back out, so me and my legs headed to the office.

Two people were there picking up their cars, a Hispanic woman in housekeeper attire, and a lawyer type, very cool in his pin-striped Armani with a Bill Blass tie loosened at his throat. He gave me a lengthy once-over. Steve, of course, did not.

I waited outside the window until the two customers left in a Volvo and a BMW respectively. Then I poked my head inside. "Ready for me?"

He muttered something, probably "No", or maybe "Hell, no." But when he looked up he said, "Have a seat."

I smiled sweetly at his grouchy response and hoped it annoyed him. "Actually, I was hoping we could look at the car. I'll understand what you're talking about better if I can see the parts. You could point out the rings and the transmission and the master...the master..."

"Master cylinder."

His eyes were so dark and shuttered, so impossible for me to read, that all I could do was nod.

After a moment he nodded back. "Fine."

I knew this was going to be an awkward meeting, but I hadn't realized just how many opportunities I was going to get to screw up. First the skirt; now the door. Did I hold it open for him? Go through first? Let him through first? If I had half a brain I would have remembered that he went in and out of this door every day. He didn't need my help. But like a fool I held it open.

"Go ahead," he told me, stopping his chair with one hand and gesturing with the other.

To my horror, a hot, embarrassing blush rose in my cheeks. So I ducked my head and did as he said. The door immediately started to slam, but he checked it with a forward wheel and rolled out next to me.

I was taller than him. Not really taller, but for all practical purposes I was. At five foot two I've never been taller than a man, not that it mattered. On the other hand, right now everything seemed to matter.

My car was parked in the last bay. She looked as good as ever, as if a cruise across the U.S.A. was no big deal, even though at the moment she probably couldn't make it out of the garage.

He opened the door, popped the hood, then wheeled around to the hood and deftly opened it. All without saying a word. He was really ticked off at me. But instead of making me feel bad, it made me mad. Doris had said he was very nice, so he couldn't act this way with everybody.

It was just me.

I decided to erase every stupid reason he had for not liking me. My mother might have been shallow and only concerned with surface appearances, but she'd taught me a few good lessons. And one of them was that old Southernism: You catch more flies with honey. So I acted like I didn't notice how rude he was to me.

I peered into the metal and rubber tangle of my car's stricken engine. "I've heard Jaguars are more complicated than other cars. Is that true?"

"Yeah."

"Why is that?"

"Eight cylinders is more complicated than four or six."

"Oh. Don't any other cars have eight cylinders? Like a Chevy V-8?"

"Yeah."

"So how is a Jaguar more complicated than that?" If he thought he could put me off with curt, one-word answers, he was sadly mistaken. I'd been grilled by the most sadistic pageant judges in the world.

"Tolerances," he finally answered.

One word. I gritted my teeth. Oh, but the man was devious. "Tolerances? What does that mean?"

He exhaled a noisy breath. "It means there's a lot less room in a Jaguar engine for error in calibrations and other adjustments. Look, Miss Hollander or Miss Landry—"

"Mary Jo."

A muscle ticked in his jaw as if he were physically counting to ten to keep his cool. "Mary Jo," he said. "Look, it's late. I've had a long day. Down there hidden on either side of the engine block are the rings. Way back there is the transmission. It's between the engine and the drive train. As for the master cylinder." He heaved himself up, leaned over the engine, and bracing himself with one hand, pointed with the other. "Under there."

He could stand up. And he was taller than me. Not macho tall like Jeff, or dapper tall like Frank. He was just the right height.

His eyes narrowed and I realized I hadn't once looked at the engine. "Why are you here, Miss Landry? We both know I can answer all of your questions about your car on the phone. If you think you can charm me into lowering your bill, forget it. I'm a businessman and this is business."

"I can afford to fix my car," I stated, barely reining in my anger. "I could practically buy a new car with what you're charging, but I'm willing to pay what it takes to fix her, so there's no need for your nasty accusations."

"Fine. Are you authorizing the repairs?"

"Yes."

"Good. Then I guess we're done."

"No, we're not!" Where had my good nature and my instinctive avoidance of conflict gone?

He stared at me, waiting. But I could feel his tension and I didn't understand—not why he was so tense or why I was so aware of it.

I tried to swallow my nervousness. "You don't like me and…and I can't figure out why."

He lowered himself into his chair—to buy time, I think. When he looked up at me again his face was a noncommittal mask. "I don't care one way or another about you. I don't care about any of the people who come through my shop. But I do care about their cars. If you need a mechanic for your

Jag, then I'm your man. If you need a best friend, I suggest you hire a shrink."

And with that he spun his chair around and rolled back to his office.

"I already have a best friend. Two of them," I shouted. In the empty quiet of the shop my words echoed down from the high ceiling.

"Good for you."

His wheels whirred in retreat; my sandals snapped in pursuit. "I bet you aren't this rude to Doris Sutherland."

He stopped and again spun the chrome and leather chair around. "Mrs. Sutherland—" He broke off, watching me stride up to him.

Usually I don't walk that fast. Without the right sports bra, my bosom bounces too much. When his eyes went to my chest then back to my face, accompanied by a new round of teeth clenching, I knew I was getting close to some nerve or another.

The glitter in his eyes warned me, however, that I might not like the coming explosion.

"All right. You want the truth? Doris Sutherland isn't built like you. Doris Sutherland doesn't throw her sex appeal in a man's face."

"That's not true,"

"What?"

"She throws her sex appeal in one man's face. I've seen her do it."

He stared at me as I were a lunatic. Then to my shock, he laughed. "I think that's more than I need to know."

"Why?" I stopped at the office door, then held it open for him. "Don't you think old people deserve to make love?"

"Maybe. But that's their business, not mine."

I continued to hold the door open. "I'm not throwing my sex appeal at you."

His good humor faded. "Could've fooled me."

"It's a problem I have, all right? It might not be on a par

with yours, but the fact remains that I always get judged because of how I look. Sometimes it's not fair."

He wheeled past me and I followed him in. He didn't want to have this conversation, and I shouldn't want it, either. But ever since Frank's death I hadn't really been myself. I was alone and for all practical purposes, homeless. I had no security, I'd cut out my drinking, and I didn't exercise as much, which might have been why I didn't know what to do with myself anymore. Maybe that's why I was letting myself get so personal with a man I didn't even know.

I watched him pull behind his desk, using it like a barrier between us. I don't know why it bothered me, but it did.

"Would you have dinner with me tonight?" I blurted out.

His hand stilled on the folder he was opening. "Dinner?"

"Yes." I hoped he didn't notice the tremble in my voice. "Even bad-tempered men in wheelchairs have to eat. My treat."

I actually got a little smile out of him. Not much, but it counted for a lot. "You must either be a glutton for punishment or desperate for company."

I smiled back at him. "Is that a yes?"

For a moment he hesitated and I was afraid he'd say no. Then he shrugged. "Sure. Why not?"

It was ridiculous how happy that made me. While he closed up the shop, I knotted my hands together and tried to remind myself how many wrinkles I'd get from smiling this big. It didn't work. He'd accepted my offer even though he didn't want to. Pretty good for a girl who'd never asked a guy out in her life.

He suggested a place on Magazine Street that had an outdoor dining patio. He rolled his chair right up to the table, and it was easy as that. No thresholds to bump over. No narrow doors to negotiate.

In his shop he was top dog, moving easily from office to workshop. Even getting in and out of his car was routine for him. He drove a '65 Mustang—a cliché perhaps. Naturally it was restored to perfection. He had heaved himself in through the driver's door and left his wheelchair in the shop. The car had hand controls, and he kept a folding wheelchair behind his seat.

I didn't offer to help him with it; he didn't ask me to.

But away from his car and shop I could see how much harder it must be for him to manage. There were a lot more limitations and that had to be difficult for a man like him.

The waitress at Café Rani knew him and knew what his favorite dish was.

"You're a man of habit," I said once she left with our orders.

"I like what I like. Most people do," he added.

I could practically hear my mother's voice. *People like to talk about themselves, so ask him something about himself.* I unfolded my napkin and arranged the utensils on the table before me. "So, how did you come to own a specialty car repair service?"

He shrugged. "I always messed around with cars." Then he just stared at me until I started to squirm and had to look away. That's when he said, "Look, Mary Jo. Why don't you just ask me what we both know you want to ask me?"

I took a quick breath and looked back at him. "Okay. Do you have a girlfriend—or a wife? Because I've been cheated on and I don't want to be a part of that for any other women."

He tilted his head and gave me a puzzled half smile. "No. I'm strictly on my own."

The enormity of my relief told me how seriously interested I was in this prickly man. "Good." I smiled at him. "That's good."

A muscle began to tic in his jaw. "Are you for real or are you just being coy?"

"I suppose I'm trying to be both. You know, I don't want you to think I'm a featherhead, but I also don't want you to think I'm easy. And I really am curious about how you came to have your business."

"And how I came to be in this wheelchair?"

His eyes were as dark as midnight and just as hard to read. I was slow to answer. "If you want to tell me."

He snorted. "I raced cars in my twenties—I was in a pretty spectacular wreck. In the space of fifteen seconds I went from race-car driver to pit crew. Later I started my own shop. Okay?"

There was a belligerence in his voice, not the firm, no-nonsense tone he usually used, but something more aggressive, something meant to hide any vulnerability. It made me like him even more. I pressed my lips together and said, "Okay."

The drinks came, followed swiftly by my salad and his dinner, and for the next few minutes we ate. Then someone he knew passed by; he had to introduce me, and after that it was easier for us to speak. I decided to stick to safe topics.

"How long do you think it will take to fix my car?"

"We're stacked up right now. Normally it would only take a few days, maybe a week. But realistically, two weeks."

"If you have so much work, why don't you hire more help?"

"I'm particular."

I bet you are. "So, what do you do besides work on cars?"

"You mean like, for fun?"

"Yes, for fun."

Again he shrugged. "The normal stuff. I read. I work out."

"I work out, too."

"No kidding," he muttered.

I smiled at him. "Is that a compliment?"

"It's an observation. Women who look like you don't get that way by accident." My smile faded as he went on. "Look, I don't know what you want from me, but I can tell you, you're wasting your time. I won't be your charity case."

"That's not what I want—"

"Then what? Fuck the crippled dude, isn't that what's going on here?"

Shocked by the sudden turn of the conversation, I sucked in a harsh breath. "No!"

"Yes." He smiled but it was cold and emphasized the sharp

angles of his face. "I've met women like you before, Mary Jo. They're the same kind who try to convert their gay friends. I mean, damn, if they can get a rise out of a gay guy, or get the crip's dick to work right, then hey, they have to be one hell of a woman." He leaned back in his wheelchair. "So why don't we just settle the debate right now and get it out of the way. You're one hell of a woman. There's not a man alive, including me, who won't agree to that. The thing is, I'm not interested in starting anything with you." He paused, breathing heavily. "So let's just have dessert and talk about cars or workout routines or whatever else you want. Okay?"

No. Not okay, I wanted to shout. Beneath the table I was strangling my napkin, anything to stop me from crying.

But maybe he was right. Frank's last act on this earth had been a horrible blow to my ego. Was that what I was looking for, the ultimate proof of my worth as a woman?

On the other hand, I'd never been a prick tease. And besides, if I needed proof of my attractiveness, I had Jeff Cole.

I forced myself to breathe, to relax my shoulders and sit up straight. Then slowly and carefully I folded my napkin and laid it beside my plate. But twenty years of classes in deportment still could not disguise the trembling emotion in my voice.

"You could not be more wrong about me. I am well aware of the fact that men find me attractive. I don't need you—" I pointed at him— "to prove it. Furthermore, the fact that I work hard to maintain my figure is no reason for you to insult me."

The young couple at the next table glanced over at us, but I was too angry to care. I leaned forward and jutted out my chin. "You have had a chip on your shoulder from the minute I walked into your office. All I have been is nice to you. But you..." My throat got tight, and suddenly the threat of tears was real. I lurched to my feet. "Goodbye."

By now all the people at the tables nearest us were watching. *Head up, shoulders back, and for heaven's sake don't trip,*

Mama's voice warned. But this was far worse than a march across some stage as second runner-up.

I managed to make it to the checkout station where I fumbled in my purse for two twenty-dollar bills.

"Is everything all right?" the alarmed hostess asked.

"The meal was fine. Unfortunately the company—"

"Was rude," came Steve's voice from behind me. "I'll get the bill."

"I said I'd treat." I kept my eyes on the hostess. "Give the rest to the waitress." Then I headed for the street.

I do not like making a spectacle of myself, but there was no avoiding the curious eyes of the courtyard audience. It didn't help that Steve followed just a few feet behind me.

Once I reached the street I debated which way to go. His car was to the right, so I headed left. I didn't have to go very far before I realized he wasn't following me anymore.

That fast all the starch in my backbone dissolved. What was wrong with me? I was behaving like an emotional fifteen-year-old chasing a guy who'd made it very clear that he wasn't interested, then pitching a hissy fit when I finally got the message. He didn't like me. He really did not like me, was not attracted to me, and probably thought I was a self-centered ditz.

The sign ahead of me said Seventh Street. Only three blocks to Fourth. Who needed Steve Vidrine anyway? But two blocks later, when his car nosed out at the corner of Washington Avenue, then waited as I approached, and my stupid heart did a stupid lurch in my chest, I knew I was fooling myself.

He'd come looking for me.

"Come on, get in," he said, leaning over to open the passenger door. "The least I can do is take you home."

"Yes," I said, not putting up even a semblance of protest. "The very least."

I gave him Bitsey's address, but other than that we didn't speak until he pulled in front of the place. His dark eyes flicked over the beautiful grounds and elegantly drooping oaks that framed the gracious old home. Dusk made it even more beautiful than usual.

"I should have figured," he said.

"This isn't mine. I'm only a guest."

"It doesn't matter." When he turned to face me his face was expressionless. "I'll let you know when your car is ready."

He waited for me to get out, the very picture of patient disinterest. He'd driven me home because it was the right thing to do, but he was making it clear ours was to be strictly a business relationship.

God, how my hand itched to slap that disinterest off his face. I'd never slapped a man in my life, and I wondered what he'd do. Then I wondered what he'd do if I leaned over and kissed him.

"Sorry I can't walk you to the door," he said.

"You could roll me. I could sit on your lap and we could bump over the brick sidewalk together."

He didn't want to laugh but he was too surprised not to. "You don't give up, do you?"

I laughed, too. "I don't know. I never had to work this hard for a guy before." Then wanting to end the evening on a good note, I climbed out of the Mustang. "Thanks for the ride."

Now as I sat with my two best friends in Bitsey's girlish bedroom, I felt guilty for not telling them the whole truth about Steve.

"You know what?" Cat said. "I think the three of us ought to plan a day together. I mean, we drove all this way, we each found our old boyfriends, and it turns out that none of us is really that interested. Well, Bitsey is, but she can't act on it yet. Anyway, there's no reason to ruin the rest of our trip. I say tomorrow we get dressed, take the streetcar to the quarter and spend the day playing tourist. We'll shop and eat and finish up with a show at one of the clubs."

"Sounds good to me, " I said.

"Should I include Margaret? Meg?" Bitsey asked.

"She won't want to hang out with us," Cat said. "Where is she anyway?"

"Out. With God knows who—Brandon, no last name."

"I wish I was twenty-three again," Cat said. "I'd do a much better job of it this time."

"Until your hormones kicked in," Bitsey said. "That's where we all screw up." She heaved a huge sigh. "I hope Meg is careful and that she doesn't get into the same sort of mess again."

"Yeah," Cat said. "It's hard not to keep picking the same kind of guy. It took me years to see that my second ex was a clone of my first ex. You know, Bits, it seems like Eddie is this really intense guy—even when he was young. In that regard, is he really so different from Jack?"

"Like Jack?" She looked at Cat as if she was nuts. "No, they're nothing alike. Matt's nothing like Bill, is he? And Jeff's nothing like Frank, is he?" she said turning to me.

"Actually, he is," I said. "But Steve's not."

That got both their attention. "Steve?" Bitsey asked. "Steve is now on a par with Jeff?"

Cat hooted with laughter. "I knew it. I knew you had the hots for the mechanic. Come on, M.J. No more secrets. What's going on with you and your grease monkey?"

I crossed my legs beneath me and stared at my knotted hands. "Steve can't walk." I looked up at them.

"What do you mean, he can't walk?" Cat said. "He can't walk?"

"He used to race cars but he was in a bad accident."

"Oh, my God," Bitsey said. "Is he in a wheelchair?"

I nodded.

"Geez," Cat said. "Is it just his legs?"

"Yes. He's got great upper body strength. You should see his arms. He can work on cars, and he's built a really good business. He can even stand up, if he has something to hold on to."

They were both silent. Then Cat said, "What about…you know, his third leg. Does it work?"

"I don't know," I answered. "Yet."

"Yet?" Bitsey echoed me.

"Let me get this straight," Cat said. "You've got Jeff Cole hot to trot, but you'd rather hang out with a guy who doesn't like you and who might not be able to do it?"

When I gave one slow nod, she started to laugh. "Oh, my God." She looked at Bitsey, then laughed again. "She must be falling in love. There's no other explanation."

Bitsey

I called Jack first thing in the morning. I'd only spoken to him once since we left. The other two times he hadn't been home and I'd left brief messages. He'd called Daddy's house once and spoken to Miss Ulna. She'd told me he was at work, and I suppose I could have called him there. But I knew he was responsible at work. It was his free time that had me worried. That's why I decided to call him at eight-thirty in the morning—six-thirty Pacific time. If he wasn't at home in our bed, then I had my answer.

I had pretty much convinced myself that Jack wouldn't be there. Maybe it was wishful thinking on my part. If he was behaving badly, then I had my green light with Eddie. Anyway, when I heard his voice, thick and sleepy, I froze.

"Hello?" He cleared his throat. "Hello?"

Suddenly panicked, I slammed the receiver down. Then unwilling to acknowledge such inexplicable behavior, I popped an old Jane Fonda exercise tape into the VCR and fast-forwarded past the stretching and went straight for the lunging and jumping.

Jack was home and that was good. So why was I behaving like an idiot?

I had to pause the tape almost right away. I'd been so antsy this morning I wasn't fully dressed, meaning no bra. I might not be built like M.J., but my bosom needed a bra for anything more vigorous than taking a shower.

M.J. came in as I was changing. "Wow. Exercising already. I'm impressed."

"What else is there to do? The reunion is next Saturday. It's now or never."

"Have you weighed yourself lately?" She stretched as she spoke, warming up to join me.

"I've lost twenty-one pounds total."

"Oh, honey, you are doing so well. Jack's not going to recognize you."

"In more ways than one," I muttered under my breath. I punched the VCR button and when Jane and her skinny friends started up again, M.J. scowled. "This has got to be fifteen years old. The fitness industry has advanced so much since this came out."

"If it worked for Jane, it'll work for me."

For several minutes we exercised in silence. Then M.J. said, "Are you going back to Jack?"

I wiped the sweat from my brow. "I don't want to talk about Jack."

"Or Eddie?"

"Or Eddie."

"Okay."

I'm not usually so testy. But I'd never been in a situation like this before.

We finished the forty-five minutes of exercise and went to our respective showers. I shared a bathroom with Meg, and I peeked in on her. She was sprawled in the four-poster bed, her blue-black hair a dark gash against the almond-colored sheets. She was my darling baby, my pretty valley girl. I hated that she had to struggle so hard to find her way. I'd had it so much easier. College, marriage, then three children. It was what was expected of me, and what I had expected of myself.

Then again, had any of those expectations guaranteed my happiness?

Obviously not.

I stared at Meg, at the scarlet streak over her brow and her pretty face that no longer showed any trace of abuse. Maybe if she struggled now she would be spared having to struggle when she was my age.

But as I closed the door I knew better. Cat had struggled as a youngster. She'd struggled through two marriages, and she was struggling still.

If only we could do our lives differently, do it all over without the mistakes.

I took off my sweaty clothes and stared at my rosy flesh. If I were Meg's age again I would…I don't know…take singing lessons. Get an old beach-cruiser bicycle and ride it everywhere. I would get an apartment in the French Quarter and live the life of a bohemian artiste.

But I was an almost fifty mother of three with a marriage collapsing under its own weight. Or maybe under my excess weight. So I showered and dried my hair and got ready for the day M.J., Cat and I had planned.

We took the streetcar downtown and started with a breakfast of grits and grillades at The Coffee Pot. From there we made a quick stop in St. Louis Cathedral to light candles for our dead relatives, then strolled around Jackson Square trying to avoid the tarot card readers, before heading for the French Market to shop.

The three of us were having a great time until I stepped out of a shop and twisted my ankle. I grabbed the door frame and let out a muffled curse. Most unladylike.

"Are you okay?" Cat asked.

"I don't know. God, I'm so clumsy. This is just what I don't need."

"Wait, Bitsey," M.J. said. "Cat, take her purse. Come on, honey. Lean on me."

With their help I managed to hobble to Café du Monde, but a bag of ice and twenty minutes later it was obvious I couldn't continue on with them.

"Listen, y'all. Just get me a cab and I'll go home. You two can go on without me."

"No. We can't let you go home alone like this," M.J. said.

"Yes, you can. I'm a grown-up, not a five-year-old. Besides, Miss Ulna will take care of me. There's nothing she likes better than hovering over people and ordering them around."

"Yeah. I can believe that," Cat said, and in a few minutes I was on my way.

There was no one outside at the house. The cabdriver didn't offer to help me to the porch. He couldn't even bother to get out of the cab. So I didn't bother myself with a tip. I hobbled up the brick walk, cursing him under my breath and let myself in. Then feeling sorry for myself, I plopped down on a rosewood bench beneath the curve in the stairs.

The house was quiet. Where was everyone? From somewhere I heard the faint sounds of melodrama. Miss Ulna might be a no-nonsense kind of woman, but she and Veronica sure loved their soap operas.

I decided not to disturb her, but when I eyed the stairs I knew that wasn't an option. So I decided to visit with Daddy instead. His door was closed. Could he be napping this early in the day? Just in case, instead of knocking, I eased the door open and peered inside.

It would have been better if I'd stayed with M.J. and Cat, even if I'd had to hobble after them, weeping in pain. Because what I saw in my father's bedroom was more painful than anything physical ever could be. Painful enough that I wanted to put out my eyes.

Just as I thought, he was in bed. But he wasn't napping. Instead he was straddling a woman—Mrs. Doris Sutherland, to be exact. He was grunting, she was making shrill little noises, and I nearly passed out. They must have had their hearing aids turned off, because I fell back against the door frame with a loud thud, and they never even looked up.

"Oh, God! Oh, God!" I'd hit my crazy bone, my arm went numb with pain, I could hardly stand up—and my seventy-seven-year-old father was fucking Doris Sutherland!

"Ulna!" I screamed, limping down the hall and into the kitchen. "Ulna!"

"What did you expect?" she said, once she had me settled into a rocking chair in the back sitting room. "You should be glad he's still healthy enough to do it."

Veronica giggled then looked guilty when I glared at her.

"That's not the issue."

"Then what is the issue?" Ulna demanded to know. She stood over me with her hands on her hips and that exasperated-with-this-child look on her face. "Your daddy has got the right to find him any little bit of happiness he can in the time he's got left. Miss Doris makes him happy, and that's good enough for me. It's long past time for you to grow up, Bitsey girl. I don't know why Mr. Jack isn't here with you, but that's not your daddy's fault, and it's not Miss Doris's fault, either."

I should have known better than to be critical of my father to Miss Ulna. She'd been running our household since I was twelve years old, and her dedication to him had only increased after my mother died. It didn't hurt, either, that he paid her a very generous salary.

But I'd been too shocked to think straight. Now, under her warning gaze I sucked in a breath and tried to calm down. "Does the rest of the family know about this?"

"You mean Mr. Chuck and Miss Virginia? They know your daddy keeps company with Miss Doris. Anything else, I can't say. But I expect they know better than to walk in on them without knocking first."

We didn't talk about it any further. She propped my foot up on a stool, and iced my ankle. I watched twenty-five minutes of *Days of Our Lives*. Marlena was still struggling with John, and Sammie was still up to her nasty tricks. But all I saw were the sexual maneuverings.

The soaps, *Friends*, *Will and Grace*, MTV. Sex was everywhere, and not just on television. It was alive and well in the downstairs bedroom of my father's house—and probably in my children's dorm rooms and apartments. Everywhere except in my bedroom.

I suppose my thinking was skewed, but when the telephone rang and it was Eddie calling for me, I was ready to say yes to anything.

"I have to drive down to the Rigolets to get a client's signature on an affidavit, " he said. "There's a great restaurant on Chef Pass. We could have an early dinner there on the way back. What do you say?"

He promised I wouldn't have to walk much, and twenty minutes later I was on my way. I decided I liked his car. It was small and we sat only inches apart. He put on a Cajun music CD. "The lead singer is one of my clients. He has a brain tumor, thanks to the chemical plant in his backyard."

"How sad. I didn't know that was the sort of case the ACLU takes."

"I wasn't always an ACLU attorney. Prior to that I specialized in consumer cases and environmental cases. Especially smaller scale class action suits."

He frowned as he concentrated on the road. "Do you realize how pervasive the problem of industrial and product pollution is to the health of innocent people? There's a reason fertility rates are down and premature births are up in this country. There's a reason deformed frogs are showing up in every state of the union. There's a reason mad cow disease and Legionnaires' disease and AIDS and SARS and so many other exotic illnesses are reaching epidemic proportions." His hands tightened on the wheel. "Every day we eat, breathe and soak in chemicals we were never supposed to get near. We're poisoning ourselves. Or more accurately, the corporations are poisoning us. And what do our so-called leaders do?" he asked, barely pausing for a breath. "Most of them are like our former governor. They do their damnedest to silence the people trying to do something about it. They close down law clinics that represent the most vulnerable citizens. God forbid the petrochemical gods be pestered by a bunch of idealistic law students who haven't yet been corrupted by money."

He veered left and flew past a car, then cut back into the right lane and exited the I-10 so fast I braced my hand on the dash. At once he slowed down. "Sorry. I get a little carried away."

I smiled, mostly in relief. "Just a little," I agreed. "But you always were pretty intense."

He grinned. "Yeah. And you were all about having a good time. Parties. Dances. Football games."

"You make it sound like I didn't have a brain in my head."

"That's not what I meant. I think maybe you lightened me up some. Made me relax." He slanted a look at me. "You made me see what else I could be—if I worked at it."

If he was trying to make me feel valuable, an important part of his life, he was succeeding very well. But I fought back the seductive urge to bask in his reflected light. "If we were so perfect for one another we would have stayed together. As I recall, once I went off to LSU, it didn't take two weeks for you to find a new girlfriend."

Again he grinned. "Ouch. What can I say? You were eighty miles away and I was twenty and horny. Besides, you were giving off 'let's get married' vibes, and I wasn't ready to settle down."

"The problem was, you had testosterone poisoning."

"What's a guy to do? Women don't want wimps." He slanted another look at me. "At least I hope they don't."

My heart was beating way too fast. "No." I swallowed and stared straight ahead at the hot shimmering blacktop of Chef Mentaur Highway. "We definitely don't want wimps."

We'd gone from urban center to shabby suburbs to rural swamp Louisiana without me really noticing. Now he turned into a shell driveway and came to a hard stop. "This is it. I'll only be a few minutes."

I watched him cross the neglected yard. He ignored the scruffy dog that barked at him, and when the door to the weather-beaten place opened, he and the dog both went in.

I hadn't really paid attention to the scenery, but now I looked around. This was the far reaches of New Orleans, a camp settlement outside the hurricane protection levees. All sorts of houses clustered on either side of the highway. Neat homes, ramshackle camps that hadn't seen paint in decades and abandoned shanties that listed like drunks before the wind. Beyond the houses lay water, Lake Pontchartrain to the north and Lake Catherine to the south. It was just the merest ribbon of land, connecting Louisiana to Mississippi, but for those who loved to fish, crab and otherwise live off the water, it was heaven.

It started to get hot in the car, so I got out. From the south a snapping breeze raced across the water and blew up a world of childhood memories. One of my uncles had kept a fishing camp like this, and as a child I'd loved the wild freedom of the place. But Mother had hated it. It was one thing for her son to fish and hunt. Those were manly arts, practiced by a long line of La Farge men. But she was not raising her daughter to behave like a hooligan. So each summer I was sent to a girls' camp in North Carolina. Later Chuck went to one in New York, and at some point my uncle died and the camp disappeared from the family.

But I remembered it now.

On impulse I tested my ankle and decided it was strong enough. I limped around the house and out onto the wood run that stretched out into the water. The surface of the lake reminded me of the ruffles on an old-fashioned pair of little girl's underpants, just touched with the slightest bit of white lacy foam. In rhythmic waves it nudged the cockeyed pilings that supported the run. At the far end an open flatboat with an oversize outboard motor tugged at its moorings.

I could have been seven again. I wanted to strip down to my swimsuit and leap into the water. Except that I was forty-eight and instead of a swimsuit I was wearing a seventy-five-dollar uplift bra and a twenty-dollar pair of control-top briefs.

I felt the vibration of footsteps coming down the run behind me.

"Nice, huh?"

Eddie. I smiled to myself, then said, "Water is always so calming."

He stopped beside me. "Is that why you came back to New Orleans? Is life so hectic in California that you need to calm down?"

I laughed at the irony. "Actually, it's the opposite. Life in California is...it's dull. And slow." A lump rose in my throat—all my tangled emotions. But I forced myself to go on as if my life wasn't collapsing around me. "There hasn't been a dull moment since I left, though. My friends. My daughter. Now my dad." I turned to him, forcing a smile. "My life is a mess, Eddie, and you're not making it any easier."

There. I'd said it.

He studied me with an unnerving intensity. "I'm not the reason you're unhappy, Bitsey."

"I know."

We stared at each other. He'd worn a pair of khaki pants and a black Polo shirt. Lawyer casual. But there was no disguising the crusading rebel in him, the rule-breaking pursuer of justice, the champion of the underdog. It showed in his ascetic's silhouette, lean with no sign of excess. It burned in his dark probing gaze. I, on the other hand, was the very picture of excess: too much money, too much food, too much time on my hands.

I couldn't help blurting out, "What do you want from me?"

A crease formed above his brows. "I 'm not sure. What do you want from me?"

"I don't know."

But I did know. Passion. Not just physical passion, though I was already feeling that in spades. My life with Jack was boring, routine. Lonely. As unsettling as the past two weeks had been, they sure hadn't been boring. Stripping M.J.'s house so Frank's brats couldn't claim her belongings, taking her car cross-country and kidnapping Margaret—that wasn't how suburban housewife Bitsey behaved.

"I think for me, you've always symbolized this ideal," he said. "The ideal woman."

I shook my head in amazement. "Are you blind?"

His eyes held with mine. "No."

I believed him. Despite my flabby, excessive weight and flabby, excessive existence, he saw a different me. The young, idealistic me. But maybe I could be that girl again. God, I certainly wanted to try.

Without stopping to think, I walked into his arms. Actually, I limped. He wanted to kiss me, but I started to cry. So we stood there. Beneath seagulls circling and crying raucously down at us, I buried my face against his shoulder and I wept like a child.

Afterward I was mortified, but I felt cleansed—and exhausted. In the car he said, "Be my date for the reunion?"

"Okay."

We drove another mile before he said, "Move back to New Orleans."

I took a deep breath before I said, "Okay."

Everything seemed inevitable after that. We didn't stop at the restaurant to eat but drove straight to his apartment. I'd thought he'd driven like a wild man before, but this trip took half the time. All I could do was close my eyes and hold on.

He pulled into a skinny driveway beside a two-story house on Bell Street, then led me up a narrow back stair to an apartment that was more office than home. Everything was books and files, shelves and boxes of them. Even the couch was piled with them. Through a messy kitchen and into the bedroom he led me, then closed the door.

The bedroom was small and, compared to the rest of the house, austere. An iron bed, a modern dresser, a television set with two red candles sitting on it. Venetian blinds covered the windows. There was no art on the walls or any attempts at decor. At least there were no files. The bed, though rumpled, had gray satin sheets and at the foot, a darker gray silk comforter with scattered oriental symbols printed in black.

It was a utilitarian place for Eddie. He slept and worked here, and occasionally had women over for sex.

I started to have second thoughts. "I've…I've never done this before," I managed to say past the dry terror in my throat.

His arms came around me from behind. "As I recall, we did it all the time. As often as we could, and not always on a bed." He kissed the top of my head, and I started to melt.

But there was still some part of me not blinded by lust. "That's different. I wasn't married then."

"No. You weren't." He kissed the side of my neck and began to unbutton my blouse. "But the fact is, you've given your marriage more than a fair shot, Bitsey. Husband, kids. The whole nine yards. Isn't it time you did something just for yourself?"

Yes. I wanted to shout the word. Yes! Something for myself. Something I should never have given up. Eddie. Me and Eddie.

We didn't even get all our clothes off. Like the teenagers we'd once been, we shrugged off just enough clothes for access. My industrial-strength panties, his Dockers and tightie whites. I sprawled backward across the foot of his bed with my skirt around my waist. He lay on top of me, kissing me, parting my legs with his knee.

Then I felt the illicit heat of him as his arousal nudged against me. I was so hot for him, sopping wet and starved for the feel of a man equally hot for me, that I feared I might suck it into me like a Eureka vacuum cleaner—suck it in and never let it go.

But one stray bit of sanity made me break our kiss. "What about protection?" I murmured as the head of his penis prodded for entrance.

"Don't worry, baby. I'm clean."

"Clean?"

He went still. "Yeah. Aren't you?"

"Of course, but…"

"Oh, you mean birth control? But aren't you too old? After all, we're forty-eight. Who gets pregnant at forty-eight?"

"Probably no one," I murmured as my Eureka fears began to wither. "But it would be just my luck."

What I didn't say was that the thought of him being "clean" meant he must have been tested, which brought up the unpleasant reality of all his previous lovers, which made me want to get the hell out of his bed, out of his bedroom, out of his house.

"I can't do this."

I shoved at his chest but he did not move. "Bitsey, listen."

He stared down at me. "You've just got cold feet. You'll be fine."

"No."

"Okay, okay. If it makes you feel better I'll get a condom."

I let him misconstrue my words, and once he was off me, I sat up. For some reason I chose that moment to remember a line of my mother's sarcastic advice: The only birth control pill you need is an aspirin clamped tight between your knees.

I squeezed my knees together and glanced wildly about for my panties. When I didn't find them right away, I abandoned the search and stood. "I want to go home."

He paused and looked up from his search of the bedside table's drawer. He was naked from the hips down. His legs were skinnier than I remembered, and hairier. The exact opposite of Jack, my guilty mind pointed out. He was still attractive, though, still sexy. Certainly more so than I was. But Jack stood in the way. I was married and no matter what Jack might have done—even betraying our vows—I couldn't do it.

"I'm sorry," I mumbled, unable to face Eddie's incredulous expression. "I'll wait in the kitchen."

"Bitsey—"

"No. I can't, Eddie. I was wrong to come here with you, so please don't try to change my mind."

I waited in the kitchen, so nervous that I almost washed the sink of dirty dishes just to occupy myself. When he came out of the bedroom he looked composed and unaffected by our botched interlude. I, meanwhile, was standing in his kitchen with no underwear on.

"Okay. Let's go." He held the door open for me.

"Eddie. I'm sorry."

He shook his head. "Don't be. I shouldn't have brought you here if you weren't ready. The thing is, Bitsey, you can't lead a guy on like that."

"I'm sorry."

I felt horrible, and the silent ride to my father's house

seemed to take forever. Between my aborted affair and Daddy's very real one, I felt like throwing up. Notwithstanding my swollen ankle, I leaped out of the car before Eddie did, so he wouldn't feel obligated to come around the car for me. I leaned down and looked at him through the open passenger door. "I won't hold you to your offer to take me to the reunion."

"No. I'll take you. This isn't high school, Bitsey. I can deal with rejection a little better now."

The first thing I did when I reached the house was hop on one foot up the stairs to my bedroom and put on some underpants. The rest of the afternoon I worried about what he meant by "dealing with it a little better now." He couldn't mean that this wasn't the first time I'd rejected him. He'd been the one to dump me.

Veronica had fixed another ice pack for my ankle, and I sat in front of the five-thirty news and then the six o'clock news, watching the television but thinking about Eddie—and Jack. Cat and M.J. arrived home just as the Super Doppler honed in on a wave of thunderstorms approaching the city.

"We brought you something," M.J. said. "Poor thing. Does your ankle still hurt?"

"It sure ought to," Miss Ulna said, bringing a tray of iced tea to us. "She wasn't back here an hour before she was up and gone again."

Cat pushed her sunglasses up into her hair. "Gone where?" Then before I could answer, she said, "Eddie."

"He took me for a ride out to Lake Catherine. He had to deliver something to a client and he wanted company for the ride. I spent the entire time sitting in the car." *Liar.*

"Hunh." Ulna grunted as if she knew the truth. But she didn't say anything else.

"Thanks for the tea," M.J. said as the woman left. She waited until Ulna was out of earshot, then she turned expectantly to me. "All right, Bitsey. Exactly what is going on?"

"We took a drive. That's all."

Cat plucked the mint leaves from her tea glass. "Did he kiss you?"

I heaved a great, put-upon sigh. "Yes. But that's all." Lying was getting to be so easy for me.

Cat and M.J. exchanged a look. Then M.J. kicked off her shoes and sat down. "Have you noticed that this trip, which was supposed to be so much fun—a Grits Girls bonding experience—has turned each of us secretive? We came to meet up with our first true loves, and in the process we've turned into sneaky high school girls."

Cat snorted. "Speak for yourself. I can't tell you anything juicy if nothing juicy is happening."

"It's not just Matt," M.J. said. "You have family here and I know you've gone to them, but you haven't shared a word of it with us."

"Fine." Cat folded her arms across her chest. "You first."

"All right." M.J. took a deep breath as if bracing herself. I couldn't imagine what she could be hiding from us—unless she had slept with Jeff the night of their date. But there was no reason for her to have denied the truth. After all, she was single and available. Unlike me.

"All right," she said again. "Steve can't walk—I told you that. I don't know if he can have sex or not. But... But I don't care if he can or not. The thing is, I'm not all that crazy about sex."

This time it was Cat and I who shared a look. 'What do you mean, you're not crazy about sex?"

"I'm just not. I never have been."

"Well, no wonder," Cat said. "Look who you were married to."

M.J. stared down at her lap. "Even before Frank."

"Even in high school, with Jeff?" I asked.

She sighed and looked up at us. "I've never had an orgasm, okay? Now do you believe me? You know, Cat, I never could understand why you kept on sleeping with Bill. To me it seemed like the main benefit of divorce was that you didn't have to sleep with the guy anymore. But that was the one connection you and Bill kept. I still don't get it."

"It was the only thing he was any good at," Cat said.

"You've really never had an orgasm?" I couldn't get over that fact.

M.J. shook her head. "So you see, that's why the sex doesn't matter with Steve."

"It might matter to him," Cat said.

"Well, that's one of the things I'll have to find out, won't I?"

We sat there a long minute, digesting M.J.'s unexpected revelation. Even though Jack and I hardly ever made love anymore, when we did it was always satisfying. Despite my insecurities about my appearance and my worry about his love for me, I always managed to lose myself in the moment. My sex life might be infrequent, but what there was of it was good.

"So," M.J. said. "What's really going on with you two?"

I took a deep breath. "I walked in on my father and Doris."

Cat's brows raised. "You mean while they were doing it?"

I closed my eyes and shuddered. "It was horrible."

Cat started laughing.

"I think it's sweet," M.J. said, but even she giggled.

I scowled at them both. "Believe me, it was not a sweet sight. That's why I left with Eddie."

After a brief silence Cat said, "And?"

I shifted the ice pack on my leg. "And, after we left Lake Catherine, we went back to his apartment."

"And?"

"And… We almost did it—till I chickened out."

"I thought so," Cat crowed. "You little liar. I knew he'd done more than kiss you."

I nodded silently. A bad wife *and* a bad liar.

"Whew," Cat said. "One of you wants sex, the other one doesn't. I wish I even had a choice."

"Come on, Cat," I said. "It's obvious something's bothering you. And it's not just Matt blowing hot and cold."

Biting the side of her lip, she nodded. "Okay. I guess it is my turn. I told you I was raised trailer trash. Well, I went to see my mom—nothing much has changed there except that she's too old to drink and she quit smoking. Doctor's orders."

"That's good," M.J. said. "The lungs can recover quite a bit, even after years of smoking."

"Yeah. Then I met up with my sister. She's sober, living in a halfway house. She actually looks like she might succeed this time. One of my brothers is in jail. The other one is a bum who should be there, too." She got up and paced to the window. "Actually, I ought to be happy. At least half my family has improved. But, I don't know. Coming home always gets me depressed. And this time, staying in a place like this." She gestured at the room. "You grew up in such a classy place, Bits. In such a classy family."

"Oh, it was classy, all right," I said. "So classy that my mother committed suicide."

I hadn't meant to say that. Not that they wouldn't sympathize. But my mother's betrayal was my own private hurt. We didn't talk about it in the family; we certainly didn't talk about it to outsiders.

But it was out now, and judging from their stunned faces, it was an even more shocking revelation than M.J.'s.

"Oh, Bitsey—"

"No." I held up a hand to forestall any words of sympathy. "Don't say anything. It was a long time ago. But since we're being brutally honest, I suppose I ought to also tell you that I take Xanax for my nerves, and Wellbutrin for depression."

"Better living through science," Cat said. "There's nothing wrong with that."

"Yes, but I hope you're careful," M.J. said, looking worried. "Xanax can be very addictive."

Somewhere in the house a telephone rang, but in my bedroom we were a silent group. "So," Cat finally said. "Are we having fun yet?"

"I am," M.J. said. "I mean, we're being honest with each other. Totally honest. And I don't know about y'all, but

I'm beginning to be hopeful about my future. That's good, isn't it?"

"Yeah," Cat said. "It is good, hon." Then she looked at me. "Now that we've been honest, what's the plan? Just don't tell me you want to meet my family."

Once more I shifted the ice pack. "Why not? You've met mine. The only difference I can see is that mine is dysfunctional rich, while yours is just dysfunctional."

Cat grinned. "That sounds like one of my lines. You're gettin' sassy, girl. It must be the haircut."

"Or the water," M.J. said. "I can't believe your father doesn't use bottled water. Doesn't he know how much gunk is dumped into the Mississippi River?"

I started laughing. I couldn't help it. Trust M.J. to turn a deep moment into a health food issue.

Just then Meg burst into the room. "Hey, y'all." She thrust the telephone at me. "It's for you, Mom. Dad."

For one agonizing moment I froze. I did not want to take that phone from her. Not now, after what had happened earlier with Eddie. What had *almost* happened, I told myself. Almost. Though I could feel Cat and M.J.'s eyes on me, at least I was assured of their concern and support. They would love me no matter what happened between me and Eddie—and Jack.

But Meg expected me to be thrilled about her father's call.

So I forced my frozen face to smile, then took the telephone and injected as much enthusiasm into my voice as I could.

"Jack. How are you doing, sweetheart? Miss me?"

His familiar voice reached through the line to stab me with guilt. "I feel like I'm living in a damn morgue around here. How's your dad?"

"Just fine. Full of beans." And how.

"And Miss Ulna and Victoria?"

"Good. Same as ever." One thing about Jack, he'd always been good to Ulna and Victoria. And to our girls. And to his secretary. I realized that it was only me he ignored. "Is everything going all right there? Do you have enough food in the house?"

"Yeah. I'm fine."

There was an awkward pause. Maybe it was the guilt, but I had the sinking feeling he was about to say something momentous, something that would change the direction of our lives forever. A part of me wanted him to do just that—a small part. The rest of me was terrified of that sort of change.

Beyond me Meg chatted with M.J. and Cat, though I suspected my friends were listening as much to me as they were to her. Then Jack cleared his throat. I stared at my lap and braced myself.

"I have to take a trip—business—up to Calgary."

I wanted to ask, what kind of business? With who? But I swallowed my panic and like the good wife I'd always been I said, "When are you leaving?"

"The day after tomorrow. I should only be gone three days. You can reach me on my cell phone if you need me."

"Okay."

"Have fun at your reunion."

"I will." After a pause I added, "Do you want to talk to Meg again?"

"No. That's okay. Bitsey?"

"Yes?" My heart began to pound and I pressed the phone closer to my ear.

"Do you think Margaret's going back to school?"

Margaret. I sighed. It was easier to talk to him about our daughter, but it also depressed me more. "I don't know if she'll ever go back to college. But if she does, I think she should have to pay for it—at least for the first semester. She's wasted enough of our money." From across the room Meg grinned and stuck her tongue out at me.

"Yeah. That's probably a good idea." After a few seconds he added. "Okay. Well. I'll call you when I get home."

Yeah. You do that, I thought after I hung up. Call me when you get home, when you've had your fun and you start feeling guilty.

"Hey, Mom," Meg said, still grinning. "Don't you think it's a little late for such a big change?"

Panic spurted through me and I jerked my gaze up to hers. She couldn't know what was going on between her father and me—or Eddie and me! Could she? "What do you mean, big change?"

"Tough love. Isn't that what you're doing with the 'we've wasted enough money on her' routine?"

It was a good thing I was sitting down, because relief made me weak. I gave her a halfhearted grin, but it was Cat who gave her a more honest answer. "The way I see it, it's never too late to change."

CHAPTER 6
The Heat Is On

Cat

I was severely depressed, and the fact that there was no real reason for it only made it worse. A character defect I couldn't shake. Then again, why should I be any different from the rest of my family? But knowledge of my defective character did nothing to lessen the depths of my gloom. Nor did logic help.

So what if M.J. had never had an orgasm? I certainly couldn't help her with that.

So what if Bitsey's marriage was going to crash and burn and her daughters were going to blame it all on her? Mothers and daughters never got along. For that matter, neither did husbands and wives.

So what if a rich, loudmouthed geezer twice my age had a better sex life than I did? Maybe things would pick up for me in thirty or forty years.

It took Miss Ulna's return to shake me out of my blue funk. "Will y'all be joining Mr. Charles and Miss Doris for supper?"

"No."

Bitsey and M.J. both looked at me.

"We're going out," I went on, every word an unsupported impulse. I looked at Bitsey. "You can hobble out to the car, can't you?"

"Sure."

"Can you drive?" I asked her after Meg and Miss Ulna left us.

"Probably. My right ankle is okay. But why?"

"Because I plan to get drunk. And you're avoiding empty calories, right?"

"And because if you drink I'll drink, too?" M.J. threw in. She wasn't smiling.

"I didn't say that."

"I said I'd drive," Bitsey repeated. "You can both get as drunk as skunks for all I care. But I won't be able to carry either of you to the car."

M.J. planted her fists on her hips. "I'm not getting drunk!"

"I never said you were," I told her.

She glared at me. "Why are you in such a bitchy mood?"

"Bitchy? Moi?" I affected a laugh. "It must be the water."

M.J. shook her head. "Joke all you want, Cat. The fact is, you hate talking about feelings. You're great with advice, especially flip advice. But talking like we've been talking today, about your childhood and all…" She shrugged and trailed off. "So where do you want to go tonight?"

Home, I wanted to shout. Except home to Bakersfield held no appeal, and home to my mother was worse.

I *was* a bitch, and I hated talking about my feelings, and it made me furious that M.J. was right about me. I slumped down in my chair. "You want the truth? I want to go back in time. I want to be born into a different family. And this time I want to marry different men."

"Men?" Bitsey asked. "Plural?"

"Man," I clarified. "I want to have married one man—the right man—and have two-point-four kids and one-point-seven pets, and live in a three-thousand-square-foot pseudo-mansion in some pristine gated community." My heart was pounding and I felt like a weepy idiot, but I went on. "I want to be Jim Carrey—the female version—in *The Truman Show*, only I don't want to ever discover the truth."

"You want to live the fantasy?" Bitsey asked.

"Damned right. What's so wrong with that?"

"But the fantasy doesn't exist," M.J. said, an earnest look

on her face. "I mean, look at me. Look at Bitsey. We lived the fantasy."

"No. You didn't have two-point-four kids," I pointed out. "And neither of you married the right man."

Bitsey let out a rude noise, kicked the ice pack off her ankle, and struggled to her feet. "That's great, Cat. Depress us even further than we already are. Not only is my marriage in the toilet bowl, but now that I've started to finally lose weight, I'm too hurt to keep on exercising."

"Oh, no you're not," M.J. said. "You might not be able to jog for a week or two, but you can lift weights and work your upper body. And you can swim laps for the aerobic benefits."

I rolled my eyes. "Good God, M.J. Does nothing interfere with exercise?"

She glared at me. "Have you already started drinking today? Because you sure—"

"No!" I lurched up and glared right back at her. "No."

"Then what is wrong with you?"

I sat down abruptly, deflating just as swiftly as I'd flared out of control. "I don't know." I sighed and shook my head. "I don't know what's wrong with me. All I know is that coming back here was a mistake. It always is."

We sat there in silence awhile before M.J. said, "Maybe we're doing this all wrong."

"No kidding," I said. "There was a reason we all moved to the other side of the country, and it obviously hasn't changed."

"No, no. The problem is, it *has* changed, only we're still behaving like it hasn't."

"You know what? I'm not in the mood for *Rebecca of Sunnybrook Farm* today."

"Just shut up for two minutes," M.J. shot right back at me. "Okay, our problems are only partly men, right? I mean, you've got your family, Cat, and Bitsey's all bent out of shape because of her dad and Doris. Plus her daughter and also her low self-esteem. Right?"

Bitsey grimaced and nodded. "So?"

"Don't you see? We're tackling our problems separately like we always did, when maybe we should be working on them together." She lifted her chin and stared steadily at me. "The thing is, we have to remember that we're the Grits Sisterhood. We're in this together." She turned to Bitsey. "I think we should plan a triple date."

It took me a while to agree, mainly because it wasn't my idea and I prefer to think of M.J. as the gorgeous one, ergo, the dumb one. But she's not dumb. In fact, she's a pretty smart cookie. We got dressed, went to dinner at Mandina's, waited a half hour for a table, then lingered an hour and a half over fried soft-shell crab and oysters, and every minute of it we planned our group date.

But it was more than merely a date. If we were going to give each other advice that was worthwhile, we needed to meet these guys that were torturing us.

Though she'd been all for the idea at first, when it came down to it, Bitsey proved to be the most hesitant. M.J. was so totally gone on Mr. Four-wheel-drive that she was sure we'd love him, too. I knew they'd like Matt. After all, he's a good-looking man in uniform. A classic hero type. But after her abortive lovemaking session with Eddie, Bitsey wasn't so sure he'd agree to come.

My response to that? All you can do is ask. After all, I wasn't certain Matt would come, and M.J. was pretty sure Steve would decline. But we were all going to give it our best shot. Our biggest problem was that we were running out of time. Bitsey's reunion was next Saturday, one week away.

So we planned our date for Wednesday. I called Matt first thing the next morning. My hands were clammy on the phone while my mouth felt like dry cotton. How perverse is the human body?

To my surprise, he agreed. "I've been meaning to call you back."

Sure you were. "Well, then, we're on the same wavelength. We'll be meeting up with my friends, Bitsey and M.J, and their dates."

"Great. What do you girls have in mind?"

"I'm not sure yet. Dinner of course." I stared out the window, watching a pair of squirrels run spirals up and down one of the giant oak trees that shaded the side of the house.

He cleared his throat. "Let me know if you come over to visit your mother before then. Maybe we can have coffee again."

My hand tightened on the phone. "All right. But I have to ask, Matt. Why did you cancel the other day? And don't say it was work, because I won't believe you."

After a short silence he said, "It was a personal matter."

"Cold feet? I mean, about dating me again."

"No, Cat, that's not a problem for me." He paused. "It was my son."

There was an odd note in his voice, something that said he hadn't merely forgotten about a ball game or a parent-teacher conference.

"I hope it wasn't serious."

He sighed. "Let's just say Alan's mother's untimely death is an ongoing problem for him."

"Maybe I could talk to him."

Now why would I make such an idiotic suggestion? I know nothing about raising kids, even less than my mother, and that's way down in the minus column. But my mouth must have been on disconnect from my brain, because I went on. "My dad died when I was fourteen." And of course that made me an expert; after all, look how calm and normal I'd turned out.

But once said, the idiotic words were impossible to retract, especially when he said, "That's not a bad idea. You wouldn't mind?"

I gulped back my utter terror of ever doing such a thing. "I'd be happy to."

That's how I came to be invited to watch a Hahnville High baseball game that night, the last one of the season. Bitsey gave me a thumbs-up, then took the telephone and went out on the back porch to call Eddie. She was afraid he'd think she was a prick tease and decide he'd had enough of her. But I doubted that. I'd met guys like Eddie before. He was basically an optimist disguised as a pessimist. He was down on everything: politics, the state of the environment, the future of the world. Whatever. But he still kept battering away at them all, trying to change things. He was a sucker for impossible causes, the harder the better.

The more Bitsey resisted, the harder he'd work to seduce her. He wasn't about to give up, especially when, after only two dates, he'd come so close.

As I expected, she was all smiles when she told us he'd said yes.

M.J.'s fellow was another matter. She called him; he said no. She borrowed my car and went down to see him; he said he was busy that night. She said what night would be better? He said something—she wouldn't tell us exactly what. But it must have convinced her, because when she came back to the house she looked crushed.

"He's not worth it," I told her. "If the jerk can't see what a great woman you are, then screw him."

Bitsey agreed, though she was more understanding about it. "He's obviously too scarred by his disability—and maybe too scared—to trust you with his feelings."

M.J. nodded. "I thought about that. It makes me sad, though. And it makes me not want to give up on him. It's bad enough he can't walk. But it's worse that he won't let anyone get close to him. He loves cars and engines, but not people. And not himself."

Bitsey and I wanted to do something with her, cheer her up. But she went for a run alone; Bitsey turned on a Pilates tape, and I went to Belladonna's for a manicure, a pedicure, and a facial. There's nothing like pure pampering to improve a girl's mood.

I left two hours early for the ball game. First I went to Wal-Mart and bought a few groceries, a new front door mat and two summery dresses for my mother. At the last minute I also threw in a pair of pink sandals into the shopping cart.

When I got to her house she was sitting in the kitchen. As before, the front door was unlocked.

"Ma, you have to lock this door. There's people out there that take advantage of the elderly. Don't you read the paper?"

She gave me a sour look. "So I get killed. So what? I'm dying anyway. At least it would be faster."

I thumped the bags down on her enamel-top kitchen table. "We're all dying, Ma. Me, you, Sissy. The Pope. That's why it's so important to enjoy every day we get. We never know which one's the last one."

When she only rolled her eyes at my profound observation, I added, "And that's why you're going out to the ball game with me tonight. Here." I thrust one of the bags at her. "Put on one of those dresses. Comb your hair, put on some lipstick and grab your purse. The Arceneaux women are going out tonight."

She looked at me like I was nuts. "I'm not going anywhere, especially with someone who's gotta be drunk."

"When did you get so particular? C'mon, Ma. You of all people know a drunk when you see one, and I am definitely not drunk."

"Oh, yeah? Well then, you're flat-out crazy if you think I'm going to some ball game with you. What do I care about ball games? What do you care about them?"

Who knows why I asked her to go with me? There was no one I wanted to keep away from Matt more than my mother—unless you counted my two brothers. I wasn't so adamant about Sissy anymore. But my mother and Matt—and his unhappy kid?

Unfortunately, like my offer to talk to Matt's son, this offer to my mother had sprung from my mouth without input from my brain.

"I'm meeting Matt Blanchard there. Remember him? His son plays for Hahnville. Shortstop, I think he said."

She frowned. "Matt Blanchard. The sheriff. Is that why you came back here? You starting up with him again?"

"That's not why I came back." *Liar*. "We're just old friends. That's all."

"He's the one that put Bubba in jail, you know."

"For what?"

We were standing on opposite sides of the table, the blue Wal-Mart bags a mountain between us.

"For what, Ma? What did Bubba do?"

She picked up the bag with the dresses and looked inside. "He wrecked his car into the front of some lady's house."

Damn. "Did he know her?"

She made a face and shook her head. "He's not mean. Just stupid. He was drunk."

"And he landed in jail. Well, I guess the third time's the charm. Or was it his fourth time? Or maybe his tenth?"

Ignoring my sarcasm, she pulled the dresses out of their bag and looked at them. "I don't like green. You know that."

"It's green and white and pink, and you do like pink."

"How do you know it's my size?"

"I guessed. Go ahead, try them on. If they don't fit I'll exchange them."

She shuffled off to her bedroom and I put the groceries away. What was I doing? First that kid, now my mother. I was not the type to get entangled in other people's problems.

Well, maybe in M.J.'s and Bitsey's. They, however, were my friends and I'd chosen to get involved in their lives and let them get involved in mine. I could almost understand the thing with Matt's kid. But taking my mother to a Hahnville High baseball game was an *I Love Lucy* episode, a disaster waiting to happen, but with no laugh track to lighten the impact.

Too late to turn back now, though. I'd put this mess into motion; I'd just have to live with the results.

As it turned out, my mother didn't look half bad in her new outfit, especially with her gray hair twisted in a chignon. There's nothing more deadly to a woman's looks than too-long, unkempt gray hair. But just put it up and, voila, instant style. To that add a touch of color on her lips and she looked fifteen years younger. I think even she was pleased, though she didn't say so.

"This dress is too big in the shoulders," she said, plucking at the sleeve as she came out of her room. "And the fabric is scratchy."

"It's cotton, Ma. Once you wash it, it'll shrink and soften up. Then it'll be perfect."

"It'll probably fade," she muttered.

It was either ignore her or slap her. I made myself choose the former. "Do the sandals fit?"

She wiggled her toes. "They'll do."

Her toenails were thick and yellowish, and too long. In contrast her fingernails were bitten to the quick. She could use the pedicure and manicure I'd had earlier. Plus a haircut. Oh, well. First things first.

"Okay. Get your purse and let's go."

She shot me a baleful look. "Don't rush me. I may not be on oxygen yet, but rushing around isn't good for me."

"Sorry," I muttered. But inside I was beginning to seethe

It took ten minutes to get out of the house and into the car. Once she was belted in, I reached for the radio. Anything to avoid what she thought passed for conversation. "What kind of music do you like?"

"Country music, of course. Garth Brooks and that handsome Alan Jackson. Somebody like that."

We found Randy Travis and after a slow drive up River Road staying five miles below the speed limit and well back from any cars, we made it to the ball field without one complaint about my driving. Problem was, I was even more tense from the combination of driving slow and waiting for her criticism than I would've been from zipping along like normal and putting up with the actual complaints.

I couldn't win, which she confirmed as we turned into a gravel drive. "Well, Cathy Ann, I guess getting older has improved your driving."

I laughed out loud at the irony. If she couldn't complain

about how I drove now, she'd point out how bad I drove before.

"What's so funny?" she asked, struggling to get out of the car.

"Nothing. Look, there's Matt." *Thank God.*

He grinned as he approached us and all at once I was caught in this massive déjà vu time warp. It was his civilian clothes, I told myself. The other day he'd worn his police uniform; today it was jeans and a red polo shirt. Damn but the boy looked good in red. And then there was my mother who'd always thought him perfect son-in-law material, if not via me, then via Sissy. To add to the aura, we were back at Hahnville High, where our teenage romance had begun.

"Mrs. Arceneaux." He leaned over and gave her a kiss on the cheek. "It's good to see you again." Then he gave a wry grin. "Better circumstances than the last time."

It was almost as if I could watch the scale tipping back and forth in my mother's head. On the one side, he was the same nice guy she'd always liked, one who had a good job and a promising future. On the other side, he'd arrested Bubba and probably, at one time or another, Hank and Sissy, too.

The scale wobbled. Bubba or Matt. Bubba or Matt.

"Yeah, this is a little better," she said, tilting her head and smiling up at him.

I could hardly believe it. She was flirting with him. I guess Bubba was plain out of luck.

He tucked her hand in his arm and at a slow pace, easy enough for her but natural for us, he led us to seats along the first base line. If I hadn't been so relieved at how well he handled her, I would have been miffed. I didn't get a hello kiss. I didn't get to hold on to that nicely muscled arm.

But that was okay. We were here, my mother was in a good mood, and just like in tenth grade, I was falling in love with Matt Blanchard.

Falling in love?

The rest of the game was a blur. Falling in lust was one thing. That I could understand. But falling in love? Through seven long innings I watched him like a hawk. He had flaws like everyone else. I just hadn't found any yet. But I would.

He bought us soft drinks and hot dogs and nachos. He pointed out his son, Alan—who looked just like Matt had twenty-five years ago—and introduced us to everyone that came up to him.

The only real disappointment of the evening was that our team lost, not that I really cared. I was floating on a cloud of sweetly suffocating feminine hormones. It was like perfume, I think, because he kept looking at me, too, like he could sniff out exactly what I was feeling—and where this would end.

The thought made me a nervous wreck. For all my smart mouth and pushy attitude, I'm no slut. There's been Matt, my two husbands and at most five other guys in the whole of my sexually active life. Compared to Bitsey and M.J. I might have been around. But the truth is, I'm pretty protective of my emotions.

With Matt, though, there was no moral ambiguity, no latent Catholic guilt. We'd slept together for twenty-three and a half months. If I disregarded the twenty-four-year gap, I had just enough time left in New Orleans to make it an even two years.

"Come on," he said. "Let's go meet Alan and the rest of the team."

In the gym outside the locker room people milled around. Some parents were trying to console their disappointed sons. A few fathers looked like they were browbeating theirs for every mistake.

We found Alan off to the side, alone, and Matt introduced us. The boy was polite enough under the circumstances. I passed off his sullen attitude to the defeat. But when Matt suggested we all go out for ice cream, I saw the flash of anger in the boy's eyes.

"I got plans."

From my dad that belligerent tone would have warranted a quick slap. Matt only said. "With who?"

The boy met his father's steady stare without flinching. "Judy."

"She's got her mother's car?"

"Guess so." Had I ever been able to imbue two words with such insolent disregard?

In the tense silence that stretched between them my mother said, "My boys played baseball, too. Let's see, Bubba was a catcher and Hank...I think he played first base."

The boy's eyes flicked to her, then down to his feet. "That's cool."

"'Course they didn't stick with it."

"Why was that?" Matt asked. Naturally he knew. But he wanted Alan to know.

My mother grimaced as if she didn't want to go there, and I felt a sudden surge of protectiveness toward her. Though I understood what Matt was trying to do, I didn't want it to happen at her expense.

"They got distracted," I said, putting a hand on my mother's arm. "You know, cars. Girls."

My mother nodded. "But mostly drinking." She looked up at Matt. "Hank Jr. could've gone to college. He was that good a ballplayer. But..." She made a face. "*C'est la vie.*"

Alan looked at her. "You mean he could've gotten a scholarship to play ball?"

"He was scouted in his junior year," I said. "LSU. USL. McNeese. But he didn't finish high school. So—" I looked up at Matt "—are we going for ice cream or not?"

"Sure," he said after a moment. "You remember where The Ice Cream Palace is?"

We met there, and I have to say, he made the evening great for me and my mother. Pecan Praline sundaes and a man brimming with stories about inept criminals makes the time pass easily. I laughed enough to cancel out the two thousand calories in the sundae.

"He's a nice fellow," Mother said as I drove her home afterward. "Even if he did put Bubba in jail. You should marry him."

I nearly ran off the road into a mosquito-breeding canal. "Marry him? Don't you think we need to date first?"

"What do you mean? Wasn't this a date?"

"With my mother chaperoning us? And his kid right there? I don't think so."

"*He* didn't ask me to go along. You did."

I turned into her driveway and killed the engine. Then I looked over at her. "Are we having a normal mother-daughter moment?"

She opened her door before answering. "How would I know?" Then she got out and I watched her into the house.

So, was the evening a success or a wash? I wasn't sure. My mother had been…bearable. Pleasant even. But Matt and his son had been a strikeout.

I shouldn't have brought my mother. He probably thought I was making sure nothing could happen between him and me.

And maybe I was. I didn't understand anything I did anymore.

"You're a pathetic loser," I muttered to my reflection in the rearview mirror as I backed out of her drive. I started back toward the Mississippi River Bridge, only to be distracted by flashing red-and-blue lights behind me.

"Hells bells, now what?" I pulled into the first driveway, a barroom, and hopped out, ready to argue that I had *not* been speeding.

It wasn't a marked car, though, and it wasn't a uniformed cop who stepped out. It was Matt in his Jeep Cherokee and his civilian clothes.

"Hey, lady," he said, leaning against the side of the SUV. "Where do you think you're going?"

A thrill of awareness shivered through me, up from my belly and all the way out to the goose bump endings of my skin. "I don't know." Oh, God, I was breathless with anticipation.

He pushed away from his vehicle and walked toward me, one slow step at a time, and stopped an arm's length away. "Are you open for suggestions?"

"Yes." I pressed my lips together. "Maybe."

He grinned. "Yes, or maybe? Which one?"

I laughed. "You make me nervous, Matt. You didn't used to, but you do now. I don't know how to act around you anymore."

He reached out and took my hand in his. "I'm glad you're back, Cathy Ann. The truth is, I'm kind of nervous around you, too. I don't make a habit of pursuing women with my lights flashing. But since you're not back for long, I figured I needed to work fast."

I had stopped breathing when he grabbed my hand, so I figured my brain had to be suffering from oxygen depletion. That's the only reason it would turn his simple statement into a plea for permanence. "I need to work fast," does not equal "Let's get married and live happily ever after," except when Matt Blanchard is holding your hand.

"Okay," I said.

"Okay?"

Like I said, I was a simpleton operating on her last two brain cells. "It's okay if you want to…" What? "To work fast."

That's when he bent down and kissed me.

Maybe I wasn't such a simpleton after all because I'd been imagining Matt kissing me all evening. Every time he smiled at me, every time he took a spoon of ice cream into his mouth. I wanted to be that spoon; I was already melting like the ice cream had.

He kissed me and I remembered all over again the pleasure of being kissed by a tall man who has to accommodate himself to a smaller woman. One of his arms circled my waist, while his other cradled my head.

It's a good thing my family history doesn't include heart trouble, because my chest hurt from the racket my heart was making. We were fused together, knees, thighs, hips, bellies and chests. But mostly mouths. His lips were warm and firm; his tongue, thrilling and bold. And as I curled my arms around his neck and kissed him back, there was one more thing. He was familiar—his taste, his scent, the feel of him against me.

This was Matt, the boy I'd once loved, a man now, who still wanted me.

He groaned as he broke the kiss. "Cathy Ann. Damn." He took a deep breath and leaned back, just an inch or two, to stare down at me. In the darkness his eyes glittered with heat. "I think you need to come home with me, Cat. What do you say?"

My arms tightened around his neck and it was all I could do not to leap up, cinch his hips with my legs, and burrow beneath his skin. "I say yes," I murmured, feeling bold and shy, and scared and sure, all at the same time.

It was like when we were sixteen, only this time I was wiser. This was my chance to fix one of my bad choices, one of the worst choices of my life.

I just hoped I didn't blow it.

M.J.

I refused to be a fifth wheel. Bitsey had Eddie; Cat had Matt. I would get Steve to go out with us, or I would die trying.

It's hard to know where this new brazen attitude of mine comes from. I have never chased a guy before. Even back in high school, as popular as Jeff Cole was, he was the one who chased me. Then in California, after dating a whole bunch of forgettable men, it was Frank who pursued me. I tried never to date married men, but he was so attentive and I was so lonely that it was easy to fall in love with him—especially when I met his wife and saw how superficial and materialistic she was.

Though I hate being labeled a trophy wife, it's hard to ignore the fact that I was one. I guess it's no wonder our marriage ended badly. Still, I was stunned when Frank died.

But that's my past. I just hope I can learn from my mistakes.

I thought about it the whole time I jogged this morning, and I realized that I've never really taken a risk before. Things have always fallen into my lap, or else I've just gone along with whatever came along. Either way, I've never set my own course. Even my career as a beauty pageant contestant was my mother's idea. Her obsession. She was Miss Raceland and Miss Sauce Piquant Festival, and she made the top ten in the Miss Louisiana Pageant. But that was it. She groomed me to achieve what she hadn't and, silly old me, I went along with it.

Forty-one years of going along with other people's plans for me. Maybe that's why I've become so fixated on the impossible goal of Steve Vidrine. I had all these years of pent-up goal-making to satisfy.

All I had to lose was my dignity, my heart and my self-respect.

But I'd lost all that with Frank's betrayal, and I'd survived. If Steve really didn't want anything to do with me, I told myself that I could survive that, too.

So I brought him lunch. Not just for him, but for the three stooges, too. Brownies for them, and po'boys for him and me.

He was elbow deep in a BMW engine when I arrived. Larry, the closest stooge to the office, was bent over a Jaguar—not mine. He banged his head on the hood when he saw me, then rubbed his buzz cut with a greasy hand as he stared at my chest.

I smiled with all the determination of a runner-up at the Miss America Pageant. "Hi. I brought y'all a little treat, you and the other guys." I jiggled the paper bag, then set it on the fender. "I hope you like brownies."

Then I waved at Steve, sashayed into his office and proceeded to spread the feast out picnic-style on his desk.

He left me waiting forty minutes—on purpose, I'm sure. It was twelve-thirty before he wheeled into the office and slammed the door behind him.

"What the hell are you trying to do?"

I was prepared for exactly this attitude. I smiled and said, "Feed you? After all, they say the fastest way to a man's heart is through his stomach."

"Oh, yeah? Well they also say you can tell a man by the company he keeps. If you notice, I like the company of cars."

"So?"

"So? In keeping with our theme of clichés, consider this—you can't teach an old dog new tricks."

"I don't believe that."

He hadn't come any farther into the office, and though it wasn't a big room, he seemed very far away from me.

He shook his head. "It's time you woke up and smelled the roses."

"Will you please stop it with the clichés. And anyway, you're mixing them up. It's 'wake up and smell the coffee,' or 'take time to smell the roses.'"

"You started it."

We stared at one another. He reminded me of a feral cat that had once lived under my mother's house. She'd been so gaunt, her ribs sticking out, her fur patchy, with a litter of kittens hidden somewhere nearby. But she wouldn't come close, no matter how I coaxed her with tuna or cooked chicken breasts. She'd rather have starved herself and her kittens than trust me.

If I couldn't convince a starving cat to eat, how could I ever convince this wary man to trust me and my motives? Despite my earlier determination, I felt the first cold fingers of defeat.

I reached for my bottle of water and opened it with an angry twist. "You know what? You do what you want. I brought one oyster po'boy and one roast beef. You can have whichever one you want. If you don't want to choose, then I will. Either way I'm eating my lunch right here—unless you think you can physically remove me."

"You think I can't?"

I wanted to cry. "I have no doubt you can, Steve. But I'm hoping you won't."

He exhaled a long breath. "You're a pain in the ass, you know that?"

I forced a smile. "I'm trying."

With one hand he wheeled around his desk. "Yeah, and you're doing a damned good job of it. The question is why? No." He raised his hand. "Don't tell me. It was a rhetorical question." He eyed the neatly laid picnic on his desk. Napkins, drinks, sandwiches. "I'll take half of each, if that's all right with you."

It was much more than all right. Maybe I was being foolish, but going half and half with the po'boys smacked of compromise, big-time. We'd shared a meal at Café Rani, but this time we were really sharing our meal, and I was almost too excited to eat. But I couldn't just sit there and watch him chew, so I picked up my half of the oyster po'boy.

He studied me over the Dagwood-thick sandwich. "So. What are we talking about today—besides you wanting me to go out with you and your friends?"

"We can't talk about that?"

"No."

"Well. Can we talk about hardheadedness and what a horrible trait it is in a person?"

"We could. But I'd be forced to point out all the ways you're more hardheaded than me."

"True." I chewed thoughtfully. "We could talk about cars."

He snorted. "Like you're really interested in that."

"Or workouts."

He bit off a big piece of oyster po'boy and stared at me while he chewed. "That sounds fairly neutral."

"Is that a car pun? Neutral," I clarified when he looked puzzled.

I was rewarded with a grin. Well, a half grin. "Maybe so, though it wasn't intentional."

We continued to eat, but the silent pauses weren't so tense now. I took another sip of water. "I like variety in my workouts," I began. "Jogging, aerobics, Pilates, free weights."

"You don't look like you're dieting." He gestured to my half-eaten sandwich.

"That's the blessing of exercise. I can eat."

He reached for his half of the roast beef po'boy. "I never did like women who talked about their diets all the time."

"You look like you have a healthy appetite yourself. How do you work out?"

He drank from his bottle and like a fool, I watched the workings of his throat. I wanted to touch him there. To kiss him there. When our eyes met, my face got warm. Could he tell what I was thinking? And if he did, did it help my cause or hurt it?

"I don't take much time for lunch," he said, ignoring my question.

"Of course not."

A crease formed between his brows. "I don't understand you."

I shrugged. "It takes time to understand another person."

"Assuming you want to understand them."

"You're not exactly an open book yourself."

He leaned back in his chair and studied me. "Why me? Why are you so determined to date me?"

"Because…" How to explain the inexplicable? My gaze swept nervously around his office. "Because, for one thing, you don't have any girlie pictures in your shop."

He lifted one dark, arrogant brow. "You haven't been in the employees' bathroom."

"And you're very particular, very detail oriented."

"And we already know you don't need a discount on your car repairs," he said.

"No. Plus." I hesitated. "Plus, you have great arms. And gorgeous eyes."

I couldn't believe I'd actually said that. Then I couldn't believe that faint hint of color that rose in his cheeks. He was blushing, and all because I'd complimented him!

Rejuvenated by the first hint of any emotion in him beyond impatience, I smiled hopefully. "Please have dinner with me and my friends, Steve. I really want you to be there."

He looked away and for a moment I thought he was going to agree, that I'd broken through his wall of reserve and proved my sincerity to him. Then he looked at me with eyes the ice-blue of a glacier.

"And afterward?" His voice was as cold as his eyes. "Afterward I'll take you home and you'll find out how sex is with a cripple?"

The venom caught me by surprise. Before I could react he went on. "Why don't we just get the sex part out of the way now?" He wheeled around to the window that looked out into the shop, and with a flick of his wrist, closed the metal blinds. Then he spun his chair so that he faced me. Our knees were inches apart. But our goals? Our intentions? They were on opposite sides of the planet.

He stared at me with the most unloverlike expression on his face, as if I were some cheap prostitute he'd hired for the afternoon. For a half-hour lunch quickie.

If I'd believed that look, I would have burst into tears, then run in shame from the room, abandoning lunch, car, everything.

But I didn't believe it. He was protecting himself because he was afraid. He didn't trust me or my motives. But how was I to convince him?

One of his brows lifted, as if his patience was wearing thin, and why didn't I just get on with it? So I did the only thing I could. Working only on instinct, I reached up and released the clip in my hair. Thank goodness I'd washed it earlier. It fell in a nice, swishy wave, and I tossed my head, just enough to make sure he noticed.

He did. But the mask that hid his emotions didn't so much as crack.

So I started to unbutton my blouse. "You'll have to tell me what you like," I said. Where those words came from I do not know.

I saw him swallow. "Same as other guys," he grunted, his eyes fixed on my face. Not my body, but my face.

The same as other guys? Frank had liked men in drag. I started to panic. I had one button undone, but the second one had me fumbling. "Shouldn't we...lock the door?" My voice sounded like a dry croak, the love call of some withered-up desert toad.

He shook his head. "They know better than to come in here when the door is closed."

I got the second button open. "What if a customer comes in?"

His eyes had fallen to my slowly emerging cleavage. When they rose back up, the glacial blue had turned to a darker, hotter color. "You're going to go through with this, aren't you?"

A breath caught in my throat. "I don't want to. Not here. But if that's the only way I can prove to you that I'm not just fooling around—"

"And screwing a guy you barely know in his office isn't fooling around? Son of a bitch," he swore.

"In case you haven't noticed, " I shouted right back. "I've been trying my hardest to *get* to know you!"

"Is that why you're divorced? You got to know too many men?"

I was too mad already to care about his insult. "My husband died paying someone else for sex. I was the faithful one. Me, not him." I lurched up and started for the door. If I didn't get out of here I was going to burst into tears. Furious tears, but even so, I did not want to cry in front of this stone-hearted, impossible man.

But he blocked my path. "Your blouse is open."

"Get out of my way."

"Mary Jo. Wait."

"What for? To be insulted? To be—"

"I'm sorry."

I heard him, but I didn't believe him. I turned away and fought the tiny slippery buttons and the too-tight button-holes.

"I'm sorry," he repeated.

"Don't be," I answered, shielding my hurt feelings with sarcasm. "I should have taken the hint the first time. I guess it's like the song. What part of no don't I understand?"

"Mary Jo." His voice was gentle now, no coldness, no hostility.

But I didn't want his pity. With my buttons fastened, and my best, first-runner-up expression in place, I turned around. "I think it's time for me to go."

"Not yet." He rolled backward and without taking his eyes off me, locked the door. My heart began to hammer in my chest. Bam, bam, bam. What was he doing?

Then he rolled right up to me and took my hand. "Come here." He tugged and I sat, right on his lap.

I cannot begin to explain the impact it had on me. The Allentown Dam had broken. Everything changed, and I felt it in every cell of my body.

For one long moment all I could think was that I'd wasted seventeen years being married to Frank. Seventeen years and I'd never felt a tenth of what I was feeling now, not a tenth of the crazy emotions or a tenth of the physical awareness.

I stared into his eyes, just inches from mine. They were the darkest shade of blue, but there were these amazing gold flecks in them, too. His hand came up to circle my waist. "Are you sure you want to do this?"

I nodded. "Yes. I don't know why, but yes."

Then he kissed me. And that's when I knew I was a goner.

Steve kissed me, this gentle, conciliatory kiss. But it didn't remain gentle. I wanted more; so did he. I threw my arms around his neck. He leaned me back, supporting my head with one strong hand, and sliding the other up from my knee to my thigh, to my waist. And all the while he kissed me.

"God, you're beautiful," he said when at last we broke apart, gasping for air.

"I think you're beautiful," I said. "And sexy." I kissed him, then reveled in the feel of his aggressive response. His mouth dominated mine, his tongue possessed me. I wanted to jump out of my skin and right into his.

And I wanted his hand on my breast. Usually I resented men's obsession with my breasts. But I didn't want to hold back anything with him.

He seemed to know everything I was feeling because he murmured, "I want to touch you all over. And taste you."

I squirmed in anticipation. Finally we were on the same wavelength. But even when I kissed along his jaw and down to his prickly Adam's apple, he kept his hand on my waist.

"Slow down, M.J. This is not the place."

"If I slow down you might change your mind."

There was a pause. Two seconds, maybe. Two years. "I won't," he said when I was strangling with dread. He was breathing heavily; his skin was hot with the damp sheen of arousal. "I won't change my mind."

I believed him. I did. But beneath my bottom there was no thick ridge. No Big Mac as Frank used to call his penis.

I didn't know how to feel about that. Up to now I'd told myself—and my friends—that I didn't care. If his penis was as affected by his accident as his legs, so what? A man is more than his penis, just as a woman is more than her breasts.

But I had never been as excited by a man as I was now. This was the very first time in my life that the idea of making love to a man felt as much about the physical act as it did the emotional closeness. Men liked to make love; women liked to cuddle. I'd always believed that was how it really was. We put up with the sex in order to get that closeness—notwithstanding Cat's screwed-up relationship with her ex.

To my amazement, I wanted to make real, physical love to Steve, and in the worst way. At the same time, now that he actually was willing, I was beginning to realize that it might be physically impossible.

"Okay, M.J." He blew out a breath and moved his hand down to my hip. "I think maybe we should cool off a little. Finish lunch."

I sat on his lap, perfectly content with my perch. "I don't suppose you could take the afternoon off."

He smiled and this close I noticed everything. The crescent lines at the corners of his eyes; the slight chip in one of his front teeth; the thick fringe of jet-black lashes that rimmed his eyes. Those eyes never veered away from mine. "I've got cars stacked on cars," he said.

"I know one very accommodating lady who won't mind if she has to wait on hers."

"Yeah, you say that now." His thumb tucked a strand of hair behind my ear. "But after you've had your way with me..."

He tried to make it a joke, but I heard the thread of doubt in his voice. "How about this?" I said. "I'll trade you your lunch hours and your evenings for—I don't know—an extra week on the car? An extra month?"

Our eyes held. I thought he was going to say something, because the air was thick with all the emotions careening between us. When he didn't speak, I did. "I'm so glad my car broke down."

He twirled that strand of hair around his finger, then stroked my throat with his thumb. "So am I," he murmured in this low rumble of a voice.

How I ever got out of his office without melting onto the floor and oozing out under the door, I don't know. He had an appointment at seven but he said he could pick me up around nine if I wanted.

I wanted.

I left lunch on his desk, waved to the three stooges and practically flew back to Bitsey's house. If I'd had on jogging shoes I would have run to work off some of the excess heat boiling inside me. As it was, I don't remember one thing about the trip to Fourth Street, or even thinking about the route.

I entered through the kitchen, made my way to the bathroom I was sharing with Cat and took a long cold shower. Me, needing a cold shower! It was amazing.

But it didn't work. Not really. For the first time in my life I stood under the streaming spray and, as I smoothed lather over my skin, over my breasts and belly, I roused myself back up to a fever pitch. I breathed in the delicate lavender scent and I imagined it was Steve's hands caressing me, and I got so excited I thought I would burst. I wanted to burst. I wanted that cataclysmic explosion, that long overdue release, that little death that the romance novels always describe with such satisfyingly heated words.

But I couldn't get there. I didn't know how. With Steve I would, though. I promised myself that finally I would have that elusive orgasm everybody talks about.

Whether I could return the favor for him, however, I didn't know. But tonight I meant to find out.

CHAPTER 7
Between a Rock and a Hard Place

Cat

Matt's house was a classic Acadian cottage—his grandparents' old place. I suppose they'd died. It had been renovated since the last time I'd seen it: a new metal roof, white paint with dark green shutters and two ceiling fans on the front porch. I caught fleeting glimpses of a porch swing, some rocking chairs and a struggling geranium in a pot next to the door. A cat ran into the house ahead of us and on a table by the door an answering machine blinked that there were five messages.

But Matt ignored the cat's plaintive demand and the machine's silent one. He closed the door, then backed me against it and kissed me.

It's hard to explain how outrageously erotic it was to make out with him.

Make out is such a teenage phrase. But that's what we were doing. Making out—without the forbidden aspect of being found out, and without the teenage arrogance of believing we were the first couple to ever discover such bliss. Without all the newness and out-of-control hormones that made our first love so incredible. Yet this was still better. Infinitely, mind-blowingly, heart-achingly better.

Oh, my God. I sounded just like a country singer, going on and on about how it felt to be in Matt's arms and eventually in his bedroom. If I could just package these feelings, I could have a career writing top-of-the-chart, country music anthems.

But I'd look into that later. At the moment I was too busy learning the length of his back and the strength of his arms. Relearning.

There was no pretense in me, no coyness. I've never been coy. I arched against Matt and wanted him with every cell in my body, and he knew it. We made it to his bedroom, shedding clothes along the way. My sandals, his belt. My blouse, his shirt. The moon slanted through an uncovered window and in its silver glow he undressed me. His hands were hot and they trembled.

I returned the favor.

Then with a waist-high field of sugar cane rustling and swaying in the breeze beyond the window, we came together in his bed.

It was every bit as furious as it used to be, but thankfully, not nearly as quick. He'd learned a thing or two—or ten—through the years, and so had I. That's not to say we lasted terribly long. I came; he came, and if I ever needed any proof that I have a strong, healthy heart, that climax confirmed it. I should have died of cardiac arrest, but I didn't.

Afterward we lay side by side in the bed—probably his grandparents' bed—sweating and staring up at the immobile ceiling fan.

He found my hand and clasped it. "That was the best time I've had in twenty years."

Completely content, I smiled up into the dark. "Only twenty?" I sighed. "I have to tell you, Matt, you've improved with age. That was—I don't know—the best fifteen minutes of my life." I'm nothing if not unsubtle.

He laughed and rolled over so that he half covered me. "That was just foreplay, sweetheart. My Cathy Ann." His tone was teasing but his eyes—oh my God, the look in his eyes made my heart stop. My Cathy Ann. That's what he'd always called me. His Cathy Ann.

He dipped his head and kissed me, this lovely, sweet, yet totally arousing kiss. But when I arched up for more, he pulled away. "That was foreplay," he repeated. "Now that we're warmed up…"

Sometime later, when we were way past warm and dangerously into overheated, we heard a car pull into the shell driveway. We might have been dead drunk on sex, but that crunching warning that his son was home sent both of us bolting from the bed.

We dressed in the dark by feel, giggling like fools, but unable to stop. Thank God Matt found the clothes we'd abandoned in the living room. By the time Alan said his own sweaty good-night to his girlfriend and reached the house, Matt and I were sipping iced tea in the kitchen.

Iced tea at one o'clock in the morning.

Alan had this curious look on his face when he came in. Probably he hadn't recognized my car. When he saw me, though, his expression turned sour.

"What're you doing up?" he asked his father. No hello to me. He was one pissed-off kid.

Matt didn't look much happier with his son's attitude. "What're you doing getting home so late?"

The boy shrugged and went to the refrigerator. Matt started to get up, but I grabbed his wrist. I did not want to be here for a fight between him and his son, especially if there was any chance I could be a contributing factor.

"It's been great catching up with you, Matt. I'll have to plan on coming back when we have our high school reunion. Next year," I added for Alan's sake. "Meanwhile, I'd better get going before Bitsey and M.J. put an APB out on me."

I stood. "I enjoyed the game," I said to Alan's back still in the open refrigerator. "Sorry y'all lost."

He grunted. Which was fine, because who understands guys anyway, no matter the age? I figured he wasn't happy that I was in his house—or more accurately, his mother's house. The weird thing is, though I've never been maternal, I wanted to reach out and hug the boy, or at least pat his arm. Something. Anything. It was bad, losing a parent. I'd told

Matt I would talk to Alan, but he didn't want to be consoled by me.

Matt started to follow me out to the car, but I stopped him on the porch. "Go in and talk to Alan. He's feeling all alone right now."

Matt cupped the side of my face. "I don't know how to talk to him anymore, not without starting a fight. It doesn't matter what I say."

"You still have to try."

I hadn't stuck the key in the ignition before I heard the proof of Matt's words. For Alan's voice, angry and loud carried out to my open car window.

"—So what? Everybody drinks. You should be proud, I'm just following in Mom's footsteps!"

I drove away as fast as I could. I even risked another speeding ticket. But I couldn't escape the questions roused by that angry teenage accusation. Alan's mother—Matt's wife—had been a drinker?

Matt had said his wife had died due to a drunk driver, and I had felt awkward asking for details. Now, though, I wondered.

Back in the Garden District a private patrol truck followed me to the La Farge "Cottage." He probably thought I was a suspicious character in my rental car.

Bitsey was out the back door before I parked. "Thank God. Now I only have to worry about two of you."

"Gee, Ma, you were worried about me?"

"You know, I really don't need that kind of attitude right now, Cat."

She followed me into the kitchen, where I tossed my purse on the counter. I was ravenous, but Bitsey was obviously still upset.

I opened the fridge, thinking of Alan. "I take it M.J. and Meg are still out?"

"Nobody bothers to call me," Bitsey complained. She pulled a chair out and plopped down, elbows braced on the table. "Do y'all *want* me to start eating again? Do y'all *want* me fat and whiny and unhappy?"

I took out a green Granny Smith apple, then put it back and turned to Bitsey. "I think you're not worried about us so much as you're lonely and not sure about your own situation."

She opened her mouth to argue, then shut it and shot me a withering look. "Whatever." Then heaving a great, put-upon sigh, she rested her chin on one palm. "So what happened? What kept you so long? The ball game couldn't have lasted this late."

"No. Matt and I hung out for a while."

A drip from the kitchen faucet marked the passing seconds as she digested that monstrous understatement. Drip, drip, drip.

"You went to bed with him," she said. "You did. That's why you look like that."

"Like what?" I smoothed back my hair and wiped the corner of one eye.

"Like you just had a giant orgasm. Maybe two."

I tried, but I couldn't contain my immense bubble of happiness one second longer. "Three giant ones," I said, then hugged my arms around me and turned around in an antsy circle. Otherwise I would have exploded with joy. I stared at her stunned expression. "I'm in love, Bitsey. I'm in love with Matt all over again. What am I going to do?"

Bitsey didn't say anything for the longest time, just stared at me. She wasn't smiling, which made me just a little nervous. "Does he love you, too?"

"I don't know. Maybe. He acts like he does." I started to bite one of my fingernails, then caught myself. "Okay. Maybe love is the wrong word. He cares a lot for me. I know that. And it could turn into love, couldn't it?"

Still no smile. Wasn't she happy for me? She drummed her fingers on the well-worn oak tabletop. "Are you moving back to New Orleans?"

I pulled out the chair opposite her and sat. "I don't know.

It's too soon to say. Does that look pathetic, moving across the country for a man?"

"No. It doesn't look pathetic. Besides, you did it before when you followed your first ex to California."

"That was different. Back then I was mainly looking for a reason to leave Louisiana."

Finally she smiled at me. "Well then, all you have to do is ask yourself, are you looking for a reason to leave California?"

Have I said before what a wonderful friend Bitsey Albertson is? Full of good, practical insight. I gave her a hug. "You're right. I didn't come here looking for a reason to leave California. But maybe I've found one anyway."

Right after that Meg came home, sneaking in until she saw the light on in the kitchen. M.J. never came home at all. I wasn't sure whether to be worried or pleased by that. But since Bitsey was doing the worrying, I decided my role was to be happy for M.J. "She's probably in bed with Steve as we speak."

When morning came and M.J. still wasn't back Bitsey got even more worried. Then she got mad. Then at breakfast she ate an overflowing plate of grits, eggs, toast and bacon. She gorged herself, and my protests and Meg's only goaded her on. Good old Charles didn't notice anything until Bitsey lurched back from the table and ran for the downstairs bathroom.

"What's wrong with her?" he demanded, even as the faint sounds of her retching spoiled what was left of my breakfast.

"Where's Doris?" he went on when no one answered his first question. "Ulna! Where's Doris?"

"Calm down, Mr. Charles," Ulna said. "Miss Doris had a doctor's appointment this morning. She told us about it yesterday. Remember?"

In the background Bitsey upchucked some more. Ulna shot a speaking look at me and Meg. We both jumped up. After all, Ulna ruled the roost here. We were just visitors. But I shook my head at Meg. "Let me go."

"She's not bulimic, is she?" Meg whispered so her grandfather wouldn't hear. "That's not how she's been losing weight?"

"No. She's just upset."

"Why?"

I just shook my head and went after Bitsey. The water was running in the bathroom sink and when it stopped I tapped on the door. "You okay?"

I heard some sniffling. "I'm a hopeless wreck. Do you consider that okay?"

"You're not a hopeless wreck." She opened the door and when I saw her red eyes and her dejected expression, I added. "Well, you do look like a wreck. But you're not hopeless."

She gave me a halfhearted smile, thank goodness. A little self-deprecating smile. Then she sniffled again. "It's bad enough I'm on a starvation diet and a boot-camp exercise regime. But now it seems like I can't enjoy eating to excess even occasionally."

"Life's a bitch."

"And then you die." Her smile faded. "I think I need to make love to Eddie again before I die."

"You okay, Mom?"

Bitsey didn't even look guilty when Meg approached us. She just smiled and said. "I guess my days of gorging are over. M.J. will be so pleased."

"Where is M.J., anyway?" Meg asked, then grinned. "Found a fellow?"

"I think she found him her first day back," I said. "The question is, has she landed him?"

M.J.

I felt like a guilty teenager creeping home so late that she can't even hide beneath the dark shelter of night. Veronica was dusting the front parlor, and when she saw me slip in the front door, she chortled. "You just in time for breakfast, child. They's all on the back verandah."

"Thanks, but I'm not hungry." I fled up the stairs, red-faced

with shame. Well, not too much shame. I knew that she
knew what I'd been up to. The rosy heat in my cheeks was
all Steve's doing. But knowing that she knew and that pretty
soon they all would, was an unnerving experience.

In the past when we Grits Girls had talked about sex, it
was usually about Cat's experiences. After all, she was the divorced one. Bitsey and I were just old married ladies. But not
anymore. They would want to know everything, and although they were my best friends in the whole world, for now
I just wanted to hug last night to myself.

Steve Vidrine. M.J. Vidrine.

Mary Jo Vidrine.

I was making myself giddy, spinning a future out of one
night. It was crazy, but I couldn't stop myself. I'd had an orgasm last night and another one this morning. Both times
thanks to Steve. If he hadn't needed to be at work, I might
have had even more.

Unwilling to come back to reality, I grabbed my robe and
locked myself in the bathroom. Then with the shower pounding my skin full force, I relived every delicious moment.

We hadn't pretended about the purpose of our date. Steve
had picked me up at nine and driven straight to his house. It
was an odd place, an old gas station farther up Tchoupitoulas Street that had been renovated into a residence. It had
one large living area with a kitchen along one side. What had
been the two repair bays were now a bedroom and an exercise room. The gas-pumping area outside was a covered
porch, made private by a tall fence covered with ivy and jasmine and rosa Montana vines.

From the outside the place looked unapproachable and
sort of forbidding. It was hard to even find the gate. Cinder-
ella's castle encircled with vines—Cinder*fella*'s castle.

But with the push of a button on the dashboard Steve ac-
tivated a remote control gate, and once we pulled into the
compound, my impression of the place changed. Though
small and hidden from its neighbors, his home was serene and
green, a veritable Eden.

I wondered how many women he'd brought here.

I wanted to believe I was the first. Foolish, I know. But as we got out of the car I vowed not to think about the past, his or mine—or the future, his or mine. Or ours. Tonight was just about tonight.

"This place is great," I said as he lifted himself into a wheelchair positioned on his side of the parking area. "How long have you lived here?"

"Eight or nine years." He came around the car. "Want the ten-cent tour?"

To his surprise I sat on his lap and put my arms around his neck. "Sure."

It ended up being the nickel tour because when he stopped at the raised fishpond and a half-dozen fat goldfish immediately came to the surface to greet him, I started laughing. "You are such a softy," I said. He stiffened and I realized how horrible my word choice was. But I plunged on. "You act so tough, so mean. But even these fish love you."

Then I kissed him on his hard, unsmiling lips—and that's all it took. We ended up in his bedroom, undressing each other. Tearing each other's clothes off, actually. His chest was even better than his arms, rippling with muscles, dusted with dark curly hair. Holding on to the arms of his chair, he hoisted himself up and let me remove his slacks.

"Don't get your hopes up," he muttered.

"Shut up," I said, kissing him, knowing I must not show any sign of disappointment. I stood and began to remove my bra and panties.

He watched my every movement with such single-minded intensity that I began to get hot all over. It was the complete opposite of sex with Frank. I mean I did what I'd always done with Frank: used my body to arouse him. But before I'd even started my innocent striptease routine, Steve rolled up to me and nudged me onto the bed. "Lie down," he said, his voice as thick and warm as a fur blanket. "Let me."

And that's when I had my very first climax. Steve lay beside me and with his finger first, then with his mouth, he caressed and stroked and licked me to my first ever. I was so shocked I think I must have fainted. Because when I came to he was lying next to me, face-to-face. And he was smiling.

"Well, that's a damned good way to start off."

Breathless, I nodded. "Very nice." My heart was pounding as much from emotion as from the physical aftereffects of what had happened. I wanted to tell him how wonderful he was, to thank him and cover him with grateful kisses and make him feel just as good as he'd made me feel. But I also wanted to make love to him in the regular way men and women make love. Torn between weeping with relief for myself and weeping with frustration for his limitations, I knew I could do neither.

He must have known what I was thinking. Maybe it was the long silence, maybe the way I blinked to hold back my tears. Whatever, he rolled onto his back and stared up at the ceiling and said, "Don't ruin it now."

I sucked in a breath so fast and hard that I choked and started to cough. I rolled away from him and sat up. He sat up, too, and pounded on my back. Then I burst into tears and *did* ruin everything.

Just to remember those awful moments now started me crying all over again. I turned my face into the needling warmth of the shower. Thank God Steve hadn't been able to run away from me.

"You okay?" he'd asked when I finally caught my breath.

"Yes." But I could tell he wasn't. "Look, Steve—"

"It's all right."

"No." I knelt on the bed facing him. "I don't think you understand."

He had this hard look on his face. Hard eyes. Hard, compressed mouth. It occurred to me how utterly vulnerable he'd made himself to me. If I had any doubts about him, they vanished. It was time for me to be just as vulnerable to him.

"The thing is," I went on. "That was the very first time in my life that I've ever had an orgasm."

He didn't say anything. Probably because he didn't believe me. Who would, considering that I look like some sex kitten who knows all the tricks. But I had to make him understand.

"I started crying because…I don't know. My emotions are just out of control. Over the top. No one has ever worked so hard to make me feel good. Me. Nobody has ever put my pleasure first like you did. And…" I twisted my fingers together. I was naked on his bed but it was baring my soul that scared the wits out of me. "I'm so afraid I can't do as much for you as you've already done for me. I want to, but I don't know how."

"Don't worry about it."

I crawled over him and straddled his thighs. "Don't pull that tough-guy routine with me, Steve. Please don't."

He lay beneath me, rigid and controlled and I was sure I'd lost him. Then he said, very low. "It's the only routine that works for me."

Those hard-wrung words pierced my heart. I suppose I reacted on instinct. This was a man who needed so desperately to be loved. Though I wanted to take him inside me and give him the same glorious release he'd given me, that wasn't going to work. So I loved him in every other way I could think of. With my lips and my fingers I loved his mouth and throat and ears. His flat male nipples and hard rippling belly. I tasted his fingers and even rolled him over and rubbed my sweaty body up and down his back.

By the time we fell apart exhausted, I was painfully aroused, and for the first time in my life, truly eager to join with a man. But that wasn't going to happen. *Don't be greedy,* I told myself. *Don't be so greedy.*

"Damn." Steve breathed out the curse, but in a good way. He pushed himself to his side and I slid into his arms and threw one leg over his hips. His penis rested between my legs, a nonparticipant in our mutual passion. But I told myself I didn't need it. I hoped he didn't, either.

We slept after that and I didn't awaken until almost dawn when I felt him leave the bed. He hoisted himself into his chair and rolled to the bathroom. When he returned he sat there a long while until I opened my eyes to find him watching me.

I smiled, utterly content. "Hi."

"Where's this going, M.J., you and me?"

Uh-oh. Pushing my hair out of my eyes, I propped myself up on one elbow. "Isn't that what the woman usually asks? Men are the ones who supposedly shy away from the C word. You know, commitment." Then knowing he was in earnest I said, "Okay. The thing is, Steve, I think I started falling for you the first time you insulted me."

His expression didn't really change. But something in his eyes did. Or maybe I just sensed it. Either way, he kept on looking at me and said, totally deadpan, "When did I ever insult you?"

Who can explain joy? At that moment I wanted to roll around in his bed and wrap myself in joy, to wallow in it and laugh like a maniac drunk with it. Remembering now in the shower was almost as good.

Somehow I'd restrained myself and said, "Let's see, there's been so many. The first insult was when you asked me what I did to my car. The second came right after, when you asked if I'd put anything in it besides gas. And the third and worst was when you deliberately ignored every lure I threw at you. You acted like I was this sexless thing, like you hated me."

He shook his head and finally cracked a smile. "Never once did I think of you as a sexless thing, M.J."

His eyes ran over me, and even in the dim light of his bedroom I felt the hot touch of them like a caress.

"How can I make it up to you?" he asked.

I knew what he was implying, but there was something else I wanted even more than his clever hands and mouth on me. "Tell me that you could maybe fall for me, too."

It was the worst sin a woman could make with a man, especially this early in a relationship. But ours was not going to be a typical relationship. That much I already knew.

He stared at me the longest time before lowering his chin in a slow nod. "I think maybe I could."

Okay, it wasn't a declaration of love or even close. But coming on the heels of my first orgasm—and the hope for another one very soon—it was enough.

I smiled back at him and when he heaved himself onto the bed, neither of us pretended we were going back to sleep. With his mouth on my breasts and his thumb on my clitoris, he brought me to another momentous climax, and my fate was sealed.

His, too, though he didn't know it yet.

That's how I came to get home so late and though I'd avoided Bitsey and Cat so far, I knew I'd have to face them eventually. When I came out of the bathroom, they were sitting on my high, four-poster bed.

"You little tramp," Cat chortled, a huge grin on her face.

I ducked my head and opened the armoire, looking for clothes. But I couldn't hide my own happy smile.

"You, too?" Bitsey said.

"What do you mean, me, too?" I glanced from Bitsey's vaguely disapproving face to Cat's satisfied one. No vagueness there. "You and Matt?"

Cat leaped off the bed, grabbed me, and we jumped up and down like a pair of silly high school girls who'd each just lost her virginity.

"Okay, okay!" Bitsey threw an eyelet lace-covered pillow at us. "Y'all are depressing me. I have one question for you, M.J. Did he make you…you know… Was it good?"

I clutched the towel to my chest. "In a word, yes *indeed* it was good!" I gave the details, the short version.

Trust Cat to cut to the heart of things. "What about little Richard?" she asked. "Does it work?"

I opened my mouth, then closed it and sighed. "No. Not really."

They shared a look. "But he took care of her needs," Bitsey said.

"Yeah. But what about him? If he can't climax…" Cat

trailed off with a shrug. "How can you tell when he's satisfied?

I understood her concern because I'd worried the same thing. But Steve had avoided the question when I'd tried to bring it up, and I did the same thing now. "He said it was good for him," I told them, using his exact words. "And when he's covered with sweat and breathing so hard he can't speak, well, I tend to believe him." I didn't have any other choice.

Cat shook her head, still skeptical. "It's hard to understand, but if you're happy and he is, too—and like, why wouldn't he be?—then I guess it's got to be good."

Yes. It had to be good. But I wanted to convince them, and maybe myself, too. "The thing is, I've had regular sex for years and it didn't ever satisfy me. Never. Steve does something for me that's more important than the sex—though that part was pretty fantastic. I don't know, I think it's because…he needs me. He really needs me. Frank didn't need me like that, and Jeff sure doesn't. And remember, they both had all their working parts. But don't go thinking this was a pity fuck—that's what Steve thought I was doing at first— 'cause it wasn't. It's like that corny line Tom Cruise said in that movie. He completes me."

Cat groaned, but it was just for show. I knew she understood.

So did Bitsey. She smiled, as if she were my mother who loved me and wanted whatever was good for me. "It's finding love where you least expect it."

I shook my head. "I don't know about love. I mean, I thought I loved Frank, and look how that turned out. But… How I felt back then, it's nothing like how I feel about Steve. Oh, God, I'm so giddy I could just faint."

"Lack of sleep." Cat smirked at me. "What do you expect when you spent the whole night fucking."

"Making love," I told her. "I feel like I've really made love for the first time in my whole life. But what about you and Matt?"

While I dressed she told us how nice he'd been to her

mom, how he'd followed her in his car, and brought her home. And also how his son had showed up and all the questions she now had about Matt's wife's death.

"That kid is really hurting," Cat said. "And as much as Matt loves him, I don't think he can solve this problem."

"So you're going to talk to the boy?" I asked.

Cat rolled her eyes. "I don't know. I mean, I'd like to help him, but I don't know how to begin."

We were all on the bed. Bitsey lay on her back staring at the high ceiling while Cat and I sat cross-legged. Bitsey had gotten more and more quiet while Cat talked. Of course I understood. Cat and I had gotten the fellows we wanted while Bitsey was still caught between guilt and desire. Jack or Eddie.

Now, though, with the subject shifted to kids, she pushed herself upright. "That boy is the key to everything, Cat. He can make your relationship with Matt hell if he wants to, so getting him to like you is a smart move. The thing is, if you're just using him, he'll know. If you're going to help him, you have to really want to help him. For his sake, not yours."

The look on Cat's face would have been funny if the subject hadn't been so serious. I grabbed her hand. "You can do it, Cat. He's just a scared kid. Just...I don't know. Try to remember how you felt when your dad died."

"It's different," she said. "I hated my dad."

"He probably hates his mom, too," Bitsey replied. "At least part of the time. That's how I felt about my mother after she died. I hated her, and yet I wanted her back. I wanted her back so I could love her, and so she could really love me. It had always seemed like there was this wall between us. And since she had never tried to cross it, I always had to be the one. Only I never could."

Neither Cat nor I knew what to say. Bitsey had told us about her mother's suicide. No details. But the fact that it was a suicide revealed a lot.

Bitsey sat up and stared earnestly at Cat. "That boy isn't going to be the one to reach out for help. I didn't when I was that age. You probably didn't, either. No matter what kind of brick wall he puts up, you have to keep reaching out to him. And so does Matt."

She got off the bed, crossed to the window and pulled the lace panel aside to stare at the tops of the crepe myrtle trees. "I know now that my mother was mentally ill. But it was all so hush-hush back then. My dad never admitted it, at least not to us kids. But if I'd known…I don't know." She turned back to us, a wry grimace on her face. "Maybe it would have helped me. Maybe I wouldn't have been so mixed up about her. Maybe I could have mourned her better instead of being so furious with her."

"This mother-daughter thing. It's a bitch," Cat said. "At least M.J. gets along with her mother."

"Right," Bitsey said. "That's why she lives a continent away from her mother and visits so often. That's why her mother didn't bother to come to Frank's funeral."

They both turned to look at me and for a moment I couldn't speak. My mother and I get along fine; we never argue, and hardly disagree about anything. But we aren't close. I cleared my throat. "I told her not to come to the funeral. There was no reason, especially considering how Frank died."

"Funerals are for the living," Bitsey said. "Not the dead. She would have been there for your sake, not Frank's."

"But it would have been harder on me if she was there," I said, feeling defensive. "Anyway, I had you guys."

But all of a sudden I realized an unsettling truth about my mother—and about myself. "I married my mother, didn't 't I? I was Frank's trophy wife, but before that I was my mother's trophy daughter—"

The words caught in my throat and I was overcome by the most ridiculous urge to weep. I'm not the weepy sort but I had to bite my lip to hold back the tears. Cat reached over and caught my hand in hers. "You married your mother, I married my father. Twice. But Matt isn't my dad any more than Steve is your mom. Right?"

I squeezed her hand and nodded. "Right. He's so opposite

her—and Frank." The tears spilled over, but I was smiling. "Steve is so—" I shook my head, unable to find the words. "You'll see. When we go out tonight."

Tonight.

I think that word sustained us the whole day. Cat went shopping. Bitsey and I exercised. Afterward I got ready for a job interview at a new exercise studio in Faubourg Marigny while Bitsey went out for coffee with her sister-in-law. Meg put in a brief appearance, slipping out with little fanfare, as though she were feeling guilty about something.

When I left the house Mr. Charles and Doris were playing checkers on the back porch while Miss Ulna and Veronica watched the soaps.

When I came back Veronica had gone home early, Mr. Charles and Doris were nowhere to be seen, and Miss Ulna was making bread pudding.

"So how did your interview go?" she asked as I perched on a kitchen stool.

"I think I may have a job. He had another person to interview, but we hit it off really well. He said he'd call me tomorrow either way."

She pushed the nearly empty bowl at me and handed me a spoon. I hesitated, but not for long. "Oh, man, is this good," I said. "I'll need a job exercising all day if I keep eating like I have been lately."

"You gonna move in with that fella of yours?"

"Oh. I don't know about that." But I was lying and she knew it. Living with Steve, being with him every night like last night. Maybe I was rushing things, but I was convinced it could work out between us. I wouldn't invite myself into his household, but I meant to do everything I could to one day get an invitation from him.

CHAPTER 8
Are You In or Are You Out?

Bitsey

I was happy for Cat and M.J. Really, I was. But it was difficult not to compare their situations with mine. They were free to have sex with their new men without one iota of guilt. Meanwhile I veered back and forth like a drunkard on Bourbon Street: taking the plunge with Eddie versus waiting until I was free of my marriage vows.

And now, sitting in a tony coffeehouse with my elegant sister-in-law caused the pendulum to swing even wider. I could continue to believe in the sanctity of marriage and risk losing Eddie, or I could thumb my nose at it all. Tonight.

"You're looking very well, Barbara Jean," Virginia said, scrutinizing me after we air-kissed hello. She's the only one in the family who uses my given name. "I hope Jack and the girls are all doing well."

"They're fine. Just fine," I said. "Elizabeth is busy at school and Jennifer loves her new job. Just like her father in that regard."

"Just like her aunt Virginia," she said, smiling smugly.

I gave her a tight smile in return. God forbid any of my children follow in their aunt Ginnie's tracks.

"How are Trey and Angelica?" I asked.

As I sat through forty minutes of my niece and nephew's most recent accomplishments—Law Review for Trey, an MBA for Angelica—I was reminded of that old joke about Southern belles who never get angry or frustrated or ugly with other people. They only smile and say "That's nice" which, when the drawl is just right, actually means "Fuck you."

I didn't rejoin the conversation until she said, "Maybe I can convince her to go back to school."

"Who? Oh. Meg?"

"Of course, Margaret. Working in a coffeehouse, for God's sake." She waved one elegantly manicured hand at the uniformed staff behind the counter. "And one of those bohemian coffeehouses, no less. I tell you, Barbara—"

"Call me Bitsey."

That pulled her up short, for a moment anyway. "Bitsey is a little girl's name. Don't you think it's time you grew up?"

"I think I'm old enough to know what name I want to go by."

She stared at me, stunned, I suppose. I've never been one to stand up to Virginia and her unwavering pronouncements about how people should think, speak and act. It felt good to do it now, though. Very good. I folded my hands on the table and went on. "As for Meg, I have every confidence that she'll eventually find her way back to college."

Virginia pressed her lips together, never letting go of her smile, and I was reminded of a hyena, grinning the whole while it eviscerated its prey. "Well. I certainly hope you're right. I'm afraid laser surgery is beyond the means of counter workers."

"Laser surgery? What are you talking about?"

The hyena smile stretched with feral superiority. "She's going to need laser surgery eventually to get rid of the tattoo."

At my look of blank incomprehension she added, "Don't tell me you didn't know?"

I think my heart stopped beating. A tattoo. On my precious child's precious skin? I had to remind myself to keep breathing.

"I saw it yesterday," Virginia kept on, rending my heart into shreds. "I suppose she's been hiding it from you." The implication being that while Meg wasn't close enough to her mother to share such information, she was close enough to her aunt Ginnie.

I wanted to kill Virginia, to scratch her evil eyes out and leave claw marks on her botoxed, chemically-peeled face. But we were in a public place and I was never particularly good at extreme physical undertakings.

Then again, I had been working out.

"I'll tell you what," I said, somehow keeping my tone pleasant and steady. "The next time I see Trey and Angelica, I'll be sure to check them for tattoos. It's the least I can do for you."

I swear I could see the hairs bristle on the back of her neck. "I hardly think a Harvard law grad is going to fool around with tattoos," she bit out. "Besides, I have a very close relationship with both of my children."

I only smiled. "That's nice," I said as I gathered up my handbag. *Fuck you.* "That's nice."

Is it any wonder I called Jack the minute I returned to Daddy's house? I'd been shaken by Cat and M.J.'s happy news, stunned by Meg's betrayal, and torpedoed by Virginia's smug gloating over my child's latest fall. Glutton for punishment that I am, I guess I needed Jack to hit the ball out of the park for me.

It took a while for the cellular system to find him in Calgary. But the connection was so clear he might have been around the corner.

"Albertson." He always sounds like a drill sergeant when he answers the telephone at work, smart, driven, effective.

"Hey, it's me."

"Bitsey? Is something wrong?"

"Wrong. No. I…um…I just wanted to make sure you arrived in Calgary all right."

"Yeah. The flight was delayed due to bad weather, but we made it here eventually."

"We?"

"Yeah. Reggie Harris from marketing is helping me with the presentation."

Reggie. As in Reginald or as in Regina? He hadn't told me much about the office lately, and I hadn't asked. But my heart sank. First Margaret had betrayed me; now Jack probably was, too.

"I hope whatever it is you have to do goes well," I managed to say. "I think you should know, Margaret has apparently gotten a tattoo."

"A what!"

"A tattoo," I repeated in a tone much calmer than I actually felt.

"Son of a bitch," he swore, and I have to admit, it felt good to hear someone else give voice to the anger and frustration I felt.

"What's wrong with that girl?" he went on. "How come everything she does has to be the opposite of what we want for her? What does she think, that she has to break every fucking rule she sees?"

"Dear, sweet Virginia was the one who broke the news to me," I said. "You can just imagine how much she enjoyed that."

"And I suppose her kids are perfect."

"Sure they are. Just ask her."

It's funny how all of a sudden I felt connected to Jack in a way I hadn't felt in ages. We both loved our girls and neither of us appreciated Virginia's smug perfection.

"Do you want me to fly down there after I finish here?" he asked.

"What?" I'd heard him but his unexpected offer took me aback. "You, come here? But why?"

"To talk some sense into Margaret."

"And what, Jack? If she has a tattoo, she has a tattoo. You can't get rid of the damned thing."

I could hear him breathing, harsh, angry breaths. "Damned ungrateful spoiled brat," he muttered.

I felt better when we hung up. I'd had enough therapy to know I'd just handed my frustrations with Meg and Virginia over to Jack. Unfortunately, because of our brief parental unity, Jack had made it harder for me to cheat with Eddie. No matter how much I wanted to be with Eddie, Jack and I were still married, at least until we were divorced.

So I compromised by deciding *not* to decide about Eddie until tonight. The six of us would go out together, we'd have a wonderful time, and then I'd either go home with Eddie or come home to my father's house.

But if my path crossed Meg's before then, she was going to get a real earful from me.

Daddy and Doris went out to an afternoon movie, not so much to save on the price of a ticket, though Daddy complained bitterly about those damned Hollywood people and their highfalutin lifestyles. Mainly though, it was because neither of them could stay awake through an evening showing.

After they left it took me an hour and a half to try on all my clothes before settling on a pale blue linen skirt with a semifitted scoop neck blouse that drew attention away from my hips and waist and onto my cleavage instead. The one real benefit of being overweight is smooth, unlined skin, on my face, on my neck, and across my collarbones and chest. M.J. had taught me how to play up my assets, and tonight I meant to use every trick I'd learned.

By the time M.J. came home—with a job lined up—and Cat woke up from a long nap, I was mentally prepared for the coming evening, no matter which way it went.

"We're meeting the guys at the restaurant at seven, right?" M.J. asked as she watched me apply a sparing amount of dry wax to my hair. I was going for attitude tonight with a capital A.

From across the hall Cat called out. "I can't believe we're actually going on a triple date."

"For dinner only," I called back, meeting M.J.'s eyes in the mirror. "Afterward you two are on your own." I dared M.J. to say anything, but all she did was raise her brows.

Cat joined us in my room. "Hey, don't you have to get ready, too?" she asked M.J.

"I showered earlier and I have my clothes laid out. Besides, I don't feel like I have to primp so much for Steve."

"Be careful," Cat said. "That's what got Bitsey in trouble."

I gave Cat a sharp look. "What do you mean?"

"I mean, have you never noticed that a lot of marriages start to go bad when one or both people let their appearance go? Don't get me wrong, honey. I'm not blaming you for anything. But—" she paused and sighed "—I think a lot of us get married for the wrong reasons."

"Like sex?" M.J. said rather pointedly.

"All right, I admit I married my husband—both of them—too fast, probably because I was having such good sex. But we know that's not why you did it. So what's your excuse? Looking for security? A sugar daddy?"

"That was bitchy," I said in M.J.'s defense.

"I'm not trying to be bitchy," Cat replied. "Really, I'm not. I'm just saying that we don't always marry our soul mates."

"So now Matt's your soul mate," I said, rolling my eyes. "Gee, and all it took was a couple of orgasms."

Cat smirked "Now who's being the bitch?"

"You started it."

M.J. held up her hands. "Stop, you two. To answer your question, Cat, I did not marry Frank to get a sugar daddy." She paused. "But I probably was looking for a daddy figure. As for Steve." A small smile curved up the corners of her mouth. It happened every time she said his name. "He likes the girl-next-door look, and I'm glad he does. But getting back to Bitsey, no matter why her marriage isn't so great, she doesn't have to apologize for wanting to look good now."

"That's right," I said. "And what's your excuse for why your husbands cheated on you?"

Cat shrugged and sauntered over to the window. "They were drunken cheaters when I married them and they're drunken cheaters now that I'm gone." She turned around and picked up my bottle of Giorgio and sniffed, then smiled at both of us. "But Matt is not a cheater. Never was, never will be."

I thought about Cat's simple remark long after she and M.J. went to get ready. Matt wasn't a cheater. Steve probably wasn't, either. Was Eddie? Was Jack? More important, was I?

It must be one of those perversities of womankind that at the same moment when I was vacillating about Eddie, I looked the absolute best I had in at least ten years—if I do say so myself. The stars had aligned: a great hair day, no monthly bloating and an outfit that made my skin glow, my eyes sparkle, and my figure look ten pounds lighter than it actually was.

I was misting on my perfume when I heard footsteps clattering up the stairs. Quick youthful footsteps.

"Margaret!"

"Yeah?"

"Could you come in here?"

Given my clipped, imperious tone, she would have to be a fool not to know I was furious. Yet she clung to the illusion of innocence as she sauntered into the room. "What's up? Hey. You look good. Where're you going?"

I looked at her, such a pretty girl despite the rebel uniform of black tank top, black short skirt and chunky Doc Marten's. Her skin was pale and clear and her blue eyes were startling against the black eyeliner and dyed black hair. But all that gorgeous, vital youth made the presence of a tattoo even worse. A crime against nature. What reason did she need to decorate that flawless skin? To desecrate it?

I fixed her with an angry glare. "Where is it?"

"What?"

I shook my head. "Don't play stupid with me, Margaret. Where's that damned tattoo?"

Her mouth pursed—not as if she was afraid of my reaction, but more as if she was resigned to it. "Good old Aunt Ginnie."

"Yes, good old Aunt Ginnie. She couldn't wait to rub my nose in it."

Margaret paused. "Is that why you're mad? 'Cause she found out first?"

"No!" *Maybe*. "I hate tattoos, Margaret. When you're old and fat, it's going to look hideous."

"It's not that big, Mom. Look." She turned around and lifted the back of her tank top to reveal some sort of Asian design with a yin-yang symbol in the middle. All told it was about four inches wide and, strictly speaking, it was actually pretty. But on a kimono, not on the small of my child's back.

She looked over her shoulder at me. "Are you going to tell Dad?"

"He already knows."

She turned around. "Aunt Ginnie called him, too?"

"I called him. Bad news travels fast," I added, hoping I sounded sarcastic.

But she only shrugged one shoulder and tugged her shirt down. "Well at least that's over with."

"Over with? You think it's over with?"

"Yeah, Mom. I do. I'm twenty-two. I have a job. I don't live with you. I can pretty much do whatever I want."

"You live with your grandfather and if you think he'll approve—"

"He'll never know. Unless you tell him."

I was breathing heavy. "Was I not supposed to know? Is that why you told Virginia, so I wouldn't know?"

"I thought she was cool with it. And it's not like I planned to tell her. We were talking, you know, and she asked if I had any tattoos, and I told the truth."

That sounded like Virginia. Search and destroy. She should have worked for the CIA. I turned back to my dresser, hurt but with no outlet for my pain. "If you didn't want me to know, why didn't you just wait to get it after I went home?"

She shrugged. "I guess I thought I could keep it hidden. It's not like we see each other all that often."

Another innocent remark. Yet it hit like a punch in my gut.

I gave her one last look and it felt like a farewell to all the years that had led up to this moment. Goodbye, Margaret— Meg. Goodbye, Elizabeth and Jennifer and Jack.

Hello, Eddie.

I gave a vague wave with one hand, dismissing her, and turned away. "I love you, Margaret. But I hate that tattoo and I always will. Go on. I have to get ready."

She straightened up but didn't leave. "The thing is, you're making this all personal and everything. But it isn't about you, Mom."

No, it wasn't. But her words only made the knife twist deeper. Nothing in her life was about me anymore and I wanted to weep from the intensity of my grief. "Go," I said, making a big production of searching for the right pair of earrings.

This time she went. I found the earrings—I already had them on. I stared through misty eyes at my reflection in the wavy glass of the mirror. I looked good. Cute outfit, zaftig figure, spunky hair. But I felt horrible, as if I'd just been abandoned on an unknown island in an unknown sea, and my only choices were to starve to death or risk drowning.

When I left the room, I still wasn't sure which fatal choice I was going to make.

Cat

Bitsey looked outstanding. I already knew that, even without much effort, M.J. would be a knockout. So when I returned to my room, it was to do some serious work on myself. I already had my hair washed, blow-dried, set, sprayed and more or less ready to go. Between a cover-up stick, base, blush, eyeliner, eye shadow, mascara, lip liner, lipstick and powder, my makeup was more or less done, too.

I was hooking a pair of sheer hose to my brand-new red garter belt, a lace and elastic beauty with just enough sequins to not be trashy, when my cell phone rang. I'd stumbled across this kinky store called the House of Lounge which, according to the salesclerk, was a favorite of Cher, Melanie Griffith and Erin Brockovich. Besides the garter, I'd bought a matching bra, skimpy panties and the softest, silkiest, shorty kimono I'd ever seen.

I winked at myself in the mirror as I reached for my phone. Matt was getting it with both barrels tonight. "Hello?" I said, hoping it was him.

"Hey, Cathy Ann." It was Sissy.

"Hey, girl. You at work?"

"No, I do the day shift. Listen, I can't talk long, 'cause we're all going to a seven o'clock meeting. But I wanted to give you a heads-up."

"About what?"

"Hank's moving back in with Ma." When I didn't reply she went on. "Did you hear me?"

"I heard you, sis. I heard you. But what do you expect me to do about it? It's her house. If she doesn't want him there she should say so."

"But she won't."

"So now you want me to tell him to stay away, right? Like he'd listen to me any better than he listens to you?"

"I know. That's why I have another suggestion."

I knew what she was going to say. I knew it, and I wanted to hang up before the words could reach through the phone line to grab me. To strangle me. But like an idiot, I hung on, knowing what was to come but unable to get out of the way.

"If you could go stay with her awhile…" Sissy trailed off, waiting.

"No." I shook my head. "No. I can't do it. Why don't you do it?"

"I would. But I can't leave this place until the judge gives the okay, and that'll be another two months. It's up to you, Cathy Ann."

"No, it's not. It's up to Mom who lives with her. If she lets Hank in, that's her choice."

"Get real. She doesn't have a choice. Remember Dad? Do you, Cathy? Well, Hank's taller, heavier, and when he's drinking, even meaner. She's too old to oppose him." She let a beat go by. "But you're not."

No, no, no, no! "Did you ever think she might prefer Hank being there over me being there?"

She made a rude noise. "Yeah, right."

"You know what they say about two women in one household. It never works."

But she wasn't buying any of it. "Cathy, listen to me. This is important. Mom's health isn't that great, but at least she's not smoking or drinking anymore, and she's watching her diet. When I graduate from here, I'm moving in with her. All I'm asking is—"

"I'm only going to be here a week, Sissy. Even if I stay with her that week, Hank will move in as soon as I leave."

"I'm working on another plan for after you leave. Damn it, Cathy, you've been gone for twenty years. Is it so much to ask that you pitch in for one week? One friggin' week?"

"That's a cheap shot, and you know it. Let me give you a tip. If you want to stay sane—and sober—living with our mother is not the way to go."

"Yeah? Well, let me give you a tip. Running away doesn't solve anything. You ran away to California. I ran away to the bottle and the needle. But I'm facing my demons. Finally I'm facing them. I forgave Mom her shortcomings a long time ago, just like I hope other people will forgive me for mine.

"Look," she went on in a gentler tone. "I know what I'm asking isn't easy. And I'm not asking for an answer this very minute. But I am hoping you'll think about it, and fast. Take it from one who's been there, Cathy. That week could turn out to be one of the best weeks of your life."

After we hung up I tried to put our conversation out of my mind. But just like when she was a little girl pestering me, tagging along—bugging the daylights out of me—I couldn't shake her off. I pulled out a silk knit tank top the color of rich clotted cream and studded with a pattern of tiny pearls around the neckline. A taupe silk skirt, dangerously high Jimmy Choo slides and a pearl cuff on my left wrist gave me the look I wanted. Sophisticated but uncomplicated. Smart but sweet. And approachable.

I closed my eyes against my image and shook my head. What a facade. The only part I got right was the "approachable" part. Beneath that silk and pearl exterior I was a messed-up idiot with a mean streak. If it weren't for the fact that I was dying to see Matt again, I would have anesthetized myself with three stiff drinks, crawled into bed and thrown the covers over my head.

Just like Mom, I could hear Sissy's voice accusing me. Just like Dad and Bubba and Hank.

Shaking off the impulse I instead added another layer of mascara, put on a pair of dangly fake pearl earrings and struck a pose before the mirror. First things first, I told myself. Tonight I was showing off the man I loved to my very best friends. We were going to have a great time. Then maybe later I'd ask his advice about Mom and Hank Jr.

"Are we ready?" Bitsey asked, poking her head into my room.

"Yep. What do you think?" I twirled around.

"Very nice." She paused, her mouth twisted to one side.

"What?" I tried to see the back of my skirt. "I don't have a stain somewhere, do I?"

"No. You look good. You look great. It's just, I don't know." She took a breath. "Be nice to Eddie, okay?"

"Of course I'll be nice. What do you think, I don't want tonight to be absolutely perfect for all of us?"

"What I mean is, he can be pretty intense. And if he gets going on some topic, like oil companies or the meat production industry or something like that…"

"I won't say a thing," I promised her. "But as for Matt and Steve, I get the impression they're pretty macho, meat-eating guys. And don 't forget, Steve specializes in high-performance gas guzzlers."

At her look of consternation I added, "Hey, I'm sure everyone will be on their best behavior—including Eddie."

We got M.J., who looked relaxed and classy in a pair of black linen capris, a black silk weskit and a pair of flat black sandals.

As we came down the stairs Meg came into the foyer. "Whoa," she said. "Y'all look like *Charlie's Angels*, all set to kick some serious male butt." Her eyes landed on her mother, then flitted away. "Don't do anything I wouldn't."

As we got in the car M.J. looked at Bitsey. "Is something going on between you and Meg?"

"She got a tattoo and I don't want to talk about it."

"Okay."

We were halfway to Emeril's Restaurant before she said, "I appreciate you giving me a ride, Cat. I didn't want Eddie coming to the house again, making Meg suspicious about us."

M.J. and I shared a look. "Eventually she's going to find out," M.J. said.

"I know. But not until I want her to."

I watched her in the rearview mirror. "So you've decided to go for it with Eddie?"

She stared out the side window. "Probably."

When she didn't elaborate, I looked over at M.J. "So. She's upset about Meg, I'm upset about my brother." I gave them the two-minute rundown. "You got any problems you want to unload before we meet the guys?"

M.J. gave a very satisfied, very contented smile. "Nope. At this moment I am happier than I ever thought I could be."

"Hunh," Bitsey grunted as we pulled into an empty parking space on the street. "Rather than hating you for being so lucky, I'm going to think positive thoughts that maybe my misery and doubt can turn out just as well."

M.J. gave her a hug once we were out of the car. "That's the attitude. Now, here we go, girls. Stand tall, walk from the hips, tilt your chin up and keep a half smile on your face." She took a deep breath and showed us how. "And never forget," she added, "that you are a queen and you *own* the place."

You can laugh at M.J.'s beauty pageant tricks, but there's no denying they work. Looking good is only one part about physical appearance. The rest is all attitude.

So I lifted my chin, smiled and glided into the restaurant.

And when the first person I saw in the entry was Matt, and he couldn't take his eyes off me, my smile turned into a grin.

He didn't look half bad himself in that relaxed macho way he had—and he wasn't even in uniform. Oh my, was I going to make him a very happy man tonight.

He took my hand and we shared a quick but meaningful kiss. "Just you wait," that kiss seemed to say. "Just you wait." I wasn't sure I could.

Nearby a muscular man sat in a wheelchair, his expression guarded, until he spied M.J. Actually, his face didn't change at all, but something in his eyes—a spark, a light—changed everything about him. And it changed my apprehensions about him. He was crazy about her. For all the roadblocks he'd tried to erect between them, it was obvious he liked her big-time. But then, how could he not?

I introduced Matt to everyone and M.J. did the same for Steve.

"Eddie must be running late," Bitsey said, as gracious as if she wasn't in the least upset. But I could see she was. As far as I was concerned, that was strike two against the crusading lawyer. The first strike was him not thinking twice about trying to seduce a married woman. I could understand why he wanted to seduce Bitsey and also why she was tempted. But I wanted him to have more honor than that, and more concern for the feelings she was struggling with. I didn't want her jumping from the frying pan, meaning Jack, into the fire, meaning Eddie. She deserved better.

The waitress was just seating us when a gaunt-looking fellow with a shock of steel-gray hair breezed into the restaurant, waved off the hostess and made a beeline for us.

"Eddie's here," Bitsey said, lighting up like a sixteen-year-old.

Have I mentioned how beautiful Bitsey is? That understated blond girl-next-door beauty that's so easy to overlook. But there was no overlooking it when she was glowing with happiness.

"Sorry I'm late," he said after he shook hands with all of us. "Something came up at the office."

The words could just as easily have come out of Jack Albertson's mouth. But Bitsey didn't seem to notice and I decided not to notice, either. For tonight I would be nice, just like I'd promised.

And I was.

Of course, it was easy for me to overlook someone else's flaws with Matt there to distract me. I was like a honeybee overdosing on nectar. Every time his knee bumped mine, his hand stroked my arm, or his fingers smoothed a stray hair back from my cheek, I got another shot of that addictive sweetness and its underlying core of erotic promise.

I love my friends, but the truth was, I wanted to ditch them, their fellows and the restaurant. Then I wanted to drag Matt into some private corner—anything to appease the hungry little sex monster inside me.

"Are you finished with this, ma'am?" the waitress asked me.

Ma'am. That's one Southernism I hate, at least when it's applied to me. "Yes." I realized I'd barely eaten a thing. "It was delicious," I added. "But I guess I'm not that hungry tonight."

Bitsey also had hardly touched her meal. Meanwhile M.J. and the guys had cleaned their plates. I guess it was obvious who felt secure in their situations and who didn't.

"Dessert?" Matt asked.

You'll do. I shook my head. "Maybe a bite of yours." I didn't mean it as a double entendre, but when his eyes got this hot look in them, I didn't mind.

Dessert and coffee took forever. The guys debated the value of the V-8 engine versus the hybrid Eddie drove. But they kept it light, agreeing that law enforcement vehicles needed the power, that keeping old cars running was an important form of recycling, and that the new hybrids were great for urban use.

"The problem is kids today still want power," Eddie said. "The advertising machine makes sure of that."

M.J. smiled at him. "Do you have any children?"

He glanced from her to Bitsey. "As a matter of fact I do. Two."

Though Bitsey's only reaction was to blink, it was enough for me to know that this was the first time she'd heard about them. Of course I had to jump in. No way was he glossing over this subject. "Boys or girls?" I asked.

"One of each," he said.

"Isn't that nice. Matt has a teenage son," I added.

"A handful," Matt added.

"Aren't they all," Eddie said, then polished off his coffee.

"Well, weren't we a handful, too?" I asked.

"I always wanted kids," M.J. said. "But it wasn't meant to be. Fortunately Bitsey had three great girls. It's been fun watching them grow up."

"Especially Meg," I put in.

While the guys did the typical fight over the bill, Bitsey and I retired to the ladies' room.

"So?" she asked as soon as we were out of earshot. "What do you think?"

"I was going to ask you the same thing," I said, trying to avoid answering her. "Do you like Matt?"

"God, yes," she said, then with a giggle, added, "He's enough to get a girl thinking about alternative uses for handcuffs."

"Good idea," I said, escaping to one of the stalls. "About Eddie," I went on, safe from view. "I gather you didn't know about his kids."

"No," she said. After a moment she added. "All he said was that he was happily divorced."

"And you didn't ask about kids?"

"I figured he would mention them if he had any. I mentioned mine."

I wondered what it said about him that he hadn't mentioned them. But I wisely kept my mouth shut.

Not until we stood side by side washing our hands, meeting each other's eyes in the mirror, did Bitsey speak. "This is hard. Harder than I thought it would be."

"And we thought the teen years were complicated."

Some of the spark had gone out of her eyes, and though I was glad she might be seeing Eddie in a clearer light, I hated that once more a man was disappointing her. I caught her arm before we returned to the table. "Have you decided what you're going to do?"

She pressed her lips together in a thin line. "I don't know. What I want… What I want is to get a little drunk, just enough that my brain will shut down and let my body take over."

"Spoken like a college freshman. But what about the next day?"

She gave me a wry half smile. "I'll think about that tomorrow, Scarlett."

Back at the table there was no discussion about who was going where and with whom. By silent consensus we split into couples. Out on the street I asked Matt, "Are we going to your house?"

"Alan's spending a few days with his cousins in Houma." He backed me against his Jeep and with his arms bracketed around me, kissed me, long and deep. "Why don't you leave your car at Bitsey's house?"

A whole night with him. I was so overwhelmed with anticipation that it wasn't until we were both in his Jeep and approaching the Mississippi River Bridge that I remembered Sissy's phone call. "I need your advice."

"About what?"

"My insane family." I quickly explained Sissy's call. He knew she was clean and sober and in a halfway house. He also knew Hank Jr. was going to kill himself or someone else if he didn't change his ways soon.

"I think you should do it."

"Move in with my mother?"

He shrugged, then waggled his brows in an exaggerated leer. "It would be mighty convenient for me."

Though my heart started this crazy tap dance, I tried to sound cool. "Convenient? Is that all I am to you, convenient?"

When he turned to meet my gaze, his joking expression had fled. "No. Fact is, you're damned inconvenient, Cat. A complication. I ought to be glad you'll be leaving soon. But I'm not."

I want you to stay.

He didn't say those words, but I heard them all the same.

It took us another twenty minutes to get to his house, a largely silent twenty minutes. He received a call from one of his deputies and checked in with someone else. Then we drove under the oaks in his front yard, and parked next to the porch.

He turned off the car engine. "If it weren't for Alan, I'd ask you to move in here. But until that can happen, I think you should move in with your mother."

I swallowed hard. "Move in here? With you?" I laughed— nerves—and looked anywhere but at him. "Aren't you kind of rushing things?"

"Hell no. The way I see it, I'm making up for lost time."

The dog stood on the porch and barked. Just once. Get on with it, she seemed to say. Come inside or drive away.

If I could have, I would have barked, too. Go with him or leave. Try to make a go of it with Matt and his unhappy son, or return to my dehydrated life in California.

Life gives you lots of choices. Sleep in or go to work. Eat fat-laden French fries or a heart-healthy salad. Go home with a great guy or kiss him good-night. Every day you get to choose. But implicit in those choices is the knowledge that it's the only life you get, so choose wisely.

One of my several marriage counselors warned me, though, that some decisions that appear small—no big deal if you make the wrong choice—can change your life forever. Have one too many drinks, get in a wreck and die. Or worse, paralyze yourself…or someone else.

I pressed my fingers to my temples. My mind was beginning to spin out of control and I had to refocus. This was an important decision.

I'd come to Louisiana on a whim, a momentary impulse. But now I was here with Matt and if I wanted to stay, I could.

But did I want to?

I wanted Matt. I wasn't so sure about his kid, but eventually Alan would grow up and have his own life.

As for my family…

He opened his door. "Are you coming in, Cathy Ann?"

All of a sudden it was an easy decision. This was Matt and he was a great guy. I'd married Stan and Bill with far less assurance of success.

I smiled at him. "I'm coming. Just try and stop me."

CHAPTER 9
Should I Stay or Should I Go?

Bitsey

Eddie and I drove out to the point. When we were in high school it had been the place to park and make out. Even though it was a weeknight, things apparently hadn't changed.

He pulled into a spot facing north across the twenty-five miles of Lake Pontchartrain, and turned off the car. "Remember this place?"

I had kicked off my shoes and with the seat belt off I shifted, curling my legs up onto the seat so I could face him. "I remember." I laughed. "Only I'm not nearly as limber now as I was then."

"You look the same to me. Even better." Then he reached out a hand to curve around the side of my neck. "Come here."

I came. Actually, we met in the middle, leaning over the console as we kissed. Boy, did I miss bench seats.

Then again, there's always the backseat.

He had my blouse open, my skirt up—thank God linen is supposed to look wrinkled—before I even came up for air. We were halfway to the backseat before I caught my breath. "Eddie, wait. Eddie!"

He sagged back in his seat and turned pleading eyes on me. "C'mon, baby. Don't do this to me again. You're killing me."

I giggled. I might be scared to death, but it felt awfully good to have a guy so worked up over me. Me! Middle-aged, overweight Bitsey Albertson. As if she were standing outside the window, I could hear M.J. exhorting me not to think such negative thoughts about myself.

"Okay," I muttered to M.J. To Eddie I said, "It was nice of you to bring me out here. For old time's sake. But... But I'd be more comfortable—" *Do it, do it, do it.* "—at your apartment."

He had the car in gear so fast its lawn mower of an engine left ruts in the shell parking area. Once we were on Breakfront Road he put a hand on my knee and squeezed it. "You sure this time?"

I nodded. But there was one nagging question in my mind. "Tell me about your children."

He made a face at the windshield. "What's to tell? Their mothers aren't very accommodating about visitations so I don't see them too often."

Mothers, as in two mothers? That didn't sound good. "Do they live in New Orleans?"

"Yeah."

"How old are they?"

He took a sharp right onto Canal Boulevard and shot me a vaguely annoyed look. "I don't know. Roy's fourteen I think. Sarah just graduated from high school."

Fourteen I think? He didn't know? I pressed my lips together. That sure didn't say much about his involvement in their lives.

On the other hand, they were old enough to call him if they wanted to. The question then became, why didn't they want to?

"The teenage years can be difficult," I ventured.

"They're fine," he said. "I guess I should have tried harder to be a part of their lives, but it's hard to have a career like mine and at the same time deal with the constant demands of two psycho exes."

He must have realized how that sounded, because he gave me a self-deprecating grin. "Don't worry, they say a lot worse about me if I'm even one day late with the child support checks."

We made a left onto City Park Avenue, but I wasn't thinking about Eddie's bedroom anymore. I was visualizing an angry fourteen-year-old miniature of Eddie and a virtually fatherless girl going off to college. I understood that his causes were important to him. But these were his children.

"I'd like to meet them someday."

"Sure," he said. "Someday." But he didn't mean it, and I felt the first flicker of anger. I wanted to shake him until his teeth rattled. Didn't he realize how his absence hurt his children? No matter what his ex-wives felt about him, he was still their father. He needed to make sure that his kids knew he could always be counted on to be there for them.

Then I remembered. Eddie's father had never been around. Eddie had lived alternately with his mother or his grandmother. That spark of anger I'd felt fizzled out. With no example to learn from, how could he be expected to be a good father?

Feeling a little more kindly disposed toward him, I decided to put the subject of his kids aside for now. But I was keenly aware of the fact that nothing would have kept Jack away from his girls. Never. No matter how bitchy I was, or how bratty they acted. Of course, aside from dying too young, Jack's father had been a great role model.

Then we pulled into Eddie's driveway, lurched to a stop, and my more immediate dilemma jumped to the fore. We were here. I was going inside with him and this time I wasn't chickening out.

We were halfway up the stairs when I heard my cell phone's distinctive *William Tell Overture* imitation.

"Don't you dare answer that," he growled, then turned me around, pressed me against his door and kissed me until I thought I'd faint.

Once inside I dropped my purse, stepped out of my shoes, and was promptly whisked off my feet. Eddie actually picked me up, all one hundred seventy-five pounds of me. To his credit, he didn't drop me; to my relief, he put me down as soon as we reached the bedroom door.

"Are you okay?" I put my arms around his waist and rubbed up and down his back."

"Okay? No. But I will be. Very, very soon," he added, rotating his hips suggestively against my stomach.

An illicit thrill streaked from my belly to every other erogenous zone I had. Even a few I didn't know I had. I started to unbutton his shirt, then paused when once more my phone made its insistence known.

"Ignore it, Bitsey," he said, tugging my blouse halfway down my arms, effectively trapping them against my sides. He knelt and nuzzled my breasts. I'd never been so happy that I could afford expensive bras. It looked like an inconsequential scrap of lace, but it had elastic and underwire and spandex everywhere that mattered.

"You are gorgeous," he murmured, then bit down on my left nipple. I must have groaned; I know I turned all juicy inside.

He looked up and grinned. "You always were a hot piece of ass, Bitsey. And like wine, you've gotten even better with age."

The man had me melting. And then William Tell called one more time.

"Wait, Eddie. Just hold that thought, okay? while I get rid of whoever keeps calling me."

He muttered a very frustrated curse, then in resignation sat back on his heels.

Feeling awful, I scurried through the dimly lit apartment, following the siren call of electronic music. It was from my father's house. "Hello?"

"Mom? Mom, where have you been? I've been calling and calling!"

The utter panic vibrating in her voice made my heart stop. "Margaret? What's wrong?"

"It's Grampy. Doris called 911 and the ambulance is here."

"What?" Oh, God. My dad. "What happened?"

"I don't know. Doris thinks it might be a heart attack."

"Oh my God. I'll be right there. Wait— Where are they taking him?"

"I don't know."

"Tell them Touro. And have them call Dr. Hanson. Rex Hanson. You got that?"

"Yes. I'll tell them."

"I'll meet you there, you hear? Tell Daddy that I'm coming."

I don't remember anything about getting to the hospital except that it took too long. Aside from a muttered, "I hope he's okay," Eddie didn't say much, which was fine with me. I didn't want him to talk, just drive.

He let me out at the emergency room and I ran in. Doris, Meg and Ulna were all there. Meg grabbed me in a stranglehold. "How is he?" I directed the question to unshakable Ulna.

"He's hanging in there," she said, but her eyes were damp and she looked shaken to the core. That scared me more than anything.

She had her arm around Doris, and I felt a spurt of anger. Why was Doris here anyway? Why was she hanging on to Ulna when we were the ones who needed her—and Ulna needed us. But one good look at Doris's stricken face banished my unreasonable anger. No trace of the elegant aging Southern belle remained. She was a scared old lady who looked ready to faint, and all because she loved my daddy.

I reached a hand to her and squeezed it. "You better sit down before you fall down. Both of you," I added. After all, Ulna was no spring chicken.

"Did anyone call Chuck?"

"I called Miss Virginia," Ulna said. "She said she'd try to reach him. He's s'posed to be flying home tomorrow anyway."

Thank God. The only one who could control Virginia was Chuck, and even he wasn't always successful.

The four of us were clustered together, waiting for some word from the E.R. doctors when Eddie arrived. He strode over to us just as Virginia hurried up. I should have panicked at the thought of them in the same room; Virginia was nothing if not a bloodhound for any hint of impropriety—witness the tattoo incident. But since I was already in a high-blood-pressure state of panic, the sight of her was actually calming. If anyone could terrify the doctors into saving Daddy, it was Virginia.

I made brief introductions, then Doris gave the details to me, Virginia and Eddie. "We had gone to an early show. Then we came home and…" She hesitated and stared down at her knotty old hands. "We took a nap."

I shared a look with Ulna. I knew what kind of naps Doris took with my father. But instead of outrage, I felt a strange sort of irony. If he should die, at least he would have died happy.

Then Dr. Hanson arrived and though he only gave us a wave as he hurried to my father's cubicle, I felt better. He'd been Daddy's doctor for at least twenty-five years.

Five minutes later he came out to talk to us. "He's had a myocardial infarction. In laymen's terms, a heart attack. That means not enough blood got to part of the heart and some of the muscle there started to die. But don't panic. Because he's been on aspirin therapy and because he got here so fast, odds are he'll recover just fine."

I looked at Doris. Because of her quick thinking, she'd probably saved him. Any lingering animosity I felt for her disappeared. Forever.

"Can we see him?" Virginia asked.

"Eventually. Just hang on while we get him admitted. He'll be going up to ICCU."

Virginia followed Dr. Hanson to the admit desk while the rest of us collapsed back in the seats. I met Eddie's eyes, then leaned toward him. "Thanks for bringing me here. You don't have to stay, though. I'm going to stay until he's all settled in."

"Does anyone need a ride home?" he asked.

"We have Doris's car," Meg said. "And Aunt Ginnie's." She stared at him without smiling, then looked at me, and I knew—just like with Virginia—that the wheels of suspicion were turning. So much for Meg's hero worship for Eddie's position on animal rights. She turned away as he gave me a very circumspect hug. Once he left she looked at me through slitted eyes. "Can I use your cell phone?"

"Sure."

Her lips were pressed flat as she held out her hand. "Somebody needs to call Daddy, don't you think?"

She knew.

"Yes," I said, recovering as fast as I could. "And also your sisters."

She disappeared and suddenly my legs were weak. It took Ulna's deceptively strong grip to stop me from collapsing. "Sit down, child. Come on. We don't need to be worryin' about nothing but your daddy right now."

Her dark eyes were so filled with compassion that I wanted to weep against her bony old chest. Weep for Meg, weep for me and my marriage, weep for my father. The thing is, Ulna probably loves my father more than I do. Why, I sometimes don't know. But he loves her, too. He loves all the women who have kept his life on an even keel. His mother, my mother. Me, and Ulna and now Doris. Even Virginia held a special spot in his heart.

I sat with Ulna and wiped my face. "He's always been a ladies' man, hasn't he?"

She chuckled. "He sure enough has. So don't you be worrying so. Those nurses are gonna take real good care of him."

Virginia came back and sat down with a frustrated oath. "Lord, why can't they have some decent chairs in these waiting rooms?"

We watched as a couple came in with a crying little boy. Across the waiting area a girl with tattoos on both arms had curled up on two seats. We heard an ambulance siren, but it was going out, not coming in. And over it all that peculiar hospital scent hovered, an invisible cloud of alcohol, betadine and Pine-Sol.

Meg was gone almost a half hour. Only when Dr. Hanson

came out and said we could ride up the elevator with Daddy to ICCU did she reappear.

"Come here, baby," Ulna said, hugging her while I went to support Doris.

Daddy looked so small and frail, shrouded like a corpse on the gurney. His eyes opened several times, but after a few seconds they would close again, as if the effort to keep them open was just too hard. As we trailed him into the ICCU, Meg hurried up to the orderly. "Wait. Wait a minute. Come on, Miss Doris. Come give Grampy a kiss."

I wanted to cry at her sweet concern for the fragile old lady. Doris tottered up to my daddy's side and clutched one of his hands while she stroked his cheek. "Now, Charles. You be good, you hear? You do whatever the doctors say, and…and you get well and come home. And when you do, why, I'll make you one of those pineapple-upside-down cakes you like so much."

Was it the mention of his favorite dessert that did it? I don't know, but his eyes fluttered open and he looked straight at her. "You promise?"

All of us gave a collective gasp. Doris gave him a sweet kiss, right on the lips. "Of course I promise."

"Y'all can't come in here," a sturdy-looking nurse told us. "Here's an explanation of ICCU's rules, visiting hours and everything else." She handed Doris a flier. "You can come back in the morning at ten o'clock." Then she hit the wall button and the big door closed on her and on my father.

"All right," Virginia said, almost before the lock had clicked. "I think we need to keep a vigil, but not all of us. One person stays here, say for a four-hour shift. Miss Doris needs to go home now. Miss Ulna, too."

"I'll stay," I said before she could start making assignments. "I'll stay tonight until the morning visit."

She gave me a tight, satisfied smile. "Fine." She checked her watch. "I'll be back at ten. Do you want me to pick you up then?" she asked Doris.

"I'll bring her," Meg said. "Then I'll stay for the shift after you. Here." She handed me my cell phone, but she didn't meet my eyes. "You might need this."

Then they left, and their footsteps—quick clicks and soft shuffles—faded down the hall. Suddenly I was alone. I lasted a half hour, consumed by worry, guilt and self-loathing, before calling Cat. I was so desperate that when she didn't answer her cell phone I had the operator look up the home number for Matt Blanchard in Hahnville. He answered on the third ring. "Blanchard here."

"This is Bitsey Albertson. I'm sorry to call so late, Matt, but…but I need to speak to Cat."

"Okay."

I heard some muffled sounds and I cringed at my utter selfishness. But it was too late to back out now.

"Bitsey? What's wrong?"

Not a hint of impatience or annoyance in those brief words. Only concern. Of course I started to cry. Fear, guilt, shame. And more fear. "My dad—" It was all I could choke out.

"What happened? Damn it, Bits! Suck it up and tell me what happened."

It was just the tough love I needed. Between my sniffles and nose blowing, I told her what I knew.

"I'm coming over right now. What hospital did you say? Touro?"

"No. No, I don't want you to come here. I just…I don't know. I just needed to talk to you. Stay there with Matt. I mean it."

"Where's Eddie?"

"I sent him home." I sighed. "I'm pretty sure Meg has figured everything out."

"Oh, shit. What did she say?"

"She didn't say anything. But she's furious with me. She won't even look at me."

"I'm so sorry, Bitsey."

"The thing is, nothing happened between us. Again."

"But the intention was there, right?"

"Right." Once again I sighed. "Maybe this is a sign that Eddie and I aren't meant to be."

"Maybe. But I doubt it. I don't believe in signs."

"Yeah, well, we'll see." I flexed my neck, feeling every one of my forty-eight years, and more. "Look, I'm okay now. So you go on back to whatever it was you were doing."

"You sure you don't want me with you?"

"I'm sure."

"I'll come see you tomorrow. Okay?"

"Okay." I felt better when I hung up.

I tried to get comfortable on the Naugahyde sofa in the waiting room, and I suppose I must have eventually dozed off. Because when my cell phone rang, I jerked up, adrenaline pumping and heart racing.

"Bitsey?" It was Jack. "How's your dad doing?"

"Oh, Jack." Just like with Cat, at the sound of his voice a huge weight of despair seemed to lift from me. "He's hanging in there. Dr. Hanson seems optimistic. But…"

"What, hon? What?"

I swallowed past the gigantic lump in my throat. "He just looks so helpless. So fragile."

"Hey. Don't you underestimate Charles La Farge. He's a tough old bird. Always has been."

"I know." I wiped my nose with a soggy tissue. "But he's seventy-seven, you know? He can't last forever."

"Nothing lasts forever."

We were speaking about my father, but his words could just as well have applied to our marriage.

"Jack," I began, needing to say something about us. About me.

"I'm coming down there," he said before I could say anything.

"No!" I squeaked with alarm. "Don't do that."

"Of course I'm coming. Your dad's been damned good to me. Besides, I can hear how shaky you are. I've already made the flight arrangements. That's what I called to tell you."

This could not be happening. "But…but your meeting."

"We presented the proposal this afternoon. Reggie can do the follow-up meetings with their staff without me. It'll be good for him."

Him. Reggie Harris was a him. As satisfying as that knowledge was, it increased my guilt about Eddie. What would I do with Jack in the middle of my love affair with Eddie? Such as it was.

"I arrive around noon," he went on. "But don't worry about picking me up. I'll rent a car and come straight to the hospital."

I sat there on the brown Naugahyde a long time after he hung up, clutching the phone and staring at a magazine rack full of *Field and Stream*, *Reader's Digest*, and *Golf Magazine*. It was a mess and needed straightening up, but the thought of making order of anything seemed impossible to me.

Not until a pair of nurses passed through the waiting room on the way to ICCU did I blink and look up. "Is there a vending machine on this floor?"

"Down the hall in an alcove just beyond the elevators."

Leaving my shoes under the bench seat, I walked to the vending machines. The floor was cool and solid under my bare feet. Cool and solid, as I needed to be.

In the alcove I stared at the glass-protected selection that I'd convinced myself was the enemy. Chips, chocolate or cookies? I spent $2.25 on one of each and proceeded to eat them all. Inhale them all. Less than ten minutes later my stomach recoiled and I had to run for the ladies' room and throw up the whole lot, plus what remained of my dinner. This was beginning to be an unpleasant habit.

Afterward, shaking, teary and a pathetic, snotty mess, I trudged back to the waiting room.

I curled up on my side and for the first time in more years than I could say, I longed for my mother. But not my mother as she was. I wanted her cool capability. But with it I wanted Ulna's quiet comfort, Cat's solid protectiveness and M.J.'s sweet, unconditional love.

Feeling very sorry for myself, I pulled out a fresh tissue,

blew my nose and tried to get comfortable. Only as I was dozing off did it occur to me that maybe Meg—and Jennifer and Elizabeth, too—wanted the same thing in a mother that I wanted.

And maybe, like me, they'd never gotten it.

Cat

The relentless romantic buried somewhere beneath the scar tissue of my heart had me married to Matt, living in his old family home, going with him to Alan's baseball games and sharing laughs and intimate secrets over ice-cream sundaes forever and ever, amen.

The hyperrealistic cynic that ruled the rest of my being had our every tryst ending with a new, ever bigger crisis: an unexpected visitor, a police emergency, a levee break. Oh, hell, why not go for broke: a terrorist attack in suburban-rural St. Charles Parish.

I tried to tell myself that reality probably fell somewhere in the middle, but that wasn't particularly reassuring.

After Bitsey's late-night phone call Matt pulled me up against him. "Everything okay?" he murmured, his breath warm against the back of my neck.

"Um, hmm." How could it not be? His presence made everything okay. My mother. Hank. Even Bitsey's dad's heart attack. If Matt Blanchard had his arms around you and his breath was tickling your neck, for that moment the whole universe fell into place.

I slept, but I dreamed of me and Sissy and Hank and Bubba when we were just kids. We were sitting at the kitchen table of our old house, playing some game—cards or Clue or Monopoly, I don't know. Mom was cooking dinner and she was laughing and singing along with the radio. A Norman Rockwell moment.

Except that in my dream I could see out the window to where a man was drowning. My dad. There was a big pond right in the driveway and he'd driven into it and now he couldn't get out. Mesmerized, I watched his desperate struggles. I couldn't hear what he was saying, but I could imagine it: Help. I'm stuck. Save me!

But I didn't try to save him. I didn't move. I didn't say a word. Not to my mother and not to the other kids. I just watched his futile flailing, watched as he grew weaker and weaker. When these huge waves started battering him, I almost called my mother. But then the waves reared up high to threaten me, and I shrank back, petrified with fear for myself.

That's when I jerked awake, drenched with sweat and gasping for breath. For a moment I thought the wave had gotten me. But I wasn't drowning and I wasn't a scared kid watching my dad die and not trying to help.

But that's logic, and in dreams logic doesn't count. With my heart still thudding from fear, I eased away from Matt and slipped from the bed. Goose bumps rose on my damp, chilled skin, but inside I was hot and churning.

It's just a dream.

But it had been so real, and I knew what it meant. How could I not?

I grabbed a shirt—Matt's—and pulled it on, then walked through the dark house and onto the porch. The old dog raised her head and her tail thumped three or four times, but she didn't get up. She only stared at me as if I was crazy for being awake. Then with a great canine sigh she laid her head back down.

Somewhere a storm was brewing. The air was thick and still with that peculiar Southern heaviness that always precedes a good gully washer. It was quiet and I didn't know what time it was. Then the quick pelt of rain began, and in a matter of seconds the night rushed from silence to a wild, wet roar.

I stood in the open door, shivering when the wind hit, but reveling in the violence of it all. I wrapped my arms close to my chest. What had I said to Bitsey—that I didn't believe in signs and omens? Tomorrow I'd have to tell her that I'd lied, that I'd been trying to deny the truth all around me, to deny fate. But I couldn't lie to my conscience; my dream had made sure of that.

My father hadn't actually died of drowning. But for twenty or so years he'd drowned himself in alcohol. And now Hank Jr. was drowning the same way, and if I let him, he'd take our mother down, too.

"Crap," I muttered.

"Cat?" Matt's arms came around me like a saving anchor in a surging sea. "You okay?"

I leaned back against him and it felt so good. Another sign, I realized. "Yeah. I'm fine. I was just thinking about all the things I have to take care of if I'm moving back here for good."

His arms tightened and even through the shirt I could tell that he was naked. Naked and pleased by what I'd just said, if his arousal was any indication.

I closed my eyes, let my head rest back against his shoulder and smiled into the storm. Then I turned in Matt's embrace, circled his neck with my arms and on tiptoes kissed him fervently on the lips.

Hank and Mama and Alan were going to make our lives rough. But Sissy was okay, and M.J. was staying.

And now I had Matt.

Like the enemy it was beginning to be, the phone rang before eight o'clock. Matt and I were awake but lying in this sweet tangle, enjoying the ultimate state of drowsy contentment. He came alert on the first ring, just like when Bitsey had called last night. He rolled over and grabbed the receiver. "Blanchard here."

When he sat up, slow and deliberate, turning his back to me on the side of the bed, I knew it was important.

"When?" Then, "Was anyone hurt?"

He started dressing even before he got off the phone, and I figured I'd better do the same. He looked at me. "Alan was involved in an accident."

"Alan? Oh, my God."

"The injuries were minor, but the car is probably totaled."

My mind was scrambling to keep up. "Whose car was it?"

He grabbed a uniform shirt and headed for the bathroom. "His aunt's. Look, I'm sorry, but I've got to make a few calls and get down to Houma,"

"Of course. Of course." I searched for my shoes then followed him. He stood in the white beaded-board bathroom with its single overhead light, his arms braced on the lavatory and his head hanging low between his shoulders. He was the very picture of dejection, and my heart bled for him. "Are you okay?"

He didn't say anything but I saw him swallow hard. I realized then that he was scared, terrified for his son, and it broke some barrier inside me. It was my turn to embrace him from behind, to press myself against him and hope my love and support provided some small measure of comfort.

"He's not hurt," I murmured. "That's something."

"Yeah. I keep telling myself that. But he could have been. He was drunk, Cat. Drunk! What in the hell was he thinking, driving drunk in his aunt's car at six in the morning?" The anguish in his eyes was hard to look at. "Car theft, driving under the influence and underage drinking."

"Don't go there, Matt. Not yet. You and he will figure it all out later." I kissed his shoulder. "Look, do you want me to drive you to Houma?"

"No." He straightened, then covered my hands and pressed them more firmly against his chest. In the bathroom mirror our eyes met and held. "No. I think he and I need some time alone."

"Okay. How about this. You drop me at my mom's house. And after you get back with Alan, bring him over there. If Hank is there, maybe a glimpse of Alan's own future will scare some sense into the kid."

Two minutes later we were on our way. True to form, my mother's front door was open and the screen door unlatched. But instead of her in the recliner, Hank held that place of honor. He was skinny with a four- or five-day beard, and he wore clothes even a ditchdigger would put in the ragbag.

This was my baby brother, the cute, blue-eyed, baseball-playing charmer? Now, with his jaw gaping open, his foul-smelling snores and drool dried at the corner of his mouth, he looked like the bums we used to make fun of when they lined up outside the Ozanam Inn waiting for a free meal. My brother the wino.

He didn't even twitch when I walked by. I found Mom in the kitchen staring into a half-empty mug of coffee. When she looked up at me, I could swear I saw relief in her faded old eyes.

"Morning. Any coffee left?"

"Yeah. I'll get you a cup."

"Don't get up. I can help myself." The sink was clean. The counter was wiped down and a dish towel draped the dishes in the strainer. Hank must have just arrived.

I sat down across from her and for a moment we were silent. Then I sighed. "Do you want him here?"

"Hell no." She turned her cup around and around in an agitated circle. "But where else can he go?"

"He can go to rehab, Ma. Like Sissy."

"But he won't!" she spat out. "Maybe you can leave your family on the street, Cathy Ann, but I can't. I'm his mother. He's my child."

I wanted to shake her and yell back, but I didn't. "Rehab's not the streets, Ma. You know, we lost Dad, and Bubba's lost for now. Do you want to lose Hank, too?"

I could tell she wanted to argue with me, but instead she seemed to wilt. "Hank won't go to any hospital. I know him. He won't do it."

"No, he won't. Not until he's got no other choice. Right now he's got another choice. You."

She bowed her head into her two hands. "You been talking to Sissy, haven't you?"

"Yeah, I have. And you should, too. She's gonna make it, Ma. And if Hank would listen to her, he might, too."

She took a shaky breath then lifted her head. "I can't just put him out."

"I can."

She let out a bitter bark of laughter. "He's not gonna listen to you."

"Then I'll call Matt. He'll listen to the sheriff."

"Don't you dare call the law on him. I don't want another one of my sons in jail."

"Nobody does, Ma."

We sat for a moment and it was strange. I was back where I'd always vowed I never would be: in the middle of one of my dysfunctional family's famous dysfunctional messes. The same impossible problems. Everything I'd run away to college and California to avoid. But somehow it was different.

Or maybe I was different.

My mother's hands were knotted together on the table. On impulse I covered them with mine. "We can do this, Mom. I can move in with you and together we can kick Hank out. For his own good. So he'll have to go somewhere else to sober up. Sissy said there's this place like where she went, but for men. It's called Bridge House."

Her hands were cold. Poor circulation or was it just the air-conditioning? Beneath the thin stretch of her skin her bones felt as fragile as a bird's. How had my mother survived this long, given the life she'd lived?

She stared at me without speaking, but then something happened that I'd never expected. We had a moment where we connected. A mother-daughter thing. It wasn't something I'd ever experienced before, but I recognized it. Like falling in love the first time. Nobody had to tell you it was love. You just knew.

She was the first to pull back, sliding her hands out from under mine, and a part of me was relieved. We'd had our moment; I needed time to recover.

I placed my hands flat on the table. "Okay. I'm taking over the spare bedroom."

She went back to worrying her cracked coffee mug. "That won't help. He 'most always sleeps in the recliner."

"Not anymore."

She watched me rise and start for the living room. "Wait, Cathy. He can get kinda rough when he's drunk."

The hair on the back of my neck pricked up and I paused in the doorway. "He ever hit you?"

She drew back as if I'd just slapped her. But she didn't deny it.

I shook my head. "Yeah, I thought so. I guess he learned that from Dad, too. Actually, it would probably make things easier if he did hit me."

"Don't say that!"

"Matt's coming by later, so you see, we could take care of this today. Throw Hank's butt in jail—"

"No!"

"—and leave him there until he agrees to go into rehab."

Full of determination, I marched into the front room. Just to make things clear, I did not want to get smacked. Been there, done that, don't need to do it again. But I was in this strange, fearless mode. It had to be Matt. There's nothing like having John Wayne on your side, even if he was driving like a bat out of hell in the opposite direction.

So I clomped noisily into the living room—and got no response. I shook Hank's shoulder. Nothing. Then I screamed in his ear. Still nothing. The man was totally passed out, stinking up the place, and probably leaving street cooties on his mother's furniture. It really pissed me off.

"Ma! Come help me."

She hesitated in the doorway. "Leave him alone, girl. Can't you see he's passed out? Pro'bly won't wake up till this afternoon."

I smiled. "Good. Come on." I flipped the lever on the side of the chair and sat him upright. He started to slide off, which was perfect. I held him in place. "Go get a big towel and a pillow."

She frowned. "Where you taking him?"

"Just to the porch."

"The porch? Everybody's gonna see him there."

"So?"

That drew her up. We'd done a lot of hiding out in my family, keeping secrets, and my mother had been the ringleader in keeping up appearances. Maybe that's why I became a decorator, to hide people's ugly walls and ceilings—and lives—beneath a surface of beauty.

But this was no time for personal introspection. "You think the neighbors don't know he's a drunk, Ma? Everybody knows. Everybody."

Silent, she turned away. But when she returned she had a big blue towel and a pillow.

It wasn't that hard to move him. Even in the doorway when his head slid off the pillow and bounced over the threshold, he didn't wake up. We pulled him off to the side so he didn't block the door. I didn't tell Ma, but I put him where I knew the sun would soon get him. Sunburned, shoeless, hungover and homeless. The more miserable he was, the more willing he might be to give rehab a chance.

Once inside, we locked the door. While Mom turned up the television and wiped her recliner down with a damp cloth, I called Bitsey.

Meg answered. "Mom is in the shower. She just got home from the hospital. So far Grampy's doing okay."

"She was there all night?"

"Yeah, but she's going to bed once she's cleaned up. Aunt Ginnie's at the hospital right now, and I'm going over there with Doris right after lunch. M.J. said she's going to visit him tonight, and I guess Mom will go back once she wakes up."

"Is M.J. there now?"

"No. She started her new job."

"Okay." I looked around my new bedroom with its dark paneled walls and single hanging light source. I was leaving an antebellum mansion furnished with gorgeous antiques for this? "Look, just tell your mom to call me."

"Where are you?"

"At my mother's."

"But your rental car is here."

"I know. The thing is, I've decided to move in with my mother."

"You mean, like, for good?"

"Just until I decide what I want to do."

"Do you want me to bring you your car? Then you could drive me back here."

"That would be great." Unless Hank woke up while I was gone. "On second thought, maybe not. But thanks for the offer. I'll get over there later and pick up my stuff. Meanwhile, tell your mom I love her. Okay?"

She was quiet a moment, then said, "My dad's coming."

I thought, oh shit, but what I said was, "That's good."

"Yeah," she said in this slow, dark tone. "I think it's very good."

After I hung up I considered Meg's words. *Very good.* Bitsey was right, the girl definitely was suspicious about Eddie.

I stripped the bed—who knew how long it had been—and stuffed the sheets into the washer, worrying about Bitsey because it was easier than worrying about the insane decision I'd made. If Hank wouldn't go to rehab I was going to kill Sissy for dragging me into this.

When my phone rang I dumped too much detergent in, then slammed the washer shut and ran for my purse.

"Bitsey, thank God. How's your dad? How are you?"

"I don't know. I'm so tired. Daddy's going to be okay, at least it looks that way. But…"

She trailed off, but I knew. "When does Jack arrive?"

I heard the sharp intake of her breath. "Noonish." Again she paused. "I'm pretty sure Meg figured out about me and Eddie."

"Yeah, I think you're right. But how?"

"He brought me to the hospital and she was already there." *Bad decision.* "Do you think she told Jack?"

"I don't know. I don't think so. God, I wish I'd never started this. I should never have come back for the reunion."

"But it's good you're here, for your dad's sake."

"No. I think it's all payback. God's been sending me messages, throwing roadblocks in my path with Eddie, but have I listened? No. I've been hell-bent on screwing the man and now my daddy's in the hospital."

"Come on, Bitsey. The two are not connected."

"But maybe they are. I don't know. I'm just so tired and confused. And now Jack's coming."

"Go to bed and get some rest, okay."

"Okay. But wait. Where are you? Still at Matt's?"

I gave her a brief update.

"Your brother has hit your mother before? Cat, please don't rile him up."

"Don't worry. Matt's gonna throw his ass in jail."

"I hope so. I like him. Matt," she clarified. "Are you staying here for him or for your mother?"

"I didn't say I was staying."

But I knew I would if he wanted me to. After Bitsey and I hung up I busied myself around the house, and when there were no more floors to sweep or throw rugs to shake, I called my office. The roaming charges were going to kill my phone bill. At what point should I change to a New Orleans service?

Oh, the tortures of personal relationships in the digital age.

By noon I was ready to jump out of my skin. I watched the midday news, then made bologna sandwiches for lunch. Bologna on white bread. Now there was a throwback to my childhood.

By one, Hank was full-faced in the sun, sweating buckets and turning a nice shade of pink. "We should move him," my mother said.

"No. He's alive and breathing. That's good enough for me."

"But people who get bad sunburns are more likely to get skin cancer."

"Ma! The man will die of liver disease long before skin cancer can get him."

She went back inside; I sat on the front steps in the shade, and tried not to think about what I was doing. I had a good job, a great apartment and a life in Bakersfield, such as it was. Without M.J, though—and maybe without Bitsey—what real reason did I have to stay there?

The sky slowly turned cloudy and around two o'clock it started to rain. Ten minutes later Matt's Jeep splashed through the rutted driveway. Alan was with him. Matt didn't get out right away. Last-minute discussion with his son, I guess. I wouldn't want to drop by my dad's old girlfriend's house, either, if I'd just had a night like Alan had had. Then I glanced at Hank, still out cold, his feet getting wet from the angle of the rain, and the irony of it struck me with giddy hilarity. Here was Alan twenty years from now. I hoped the kid got the similarity.

Matt got out and hurried up to the porch. He glanced at Hank, then gave me a hug.

"You okay?" I asked.

"Yeah." Then he shook his head. "No."

"Is Alan coming in?"

"I don't know. He's ticked off that I didn't bring him straight home."

I grimaced. "He doesn't like you dating me."

Matt looked at me. "I've dated other women since Julie died."

Julie. Had I ever known her? "Did he like any of them?"

He shrugged. "It never lasted very long, so he never met any of them."

That was interesting. "Eventually he'll come in, if only to use the bathroom. I'm guessing he's got a pretty bad hangover."

Matt snorted. "I'd say he deserves it. He damned well gave me a headache."

Not a minute later the passenger door opened and Alan stalked up, shoulders hunched and hands shoved deep in his pockets. He looked pretty bad. Pasty skin with a nauseous green cast. I decided to go the Southern hospitality route.

"Hey, Alan. How're you doing? Would you like something to eat? If you're hungry I can make you a bologna sandwich."

Already he wasn't too happy to see me. But the mention of bologna made his lips pucker. He looked like he wanted to puke. "No thanks."

Then he caught sight of Hank and came to a stumbling halt. His eyes grew huge. "Is he dead?"

I smiled, not a nice smile. "Not yet. But a couple more drunks like that and he will be. And if he comes around here bothering my mother again, I may have to kill him myself. Sure you don't want that sandwich? Or maybe some cereal and milk?"

His face contorted and abruptly he whirled away. At the first sound of his retching I opened the screen door. "Looks like my work here is done," I murmured to Matt.

He gave me a wry grin and followed me inside. "By the way, something else has come up that you need to know about."

He had quit smiling. I knew it couldn't be about Hank, at least not yet. And Bubba was already in jail. "What do you mean? Something with Alan?"

"Something with your friend M.J."

His expression had turned serious. Coplike. I got this sick feeling in my stomach. "This is law enforcement business, isn't it?"

He nodded. "There's a report out from California about a stolen Jaguar that could be headed to Louisiana."

"What? That is so not true. God, I hate Frank's kids. It's her car. Her husband gave it to her at least ten years ago. She did not steal that car, Matt. She didn't."

"Someone in Bakersfield says otherwise." He paused. "Auto theft is a felony, Cat."

"Oh, my God. You're not serious, are you? This is a civil dispute, not a criminal matter."

"You're probably right. But that's for a judge to decide. The way it stands now, if that car should turn up in St. Charles

Parish, I'd have to impound it and report it found to the Bakersfield police."

St. Charles Parish. That fast my fear dissipated. The Jag was in Steve's shop in Orleans Parish—as Matt well knew.

"Okay." I smiled up at him, then stretched on tiptoe to kiss him. "Okay. I'll let her know. But I'm pretty sure you'll never see that car in your jurisdiction."

"Good. But tell her that if I got the notification, the New Orleans Police did, too."

I was getting hit with problems so fast my head was spinning. But this was M.J.'s problem to tackle; I had Hank et al.

To my surprise my mother had a pitcher of iced tea ready and a plate of Big Sixty Lemon Creme cookies on the table. Matt sat down, but while she fussed over him, I went back to the porch with a glass of water for Alan.

He was leaning over the porch rail, braced on his arms with his head hanging down.

"You look just like your dad."

He stiffened and straightened up. But he didn't look at me. "Everybody says that."

"I don't mean your hair or your eyes. I mean you look like he did this morning when he got the phone call about you. He stood just like you are now, head hanging low, and so dejected and miserable that I wanted to hug him."

He shook his head, a slight movement, but I saw it.

"I brought you a glass of water in case you want to rinse your mouth out." I set it on the rail next to him.

After a moment he took it, rinsed, spit and rinsed again. "Thanks."

"You're welcome."

I saw his Adam's apple bob up and down, but this time I was pretty sure it was from emotions.

"I'm glad no one was hurt," I said, settling gingerly into a green plastic chair with a serious crack up the back.

He shrugged. He didn't want to talk with me, but I wasn't letting him get away that easily. "My brother Hank—" I gestured to the other side of the porch "—after three DUIs his license got pulled. He's been in a lot of fender benders, but luckily only one bad accident."

Alan glanced at Hank, then at me. "He kill anybody?"

"Almost. He drowned my mother's car in a bayou. The only reason he didn't drown with it is because some good Samaritan risked his own life to save him."

Hank chose that moment to snort and roll over. When his face clobbered the bottom of the railing, he shot up, cursing like it was a contest and he was determined to win.

"Son of a bitch!" He stared wildly about, then spying me and Alan, pulled himself to his feet and scowled. "Who the fuck are you?"

I gave him a huge, fake smile. "Aren't you going to welcome me home, little brother?"

His brows drew together above his eyes and he rubbed his mouth with the back of one hand. It threw him off balance and he had to grab the railing to stay upright. "Cathy Ann?"

"Yeah, Hank. Cathy Ann," I said in a sweet, singsong voice. "I've come home to live with Mama."

He stared bleary-eyed at the door as if he wasn't sure where he was. then it must have come back to him because he swung his head around to stare suspiciously at me. "How'd I get out here?"

I crossed my arms. "You were hogging Ma's favorite chair. And since I'm in the spare bedroom now, the only place left for you to sleep is on the porch."

It took a few seconds for my words to sink in and I braced myself. He looked so much like our father. Stooped and gaunt, but with a wiry strength.

I had to remind myself that this was my brother, not my dad, and that the red-hot rage building in me was misdirected toward him. I'd been afraid of my dad and I'd hated him, too. But I wasn't afraid of Hank. I pitied him and I really did want to help him.

Boy, had I changed!

"I know what you're doing." He growled the words. "You're trying to kick me out of my own house."

I smiled, this time utterly sincere. "It's Mom's house, not yours. But yes, you've got it absolutely right."

Hank's hand tightened into fists and fury emanated off him like heat waves off an August sidewalk. Beside me Alan shifted. A part of me was sorry he had to witness this. But maybe it was for the best.

"No way," Hank vowed, advancing on me with unsteady steps. "Just 'cause you're back doesn't mean you're runnin' things around here."

"Actually, it does," I said, filled with reckless bravado. "I'm moving Mom out of this dump and into a condo with me." I was? "It's time for you to start taking care of yourself, Hank. Past time."

"Fuck you! I take care of myself!"

"And doing a pretty good job of it, I see. Bathed lately?"

He came at me faster than I expected. Fortunately Alan had teenage reflexes and pulled me aside. When Hank hit the porch rail it took only a little nudge from Alan to tip Hank right over the edge.

"Shit! Shit!" he screamed. "You bitch. You fucking bitch!"

It was only a four- or five-foot drop and his fall had been buffered by an overgrown bush. Problem was, it was a prickly holly bush and he was upside down in it.

"Help me. Help!"

"What on earth?" Mama came tearing out of the house. "Hank?"

"No, Mom. You go inside." I steered her back through the front door while Matt vaulted the rail to get to Hank. Meanwhile all the excitement had gotten to Alan's stomach and he was back to puking over the other side of the porch.

All in all, not a particularly serene day for my family. But when had it ever been?

CHAPTER 10
On the Brink

M.J.

Only twenty-four hours had gone by since our triple date. But when Cat met me and Bitsey for dinner at Rockie's, it seemed like each of our worlds had been turned upside down. Jack had arrived earlier, and tonight he would be sleeping in Bitsey's room as if nothing in the world was wrong between them. Cat had come to collect her things and was moving in with her mother. As for me, it seemed I was now a felon liable to be arrested the minute my car rolled out of Steve's shop.

That's why the three of us had ditched everyone else tonight. We needed a powwow, some good Grits Girls time. Maybe together we could figure out our crazy lives.

I watched as Bitsey picked listlessly at her shrimp salad. "Have you eaten anything today?" I asked. "Because you're looking thinner by the day."

"Nothing like disaster to affect your diet," Cat said, pushing her plate of linguine aside. "Hold the food, bring on the dessert." When I gave her a pointed look she grimaced. "Sorry. But I've had a rough day. I *need* a hot fudge brownie à la mode."

"Same here," said Bitsey. "But at the moment I don't think my stomach could take it. You know, life was easier when I could eat myself into oblivion."

"No it wasn't." I waved my fork at her. "You and food were like me and exercise—and me and alcohol," I added when

Cat raised her brows. "We went overboard with them as a way of stuffing our emotions."

"Stuffing our emotions," Cat echoed. "What, you've already found a therapist?"

"I've been reading," I admitted. "Steve doesn't talk about his feelings. You know, about being in a wheelchair. So I thought I could read up about it, try to see the situation from his perspective."

And despite my previous assurances to them, I was still worried about whether or not he truly enjoyed sex under the circumstances. But I wasn't ready to bare those fears to anyone just yet. First I had to figure out why, when I'd never really enjoyed regular sex before, I now obsessed constantly about doing it with a man who wasn't able to.

Bitsey sighed and propping her elbows on the table, she rested the side of her head in her hand. "I don't think anyone can ever really understand anyone else. I mean, do we really even understand ourselves?"

Cat looked at me. "I think Bitsey needs to go first. Her situation is the diciest."

"Fine with me," I said. Especially since I didn't want to talk about me.

Bitsey snorted. "Diciest. There's an understatement." Again she sighed. "All right. I called Eddie and told him Jack was in town. Actually, I told his voice mail, which was good because if he'd asked me to come over or to dump Jack or anything else, I would've done it." She ran her hands through her messy hair, making it messier and cuter. Bitsey was looking better every single day.

"What about those kids of his?" Cat asked.

"That's right," I said. "When are you going to meet them?"

"Probably never." Bitsey shook her head. "I don't think Eddie is that involved in their lives."

"That's not good. Kids need their dads," I said. "I spent most of my childhood wondering why my father dumped me and my mother. That's probably why I married Frank. At the time I needed a father more than I needed a husband."

Bitsey gave me one of her sweet, motherly smiles. "Yes. We know. The question is, does Steve fill the role of father or lover?"

"Oh, no you don't," I said, shaking my head. "We're dealing with your issue first. Remember?" Then I couldn't help it. I giggled, leaned toward them and whispered, "Lover."

It was true. Despite my worries about how much satisfaction he was getting, the orgasms he gave me were amazing. All day I'd moved around in this warm glow, as if there was a golden halo of light around me. I wanted to move in with Steve and be with him every minute of the day and night.

But I knew that was the wrong approach. First of all, Steve was nowhere near that level of commitment. Second, I knew we needed to meet as equals. I'd had one marriage where I'd been totally dependent, but never again. Already I had a job. Plus I'd found two different apartments that might work out for me—both on the ground floor and wheelchair accessible. I was thinking about our relationship from his perspective, not just mine.

I felt as though at forty-one years old I'd just graduated into the world of adults. And it felt good.

Trust Cat to burst my optimistic bubble. "Is he gonna freak out when he finds out the Jag was stolen?"

I straightened up. "I'll let you know after I tell him." I turned back to Bitsey. "Okay, about Eddie."

Bitsey made a face. "Like I said, I called him this morning and he hasn't called back. Not that I really expected him to."

"What do you mean? The least he owes you is to return your calls," I said. "What about the reunion? Is Jack going with you?"

"We haven't talked about it. He and Meg are at the hospital with Daddy and Doris." She glanced down at her fingernails. "Jack was very sweet when I saw him." She paused. "And Daddy was so happy he'd come." She looked up at us and in the uneven restaurant lighting I could see the shimmer of unshed tears in her eyes. "He and Daddy have always gotten along so well."

It took hard, cynical Cat to express the vague question circling around in my head. "Are you sure you really want to leave Jack? Never mind about Eddie. I'm talking about you and Jack."

Bitsey grimaced. "You know, Cat, you've got your nerve asking me that. You're the one who never has anything good to say about Jack. Now you want me to stay with him?"

Unfazed, Cat leaned forward, her face earnest. "What I want is for you to be with a man who appreciates you, who loves you and worships the ground you walk on."

Bitsey leaned back in her chair. "Right. That's a pretty tall order for any man."

"That's true," I put in. "But maybe Jack loves you more than you think, Bitsey. He may have been taking you for granted, but that doesn't mean he doesn't love you."

"The question is," Cat said. "Are you sleeping with Jack tonight? You don't have to answer me now, but tonight…" She trailed off expectantly.

Bitsey shifted in her chair. "I'll probably sit with Daddy tonight."

I shook my head. "I heard Meg say she was staying."

Bitsey rolled her eyes dramatically. "God, that girl is messing up everything."

"Gee, I wonder why." Cat smirked.

I laughed. "Isn't that what Meg said we were doing after we'd kidnapped her? Maybe she's returning the favor."

Bitsey stared intently at us. "Do y'all think Eddie's the wrong guy? I need the truth." In the background Aaron Neville's falsetto warbled, and the aroma of garlic and cheese filled the busy room. We might have been sixteen-year-olds again, eating at a pizza place and worrying about guys. I looked at Cat; she looked at me. As one we turned to Bitsey.

"I don't know," I said.

"He might be," Cat said. "Look, why don't you seduce Jack tonight—don't interrupt, just listen," she said when Bitsey's mouth dropped open. "Seduce him or at least try to. If you can't do that, well at least you'll know whether Jack is the wrong guy."

Bitsey had this look on her face, like, "You can't be serious."

But not me. "Wow. That is such a good idea."

"Thank you, thank you." Cat gave me a mock bow. "Now. My turn."

"I don't get to respond to that preposterous suggestion?" Bitsey snapped.

"No," Cat and I said in unison. I turned to Cat. "Your turn."

She brought us up to date on the Matt-Alan, Mama-Hank mess. Despite her attempt at pique, Bitsey was too nice not to give her total attention to Cat's problems. "No matter how I try to avoid liquor and the people who overdo it, I always get drawn back in," Cat finished.

"Maybe that's your role in life. Wait, wait," I said when she got this skeptical look on her face. "You wouldn't let Bitsey argue, so you can't, either. The thing is, I'm beginning to think that the reason we go through life so unhappy all the time is that we're usually fighting our true nature. I mean, look at me. My whole life has been about my appearance. Naturally everybody I've attracted has also been all about my looks. Except you guys, of course." I smiled at them, filled with such intense love for these two friends of mine. "Even then if I hadn't been from New Orleans like you two neither of y'all would have given me a chance, either."

Bitsey nodded. "Though I'd like to think otherwise, that's probably true. You have to admit, M.J., the way you look is pretty intimidating to most women." She patted my hand. "But once we got to know you, we loved you."

"And I love you, too. Both of you." I grabbed their hands and like a living, breathing river, our friendship ran its gratifying course through us, friend to friend to friend. It was one of those lovely family moments that I'd longed for so much as a child. My mother and I had never managed to create that warm, wonderful, no-strings-attached bond, and neither had Frank and I. But with my Grits Girls...

"Anyway," I said when the overwhelming emotion moved out of my throat. "I've decided my calling is to look past the surface of people and help them be the best person they can be and find contentment with who they truly are. That's what I want for me and for Steve and for y'all, and everyone who comes through my classes."

Bitsey was smiling when I finished. "If you're half the inspiration to your students that you've been to me, you'll do great."

"Yeah," Cat said to her. "Except that you're not all that content with yourself right now."

Bitsey gave her an annoyed look. "At least I'm working on it. What are you doing?"

"She's not running from her family anymore," I put in before Cat could snap back. "Right?"

Cat closed her mouth, then after a moment nodded. "Right. For some reason I missed out on the addiction gene that curses everyone else in my family." She glanced down at her plate. "You know, while I was dosing Alan with Pepto-Bismol, it occurred to me that if I hadn't run away from my family, he could be my son. Mine and Matt's."

She looked up at us and I think I saw deeper into Cat's soul than I ever had before, down to the places she'd hidden from us for all the years of our friendship. "So you're staying here," I said. "For good."

She straightened up as if to contradict that last part about "for good." Then she sighed. "Yeah. I think I am. No more running for me—no matter what happens with Matt. Because I'm staying for me and my mother and Sissy and even Hank. And Bubba if he ever gets paroled. And maybe for Alan, too."

The waitress came for our dishes, then brought dessert. One hot fudge brownie à la mode with three spoons. Bitsey didn't look very happy, but it wasn't about the dessert. As we dug in she looked at us over her loaded spoon. "If y'all are staying here, then I'm staying, too. I only managed the last few years because you were both there to prop me up. But with my girls gone and you two gone, there's no way I can stay in Bakersfield with just Jack."

"Don't be too quick to run away from your troubles, " Cat warned her. "It may feel right at the time, but it ain't necessarily so."

I scooped up a big drippy spoonful of brownie. "Here's to facing our demons," I said.

Cat was quick to join me in the toast; Bitsey was slower. "Here's to true friends," she added, "who help you face those demons." Then we ate, practically licking the saucer clean.

In short order we waved Cat off as she drove back across the river to her mother's house. Bitsey and I went home to her father's house where she dropped me off then went on for a visit with her dad.

As soon as I reached my room I called Steve. I needed to tell him about my so-called stolen car. "Hey, there," I said when he came on the line.

"Hey yourself. You home?"

"Yes. We had dinner, just us girls."

"How's Bitsey's father doing?

"Better. He doesn't need surgery and he'll probably come home by Monday."

"That's good."

There was a quiet pause and in the background I heard Aerosmith singing "Amazing." It made me smile. "Listen," I said. "I need to talk to you about something. Can I stop by the shop in the morning?"

"Why don't you tell me now?"

"No, I'd rather us do this face-to-face." As soon as I said the words I realized how bad they must sound to him. "It's not what you think. It's not about us."

"Then what?"

Just two words, but his voice sounded so flat I knew he was already imagining the worst: I'd gotten him in bed; now I was breaking it off. "It's not about us," I repeated. "I'm still staying here and dating only you, even if I have to chase you down to prove it every single day."

Another pause, then he said, "I don't get you, M.J."

A giggle bubbled up and I knew we'd be okay. "Oh, you get me, all right. You get me just as often as you want to get me."

I heard him chuckle. "If that's true, why'd you dump me for your girlfriends tonight?"

Grinning ear to ear, I started to undress. "I can't let you get a big head or get overconfident about me, you know. Then you'd be taking me for granted, and I could never stand that."

"I can pretty much guarantee I'll never take *you* for granted."

Music to any woman's ears. I kicked off my shoes and unzipped my pink silk capris. "So. Whatcha doing?"

"Reading. Talking to you."

"I see." I closed my eyes. "What are you wearing?"

Like a dimmer switch turned without warning onto high, the electricity between us crackled through the phone line. "Not much," he said in a voice that made my insides go all hot and juicy. "What about you? What are you wearing?"

"Oh, just about the prettiest lavender bra and panty set you've ever laid eyes on."

I heard something that sounded sort of like a growl. "Lace?"

"Mm, hmm. With little rosettes at the base of the straps and just beneath my navel."

"Is it a thong?"

"Yes," I lied. Men might love thongs, but as far as I was concerned, they were a twenty-four-hour wedgie. But if it made him happy...

Another growl. "Do your nipples show through the lace?"

I'd never understood the idea of phone sex. Until now. We ended up spending over two and a half hours on the phone. I didn't hear Bitsey come home, or Jack. All I heard was

Steve's voice dark with passion, hot with urgency, hoarse with need.

When we finally said good-night and I lay in a sated stupor, it occurred to me that I was going to lose my deposit if I took an apartment with a one-year lease. Because even if Steve and I did this every night, it would never be enough. I needed his presence, his touch and his love to fulfill me.

His love?

For a moment my euphoria dimmed. I'd made huge strides with Steve, but it was mostly all physical. Gaining his love—his trust, his faith, his commitment—was a different kettle of fish.

"Don't think about that today, Scarlett," I murmured into the sultry night air. The worst thing I could do was to rush things with Steve.

After all, I had all the time in the world.

Bitsey

Jack left his rental car for Meg and rode with me back home to Eighth Street. I drove—my weak attempt to show that I was in control, which I wasn't. It made my gesture even less effective when he didn't even attempt to take the driver's side.

There had been no mistaking Meg's intense observation of my every interaction with her father. Whether or not she'd told him her suspicions about me and Eddie, I didn't know. I toyed with the idea of asking her, but in the end I chickened out. It was one thing for me to interfere in her life. After all, I would love all my girls no matter what they might do. But I wasn't so certain Meg would feel as generous toward me.

I'd felt her eyes watching us leave the ICCU. Even now, back at Daddy's house, empty except for me and Jack, I felt her presence still. Well, not her presence exactly. More like her thoughts. No child of any age ever wants her parents' marriage to end.

Jack headed for the bar in Daddy's study. "Damn. What a bitch these last few days have been. You want a drink?"

"No." Then I reconsidered. "Actually, yes." If I was going to follow through on Cat's suggestion I needed something to fortify myself. "Make it a double."

He raised his eyebrows at me. I've never been much of a drinker. To his credit he just poured the drink without comment.

I hooked my purse on the newel post and kicked my slides off in the foyer, then followed him into the study, watching him as if I could figure out what he knew—or didn't know—if I just paid close enough attention. It was odd, because as he poured Southern Comfort for himself and rum and Coke for me, I realized that I hadn't really looked at Jack since he'd arrived. I'd been avoiding him, both his physical touch and the even more intimate touch of his eyes. Guilt, of course. If he looked deep into my eyes I was afraid he'd know the exact extent of my transgressions.

Why wasn't he that transparent to me?"

He bent to open the small refrigerator built into the mahogany paneled wall, and my gaze narrowed. Was it my imagination or had he lost weight?

"Here you go." He handed me the tumbler. "Two ice cubes, just like you like it."

"Thanks." I retreated to a big wing chair, confused even more.

He took the chair opposite mine. "How are you doing, hon? I know this has been hard on you."

I nodded and sipped, and nodded some more. "At least he's improving."

It was his turn to nod. "When's that reunion of yours?"

"Tomorrow, I think. Wait. What day is today?"

"Friday."

"Okay, then. It's tomorrow."

"I brought a suit so I could go with you. If you want me to," he added.

"I don't know if I can go now." *Coward!*

"Sure you can go. Like you said, your dad's improving."

I took a big gulp of my drink. "All right." Then, because I was feeling tongue-tied around the one man I should least feel tongue-tied around I said, "Have you lost weight?"

He grinned. "You noticed."

"Of course I noticed."

"When I saw how well you were doing with your diet—"

"And exercise."

"Diet and exercise, " he amended, "I decided I'd give it a try."

"Why didn't you say anything about it?"

He shrugged his shoulders. "I was afraid I'd fail at it. Gain weight instead of lose it."

I tilted my head at him. Jack fail at something? Since when? "How much have you lost?"

"I don't know. About ten pounds or so. How about you?"

"I haven't weighed myself in a couple of days. Over twenty, though."

He nodded and his eyes ran over me. "You are looking very good, Bitsey."

I felt a flush of heat climb into my cheeks. Jack and I hadn't sat and talked like this since I don't know when. "Thank you." It was all I could think to say.

"I missed you," he went on, shocking me further still. "I think this is the longest we've ever been apart."

"Not really." I blurted out.

"No. I'm pretty sure we've never been apart more than a week or so." His gaze sharpened when his smile didn't receive an answering smile from me. "What?"

It was time to be honest with him, I told myself. I polished off my drink, set the glass down and took a deep, fortifying breath. "The truth is, we haven't exactly 'been together' in years."

I thought he was going to argue, but instead he sighed and said, "I know." It scared the dickens out of me. This sort of personal honesty was not something Jack and I had shared, not in a long time.

I frowned down at my hands. "We've been living parallel lives. Side by side, but not really in sync."

"Yeah. I know."

Like a chasm the silence stretched wide between us, not a wall, but a black, bottomless canyon that threatened to swallow anyone who tried to cross it. But I had to try, so I took another shaky breath—then straightened up in the chair. "Jack—"

"No. Let me go first."

He leaned forward, planted his elbows on his knees and gripped his hands together. His knuckles were pale with the tautness of his grip. "I should have changed my plans to come to the reunion with you in the first place. I've been letting work take over my life and just ignoring what's going on between us. Or what *isn't* going on between us."

Wow. I had not expected that. "Okay." My voice sounded a little shell-shocked, but not nearly as shell-shocked as I felt. "What made you come to that realization?" I finally asked, steeling myself for Meg's version of me and Eddie—not that her version could be much worse than the truth.

Jack stared down at his hands, then back at me. "You know that guy I was with, Reggie Harris?"

"No. I've never met him."

"No, you haven't. Well, he and his wife are getting divorced. For no good reason that I can see. They do okay financially. Their kids turned out fine. They're just like us in a lot of ways, married a long time. The thing is—" he cleared his throat "—I don't want us to turn out like them, Bitsey. I don't want to be a fifty-year-old divorced guy."

I was too flabbergasted to say anything, so I got up and fixed myself another drink. Jack still wanted me. But so did Eddie. I felt dizzy with the knowledge, for in my wildest dreams I could never have come up with this scenario. The problem was, I had to decide what I wanted and I didn't know what that was.

I turned to face him and said the first thing that came into my head. "Have you ever cheated on me?"

He recoiled as if he'd been punched. "No!" Then a telling flush crawled up his face and his eyes veered away from mine. "Almost."

Almost. Oh, God. Like a slap in the face I was hit by betrayal first, then rage and finally by guilt. A fast and furious succession of emotions that left me trembling.

I cleared my throat. "Almost?"

He shook his head. "I'm not going to lie to you. I thought about it. But I didn't do it." His eyes were damp with feeling. "I swear, Bitsey. That's as close as I came."

I sank back in the chair, strangling the glass in my hands. "I…came close myself."

His mouth gaped open and I had to suppress a hysterical giggle. He hadn't expected that.

"Close?" He croaked out the word. "When— No." He put up one hand. "I don't want to know the details."

The silence stretched out again, but for some reason the chasm didn't look so wide or deep or scary. I took a little sip of the rum and Coke, then put the glass aside.

"So," he said. "Where do we go from here?"

I took off my earrings, one at a time. "Why don't we go up to bed?"

"To bed?"

Our eyes met, and it was the strangest thing. I wasn't afraid of what would happen anymore. If it didn't work with Jack, there was always Eddie, and if it didn't work with Eddie—and in a moment of clarity I realized that it probably wouldn't—I would manage on my own. I had friends. I had family.

We walked up the stairs side by side. That's one of the nice things about grand old houses. They need constant maintenance; they're thankless money pits. But you can walk up the stairs side by side with your husband, bumping shoulders, touching hands, your steps in sync in a way they never are in modern houses with their narrow halls and single-file stairs.

It occurred to me that my marriage might not have drifted

so badly if we'd lived in this house—or at least one that had wider stairs leading to the bedroom.

I didn't have to tell Jack which room was mine. Just as I didn't have to tell him how important my father was to me, or how upset I was about Meg's tattoo. But when he turned on the overhead light, I turned it off and turned on a lower wattage bedside lamp instead.

I looked a lot better in clothes these days, but unless my instincts were way off, we were about to get naked.

His arms came around me from the back and after he kissed my neck he rested his head on my shoulder. "God, I've missed you."

"That's hard to believe."

"I know." He kissed my neck again and I could feel his heart beating against my back. It felt good. Intimate.

"The time you came close," he said in a low, still voice. "Was it recently?"

I stiffened, but I answered honestly. "Yes. The time you almost, was that recent?"

He shook his head. I felt the back-and-forth brush of his face against my hair. "All right. No more questions," he said. "Except for one." His arms tightened around me. "You aren't staying here, are you? You're coming back home with me."

I turned in his arms, looped my arms around his neck, and stared into his anxious eyes. "That depends on you, Jack."

I meant it to be a teasing come-on, but I obviously failed because his brow creased in concentration. "What does that mean? You're taking no responsibility for the state of our marriage? It's all on me? That's not right."

"What are you saying? That you feel taken for granted?"

"Well, yeah. A lot of times I do."

"Well, so do I," I snapped, starting to get angry.

"Then let's stop doing that to each other." His hold on me shifted and all of a sudden he was dancing me around the room. My husband the nondancer, and with no music, either.

That fast he turned what could have become a fight into a seduction. He started to hum; I started to giggle. If this trip back to New Orleans had been all about high school, this moment was rooted in college. My dorm room in Acadian Hall at LSU, answering a furtive knock to find Jack had snuck into the all-girls dorm. We'd danced to a very sexy Barry White song.

"Remember that night?" Jack murmured.

"Oh, yes."

Then he kissed me and I swear I felt as giddy as the girl I'd been back then. Scared, excited. Sneaking around in my daddy's house, not that Daddy would disapprove. God knows he was still horny enough.

"Will we still be doing this when we're in our seventies?" I asked.

"Damned straight. When I go, I want it to be in bed with you."

I laughed out loud. "Oh, thanks. Just what every woman wants, a dead husband on top of her."

He waltzed me back to the bed, rubbing up against me with each delicious step. "Don't worry, honey, I'm not dead yet."

And he wasn't. If anything he'd turned back the clock twenty-five years. I don't know if it was his ten pounds, my twenty-plus, or just the scare our marriage had gone through. Maybe it was all three. I know I put a lot more effort into pleasing him than I had in a long, long time.

Afterward, with the air in the bedroom feeling twenty degrees hotter than when we first came in, we lay side by side in my girlhood bed, exhausted, sated and feeling pretty damn good.

"I love you, Jack," I said, not looking at him because I felt ashamed for ever doubting that fact.

He rolled over to face me. "I love you, too, Bitsey."

Our eyes held in the comfortable loving way they used to. "Do you think it's this house?" I asked.

"Do I think what's this house?"

"I don't know. This romantic interlude."

He grinned and he looked like a cocky college kid again. "You mean the great sex?"

I grinned right back. "Yes. The great sex. Is it this house? I mean my mother worshipped the ground my father walked on. Doris obviously feels the same way about him."

When I didn't go any further Jack continued, "And now you obviously worship the ground I walk on."

Before I could react with an appropriate show of outrage, he rolled on top of me and kissed me breathless. "You do, don't you? I know I worship you." The teasing light disappeared, to be replaced by complete earnestness. "My life is nothing without you, Bitsey. If I ever let you think otherwise, I'm sorry. I'm sorry."

Without going into further detail, suffice it to say that I slept better that night than I had in months. Years. When I finally awakened, the sun was bright against the window sheers and the phone was ringing in the hall. I heard a voice, Miss Ulna, I supposed. But it was Meg who poked her head in our room.

"Mom. It's Aunt Ginnie for you."

I struggled upright, holding the floral-print sheet up to my chin. "Is Daddy okay?"

"Yeah," she said. "He had a good night."

"Thank God."

I thought Meg would smile when she saw her father beside me but instead her brows furrowed down in a scowl.

I gave her a pointed look. "Tell her I'll call back in a few minutes. Okay?"

She ducked out without answering. I slid out of the high bed, feeling wondrously sore and wondrously relaxed. My father was fine and my decision was made: I was staying married. Now I only had to worry about Meg—and whatever it was Virginia wanted.

Daddy was sitting up in bed when Jack and I arrived at the hospital. We'd passed Virginia in the lobby glued to her cell phone. My brother, Chuck, was sitting in the only chair, reading the *New York Times* while Daddy read the local sports page. He looked up and grinned when he saw us, then threw down the paper. "Damn summertime. Baseball's not nearly as much fun as football."

"That's probably a good thing," I said, kissing his cheek. His skin looked leathery, but it felt fragile and very thin. He looked better, though. Much better.

"Hey, Bitsey girl," Chuck said, standing to greet me. I hadn't realized how happy I'd be to see him, and he must have felt the same because we clung to one another.

When we came apart he smiled down at me. "I heard you were looking good, but damn I'm not sure I would have recognized you if you hadn't been with Jack."

No need to dwell on the multiple ironies of that remark. He meant it innocently enough as a compliment so that's how I took it. It was even sweeter given that his source of information had to be Virginia.

"So what are we going to do with him?" I gestured to Daddy.

Naturally Daddy puffed up, as much as a one-hundred-twenty-six-pound seventy-seven-year-old man can puff up when he's naked under a wrinkled mint-green hospital gown. "*Do* with me? *Do* with me? Nobody's *doing* anything with me."

"Don't worry, Daddy. I'm not shipping you off to Château de Notre Dame. Just yet," I added. That was the Catholic retirement home most uptown Catholics chose when they couldn't live on their own anymore. "You've still got Miss Ulna and Veronica."

"Damn right."

"But you might want to consider someone for at night," Chuck suggested. "Just in case."

"I already found somebody," he said. At our twin expressions of surprise he grinned like a bad little schoolboy.

"You have?"

"Who?" Chuck asked.

"I bet it's a woman," Jack put in, winking at my dad, who winked back.

"Doris!" I exclaimed. "She's moving in with you?"

"If you mean are we shacking up, hell no," Daddy replied.

"I've decided to make an honest woman of her. We're getting married," he added when I just gaped at him.

"Hey, isn't that something," Jack said. "That's great!" He shook Daddy's hand and slapped him on the back—but gently, I noticed. All the motions of macho congratulations, but toned down.

I followed Jack's lead and gave Daddy an effusive hug, and so did Chuck. But though Daddy's unexpected announcement took center stage, I found my focus turned more on Jack. He seemed so different. Or was it me? Had I just been blind to his good points all along?

Maybe I'd been too unhappy with myself to see them.

Maybe I'd invested so much time and emotion on the children that when they'd grown up, instead of focusing it back on him, I'd given it all to my girlfriends.

Not that I would ever give up Cat and M.J. I stared askance at Jack. I wanted our marriage to work, but if the cost was giving up my friends, it was a cost too high to pay.

Slow down, I told myself before panic could set in. I hadn't given up Jack for the girls or the girls for my friends. Why worry that I had to give up my friends for Jack?

It occurred to me then that perhaps the enduring problem of my life was not the people in it, but how I balanced them. Maybe it was time for a new balancing act. I'd begun to do that with food and exercise, and with great results. Why not do the same with the people I loved?

"We'll just have to get used to having a stepmother," Chuck said, draping an arm across my shoulder. "Right, sis?"

"Right." I hugged him back. "Not that it will be very hard to get used to her. Doris is a lovely person. Perfect for Daddy."

After a while Chuck left. Jack and I stayed with Daddy until Ulna and Doris arrived and more congratulations were exchanged. It was all lovely and pleasant except for the two clouds hanging over my head. Eddie and Meg would have to be dealt with one way or the other. After all, tonight was the reunion.

"Excuse me a minute, will you?" I asked Jack. Outside,

standing with the smokers, sweating in the one hundred and ten percent humidity, I called Eddie. Of course I got his machine. "It's Bitsey," I began. "I just wanted you to know that my father is doing fine." I cleared my throat. "I'll be going to the reunion tonight with Jack," I went on. "Since he—"

"I thought you might," he said, picking up his end of the line. I heard him punch a few buttons and the recorder stopped. "So," he said. "Is that it? We're done?"

I sighed. "Oh, Eddie, this is not how I planned things. But yes, I guess that's it for you and me. But tonight…I hope we can still be friends."

"Sure," he said. "No problem."

No problem, I thought when we hung up. No problem for him if I stepped out of his life. After all, he stepped out of mine a long time ago. And more recently he'd stepped out of his kids' lives.

No emotional fuss for Eddie over them, so why should I expect any emotional fuss over me?

Feeling unaccountably angry, I called Cat.

"He's trying to save face," she told me. "What did you want, for him to beg and plead for you to choose him?"

"Yes. No." I shook my head. "Not really. You're right. I'm an idiot."

"Look, Bits, you go tonight and have a wonderful time. With Jack."

"You mean it, Cat? I mean, really. Are you okay with me and Jack patching things up?"

"Yes. If that's what you want, then that's what I want, too. But only if things really do change between you two."

I smiled at my smoke-bound companions. "They will," I assured her. "They already have."

CHAPTER 11
Bed Head & Boob Jobs

Cat

Hank had slunk off sometime during the afternoon, but only when he got it through his pickled brain that I would not let him back in Mama's house. He was furious, cursing us at the top of his lungs. Two neighbors came out to see what all the hubbub was about, but they didn't interfere. At least Hank wasn't stupid enough to mess with the sheriff. He sat under a Japanese plum tree for a while; he might even have fallen asleep. But at some point when Matt and I were inside, Hank Jr. disappeared.

All during Hank's carrying on, Mama sat in the kitchen, not crying any visible tears. She wasn't much for crying except for herself. But inside I knew she was a wreck. She'd shredded a pile of paper napkins and drank at least a gallon of coffee.

Meanwhile Alan had cleaned himself up in the bathroom and eaten some cinnamon toast my mother fixed for him. They were an odd pair, my beaten-down mother and Matt's hungover son.

"That's what comes of letting liquor and drugs rule your life," Mama was saying when I came in. "His daddy ruined his life—and mine. And now Hank Jr.'s life isn't worth a pile of crap."

"Yes, it is, Mama. If he does like Sissy he can get his life together again."

She sent me a ferocious scowl. "And how's he gonna do

that if he can't even come to his own mother's house when he's sick?'

"He'll go to another house," Matt said. "I called a friend of mine in Orleans Parish and we can get him in Bridge House. If he wants to go."

"He won't do it," she muttered.

"Then he can keep on making a public nuisance of himself and I can arrest him for public drunkenness. I guarantee, any judge in this Parish will send him, signed, sealed and delivered to Bridge House if that's what I suggest. Either way, he's done sponging off you, Mrs. Arceneaux."

"Actually, Ma, arresting him would be a good thing. Sissy explained that if a judge puts Hank Jr. in a rehab program he can't just bail out. He'd get the help he needs."

At least she listened. My mother would never admit she was pleased by any of this, but I could tell she felt a certain relief, if only from having the decision taken out of her hands.

"How long will he have to stay there?" Alan asked.

Three sets of eyes swung his way.

"A year or so, " Matt finally said. "That's what most judges rule."

"It would have saved us all a lot of grief—and him, too—if the first time he was arrested for DUI he'd been sent there." I took Mama's hand. "He's lost almost twenty years being a drunk."

Alan's brow was pulled together in one dark line. He got up from the table and walked to the back door, his back to us. "At least he's not dead."

I felt Matt stiffen. The mother thing, again. Alan's mother, Matt's wife. Though I didn't want to hear any of this, I knew it needed to be aired. I took a breath. "You miss your mom, don't you?"

He didn't answer.

My mother stared at me and shook her head. But I frowned and nodded mine. She rolled her eyes. Then to my amazement she said, "It don't seem fair how some people live in spite of all the foolish, downright stupid and mean things they do, and others, well, they're not so lucky."

Alan didn't move a muscle, but from where I sat I saw a tear roll down his cheek. "Life isn't fair, " he muttered in a gruff voice. "That's what everybody says, and it's true."

My turn. "The worst part is, some of us take forever to figure out we're making the same mistakes over and over again. Did I tell you, Alan, I've been divorced twice. Twice. It's embarrassing. I'm forty-three years old and I'm only just now realizing that I've been dating and marrying and divorcing men just like my father—and my brothers. Pathetic, isn't it."

He shot a sharp glance at me. "My dad isn't like that."

I smiled at him. "Yeah, I know. I think maybe I'm finally wising up." My smile faded. "I hope you don't mind us dating."

He shrugged. Teenage speak for "it doesn't matter to me—or at least that's what I want you to think."

"I've decided to move back here," I went on. "A long time ago I ran away from my family." I said this part to my mother. "But it's time I came back. So I guess you'll be seeing a lot of me. All of you."

Matt caught my hand in his, and my mother, seeing his movement, smiled at me. It did something to me, knowing she approved of me and Matt and my return home. Alan glanced at us, then away. I wanted to help him, but I wasn't sure I could. For all I knew, despite his momentary toleration of me, my presence could be reopening all his wounds about his mother's death.

Matt pushed back from the table, but before he could say he had to leave, my mouth opened and I blurted out. "I think I'm going to start going to Al-Anon again. You know, to help me learn how to deal with Hank, and to figure out why I keep messing up all the time myself. I hope you'll come with me, Ma. And Alan, I know there's this group called Alateen. If you want to go I'll—"

"I don't need that! Just 'cause I got drunk, it doesn't mean I'm an alcoholic!"

"No, no. Alateen's not about whether *you* drink. It's for teenagers whose parents have drinking problems."

He scowled at me. "What's the point? My mother's dead."

"Yeah. And you're still dealing with the aftermath. You're still grieving."

We left it at that. Matt had to go in to the office, but he promised to call me later. I walked him out to his Jeep. "I'm going over to Bitsey's for a while, to help her get ready for her reunion tonight. While I'm gone, could you have somebody drive by here every so often, just in case Hank tries to get back in?"

"Sure." He gave me a quick kiss, then sighed. "I hope leaving Alan at home alone isn't a mistake."

I watched them drive away until the Jeep merged into the traffic and was gone. Then slowly I surveyed my mother's little kingdom: scraggly lawn, rusty truck, broken-down furniture on the front porch. Was she ready for a condo in a swanky development? Was I? It occurred to me that I needed to quit my job, break my lease, pack up my apartment and drive my car to Louisiana. Not to mention finding a job.

But not today, I told myself. Today I would settle Mama down, then go see Bitsey and M.J. Monday was soon enough to deal with all the rest.

Bitsey was in a tizzy, but happy despite everything that was going on. I could see it in her sparkling eyes and flushed cheeks. M.J. was there, too, but I could tell she was preoccupied.

"What's up with you?" I asked her.

"I haven't told Steve yet about my car being stolen. Not that it *is* stolen. But I don't want him to get in trouble."

"He won't care about the car," Bitsey said, coming out of the enormous walk-in closet dangling a turquoise dress, a pair of strappy black sandals and a gorgeous black burn-out velvet stole. "He's too crazy about you to care about stuff like that."

M.J. made a face. "Except that he'll wonder whether I'm

using him to keep it hidden. He's always suspecting me of ulterior motives. The thing is, that car is mine and I'm not giving it up."

Bitsey and I shared a look. "Okay, it's yours," I said. "We all agree and we'll help any way we can. But for now, we need to get Bitsey ready. Where's Jack?" I asked.

"He had to run to Walgreens," Bitsey said. "He quit smoking and he's on the patch. Did I tell you that he's lost ten pounds? He said I inspired him."

M.J. clapped her hands together. "That's wonderful."

My reply was more sanguine. "He's afraid of losing you. But that's good. He should be afraid."

Bitsey slipped out of her housecoat and stepped into the dress. "He doesn't have anything to be afraid of. Not anymore," she said.

"Don't give in too fast, Bits. Make sure he's changed and that he puts as much value on your marriage as you do."

Unperturbed, Bitsey turned her back to M.J. to be zipped up. "Actually, I think he may value it more than I do. Don't get me wrong, I want things to be good between us. But I know now that he does, too."

I hoped she was right, but I wasn't convinced, especially when Meg barged into the room.

We all turned to look at her, and I swear, she looked in worse shape than she had when we kidnapped her. No black eyes, and I didn't think she was loaded or anything like that. But she was wounded; I recognized the look. Meg. Alan. And once upon a time, me.

Meg might be twentysomething, but deep inside she was hurting as only a scared kid can hurt.

Your parents do that to you. People talk about their kids and the pain junior's childhood miseries inflict on them, but there's this flip side, the devastation only your parents can deliver—like when they crack or fail or forget to catch you when you fall.

That's the look Meg had. *You're supposed to be the strong steady one, Mom. How can you dare to have a life beyond being my mother and Daddy's wife?* She didn't have to say the words out loud. We got the message strong and clear. Even sunny M.J.'s smile of greeting faded.

There was this long awkward moment where Meg just stood in the doorway staring at her mother, who looked, I have to say, absolutely gorgeous. Her dress was perfect, taking another twenty pounds off her. Her hair was *Marie Claire* cute, and her makeup played up her natural, girl-next-door prettiness. In short, she looked just like what a former high school cheerleader should look like thirty years later.

Meg's gaze ran up and down her mother, and her frown deepened. "You look nice," she said in a tone that implied complete disapproval.

"Doesn't she?" M.J. said. "Your dad is going to drool when he sees her."

Meg raked her hands through her black, spiky hair. "Yeah. Him and that Eddie guy." She glared at her mother. "I thought you were just curious when we looked him up on the Internet. But you had another motive, didn't you? All the time you were planning to hook up with him."

That should have been our cue to split. But M.J. wasn't budging, and that meant I got to stay, too.

Except for the guilty color in her cheeks, Bitsey didn't react directly to Meg's accusation. "Eddie's on the reunion committee, Meg. I knew before we even left Bakersfield that I would be seeing him."

"Oh, and that makes everything fine. Your whole reason for coming to the reunion was to see him again!"

"That's not true."

M.J. and I didn't say a thing.

"Okay," Bitsey conceded. "It's partially true. Wait—" She grabbed Meg's arm when the girl turned to storm off. "Wait."

"For what? To watch you make a fool of Daddy? God! I wish you were still fat and frumpy."

If it hadn't hurt Bitsey so much, Meg's words would have been funny. "Nanny, nanny, boo, boo. I wish you were still fat." But they did hurt Bitsey, and they made me see red.

I planted my fists on my hips. "Shut up, Meg. And quit acting like a two-year-old."

She whirled on me, not the least bit intimidated. "Haven't you done enough, Cat? None of this would have happened if you and M.J. hadn't egged her on. But no, you *had* to drag her back here where she could hook up with that sleazy lawyer."

"Now he's a sleazy lawyer? And all along I thought you liked him and his animal rights lawsuits," I said snidely, acting just about as mature as she was. Alan could have given us both lessons in adult behavior.

Bitsey held up her hand. "I can handle this, Cat."

"No. You can't," Meg said, shaking out of her mother's grasp. "You've messed everything up. Everything!"

"And now I'm going to fix it."

M.J. glanced at me. It really was our cue to leave. But before we could sidle to the door, Jack poked his head in.

"Fix what?" he asked, staring at Bitsey. When she froze, just like the rest of us, he looked at Meg. "Fix what? What are you talking about?"

The fact is, as much as Meg wanted to bust her mom's chops, she still wanted her parents to stay married. That made her an accomplice in our little deception—an unwilling accomplice, but an accomplice all the same. After flashing us a panicked look, she turned to her dad, a determined smile on her face.

"Fix…her hair," she said. She again passed a hand though her own hair. "I…uh…have this great hair product. It's called Bed Head."

"Bed Head?" Jack made a face. "It's called Bed Head?"

Inside I groaned. Given the circumstances, it was a most unfortunate product name. But I had nearly as much invested in this deception as Bitsey and Meg. "Oh, yeah. I've heard of that stuff. It's supposed to have great hold. Do you have any in your room, Meg?" Hint, hint.

"I sure do." She turned back to her mother. "I'll go get it right now."

Then she left and it was Bitsey, M.J. and me, all looking at Jack.

I think he had a pretty good idea of what was going on. He covered it pretty well, though, giving Bitsey the once-over, letting out a wolf whistle and making everything easier for all of us.

"Wow. You look great," he told her. "Better than great."

Bitsey went along with it by turning a quick pirouette. "Thanks, but without M.J.'s and Cat's help, I'd still be an old fat frump."

"That's not true," I said. I was going to kick Meg for putting that image back in Bitsey's head.

"You worked really hard for this," M.J. added.

But no amount of compliments or our jovial send-off could dispel the strain between them. M.J.'s efforts with the Bed Head gel were fake; Meg's enthusiasm for M.J.'s efforts was fake. Worse, Bitsey's and Jack's determined smiles were fake. Ironically, the only thing that gave me a glimmer of hope for how the evening would go was the very fakiness of Jack's smile. He was trying, and that meant he wanted things to work out between him and Bitsey.

Bitsey

On the way to the reunion at the Audubon Tea Room, we stopped by the hospital to see my father. Virginia was already there, which made me glad we weren't staying.

"Damn, girl. You look like a million bucks," Daddy said. "Good thing you came when you did, Jack, otherwise one of her old boyfriends might try to steal her away from you."

He laughed uproariously and his eyes crinkled with appreciation of his own humor. But within the folds of his old eyes I saw the sharp glint of knowledge. Of warning.

Did it come from personal knowledge? I was certain my mother had always been faithful to him. I'd bet my life on it. I'd never wondered, though, whether he'd been faithful to her. I wondered now. Had the misery that pushed her to suicide come from inside her, or from outside? From him? Had he abandoned her, either physically or emotionally?

Something in my chest hurt to even consider such things. The truth was, I didn't really want to know. At the same time I felt a mammoth relief that I hadn't completely betrayed Jack. Not completely.

On impulse I slipped my hand into the crook of Jack's arm and pressed a quick kiss to his cheek. He smelled of Old Spice, Irish Spring and Mennen deodorant. He's nothing if not a traditionalist. They were all subtle, but uniquely, familiarly him.

I felt his curious eyes on me, but I stared at Daddy. "Jack's not getting rid of me that easily," I said.

"You do look nice," Virginia said, as if she was amazed by the fact. "That's a gorgeous dress. Where did you find it?"

"Why thank you, Virginia. I bought it at Darrell's Designs. You know, the shop up on Magazine Street."

"Really? I thought you had to book him months in advance, and that he mainly did Carnival gowns and wedding parties."

"Oh, no. He'll do anything you want." Or more accurately, anything M.J. wanted. She'd waltzed in, oohed and aahed over several of his designs, and before the poor man knew it, he'd agreed to rush through a cocktail dress for little ol' me.

"You should make an appointment with him," I told Virginia. "You must have a big reunion coming up yourself. And do tell him I sent you."

I wasn't sure what she hated more: me condescending to her, or me reminding her that she, too, was aging, and that high school reunions were a dead giveaway.

She gave me a tight smile, then turned her attention to Jack. "Did you hear? Dad is going home tomorrow."

Daddy puffed up like a little banty rooster. "Damned straight I'm going home. I got a lot of people relying on me. A lot of women."

"Well, I'll be out of your hair soon," I said. "After tonight it will be time for me to get back home. With Jack."

We left after that, but the minute we slid into the front seat of Daddy's car, Jack turned to face me. "You're flying home with me?"

"Yes. Assuming I can get on your flight."

We stared at one another a long, awkward moment. I imagined all our spousal sins circling around us like dust motes in the stale car air. The sharp words. The little white lies. The times one or the other of us pretended to be asleep. Or pretended to have an orgasm.

I tried to roll down the window, but of course it was electric and I couldn't. As if he, too, saw the dust motes, Jack turned on the car and pressed the buttons to open both front windows. Parking-garage air drifted through the front seat, still hot and a little smelly, but the dust motes of our marriage blew away. I leaned over, and bracing my hand on his thigh, I kissed him on the mouth, a nice, juicy kiss with lots of tongue.

From the corner of my eye I saw his appropriate parts leap to attention. Okay, we were getting somewhere. Before I could pull away he caught me by the shoulders and drew me back for another overheated kiss.

"I think we need the air conditioner," I murmured when we came up for air.

"I think we need a quick trip home," he said, leaning back and reaching for the shift.

I put my hand over his. "Not so fast." I looked around. Cars as far as the eye could see, but no people. "What do you say we do it here?"

He didn't believe me until I wriggled my skirt up past my hips.

Now, we all know that my thighs and hips will never be my best features, but from the look on Jack's face, he didn't care. I was thinner than I'd been in years; I had bypassed stockings in favor of a tan that was only partially supplemented by Sunless Bain de Soleil; and I had on a pair of the pinkest, flimsiest panties I'd worn since the birth of our first child.

I turned to face him, pulling my knees onto the seat and taking my sandals off, very slowly. "Do these seats lie flat?"

They did, at least they went flat enough for what we had in mind. Jack shimmied out of his pants and into me so fast you would think we were a pair of teenage gymnasts. It was a good thing it didn't take long. But then, not including last night, we hadn't had sex in a month and a half so there was still a lot of pent-up energy there.

I could tell he was going to come before me. You're married that long, you know the signs. But I had other plans. So when he zigged, I deliberately zagged, and out he popped.

"Damn," he swore. He grinned down at me. "Come back here, you."

I cannot really explain how joyous I felt at the moment. My husband was after me as if we were still college kids. "We'll be late for the reunion."

"So? Come here."

"Jack!"

The resisting was just as much fun as the doing. I came and so did he. Afterward we were such a hot, sweaty mess we had to drive home first to straighten ourselves out, giggling the entire time like a pair of immensely pleased-with-ourselves kids.

Jack had to change his suit. His pants were creased where they were never meant to be creased, ironed between his overheated thighs and mine. I needed fresh makeup and a new pair of panties. We'd torn the other pair.

"Go without them," he told me. "Please?"

On impulse I agreed. But, oh, my God, when we finally arrived at the reunion, I felt as though everyone could tell— Bitsey La Farge isn't wearing underpants! Worse, I was certain they knew exactly what we'd done on the third floor of the Touro Parking Garage, in the front seat of my father's 1999 Seville.

But really, I didn't much care what they thought. In fact,

I was pretty damned pleased with myself. Jack held my hand as we arrived, and kept his palm on my waist or his arm draped over my shoulder the whole time. It was as if he had to keep touching me.

We had that glow, I think. That in-love, just-made-love glow.

Lurking at the edge of that lovely, golden haze of rediscovery, however, was a tricky shadow. Eddie.

Since we were late to arrive, the Tea Room was already crowded. I saw two of my cheerleader sisters, my favorite English teacher, half the football team and almost all my old girlfriends. From group to group I flitted, remembering this face, not recognizing another. Everyone recognized me, though, and I decided to take that as a compliment. M.J. would expect me to.

I was introducing Jack to Liz Mathieu, yearbook editor, senior class president and still a size six, when I spied Eddie. He stood outside the main room, on the covered breezeway where the smokers all gathered. He wasn't smoking, though; he was talking to a petite redhead I didn't recognize.

With the same radar she'd possessed at eighteen, only honed by thirty years more practice, Liz locked onto the source of my distraction. "Oh, my God!" she exclaimed. "Look. There's Eddie Dusson. Remember him, Harley Ed? Oh, but of course you do," she went on, her green eyes as sharp as glass. She turned to Jack, leaning in conspiratorially. "Eddie was Bitsey's beau way back when. Have y'all ever met?"

Jack followed the direction of her eyes. "I don't think so. Have we, Bits?"

Give me an Oscar. No way was I letting on anything. "No. Who's that he's talking to? Oh, look. They're bringing out crab cakes. I love crab cakes."

But Liz was undeterred by my smoke-screen interest in food. She squinted at Eddie and I wanted to say, either wear your glasses or get laser surgery.

"Well, I'll be. That's Suzanne Grimsky."

It was my turn to squint. "No."

"Oh, yes." Liz nodded. "The reason you can't tell is that the only thing the same about her these days is the red hair."

I could not believe it. This Suzanne looked nothing like the old Suzanne. She'd been one of those unfortunate girls with huge hips and no chest.

"Liposuction and two boob jobs," Liz murmured. "Amazing, huh?"

"Wow."

"Yeah," Jack said. "Wow." But he slid his hand down over my rear end when he said it.

"Eddie obviously thinks so, too," Liz said, going right back to her original target. "You know, of course, that he's been divorced. Twice."

"Yes," I said. "And he has two children he never sees." *Meow.*

I watched him laugh with Suzanne and then the most amazing thing happened. I realized that I wasn't jealous. I would rather rekindle my marriage with Jack than rekindle anything with Eddie.

With that knowledge came the conviction that I needed to introduce them. Let Eddie know I really was with Jack— not that he would much care. Mainly it would show Jack that I was with him one hundred per cent. At least I hoped he'd take it that way.

But before I could extricate us from Liz, she grabbed my arm. "Look. There's Arnie Fisk. Remember him?"

"Arnie Fisk? Arnie Fisk? Oh, right. The skinny guy who was always the team trainer but never played any sports himself." I looked toward the registration desk but didn't see him. "Where?"

"The brunette," Liz said, stifling a giggle. "The one in the twin set and zebra-print miniskirt."

"Damn," Jack said. "That's a guy?"

I couldn't help gasping. "Shades of *Come back to the Five and Dime, Jimmy Dean, Jimmy Dean.*"

"You saw that play, too?" Liz exclaimed. She stared at

Arnie. "He calls himself Arnette now. I think he edges out Suzanne for most changed, don't you?"

I hooked my arm in Jack's. "Probably so. But you probably win for least changed, Liz."

"Why thank you." She preened as I waved my fingers bye-bye and pulled Jack away.

"I assume that was not a compliment," he murmured as we angled across the crowded room. A warm tickle of satisfaction bubbled up in my chest, and I laughed out loud to know how well my husband understood my subtleties.

"She was a self-righteous gossip then and she's a self-righteous gossip now."

"I thought all women gossiped."

"Watch it, buddy." Then I relented. "We all do gossip—not that men don't. But it's the attitude that counts. People like Liz enjoy other people's misery, and that's wrong." Especially if that gossip was focused on me.

I could feel Liz's eyes on my back as we approached Eddie. I started to get nervous when he didn't even blink when he saw me. Suzanne's eyes lit up with recognition. "Bitsey?"

"Hey, Suzanne." We hugged, air-kissed, and in the middle of it all, I introduced Jack, and he and Eddie shook hands.

"So you're the lucky guy who married our Bitsey," Eddie said.

Jack draped his arm possessively across my shoulder. "Yeah, I am."

They stared at one another and adrenaline pumped my racing heart rate up another ten notches. Like poisoned fumes, testosterone circled in a cloud around us.

Eddie smiled, an opposing lawyer in the courtroom sort of smile. "I hope you'll let her dance once or twice with an old friend."

I held my breath.

"Let her?" Jack said. "*Let* her? Bitsey makes those sorts of decisions herself."

Good answer. I relaxed against Jack and smiled at Eddie.

"By the way," Suzanne said. "Have y'all seen Arnie Fisk?"

"People change," I said. "Arnie. You. Me."

"Have you changed?" Jack asked Eddie.

Eddie shifted his weight from one leg to the other. "Somewhat."

"Come on, Eddie." Suzanne tapped him on the arm. "You've changed from a motorcycle-riding hellion into a respectable attorney."

"But he's still a rebel," I said. "More dedicated to his causes than anything else."

"Is that why you two broke up?" Suzanne asked the question, but I could tell Jack wondered the same thing.

Eddie shrugged and stared at me. "Bitsey was ready to settle down at eighteen, I wasn't."

"It was high school. The bad boy had already won the cheerleader. He was ready for bigger battles, loftier goals." I laughed. "It was all so long ago, who can remember the details?"

"Speaking of dancing," Eddie said. "I believe they're playing our song."

Sure enough the opening strains of "Unchained Melody" filled the air. Not that it was our only song. But it had been one of them. "Shall we?" he asked, holding out his hand.

Every muscle in Jack's body went rigid. I felt it in his arm but knew it went throughout him. My first inclination was to decline Eddie's offer. Except that Eddie would see that as a sign that I was scared. But if I accepted...

The thing is, I didn't want to accept. I didn't want to dance with him or be close to him in any way.

Jack answered before I could. "I think this is my dance." Then he swept me around and with moves I never knew he had, danced me backward through the crowd toward the dance floor. My white knight.

Somebody wolf-whistled. A few other couples joined us and once again I was the belle of the high school ball, the popular girl that all the guys wanted. But only Jack was getting me.

"What did you ever see in that guy?" he asked as Bobby Hatfield hit the high notes.

I leaned my head against his shoulder. "The usual stuff that attracts young women. Good looks and a bad attitude."

"Huh. And what attracted you to me?"

I let my fingers slide up into his hair. "Good looks and a better attitude."

I hoped that would appease him. But after a moment he cleared his throat. "Is there anything I ought to know, Bitsey?"

The song ended but we didn't move. I looked up at him. "I might ask the same question of you."

"You're the one Meg is mad at. I have to wonder why."

I took a breath, held it, then exhaled. "She's afraid I'm going to divorce you."

Another song started, something fast. But we didn't move. "Are you?"

I shook my head. "No way. I've got a lot of lost time to make up."

"Yeah." He pulled me so close I felt his heart beating against the wall of his chest, beating in time with my own. "Me, too."

To put it mildly, I had a better time at the reunion than I ever could have imagined. Eddie left fairly early. With Liz. They deserved each other. Meanwhile, Jack and I stayed till the very end, laughing, dancing and generally having a terrific time.

We were so exhausted we crawled immediately into bed. But though Jack fell asleep right away, I still needed to deal with Margaret. So I crossed the hall and curled up in her bed. I must have dozed off, because when I awakened, she was staring at me, a frown on her pale face.

"Oh, good." I pushed myself up on my elbows. "You're home."

"Where's Daddy?"

"Asleep."

"Why're you in here?"

"To talk to you. To let you know that…that I didn't betray your father."

She rolled her eyes, then turned away. "Yeah, right."

"I was tempted, Margaret. I won't deny it."

She whirled around. "But you shouldn't have been!"

Her whole body was rigid with anger, with disillusion.

I sat up in her bed. "I'm not perfect, Margaret. Neither is your father. But if we're willing to forgive each other and work to better our marriage, then…then it doesn't matter what *you* think."

I hadn't meant to get so angry. But damn it, this was *my* life and *my* marriage. "I love your father and he loves me, and the fact is, if not for Eddie, I'm not sure we could have mended our marriage."

Her eyes had gone huge, and swam with emotions. "Okay," she finally said, her lips trembling. "Okay. But I don't want you to ever talk about *him* again. I mean it. Not ever!"

Such an easy promise to make. I smiled and climbed out of the bed. "Don't worry. I won't. Now, can I have a hug? I'm tired and I want to get to bed—"

She was in my arms before I could finish, and oh, how wonderful it felt. "I love you, Magpie," I whispered into her streaky black hair.

"I love you, too, Mom," she said, hugging me back. "And I'm glad everything's okay."

"Me, too." I smiled, amazed at how lucky I was. How blessed. "Me, too."

CHAPTER 12
Walking to New Orleans

M.J.

It's awfully hard to exercise outside in New Orleans in the summertime. The humidity is so high that instead of your sweat cooling you down, it bakes you like stuffed grape leaves in a steam bath. Overheating and heat stroke is a real threat because ninety degrees here is hotter than one hundred ten degrees in California. That's why Steve and I decided to do our first workout together in the evening.

I'd seen Bitsey off for her reunion. She looked spectacular. Even better, she and Jack looked good together. I was feeling very optimistic about those two—I suppose because I wanted someone's marriage to work out. Mine and Cat's certainly hadn't.

But I wasn't going to dwell on anything negative. Good thoughts, I told myself after Cat dropped me off at Audubon Park. Steve was meeting me there where we'd do a couple of laps—him in his wheelchair, me jogging. Then while we were cooling down, I planned to tell him about the Jaguar.

He was already there, doing pull-ups from his chair. I stopped short of approaching him so I could watch the wonderful flex of his arms and shoulders. He wore a loose gray tank top and a pair of lightweight navy sweatpants. I'd only seen his bare legs in the shadows of his bedroom. But it was enough to know they'd lost a lot of muscle mass. He exercised them daily on a machine set up in his bedroom. But that was therapeutic exercise meant to keep up his circulation and flexibility. When I'd asked him about it he'd explained in a flat, unemotional voice that he exercised to prevent atrophy of the muscles; he'd never walk again.

His real exercise worked his upper body. Pull-ups, weight training, a weekly wheelchair basketball game and speed racing in a specially built chair.

And, oh my, had it ever paid off. As he pulled up and lowered himself, so fast it seemed effortless, the slanted sunlight glinted off his damp, flexing muscles, emphasizing the sharply cut definition.

I swallowed hard. My goodness, but he was one beautiful man.

A trio of young women jogged by, sending appreciative glances his way. "Too bad about that chair," I heard one of them say as they passed me. "Such a waste."

I was so stunned that all I could do was gape at her as she jogged away. I wanted to chase her down, tackle her and slap the words right down her throat. But of course I didn't do anything but glare at her. Snotty Tulane brat. Did she think she was immune to tragedy? Did she believe life was one wide smooth highway that never took a sudden turn uphill or off road?

Get a grip, I told myself, shocked by the violence of my feelings. It *was* too bad about the wheelchair. On the other hand, would Steve be the man he was now if he hadn't been dealt that rotten hand? Would I know him?

Would I be falling in love with him?

When I turned back to Steve, he was looking straight at me. All my philosophical musings evaporated. He smiled, but there was this challenge in it, as if he figured this was the situation that was going to send me screaming in the opposite direction. How long was it going to take to earn his trust and erase that doubt from his mind?

Considering what I had to tell him tonight about my Jaguar, a very long time.

He situated himself in his chair, then rolled backward. "You do pull-ups when you work out?" he asked.

I approached the various height bars. "No. But I'll give it a try."

"It's easier if you grip the bar with your palms turned toward your face."

"Really?" I jumped up and grabbed the bar, then placed my hands in the opposite position, which I vaguely recalled from my high school PE classes as being a lot harder on the forearms. But I wanted to impress Steve, to show him I wasn't the little cream puff he still thought I was.

The first one was hard.

"Put your hands a little wider apart, " he said. "Shoulder width."

It helped and I managed five pretty well—until I made the mistake of looking at him. He was watching me so intently. Then he grinned and lowered his wicked gaze to my chest, and that's when I lost all my focus. When your nipples pucker in arousal, the pecs forget that they're supposed to be helping the biceps and flexors. I tried one more pull-up but only ended up dangling in front of him.

Holy cow, was that exciting, as if I was helpless and exposed, and all his. He was aroused, too. If the night had been darker, the hot awareness between us would have crackled like lightning.

He rolled forward and I dropped down, and there was this long, intense moment between us.

"I don't think I can jog if you keep looking at me like that," I said in this strangled voice.

"That's okay. At the moment I'm thinking we should just go home."

Go home. Goodness, did I like the sound of that.

Just then a couple of guys sauntered up, checking me out. I was used to it, but I wished they would disappear. One of them jumped up to the highest bar and started a show-off series of pull-ups.

Unimpressed, I sat down on Steve's lap, much to his surprise. But he rose to the challenge. With one hand he wheeled us around, then he propelled us onto the jogging track and took off at a very fast, very scary speed.

"Slow down!" I gasped, clinging with a death grip to his neck.

"Why?"

I buried my face against his neck. "Because my weight will throw off your center of balance."

I felt his chest shaking with laughter. "You threw me off

balance the first day you walked into my shop, M.J. Why change things now?"

It was the most romantic thing anyone had ever said to me, and I swear I could feel my heart swell with emotion. He did slow down, though, enough that I wasn't afraid we'd tip over.

It was odd, going around the park on wheels. I'm not very tall, but it was still a new perspective. Lower. Smoother. People looked at us. Some smiled. Some looked away, acting as though we were invisible. That was their problem, I decided.

"I have something to tell you," I began. I'd meant to wait to tell him about the stolen car in his shop, but I decided to go for it. After all, he couldn't turn away from me when I was sitting in his lap. "It's about the car."

"You can't pay me. I knew it."

"No. I can pay you. In advance, if you want."

"Okay. If it's not about payment, then what?"

We had come around the front end of the park and were starting the long way back toward Magazine Street. He was turning the wheels with both hands and I felt the rhythm of his flexing muscles against my side and arms. It was a nice rhythm, like a porch swing or a rocking chair. I hated to upset the comforting embrace of it.

"It's about who owns the car. There's a dispute about it."

"Because of your husband's estate?"

I nodded. "His kids hate me, so…they've filed auto theft charges against me."

The rhythm stopped and we coasted. I'd forgotten how hot it was, but all of a sudden I was sweating.

"I'm working on a stolen car?"

"It's my car," I insisted. "Frank bought it for me."

The wheelchair stopped. "Exactly when were the theft charges filed?"

"I don't know." I got off his lap. "I just found out about it yesterday."

"From who?"

"Cat found out from Matt."

"From a cop? Great."

"Since it's not in his jurisdiction he told Cat he wouldn't say anything to anyone about it."

"Well, that's good." He started rolling again and I fell into step beside him. "So what do you want to do?" he asked.

"You're not mad at me?"

He slanted a look at me. "To tell you the truth, M.J., so far you've been just a little too good to be true."

I wanted to take offense at that, but instead I started to smile.

He went on. "It's kind of a relief to know you've got a bad side, too. Damn. Me, of all people, hooked up with a car thief."

"I'm not a car thief!"

He crooked one dark brow at me. "Maybe, maybe not. Let's take a slow lap while I think about this."

His slow lap was a fast lap for me, and it took all my effort to keep up. There's a reason the wheelchair racers always finish way ahead of the other racers: they're faster. By the time we made it once around the nearly two-mile circuit I was really pushing it. We stopped for water. He was barely sweating, but I guess he noticed I was drenched. "Look. Why don't we go the next couple of laps at our own paces? How many more laps do you have in you?"

"One." I hoped.

"Fine. I'll take a couple of fast laps and meet you at the car."

He passed me three times. I was jogging very slowly on the dirt path that meandered alongside the wide paved path. When I reached the car I walked up and down, cooling off while I waited for Steve.

I was conscious of the exact moment when one of the guys from before decided to approach me. Mr. Pull-ups. "How ya doing?" he asked. I gave him a tight smile and kept on walking.

You'd think I'd be good at shaking off unwelcome advances from guys, but I've always found it excruciating. I don't want to shoot them down; I just want them to go away. But when he matched his pace to mine and said, "What's your time around the park?" I changed my mind. I did want to shoot him down. He'd seen me ride off in Steve's lap, yet he still didn't get it.

I turned abruptly to face him. "Eight-minute miles. But my boyfriend does it in four, except when I'm in his lap. Then it's five minutes. You know, I saw your girlfriend go by earlier."

His smarmy grin faded. "My girlfriend?"

"Yeah. Great figure but not too many brains. Like you, she couldn't figure out that there's more to a great guy than a pair of working legs."

Then I turned away, and spying Steve coming up the path, jogged up to meet him.

"Somebody you know?" he asked when we met at the car.

"Nope." I got in the passenger seat without explaining, and waited for him to do his thing with the wheelchair. I was furious with that presumptuous guy and still upset about the comment that smug girl had made. I wanted to protect Steve from them and all the other stupid people in the world that only saw him as a guy in a wheelchair. But I couldn't protect him.

Then with a perverse twist it occurred to me that by not watching Steve's wheelchair-to-car routine I was wincing away from his disability, too. And by wanting to protect him... Was I sending out signals that I thought he wasn't a complete man?

That was the last thing I wanted to do. I realized, sitting there in the hot car with my sweaty thighs sticking to the seats, that if Steve and I were ever to meet as equals, we had to really be equal.

Once he was situated in the car he put the key in the ignition. But with a hand on his, I stopped him. When he looked over at me I said, "Do you enjoy sex with me?"

His eyes went from a clear, questioning blue, to hard, opaque granite. That immediate need to protect himself brought a lump of emotion to my throat.

"Do you doubt it?" he asked.

"No. But..."

"But?"

"But...I guess if I'm ever going to feel like I satisfy you, I'm going to have to know how it works for you."

He turned away and stared through the windshield. In the open field beyond us, a pair of teenagers tossed a Frisbee back and forth through the fading light while a dog chased madly between them. For the dog it was a futile effort, but the game little animal wouldn't give up. Neither would I.

"What's to understand?" he asked. "I like touching you, seeing you excited. I like doing that for you and watching you come."

Just hearing his low, rumbling voice describe what we'd done set my heart thudding as if I'd run a five-minute mile. "I like doing that for you, too, Steve. But I realize that as long as I wonder if you're satisfied—just like I avoid watching you get in and out of your chair—well, I wonder if I'm handling you with kid gloves. It's like a wall between us, your unwillingness to discuss what's going on with you and my unwillingness to ask."

He didn't say anything, just sat there, letting me see his profile. One side of him only.

I twisted my hands together in my lap. "I know we haven't been together very long, Steve. But the thing is, I haven't felt like this about anybody before. I think I—"

"Don't." He bit the word out, stopping my declaration of love. I should have known better, but I'd gotten caught up in emotion. Why was I such an idiot?

"Don't, M.J." His jaw clenched; my heart turned to lead. But I couldn't just sit there and say nothing.

"Okay. I got off track there for a moment. So, back to the subject. We were talking about sex, about how I can satisfy you in bed."

I held my breath, waiting for his response. He wasn't ready to be loved or to give love, so I would just have to be patient—and use our sex life to batter down his defenses.

He gripped the steering wheel with both hands, then flexed his fingers. "Do you plan to pursue this subject the same way you originally chased me?"

I nodded. "Yes."

He turned to face me then, his brows lowered, his eyes dark. "Okay, let's get this over with. I never did want to get involved with you, M.J. You know that."

I caught my breath. Was he breaking up with me?

He went on. "Letting you get close to me physically was damned hard. But doing it was a lot easier than talking about it now."

I swallowed hard. "But you're glad you let me get close to you physically. Aren't you?"

A reluctant smile turned up one side of his mouth. "Yeah. I am." After a pause he blew out a breath. "Okay. Here's the deal. A hard-on that leads to ejaculation isn't all there is to a guy having an orgasm. Ejaculation is the physical reaction. Orgasm happens in the brain. You get me to that point, M.J. I have an orgasm. Never doubt that."

"But how can you tell? And how can I tell that you're satisfied?"

"Same as I can tell with you. The sounds you make. The way you thrash around and arch up. It's the same for me. Something inside me builds, like to a breaking point. Then…it does break. But in a good way. Damned good." His eyes held with mine. "Do you want to know which move really sends me over the edge?"

I nodded, captivated by the intense look on his face.

"Remember when I was facedown on the bed and you rubbed your whole body over mine?" I started to blush and he laughed. "Yeah. That was a real turn-on." Then he reached under the seat and pulled out a yellow plastic bag. "I was planning to give this to you later. But maybe now would be better."

I opened it, then looked up at him. "A dildo?"

"I… Well, I know you're getting shortchanged."

"I'm not!"

"Yeah. You are. I don't care what sex was like for you with your husband, M.J. I want it to be better than that with me." He grabbed the steering wheel again and twisted the key in the ignition. "What do you say we go test it out?"

He backed the car out, then circled around to Magazine Street. In my lap I held the Mighty Magic Personal Vibrator close, extra batteries and all. But in my heart I held this man much closer. He might not be able to express his feelings for me, but he couldn't be so incredibly generous and unselfish if he didn't care.

He flipped the left-turn blinker on, then glanced at me as he waited for the traffic to clear. "Put on your seat belt." His voice was low and even, but his eyes were alive with unspoken emotion. "I wouldn't want anything bad to happen to you, M.J."

Dutifully I clicked the seat belt in place. But inside I fought down the rise of happy tears. It might not be a declaration of love, but it was a beginning.

CHAPTER 13
Home Again

Cat

Being back in Southern California felt surreal. I'd been gone almost six weeks, but it felt more like a year. After the plump humidity of the deep South, the minute I stepped off the plane at LAX my skin felt as if it was being sucked dry.

Even more surreal, the first phone call I got was from Bill, my second ex. It's like he has this radar that says, "Dumb broad back in town. Go for it." Except that I was finally beginning to wise up.

Just the sound of his voice made my skin crawl. "Sorry," I broke in before he could start his "I miss you babe," routine. "I think you should know that I'm not into men anymore. You cured me of that, Bill. I mean, you chased anything in skirts, so I thought, 'Hey, what's the appeal?' and decided to do the same thing. And you'll never guess. M.J. and I are a couple now. Can you believe it? You know, it's too bad you never got to see her naked. She is really something. Oops. Gotta go."

Somehow I didn't think M.J. would mind.

He called back. Twice. But I didn't bother to pick up and I disconnected the answering machine. I had work to do, years and years of stuff to sort through. After all, the movers were coming in two days.

The doorbell rang. Bitsey, all smiles and another eight pounds thinner. She'd been back two weeks and from the looks of her it had been a good decision. We hugged like we hadn't seen each other in ten years.

"Oh, my God, do I miss you guys!" she exclaimed.

"You have to move back to New Orleans," I told her. "You have to. I need you there and so does M.J. Besides, she's not going to believe how good you look unless she sees you with her own two eyes." I shook my head, just staring at her.

"What?" she said. Her cheeks started to go pink.

"I don't know. It's not just that you're slimmer. I mean, you look good, Bits, but…. You look…"

"Happy." We both said the word at the same time.

She smiled then hugged me again. "Life is so much better with Jack these days."

"He nearly lost you. He knows now that he can't take you for granted anymore."

"True. But I can't take him for granted, either."

She'd been saying that every time we talked on the phone, which was daily, and though I'd never seen her as anything but loving and giving, I was beginning to accept her statement as true. I loved Bitsey and saw her as close to perfect. But I could also see that she'd played her own part in her marriage's near tragedy.

But she was happy now.

"So, what are you keeping?" she asked, surveying my living room, which now seemed like a room from my distant past, frozen in time. A Good Interior Designer Lives Here, the caption on the photo would read. Everything was so neat and arranged, like for a photo op. But I hadn't been living in this place, I'd been existing. My real life, messy and disorganized, uneven but with more highs and lows, waited for me in New Orleans.

"I think I'm only taking the art and the clothes," I said, ending the internal debate I'd been waging for the past three weeks.

"Are you sure? What about the French armoire? And that darling silver-leafed hall table? You redid that one yourself."

"I'm selling it all," I said. "That designers consignment

shop in the arts district will take most of it—unless there's something you want."

Once more she surveyed the living room. "I'll buy the hall table from you. I always did love that piece."

"It's yours, then. But I'm not selling it to you. If you want anything, you can have it. Just don't start the money thing with me."

We argued for a half hour. It was so much fun! In the end she took the hall table, a pair of blown-glass candle braces and a darling little turn-of-the-century Hungarian hooked rug.

"So how is Matt?" she asked once we were done with the house stuff and we'd settled down with fresh brewed café au laits.

"Matt's wonderful." I sighed. "Alan's been going to Alateen. He didn't want to go at first, but he didn't argue the last time I took him. It's been good for me, too, because it forces me to go to Al-Anon—which I need."

"And your mother?"

"She's…okay. I talked to her doctor and her health isn't that great." Actually, it was terrible. "I want her last years to be as good as possible. She's moving into an apartment across the hall from me. We need our own space."

"But what about Matt? I thought he wanted you to move in with him?"

"Yeah. He does. But I think he and Alan need a little more time with just them. My turn is coming, Bits, and I can afford to wait. Don't forget, Alan will be leaving home in a couple more years."

She gave me a long, steady look. "My goodness. I think my baby girl is growing up."

"Shut up. Speaking of your babies, Meg got another tattoo."

"What!"

"Just kidding." I ducked when she threw a pillow at me. "But she does have a new boyfriend, and he *is* covered with tattoos, so prepare yourself."

She let out a pained groan and slumped down in the love seat. "What am I going to do with that child?"

"She's her own person, Bitsey, and she's gonna do exactly what she wants."

"No kidding. What does Daddy think?"

"He hasn't met tattoo man yet. I only know about him— by the way, his name is Raven—because I saw them together at the coffeehouse. He was very polite."

"Right. Oh, well. So, have you seen Daddy and Doris?"

"I dropped by there the day before I left. He looks really good now that he's been home awhile. I talked to Miss Ulna yesterday. She told me the wedding invitations are in the mail."

Just then the phone rang and, I kid you not, it was M.J. "I got the invitation," she said. "The weekend of July Fourth. You will be back in time, won't you?"

"Hello, M.J. Yes, I will. The movers are coming day after tomorrow and I plan to be back early next week." I waved Bitsey into the bedroom to pick up the other extension.

"Hey there, M.J."

"Bitsey! Goodness but I miss you."

"I'm planning on staying a week and a half for Daddy's wedding."

"That's not long enough," M.J. wailed. "I need both my Grits sisters with me. Can't you talk Jack into transferring here?"

"Actually," Bitsey said, "there's a rumor that Jack's company is downsizing again. Even though he's a couple of years from qualifying for full retirement, he told his boss that he's open to an offer. You know, the golden handshake."

"Are you serious?" I asked while M.J. squealed with delight. "Jack would leave his job and move back to New Orleans?"

"He'd probably get another job there. He's not the type to play golf all day. But the truth is, between his retirement income, our equity in our house and my trust fund, we could manage just fine."

"When?" M.J. asked "When is this going to happen?"

"I don't know. Maybe by Christmas. More likely in the spring. I'll keep you posted. But, tell me about you and Steve. Is the car fixed yet?"

M.J. giggled. "He's got it purring like a contented cat."

"Are you talking about the car or yourself?" Bitsey teased.

"Both. I have a lawyer working on the ownership dispute. Oh, and wait till you hear what Wendy did…"

I stood there in my living room, holding the telephone to my ear, and just listened to them talk. M.J.'s sweet exuberance, Bitsey's sweet comfort. My two best friends, and soon we'd all be together again. But this time we'd be together and happy.

But if we were happy, did that mean we'd see less of one another? Rely less on one another? Had our closeness been based on the unhappiness in our lives?

I felt a sudden hollowness in my chest. To some extent it had, and it was a bittersweet realization. Now that we each had the right man in our lives, more of our time would probably be spent with them.

"…I can tell sometimes that Steve still doesn't believe I plan to stay with him," M.J. said. "He still expects me to get tired of him and move on. And God forbid I make any noises that sound remotely like 'I love you.'"

"It's just going to take time," Bitsey told her. "Remember, you haven't even been together two months."

"I know, I know. But he means so much to me and I just want to tell him."

"Yeah, I can understand that," Bitsey replied. "But take it from one who learned it that hard way—sometimes actions speak louder than words."

"You're right." M.J. sighed. "You're right. So how are things between you and Jack?"

"Oh, he's great," Bitsey said. "Though he'll never be perfect. The other night—you won't believe this—he was reading some magazine during dinner. Reading some business journal at the table! I snatched it away from him, threw it across the room and said, 'Hello, Mr. Albertson. I'm your wife. Remember me?' You should have seen his face."

I chuckled and rejoined the conversation. "Were you naked when you did it?"

M.J. hooted with laughter. "That would get his attention."

Bitsey laughed, too. "Give me another thirty pounds off these hips and I might try it."

And that's when I knew, men or no men, happy kids or sad, healthy parents or sick, contented marriages, divorces, even widowhood—through it all we three would always need each other for advice, for support, for laughter and for tears.

"I read an interesting article in *Cosmopolitan*," I said.

"Come on," Bitsey said. "You still read that?"

"I picked it up at the airport, okay? But you would've picked it up, too. 'Twelve Moves That Will Drive Your Man Crazy in Bed.'"

"Ooh," M.J. said. "Tell me more."

"What's the matter?" I teased her. "Aren't you still achieving the big 'O' on a regular basis?"

"And how. But I still want to know what the twelve moves are."

"I'll mail you a copy of the article," Bitsey said, "After I make a copy for myself."

"Don't mail it," M.J. said. "I want hand delivery. I want us to discuss it over coffee just as soon as you two get back here. Just like always, the three Grits Girls talking dirty and drinking Bitsey's special cinnamon café latte."

I laughed out loud. "Okay by me."

"Me, too," said Bitsey.

"I can hardly wait," M.J. said.